RICH'S FAREWELL
TO MILITARY PROFESSION

RICH'S FAREWELL TO MILITARY PROFESSION 1581

Edited by

THOMAS MABRY CRANFILL

AUSTIN
UNIVERSITY OF TEXAS PRESS
1959

Library of Congress Catalog Card No. 58–7232

Published with the assistance of a grant from the Ford Foundation under its program for the support of publications in the humanities and social sciences

ISBN: 978-0-292-73492-0

To the memory of

HYDER EDWARD ROLLINS

PREFACE

FEW editions of Elizabethan works could have been more generously sponsored than the present volume, which was made possible by a research leave from the University of Texas Research Institute in 1947–48 and by research fellowships at the Folger Shakespeare Library in 1947–48 and the Huntington Library in 1949–50. Grants from the Arts and Sciences Foundation and the Research Institute of the University of Texas and from the Ford Foundation's program for the support of scholarly publications in the humanities and social sciences have helped defray the expenses of publication.

For advice in bibliographical matters I am indebted to Dr. G. E. Dawson, Dr. J. G. McManaway, Dr. E. E. Willoughby, and Dr. P. S. Dunkin, all of the Folger Shakespeare Library, and to Professor W. A. Jackson. For encouragement and counsel I am grateful to Professors H. E. Rollins and V. B. Heltzel and to Professors D. T. Starnes and H. H. Ransom, my colleagues at the University of Texas.

Thanks are also due the Folger Shakespeare Library for allowing us to reproduce the title-pages of the second, third, and fourth editions of Rich's *Farewell* and excerpts from the text of the fourth edition. The text of the unique copy of the first edition of the *Farewell* is printed by the kind permission of the Curators of the Bodleian Library.

T. M. C.

Austin, Texas
December 19, 1957

CONTENTS

FACSIMILES

INTRODUCTION

INTRODUCTION

THERE has recently been a remarkable revival of interest in Barnaby Rich (1543–1617), captain, courier, privateer, real-estate agent, informer, and author of short stories, prose romances, character sketches, prose satires, pamphlets on Ireland, intelligence reports, anti-Roman Catholic tracts, and verse. During the last twenty-five years his long, varied, and interesting career has inspired all manner of comment in articles, theses, and books. Two doctoral dissertations have been devoted entirely to his life and works, and three others have dealt with him in sizable part. In a spate of articles scholars have dealt with the sources of Rich's tales, with plays based on the latter, with textual and editorial problems concerning the *Farewell*, with Rich as a military scientist and a satirist, with Rich as a journalist and companion of Thomas North, with a report by Rich to King James, and with Rich's relationship to his sovereign. In addition, a book on the good captain's life has recently appeared.[1]

The time has come, it would seem, for a modern edition of Rich's most celebrated work, *Riche His Farewell to Militarie Profession.* "Apolonius and Silla," the second tale in the *Farewell* and neither the best nor the worst in the collection, has been reprinted, often badly, scores of times because it is the principal source of *Twelfth Night.* But there has been no edition of all the stories with Rich's engaging prefatory and concluding sections since J. P. Collier's, published for the old Shakespeare Society in 1846 and consequently difficult to obtain. Of all four early editions, only six copies, three of them woefully imperfect, survive, and these are in rare-book libraries where they are inaccessible to all but the most fortunate students of Elizabethan fiction.

[1] The authors, titles, and places and dates of publication of most of these studies are cited elsewhere and may be found by referring in the Index to B. E. Boothe, Dorothy H. Bruce, T. M. Cranfill, E. M. Hinton, D. T. Starnes, and J. S. Weld. Not cited elsewhere are Dorothy H. Bruce, "Barnabe Riche and His Acquaintances" (Stanford University dissertation, 1944); T. M. Cranfill, "Barnaby Rich's *Farewell* and the Drama" (Harvard University dissertation, 1943); Sir James Craigie, "A 1594 Edition of Barnabe Riche's *Farewell*," *TLS*, November 1, 1934, p. 755; H. J. Webb, "Barnabe Riche—Sixteenth Century Military Critic," *JEGP*, XLII (1943), 240–52.

To be hard to come by is a fate which the *Farewell* does not deserve. Not only were Rich's tales unquestionably best-sellers in his own day, but they evidently continue to delight scholars, critics, and even casual readers today, if one may judge from the praise they still inspire.[1]

[1] See below, pp. lviii f.

RICH AS A BORROWER

EVEN in a day when plagiarism was not yet a word, let alone a sort of crime, and when few put pen to paper without first canvassing and tapping assorted models, the extent of Rich's borrowings was prodigious. So it must have seemed to Rich himself: as if prompted by a queasy conscience, he felt obliged to comment on the subject in a prefatory section of his first publication. "Although, gentle Reader," he freely and disarmingly confesses in *A Right Exelent and Pleasaunt Dialogue, betwene Mercury and an English Souldier* (1574), "I haue done as the Iay, who decked her selfe with the fethers of other Byrds, to the ende, she might seeme to be the more glorious, yet I doubte not but if euery Byrd should pluck his fether from this my deuise, it would not be left altogither destitute, nor so vtterly naked, but ther would yet remayne something worthy to be perused."

Plucking and identifying the feathers which adorn the five stories in the *Farewell* (the first, second, fifth, seventh, and eighth) which are not adapted from Cinthio's Italian is both a diverting and an instructive exercise. The catalogue of discoverable sources, Continental and English, shows that verse and drama as well as prose were grist to Rich's mill. Clearly demonstrable are his debts to Painter, Pettie, Gascoigne, Lyly, Udall, Golding, Underdowne, Cinthio, Belleforest, and Straparola.[1] Why other authors of Elizabethan best-sellers published before 1581 do not appear on this list may be explained by Rich's revelation "To the gentle and friendly Reader" of his second book, the *Allarme to England* of 1578, a year when he was probably engaged in writing the *Farewell*: "Surely I must confesse I haue vsed the helpe of sundrie writers, but not of so many as I would haue done, if I had bene in place where I might haue come by them: for what I haue written, was onely done in *Ireland*, where there is no great choyce of bookes to be had."

The books that did somehow find their way to that literary desert

[1] Specific borrowings are indicated in my notes, as in those to 48. 7–28 and 87. 27–36 (such references are to pages and lines of the facsimile text). The sources of each of the tales not adapted from Cinthio are discussed below, pp. 339–50.

island, to serve such castaways as Rich, Bryskett, Fenton, and Spenser as intellectual pabulum, must have reflected a fairly careful choice. Presumably, then, the sources that went into the making of the *Farewell*, also composed in Ireland, so Rich confides (10. 19 f.), provide an interesting, though doubtless incomplete, index to what the exiles deemed of special value as entertainment and literature and therefore worth importing.

The scarcity of books at Rich's disposal may account for the fact that he worked certain of his sources overtime. Painter's *Palace* never failed him when he required help in christening a hero, delineating a character, evolving a plot, or, above all, constructing dialogue and soliloquy. Obviously convinced that Painter's rhetoric was more elegant than anything he himself could devise, he transferred torrents of words from the *Palace* to the *Farewell*. Of Painter's 101 stories, more than two dozen, a not unimpressive proportion of the total, are represented in Rich by borrowings great and small. These are not distributed evenly throughout the *Farewell*. Painter's hold on Rich is unrelenting in the first tale (where it is discernible on thirty-three of the forty-three printed pages), still powerful in the second, and substantial in the fifth, but almost negligible in the seventh and eighth.

As Painter's influence waned, Pettie's waxed. Rich used all twelve of the stories in the *Petite Pallace*, not to mention the introductory sections. Verbal echoes of Pettie are slight though unmistakable in the first story, louder in the second, reverberating in the fifth, and thunderous in the eighth. Apart from words and bits of plot and characterization in the *Petite Pallace*, there were, of course, to be emulated Pettie's famous attitude toward the ladies in his audience and his style, and the influence of these on the *Farewell* is pervasive. Dozens of passages, some lifted verbatim from the *Petite Pallace*, others composed with one eye on Pettie's page, are so dotted with alliteration, antithesis, and proverbial lore as to suggest that Rich regarded felicity of style and Pettie's brand of euphuism as practically synonymous. Like Pettie, moreover, he is much given to interrupting his narrative (as at 84. 5) to smirk at his gentlewomen readers and to offer—in a tone now confidential and insinuating, now coy, now saucy—arch commentaries on the action.

His surprisingly wholesale borrowings from Painter and Pettie may be due as much to necessity as to choice. Since in Ireland he was, by his own admission, poor in books available for ransacking, why should he not make the greatest use of what few he had? Such a need for economy would also explain his treatment of other sources. Several stories in Belleforest and Cinthio were made to do double or even triple duty—Belleforest's melancholy "The Lady of Chabry," for instance. After translating and printing this particular story as part of his first book in 1574, Rich then turned to his own translation for substantial help in writing the first, second, and fifth tales in the *Farewell.* In like fashion, Cinthio's "Cesare Gravina" supplied certain details of plot for the first story in the *Farewell*, while certain others, unused in the first but apparently husbanded with remarkable care, appear in the last. From Belleforest's story of Nicole and from the Eustace-Placidas legend Rich also wrung an uncommon amount of service; the former is a principal source of both "Apolonius" and "Phylotus," the latter of both "Sappho" and "Apolonius." Thus ingenuity meliorates poverty: even not quite enough may be as good as a feast.

However limited Rich may have thought his raw materials to be, they are nevertheless profuse, complicated, and unwieldy enough to inspire wonder that they could have been reduced to any convenient, usable order. When Rich "forged" a story, to use a word with which he himself aptly describes (19. 13) his method of composition, he was in effect fusing elements from a welter of sources into a tale of his own. Instead of scurrying through the pages of a dozen models, selecting here a bit of plot, there a character, and there an appropriate speech, he resorted to a commonplace book, that invaluable aid without which few Elizabethans ventured to engage in composition. Scores of items that Rich clearly committed to his notebook and transferred thence to the *Farewell* are identifiable; but specific sources await detection for others (those beginning at 120. 31 and 47. 5, for example) which are also evidently gems of the commonplace book. As Rich readily confesses (205. 31–33), he was himself unable to recall from time to time precisely where and when he had gleaned this or that incident. But what could such lapses of memory matter to a tireless, unashamed borrower who, though eclecticism and improvement of his models may have been of some concern to him, was primarily interested in "forging" a good tale?

To read in order the five stories Rich says he "forged onely for delight" is to discover that his technique in "forging" improved with practice. "Sappho," the first selection in the *Farewell* and probably Rich's first essay at writing an "original" tale, contains faults that betray him as a beginner. Its length, caused partly by the some two dozen lengthy sources which went into its making, seems exorbitant, the transitions from one section of the plot to another (as at 35. 12–22) gauche, and the interruptions of the narrative with homilies or endless amatory debates tiresome. So Rich himself regarded them, for he apologizes (at 24. 25–30 and 67. 28–33) for his prolixity and discursiveness. These blemishes may have offended his contemporaries less than he feared, since no unhurried Elizabethan who could placidly make his way through such fiction as the *Aethiopica* and the *Arcadia* was likely to be disconcerted by a tale a mere sixty-three pages long. And the flights of rhetoric in a homiletic or amatory vein that strike the twentieth-century reader as unbearably grandiloquent doubtless impressed the Elizabethan as morally and stylistically grand.

"Apolonius," the second tale, is neither the most nor least attractive in Rich's collection, though as the source of *Twelfth Night* it is certainly the best known. From twenty-odd tales Rich was able with reasonable deftness to devise a narrative of his own that is marred little by the faults which beset "Sappho." On the contrary, "Apolonius" is often characterized by sprightliness and charm. Even so, Rich became a "forger" of remarkable suavity and finesse only in his fifth story, "Two Brethren." The casual reader of the *Farewell* in search of entertainment would be well advised to begin with this story rather than with "Sappho." Here Rich was a highly competent, even adroit, borrower, felicitous in both the choice and the adaptation of his eight sources, and the result of his skill is a tale as hilarious as the best of the French fabliaux.

The soberer seventh "history," "Aramanthus," is evidently the most original of Rich's eight tales; it depends on only three models that have been identified with certainty. The paucity of sources probably accounts both for the brevity of "Aramanthus" and for its unity, qualities for which Rich's other tales are not particularly distinguished. That Rich employed only three discoverable sources in writing it suggests that as he gained experience in storymaking he also gained confidence and was willing to rely less on others, more on his own resources. He manipulated the three sources he chose, however, with the same technical proficiency which he exhibited in "Two Brethren" and was to display again in "Phylotus," the eighth and final tale. This rollicking, richly comic narrative is a smooth blend of such widely diverse ingredients as two *histoires* by Belleforest, *novelle* by Cinthio and Straparola, a story from Golding's *Ovid*, five stories by Pettie, and a play by Gascoigne. Yet this formidable lot of sources, which would perhaps have confused the relatively artless, inexperienced author of "Sappho" with their number and variety, failed to daunt the author of "Phylotus." No longer apprentice or journeyman, he left upon the last tale in the *Farewell* the stamp of the master "forger."

CINTHIO, L. B., AND THE *FAREWELL*

At some time during his compilation of the *Farewell* Rich must have considered how he might make his collection sufficiently long and varied. When he decided to include versions of three *novelle* from Cinthio's *Gli Hecatommithi* (1565), he did much to solve his problems. The five stories "forged onely for delight" plus Cinthio's three make up a work of very respectable length. Rich also managed to deploy the *novelle* to considerable advantage. After the long, stately "Sappho" and the nervous, complicated "Apolonius," the reader is grateful to encounter in the third story, "Nicander and Lucilla" (Cinthio's Decade VI, Novel 3), a brief, well-unified narrative with an almost lyrical sweetness and simplicity. Next come the hectic high adventure and exotic setting of "Fineo and Fiamma" (Cinthio's Decade II, Novel 6), after which one is signally prepared to relish the cynicism, the hilarity, the bawdiness—and the England—of the fifth tale, "Two Brethren." The position of the sixth, "Gonsales and His Vertuous Wife Agatha" (Cinthio's Decade III, Novel 5), a dignified account of a preternaturally faithful wife, similarly enhances that tale and also "Two Brethren" and "Aramanthus," the quaint, archaic seventh tale. Though to credit Rich with the same sort of acumen that inspired Shakespeare to devote a scene to the porter after Duncan's murder might be going too far, still the sensitiveness to contrast he exhibited in determining the order of his tales deserves high praise.

Rich provides a cryptic note on the three "Italian Histories" with which he thus agreeably leavened the *Farewell*: they were, he confides (19. 16 f.), "written likewise for pleasure by maister L. B." Why he should ascribe three of his stories, by no means the least attractive of the lot, to L. B. unless L. B. had indeed been somehow responsible for them is hard to explain, particularly since what he says about his own work usually proves to be true. Had he chosen to make his statement pointed instead of obtuse, he would presumably not have said, vaguely, that the *novelle* were "written" by L. B. but were "translated" by him.

What name he would have substituted for the initials is less clear.[1]

[1] Emil Koeppel suggests that the initials stood for no name at all but were a literary trap Rich contrived in order to send prying readers on wild-goose chases. Thus he hoped to

Edmond Malone proposed the only noteworthy candidate when he wrote a footnote to L. B. in his copy of the 1606 edition of the *Farewell*, now in the Bodleian: "Probably Lodowick Bryskett." The conjecture is brilliant. It merits serious consideration, since the question of who was at least partly responsible for so high a proportion of Rich's stories as three out of eight is one of considerable importance.

In dull Ireland, Bryskett, like Rich, busied himself with writing—specifically, with translating Cinthio's "Tre dialoghi della vita civile," and these appeared between Decades V and VI of *Gli Hecatommithi*, the very work by Cinthio from which Rich's "Italian Histories" came. Published in 1606 in Bryskett's version and entitled *A Discourse of Civill Life: Containing the Ethicke Part of Morall Philosophie*, Cinthio's cheerless treatise had attracted Bryskett much earlier.[1] He may indeed have come to know it as early as the years 1572 to 1575, during which Sir Henry Sidney employed him to exercise his fluent Italian in accompanying young Philip on a grand tour of the Continent. While the party was in Italy, Hubert Languet, the celebrated French scholar and Sidney's intellectual patron, plied the youth with letters encouraging his interest in moral philosophy, and Bryskett unquestionably shared the letters and the interest of his young master.[2] Armed thus with an opportunity to acquire Italian works on the subject and with the incentive to do so, Bryskett perhaps returned from Italy with both Cinthio's work and the resolve to translate it.

After three dazzling years abroad with Sidney, Bryskett found life in Ireland excessively dreary.[3] He doubtless welcomed a chance to

conceal his borrowings from Cinthio. Morton Luce regards the initials as "possibly a slip for M. B., i.e., Matteo Bandello." See Koeppel, "Studien zur Geschichte der italienischen Novelle in der englischen Litteratur des sechzehnten Jahrhunderts," *Quellen und Forschungen*, LXX (1892), 48, and *Rich's "Apolonius & Silla,"* ed. Luce (London, 1912), p. 49.

[1] "The booke written first for my priuate exercise, and meant to be imparted to that honorable personage [Lord Grey of Wilton, died 1593] . . . hath long layne by me," so Bryskett reveals in his dedication to Sir Robert Cecil. According to H. R. Plomer and T. P. Cross, *The Life and Correspondence of Lodowick Bryskett* (Chicago, 1927), p. 78, "it seems probable that the translation was made as early as 1567," though these biographers fail to give evidence indicating the probability.

[2] See S. A. Pears, *The Correspondence of Sir Philip Sidney and Hubert Languet* (London, 1845), pp. 7, 11, 19, 26–28, 37, 51 n., 52, 57, 60, 64, 67.

[3] In the dedication to his translation of Cinthio he gloomily validates Rich's complaint about the scarcity of books in Ireland by speaking (sig. B2) of "this barbarous countrie of Ireland . . . where almost no trace of learning is to be seene, and where the documents of Philosophie are the more needful, because they are so geason."

escape the tedium by "writing for pleasure." Did he, then, escape by translating Cinthio's *novelle*, which were conveniently at hand, as well as the treatise? In answer one can only echo Malone's "Probably," and add that, if he did, his manuscript versions of the stories should not have been hard for Rich to come by. Both minor lights in the small galaxy of literary figures relegated to Ireland by military, political, or economic exigencies, Rich and Bryskett were in the same places in Ireland at the same times and could scarcely have escaped being friends. Apart from their common interest in literature, there were other strong ties which should have bound them together. Both suffered the persecutions of a common enemy, Adam Loftus, archbishop of Dublin, and both enjoyed the favor of the same patrons, Sir Francis Walsingham and Sir Robert Cecil.[1]

One of the three "Italian Histories" in the *Farewell* provides internal evidence which seems greatly to reinforce Bryskett's claim to the stories. The hero and heroine of "Fineo and Fiamma" are natives of Savona and Genoa, respectively. At the beginning of his tale Cinthio simply gives the name of the cities, thinking it no more necessary to identify them further for his readers, I suppose, than an English author would have felt obliged to gloss Dover. But to Cinthio's mention of the towns someone, presumably either L. B. or Rich, added in the English version a political and geographical note no doubt welcome to the untraveled English reader. Savona is, it is explained (106. 16–18), "a Citie Subiecte vnto the State of Genoua, and distaunte from thence aboute thirtie miles." The information thus supplied was accurate. Savona had been subservient to Genoa since the conquest of 1528, and it is twenty-seven miles from Genoa. Though Rich never visited Italy, so far as is known, Bryskett was prepared to furnish such a footnote from personal observation, his stay in Italy with Sidney having included an excursion out of Padua to Genoa.

The firsthand knowledge of Genoa and its environs which Bryskett possessed may be reflected again by a further addition in the same tale. The heroine escapes from Genoa in a small boat of her father's. In this boat, according to another explanation (109. 37–110. 2), which is either

[1] On these connections, see E. M. Hinton, *Ireland through Tudor Eyes* (Philadelphia, 1935), pp. 41–43, 57–61, 86–91; Plomer and Cross, pp. 17–27, 30, 54 f., 65–70, 72 f.; and the *DNB* articles on Rich and Bryskett.

L. B.'s or Rich's—not Cinthio's—the father "was wont to take the aire vpon the sea, in tyme of faire weather, and to goe to their houses of pleasure, whereof that coaste is verie plentifull, and theim of exceadyng beautie." Whether Rich was able to volunteer this again accurate information about the use of Genoese yachts and Ligurian resort villas we cannot be sure. Bryskett, on the other hand, had seen them and as the attendant of the resplendent Sidney had perhaps even been entertained in them.

Bryskett was not one to make a secret of the fact that he was a man "bred and trained . . . in learning . . . that thereto hath added the experience and knowledge, which trauell and obseruation of many things in forraine countries must breed in him that hath seene many places, and the manners, orders, and policies of sundry nations."[1] But if this learned traveler was Rich's L. B. and if he was responsible for the glosses on Genoa and its satellite, why did he not display his knowledge of Italy in the first "Italian History," which is set in Ferrara? Why should Genoa twice set him happily to adding information and Ferrara move him to no explanation at all?

The clue to his knowledge of Genoa and his special interest in it may lie in the fact that he was the son of the wealthy Italian-English merchant Anthony Bryskett, who was born of a good family in Genoa in 1506, came to England about 1523, and became a British subject only in 1536. Hence had Lodowick been unable to glean information about Genoese affairs at first hand, he doubtless could have at second. It may have been as much the son of the well-born Genoese as Sidney's traveling companion who evinced an interest in Genoese villas by the sea.[2]

The case for Lodowick Bryskett is thus strong. It seems improbable that a likelier candidate can ever be nominated. Some might insist that if he is to be accepted as L. B. certain differences between what he is known to have translated and the translations in the *Farewell* must be accounted for. In *A Discourse* there are, for example, relatively few of the doublets and Briticisms which enrich the stories. The stories, too,

[1] The words are supposedly those of Sir Robert Dillon, whose encomium is modestly quoted by Bryskett himself in *A Discourse* (sig. D4).

[2] Even before his tour with Sidney, Lodowick had been sent to Italy by his father on family business, but whether specifically to Genoa is not known. For details of Anthony's life and business, see Deborah Jones, "Lodowick Bryskett and His Family," in *Thomas Lodge and Other Elizabethans*, ed. C. J. Sisson (Cambridge, Mass., 1933), pp. 254, 269; and Plomer and Cross, pp. 1, 3.

exhibit little of the painstaking care to which, Bryskett continually asserts, a translator should be solemnly committed. In *A Discourse* he speaks (sigs. E3v, E3, E2v) of "the precise rules of a translator," of "blots and vnderlinings" in his manuscript, and of "a thing so studied, and aduisedly set downe in writing, as a translation must be."

This scrupulosity is everywhere evident in *A Discourse*, which is often a servilely faithful rendering of Cinthio's Italian, yet is seldom apparent in the "Italian Histories," which are usually faithful to neither the letter nor the spirit of their originals. Since one could argue that fiction and the serious philosophical tract are different categories of literature, each might have required from the translator a different approach, the fiction exacting from him considerably fewer pains than the tract. But such arguments for and against Bryskett's claim are not very fruitful because they cannot be based on L. B.'s versions as they existed before they were modified for inclusion in the *Farewell*.

Beyond question, L. B.'s versions underwent extensive modifications, and the hand of the modifier is not difficult to recognize as Rich's. In the three stories as they stand in the *Farewell* there are turns of expression, even whole passages, so characteristic of Rich that they could have been written by no one else. One example must suffice for illustration. Whenever Rich's protagonists attain the consummation of their love or otherwise fall upon any notable good hap, Rich seldom neglects to mention "the joy and contentation" of all concerned. Two leading characters in "Apolonius" spend the night together "with suche ioye and contentation, as might in that conuenient tyme be wished for" (78. 4 f.); and some pages later, one hastens to add, they are married "with greate ioye, and contentation to all parties" (88. 33 f.), the unfolding of the plot having meantime rendered their original happiness dim and a new beatitude possible. In "Sappho," too, one heroine, at last sure that she is beloved, is "all rauished with ioye and contentation" (43. 9), while a second heroine, reunited with her husband, finds herself unable to speak "for ioye and contentation" (58. 17).

As a result of the bliss thus abounding in the first two tales, one is not unprepared to read in the third and fourth (two of the Cinthio stories) that Nicander and Lucilla are married "with the infinite ioye and contentment of the twoo yong louers, who had long wished and desired that happie daie" (104. 30–32), and that Fineo "wedded Fiamma and tooke her for his wife, to the vnspeakable ioye and contentation of bothe their hartes and myndes" (119. 3–5), even though Cinthio fails to give these details of their felicity. Of both weddings Cinthio's report is quite simple: "Si celebrarono le nozze," and "Fineo . . . sposò la giovane, e per mogliera la si prese,"[1] statements that L.B., had he been following Bryskett's usual method of translation, would doubtless have rendered with equal simplicity and starkness, "The marriage was performed," and "Fineo married the girl and took her for his wife." But simplicity and starkness were not for Rich. He was not an author to let slip his chance to exercise a favorite phrase.[2] For him, nuptials unaccompanied by joy and contentation were not proper nuptials at all.

Enough of such departures from the original are clearly Rich's to prove that he energetically applied himself to adapting the stories for his collection.[3] He thus made them his own, by Elizabethan standards—and yet he made a point of asserting that they were "written" by L. B. The "written" raises many questions but answers none because L. B.'s versions are not available for comparison with Cinthio's and Rich's. How literal were L. B.'s translations? Did he supply many comments like those on Genoa and Savona which seem to point to Lodowick Bryskett? Did he give Rich oral advice and suggestions along with the manuscripts? Did Rich consult Cinthio's Italian as well as L. B.'s English?[4]

Such questions are unanswerable. Without L. B.'s manuscripts his share in the stories as they now stand in the *Farewell* can never be precisely assessed. We must be content with Rich's generous though brief ascription—and with the knowledge that the stories did not appear in their present form until Rich had expended much of his energy and

[1] *Gli Hecatommithi*, reprinted in *Raccolta di novellieri italiani* (Torino, 1853), II, 326, I, 304.

[2] Particularly a phrase borrowed from "Rhomeo and Juletta," his favorite story in his favorite source, Painter's *Palace* (see the notes on 43. 9 and 47. 27–29). For other traces of Painter's *Palace* superimposed on Cinthio's prose, see the notes on 94. 27, 116. 15–17, 117. 5–7, 165. 6–10.

[3] For further examples, see the notes on 90. 26 f., 91. 10 f., 95. 36 f., 96. 9 f., 100. 32 f., 100. 36, 109. 2 f., 153. 6–8, 161. 26. Also attributable to Rich are the poems in "Nicander and Lucilla" (91. 36–93. 2, 93. 13–94. 8).

[4] There is no reason to pronounce Rich, who was at home in French, incapable of reading Italian. In addition to the three "Italian Histories" in the *Farewell* he made considerable use of at least two and probably three more of Cinthio's *novelle* (see below, pp. 339, 343 f., 348, which, so far as I can discover, were available to him only in Italian—unless L. B. had translated them too.

talent upon them. For the sake of convenience in discussion let us therefore take the point of view of an Elizabethan and proceed as if Rich alone should be held accountable for all that appears in his adaptations. Otherwise it would be necessary continually to observe that this or that deviation from the Italian is due possibly to Rich, possibly to L. B., or possibly to both. Throughout the remainder of this section, then, "Rich" is to be understood as a contraction of "Rich and/or L. B."

The garnishing of Cinthio's weddings with joy and contentation is merely one indication of what a careful study of the English and the Italian will make increasingly apparent—that Rich seems never to have hesitated to take astonishing liberties with his text. Unlike those Elizabethan translators who, pursuing their patriotic duty, edified their fellow-countrymen by carefully and conscientiously Englishing "serious" foreign works of history and philosophy, Rich is primarily interested in telling a good story. The main obligation he feels that he owes to a reader is to entertain him. He consequently does not often overlook an opportunity to heighten the drama, to intensify Cinthio's language, or to raise the emotional pitch of the original, which he almost invariably succeeds in rendering more attractive. An examination of his modifications is rewarding because it reveals not only how Rich's mind functions but also how an Elizabethan man of letters approached the problem of adapting foreign fiction for home consumption.

Rich effects many of his changes simply by adding to what he found in Cinthio. He shows a distinct predilection for piling Ossa on Pelion. Misery in any form often affects him as do Cinthio's joyous marriages. Witness what becomes of the hero's pathetic injunction to the heroine in Cinthio: "Therefore let me die, and you live." Rich's hero clamorously implores, "therefore (my deare) suffer me to dye before, and content thy self to liue, *and vouchsafe sometyme to remember thy vnfortunate Fineo when he is dedde*" (117. 21–23).[1] Whenever these misery-ridden characters seek to better their lot by any sort of suasion, Rich usually endeavors to increase the eloquence of their pleas, as when he exuberantly piles Ossa, "He assured hym that he would neuer . . . confesse of whom he had the poison, *but would rather suffer his tongue to be pulled*

[1]The italics distinguishing Rich's modifications are mine. The Italian upon which the quotations from Rich are based may be consulted in the notes to the passages identified in parentheses. For similar expansions of misery see the notes on 90. 10, 90. 17–19, 113. 37.

out of his hedde, or endure any torment that might be deuised" (155. 22–25), upon Cinthio's Pelion, "He promised him never to tell that he had obtained the poison from him."[1]

By adding concrete, specific, realistic details again and again, Rich shows a practical turn of mind. In Cinthio one reads, "And because he was young and of good strength, having brought with him some things so that he could lift the stone which closed the tomb, he opened it." But Rich equips him with tools more adequate than "some things" for performing this feat: "And because he was a yong manne of verie good strengthe, and had brought with hym *instrumentes of iron* to open the Toumbe, and lifte vp the stone that couered it, he gatte it open" (158. 18–21). Having raised the stone, Cinthio's young man carelessly enters. Not Rich's. Though not a more experienced ghoul, he is at any rate a more practical one. He hoists the stone, "*and hauyng vnderpropped it surely*: he went into the vaute" (158. 21 f.).[2] In my opinion, such additions give reality to action which in Cinthio seems remote.

A desire for an elegance in style like George Pettie's evidently inspired a good many additions. Proverbs, alliteration, and doublets, those marks of euphuism that stud Rich's "original" stories, are everywhere to be found in the "Italian Histories," though not in Cinthio. In one addition Rich was able to indulge a euphuist's appetite for both the proverbial and the alliterative. Cinthio's Nicandro fears "that Lucilla had left him," while the English Nicander's trepidation is aggravated by his knowledge of womankind's proverbial fickleness: he is afraid "that Lucilla (*waueryng as women vse to doe*) had forsaken hym" (91. 26 f.). Cinthio, whose interest in proverbs and alliteration seems to have been negligible, might have rubbed his eyes again to see a simple noun like "gain" burgeon into the alliterative "prey for their profite" (108. 29).[3] But the euphuisms that might have perplexed (not to say irritated) him most are the scores of doublets replacing the single words and phrases he made do in Italian. Single nouns, adjectives, verbs, or phrases repeatedly yield such graceful though tautological pairs as "prime and

[1] For other considerably augmented persuasions, see the notes to 99. 17–22, 99. 29 f., 156. 9 f.

[2] For other additions revealing Rich's practicality, see the notes on 110. 23 f., 111. 8, 115. 29 f., 115. 33, 117. 36, 151. 34–36, 156. 20 f., 158. 21 f.

[3] For other English proverbs in the "Italian Histories," see the notes on 107. 29, 150. 35, 151. 15 f., 152. 12 f.; for other alliterative phrases, see the notes on 90. 16, 95. 5.

flower" (89. 22 f.), "stout and valiant" (107. 6), "dooe wishe and would bee glad of" (99. 11 f.), and "refused his consente, and shewed hym self contrary to" (106. 23 f.).

Not all these pairs can be explained by Rich's undeniably strong instinct for following a literary fashion or by a desire simply to enhance the sound and pattern of his prose with words and phrases in couples. Some may be due to a preoccupation with the Renaissance idea of "copy" (i.e., *copia*) that impelled the lexicographer to gloss a foreign term with a great abundance of native words and the translator to render a single foreign word for which he knew more than one meaning into two English words.[1] Some of Rich's doublets may even be the result of consulting a bilingual dictionary. Without pretending to prove that either the translator or the adapter of the "Italian Histories" used William Thomas' *Principal Rules of the Italian Grammer, with a Dictionarie for the Better Understandynge of Boccace, Petrarcha, and Dante* (1567), to which an Englishman dealing with Italian shortly before 1581 was most likely to resort, one may see from the following samples how suggestive such a dictionary might have been:

THOMAS	RICH
Macchiare, to spotte or steigne	to staine or spot (*macchiare*; 101. 34 f.)[2]
Podestà, a potestate or principall officer of a towne	Magistrate, or cheef Officer of the citie (*podestà*; 107. 37 f.)
Toglierre, torre, or tor, to take away	take from hym or barre hym of (*torre*; 151. 23 f.)
Inditio, a token or likelyhoode	token or signe (*inditio*; 157. 32)
Inditioni, signes	
Mercede, rewarde or wages	rewarde and hire (*mercede*; 160. 31)
Affligere, to punishe or torment	torment and afflicte (*affligea*; 114. 3 f.)
Costume, use or custome	maner or custome (*costume*; 113. 26)
Costumato, manered or accustomed	
Noievole, displeasant or hurtful	displeasant and . . . vngrateful (*noiosi*; 152. 8)

[1] On "copy" in lexicography, see D. T. Starnes, "Thomas Cooper's *Thesaurus:* A Chapter in Renaissance Lexicography," *University of Texas Studies in English*, XXVIII (1949), 42–45. For the prodigal use of doublets by such translators as Hoby, Amyot, North, Florio, and Holland, see F. O. Matthiessen, *Translation: An Elizabethan Art* (Cambridge, Mass., 1931), pp. 40, 67, 78, 126, 190.

[2] Preceding the usual references to Rich's page and line are the words in Cinthio which yielded the English doublets.

THOMAS (*continued*)	RICH (*continued*)
Saettia, a certein barke or fuste	Foiste or Galley (*saettia*; 111. 31)
Auenire, or Aduenire, to come unto, to chaunce or happen	should happen and come to passe (*avvenisse*; 100. 30)
Spegnere, to put out or extinguishe	extinguishe, or quence (*spegna*; 118. 29)
Ammollire, to mollifie or make soft	mollified and wrought to be tender (*si ammolisci*; 152. 19)

In the last two samples may lie a clue to the genesis of yet another kind of doublet in Rich. Observe that "extinguishe" and "mollified" are linked with simpler language. Had they not been, their meaning might have eluded some readers. Such consideration for the untutored, to whom Rich's appeal was great, seems to have led to a similar thoughtful coupling of other words, usually of Latin origin, with plain, forthright English, as in "reprehend and chide" (152. 5), "composition . . . [or] mixture" (155. 33 f.), "Artificer or craftes man" (94. 31), and "commoditie or quiet" (149. 16).

These prudent addenda are amusing as well as sensible; one smiles at them. But with additions of another sort Rich gains one's respect. More interested than Cinthio in the psychology of his characters, he adds details of characterization that are far from crude. There are just enough of these to make the reader wish that Rich had completed the fleshing of Cinthio's skeletons. To the bare statement of a character's behavior Rich sometimes adds a complete exposition of the mental processes which precede and motivate the character's actions. For example, where Cinthio's King of Tunis is merely advised of the flight of his two favorite captives, Rich's king puts two and two together: "*Fiamma beying missed and Fineo likewise*, the kyng (was aduertised of their eskape) *who perceiuying the Marchauntes to be gone also, rested assured that it was a sette match made for the stealyng of Fiamma awaie*" (115. 38–116. 4). Rich thus better prepares his reader for what follows: the king's violent rage and sanguine pursuit of the fugitives seems consequent and justified.

At the beginning of the tale the objects of his hunt, we are told, would have married had not the heroine's father opposed the match. Here Cinthio leaves us, offering no explanation of the old gentleman's opposition (without which there would have been no encounter with pirates, no selling into slavery, no adventures in the King of Tunis' harem—in short, no story at all), and plunges directly into the action of the tale. Rich does not similarly scant the all-important parental hostility that makes the protagonists' odyssey necessary in the first place. Instead, with no hint from Cinthio he suggests (106. 25–31) four substantial reasons why the old man should object to Fiamma's marriage, thus transforming an inexplicably perverse and intolerant old tyrant into a very human father. First, he has a natural desire to see his daughter make a better match; second, he cannot bear to have her marry a man who would take her to live out of town; third, he displays a normal xenophobia; and, finally, he is enough of a snob to balk at receiving a citizen of a subservient state as his son-in-law. Here, it seems to me, are touches that are something more than skillful; they are, in a very real sense, creative.[1] They render Fiamma's father—an uninteresting, stilted puppet in Cinthio—a man of breath and feeling.

Rich's lively interest in motives and mental processes is accompanied by a deep concern for the moral and religious climate in which his characters dwell. Time and again not only additions but deletions and rearrangements as well reveal, in a most engaging way, the powerful bias which inspired them. In one addition he makes it clear that he considers only nature on the rampage worse than the Mohammedan beasts which infest "Fineo and Fiamma": Fineo decides "that it was better for hym to be in the power of men, *though thei were Infidels*, then in the power of Seas and windes" (108. 36–38). At the end of the story all agree that "God and Nature" (119. 18) had created Fineo and Fiamma for each other, but not before Rich has piously reversed Cinthio's word order ("nature and God") to give God precedence over the pagan deity. The prostitute and lecher in "Gonsales and His Vertuous Wife Agatha" receive shrift as short as the infidel's. Cinthio's calm, matter-of-fact introduction of them early in the tale sets Rich off (148. 26–149.4 and 149. 21–25) on passionate though brief homilies concerning their failings.

His reaction to the religion of Cinthio's characters, who are as a matter of course Roman Catholic, is also heated. Anything smacking

[1] For other admirable, perspicacious additions which endow Cinthio's shadowy figures with character, see the notes on 111. 16–19, 148. 26–149. 4, 149. 13 f., 150. 25 f., 156. 25–29, 156. 34 f., 157. 13–15, 163. 37 f.

of popery, like Cinthio's references to the ritual of taking the veil, to going to mass, to observants, and to Pope Adrian, is expurgated with almost morbid scrupulosity.[1] What place could it have in the collection of so vociferous a Protestant as Rich, the author of the bitterly anti-Roman *The True Report of a Late Practise Enterprised by a Papist* (1582) and *A Catholicke Conference betweene Syr Tady Mac Mareall, a Popish Priest of Waterforde, and Patrick Plaine, a Young Student in Trinity Colledge* (1612)?

Rich is not so engrossed in matters of religion, style, and characterization that he neglects the technical and mechanical problems involved in readying the "Italian Histories" for the *Farewell.* Cinthio usually prefaces each *novella* with a one-paragraph post-mortem on the preceding tale, underlining the virtue of the heroine, castigating the wickedness of the villain, and in general calling the reader's attention to any moral he might have missed. Rich, of course, omits this autopsy. In "Nicander and Lucilla" he compensates for its omission and establishes the time and place of the story by borrowing from Cinthio's Decade VI, Novel 2, which immediately precedes "Nicander and Lucilla" in *Gli Hecatommithi*, an introduction (89. 13–15) that is ornamental, resounding, and authoritative in tone.

As a rule Cinthio's tales contain only two paragraphs, the first consisting of the post-mortem, the second recounting a whole story from beginning to end. After dropping the first, Rich takes the liberty of dividing the second into more or less logical paragraphs. In less obvious ways, too, he displays an awareness of the niceties of composition and storytelling, as when he transposes a sentence or two to eliminate an exasperating interruption in Cinthio's narrative, supplies connectives for the sake of smoothness, and turns declarative sentences into rhetorical questions to gain variety, emphasis, and a dramatic effect absent in the Italian.[2]

In the English versions there is much to charm and delight students of Elizabethan diction. There is something of the flavor of the King James Version of the Bible in "But Fineo *bad her bee of good comforte* ... [and] saied" (117. 17 f.) for Cinthio's "But Fineo said to her"; in "He

[1] See the notes on 100. 37–101. 2, 91. 22–25, 158. 10 f., 101. 23–102. 12. For other modifications which are in effect moral or religious comments, see the notes on 116. 21, 116. 24 f., 118. 26, 150. 3–5, 151. 19.

[2] See the notes on 162. 23–33, 102. 32, 108. 21, 162. 6–10.

framed hym self to beare *with pacient minde, that heauie yoke of his* captiuitie" (109. 4 f.) for "He patiently endured this cruel servitude"; and in "Trouble not your self, *nor greeue not*" (99. 5 f.) for "Do not be distressed." When Cinthio's stark "replied to him," "wicked woman," "courtesan," "old man," "old woman," and "villain" become, respectively, "saied to him boldely and roundely againe" (107. 23 f.), "thou naughtie packe" (162. 6 f.), "baggage strumpette" (165. 14), "th'old carle" (90. 20 f.), "This olde hag" (152. 12), and "mischeeuous knaue" (110. 22), the effect is not so elevated as to be Biblical, but it is none the less vigorous.

This kind of hearty, colloquial speech rings everywhere through the avenues of Rich's Genoa, Ferrara, Seville, and Tunis and transforms Cinthio's relatively sedate Italians, Spaniards, and Tunisians into robust Elizabethans. Witness the metamorphosis of the suave, gracile Ferrarese lord in "Fineo and Fiamma" into a lusty young Englishman: "[Don Hercules] beganne to allowe and commende his owne iudgemente, in that he had placed his loue vppon *so excellente and rare a peece*" (98. 21–23). Is it any wonder that when such a lad calls uninvited on the sleeping, innocent heroine she awakes with the scream, "Out alas sir" (98. 31), and not "Oime, Signore"? Or that the tears which follow when she realizes her predicament should evoke, not "like dewdrops on morning roses," but a simile with a Chaucerian touch—"like droppes of dewe hanging vppon Roses, in a Maie mornyng" (99. 2 f.)?[1] Even the prostitute of Seville in "Gonsales and His Vertuous Wife Agatha" is denizened when in a quarrel with Gonsales we find her "aunsweryng hym thawartly" (162. 5) instead of "replying to him arrogantly," as Cinthio has it. Like any whore of Shoreditch, in Rich she entertains clients impartially if they come "with their handes full" (150. 7), a phrase which promises a far more exciting fee than Cinthio's pedestrian "with plenty of money."

Rich shows little patience with Cinthio's elegant euphemisms. Despite these he recognizes, and relishes, the risqué elements in the *novelle* and makes the most of them. Where Cinthio primly describes Lucilla's fear lest Nicander should discover that Don Ercole "was casting his eye upon her," Rich comes right out with an exuberantly slangy passage: his

[1] For other departures from the original in which Rich's gift for figurative language is apparent, see the notes on 95. 20 f., 96. 29, 97. 37, 155. 22–25.

Lucilla worries lest Nicander "perceiue, that this yong Prince *hunted after that haunte*" (91. 18 f.). According to Cinthio, Lucilla's mother, considering the poverty and temptation apt to beset an orphaned, foot-loose girl, predicts that to die and leave her daughter impoverished and unchaperoned might "make her become a woman of the world." Woman of the world, indeed! Rich describes in plainer terms the fate to which such a misfortune may reduce a girl: she may well "be brought to yeelde her self into the handes of some suche one, as would not haue due regard vnto her calling, but bring her vnto the spoile" (95. 24–26).

Rich seems to strive instinctively to achieve the picturesque and the robust. He is not content with a mere "dead"; he writes "starke dedde" (155. 37). In rendering "speak" as "open my lippes" (96. 29), he reveals the Elizabethan's love of action. Too energetic to accept Cinthio's decorous "that evening he put it [the sleeping potion] secretly in her food," he prefers "at Supper he did *caste* it there vpon her meate" (156. 12). This taste for the athletic occasionally leads to quite extraordinary lengths. Sent to arouse Agatha from her Juliet-like sleep, Cinthio's maidservant, a timid girl in the Italian, "put her hand on her and, touching her gently, said: Arise, Madame." But Rich's servant, having called her mistress in vain, "laied her hand vpon her, and *giuying her a shagge*, she saied withall, Mistres awake" (157. 5 f.). When she reports the failure of the "shagge," she is ordered to return and shake her mistress till she awakens. Cinthio spares us the carrying out of this injunction. In Rich, however, there follows the sort of performance to be expected of an Amazon, not a well-trained domestic: she "rolled and tumbled her in her bed, and all in vaine" (157. 16 f.) and then had the temerity to admit that she had "rolled her vp and doune the bedde, and that yet she stirred not" (157. 20 f.).

Because such vigor and imagination are lavished upon what were, to begin with, three of Cinthio's best tales, the finished products in English are most engaging. That these three out of Cinthio's nearly endless century should have been selected for treatment speaks well for Rich's taste. That he managed with almost every modification, whether addition, deletion, expansion, or rearrangement, to improve the original is also remarkable and worthy of the highest praise. To compare the English with the Italian is to learn respect for the Elizabethan art of adapting Continental fiction for English readers, an art which deserves further study. "Nicander and Lucilla," "Fineo and Fiamma," and "Gonsales and His Vertuous Wife Agatha" are not only great credits to Rich and most attractive additions to the *Farewell* but fine examples of that art and notable contributions to Elizabethan fiction as well. Not the least praiseworthy feature of the "Italian Histories" is that as fiction they are entertaining to the modern reader, and that is more than is usually said for *A Petite Pallace of Pleasure*, *Euphues*, and the *Arcadia*.

RICH AS A LENDER

COLLIER entitled his reprint of Rich's tales *Eight Novels Employed by English Dramatic Poets of the Reign of Queen Elizabeth.* Though a cross to library cataloguers, the title nevertheless proclaims the most important thing about the *Farewell* in the eyes of Collier and of many a scholar after him. Actually, Collier greatly underestimated the borrowings from Rich. In his preface he discusses the relationship of the *Farewell* to only three plays. If he had been aware that not three but at least ten, dating from 1598 to 1633, are related to Rich's stories, he might have revised his title to read *Eight Novels Employed Again and Again by English Dramatic Poets of the Reigns of Queen Elizabeth, King James I, and King Charles I.*

It is unlikely that the number of plays will remain fixed at ten. After reading the *Farewell*, students with a wider knowledge of Jacobean and Caroline drama than mine will most probably be able to extend the list offered below. Even at present, however, there is much justice in Collier's remark that the *Farewell* "must have been popular, and may, in some respects, be considered a second 'Palace of Pleasure.'"[1] As a happy hunting ground for playwrights in search of a plot, Rich's collection was indeed a second *Palace*. Among all the works of Elizabethan fiction only Painter's collection attracted more dramatists than Rich's—and Painter offered 101 selections to Rich's 8.

Why the *Farewell* had a special appeal for playwrights may be readily understood by those who have patiently followed the stylistic flights of Pettie and Lyly or the involutions in the plots of Underdowne and Sidney. By Elizabethan standards all the stories in the *Farewell* except the first one are concise. Furthermore, like most good tellers of tales, Rich conceived of a story as a series of scenes. These he developed sometimes by means of stately utterances borrowed from Painter, Pettie, or Cinthio, sometimes by means of the racy, colloquial dialogue at which he himself excelled. He further underlined the dramatic potentialities of his narrative by inserting many passages (as at 157. 13–15 and 189. 15–18) which smack of the stage direction.

[1] *A Bibliographical and Critical Account of the Rarest Books in the English Language* (New York, 1866), III, 302.

Occasionally he even showed some skill in the delineation of character, rarely a matter of great concern to his fellow-Elizabethan short-story writers. Observe, for instance, how in the fifth tale the doctor suing for Miss Dorothy's favor diagnoses and prescribes, the lawyer argues and pleads, and the soldier talks with aggressive bluntness. It is in no way surprising that such characters as these, the robust scenes in which they participate, and the sprightly speeches which they utter caught the eyes of the authors of the following plays.

A *The Weakest Goeth to the Wall* (1600)

Collier first observed that "Sappho Duke of Mantona," the first selection in the *Farewell*, and the anonymous comedy *The Weakest Goeth to the Wall* are somehow related. He suggested that the story may have existed before 1581 as a drama which was the source of both "Sappho" and *The Weakest.*[1] Sir Walter Greg, who edited the latter, asserts that the story is the basis of the comedy without advancing the evidence that led him to this conclusion.[2] Two recent investigators have put the matter beyond doubt by adducing evidence which may be summarized here.[3]

At least two dozen widely scattered sources went into the confecting of "Sappho."[4] Partly as a result of their number and variety it is the most complicated tale in the collection. Yet the author of *The Weakest* followed Rich's meandering plot with sufficient fidelity to prove that he either relied on "Sappho" or consulted the same two dozen sources Rich utilized. In addition, Rich's words as well as his plot found their way into the comedy. Though the playwright was not so smitten with Rich's rhetoric as Rich was with Painter's, he obviously composed some of his blank verse with the *Farewell* open before him, and he even did Rich the honor of giving a low-comedy character the name Barnaby and allowing this clown to quote a celebrated line from the *Farewell.*[5]

[1] See his edition of the *Farewell*, p. x.

[2] See his edition, Malone Society Reprints (Oxford, 1912), p. vi.

[3] See D. T. Starnes, "Barnabe Riche's 'Sappho Duke of Mantona': A Study in Elizabethan Story-Making," *SP*, XXX (1933), 472, and T. M. Cranfill, "Barnaby Rich's 'Sappho' and *The Weakest Goeth to the Wall*," *University of Texas Studies in English, 1945–1946*, pp. 166–71.

[4] See below, pp. 339 f.

[5] On Barnaby Bunch and his quotation of 8. 13, see below, pp. lvi f. For passages from the play which echo the story, see the notes on 26. 37, 31. 13–32, 35. 2–10.

A study of *The Weakest* and its relationship to its source has produced no clues to the identity of the author of the comedy, which has been variously attributed to Webster, Dekker, and Munday.[1] Whoever he may have been, he spun well of the stuff he found in "Sappho." Except for those plays for which Shakespeare was in part indebted to Rich, *The Weakest* is the most attractive drama inspired by the *Farewell.*

B *How a Man May Chuse a Good Wife from a Bad* (1602)

How a Man May Chuse was an exceedingly popular play, running through seven editions by 1634. Though it was published anonymously, most critics believe that the author was Thomas Heywood, a man of vast experience in appraising plots which appealed to audiences.[2] The comedy was very influential. The authors of several later dramas borrowed from it, and its effect on stagecraft was considerable.[3] Indirectly, then, its source exerted an appreciable influence on Elizabethan and Jacobean drama.

Scholars have long agreed that the source of *How a Man May Chuse* is the story of the preternaturally virtuous wife Agatha and her depraved husband, whose adventures are recounted in Cinthio's *Gli Hecatommithi* (Decade III, Novel 5) and in Rich's adaptation of Cinthio's *novella,* "Gonsales and His Vertuous Wife Agatha," the sixth tale in the *Farewell.* However, there seems to be some uncertainty whether the dramatist obtained his plot from Cinthio's version or from Rich's.[4] Happily, the uncertainty may now be dispelled by evidence that the playwright culled bits from other stories in the *Farewell* and also used

[1] See M. L. Hunt, *Thomas Dekker: A Study* (New York, 1911), pp. 42–45, and *The Cambridge History of English Literature* (New York, 1933), V, 351 f.

[2] See F. G. Fleay, *Biographical Chronicle of the English Drama* (London, 1891), I, 290; A. C. Swinburne, *The Age of Shakespeare* (London, 1908), pp. 242 f.; J. Q. Adams, "Thomas Heywood and *How a Man May Choose a Good Wife from a Bad,*" *Englische Studien,* XLV (1912), 30–44; and *How a Man May Chuse,* ed. A. E. H. Swaen, *Materialen zur Kunde des älteren englischen Dramas,* XXXV (Louvain, 1912), vii–xiii. For dissident opinions, see F. E. Schelling, *Elizabethan Drama* (New York, 1908), I, 331, and Otelia Cromwell, *Thomas Heywood: A Study in the Elizabethan Drama of Everyday Life* (New Haven, Conn., 1928), p. 200.

[3] See C. R. Baskervill, "Source and Analogues of *How a Man May Choose a Good Wife from a Bad,*" *PMLA,* XXIV (1909), 717 f., 730 n., and *The Faire Maide of Bristowe,* ed. A. H. Quinn (Philadelphia, 1902), pp. 11–14.

[4] In Baskervill's opinion, pp. 711 f., "It would be hard to decide which is the immediate source. . . . But the slight evidence is all in favor of his borrowing from Riche."

some of Rich's additions to Cinthio's *novella.* At least nine passages indicate the dramatist's knowledge of the *Farewell.* These may be consulted in my notes, as may a few samples of the playwright's blank verse which show how Rich's prose lent itself to that form.[1]

C *The Old Law* (written about 1599,[2] published 1656)

In *The Old Law*, by Middleton, Rowley, and Massinger, there is a hitherto unnoticed parallel to Rich's "Agatha" that deserves mention. Like the story, the play contains a mistreated wife named Agatha who suffers much at the hands of a husband who wishes her dead so that he may marry a courtesan. The Agatha of the comedy furthermore emulates Rich's heroine by pleading for her husband at the trial to which he is ultimately brought.[3] Here the parallel stops, and the differences between Rich's and the playwrights' treatment of Agatha's predicament are great. To mention only one, Rich's heroine has beauty, refinement, and nobility, while the "old Ag" (IV. i. 106 f.) of the comedy, though faithful, is a simple "old piece of flesh" (IV. i. 14), aged fifty-nine, and a principal only in the farcical subplot. Even so, the playwrights' familiarity with the Cinthio-Rich tale cannot be doubted. Whether they knew it in *Gli Hecatommithi*, in the *Farewell*, or in both there seems to be no way of discovering.

D *Philotus* (1603, 1612)

Since *Ane Verie Excellent and Delectabill Treatise Intitulit Philotus* and Sir David Lindsay's morality play, *Ane Pleasant Satyre of the Thrie Estaitis*, constitute the scanty corpus of extant early Scottish dramatic literature, both have received a good deal of scholarly attention. Yet the problems of the authorship, date of composition, and source of *Philotus* have remained unsolved, though it has been four times edited since 1792.[4]

[1] See the notes on 31. 20–22, 33. 23–27, 41. 8–10, 155. 33 f., 156. 19 f., 156. 21–23, 158. 37–159. 2, 161. 26, 161. 37–162. 3, 162. 14–16, 162. 24–29, 163. 13–18, 165. 16–22, 197. 7–11.

[2] See E. C. Morris, "On the Date and Composition of *The Old Law*," *PMLA*, XVII (1902), 2, 67.

[3] V. i. 568, 574 f., in *The Works of Thomas Middleton*, ed. A. H. Bullen (London, 1885), II, 240.

[4] See J. Pinkerton, *Scotish Poems Reprinted from Scarce Editions* (Edinburgh, 1792),

One scholar ascribes it to some author before 1530, but later retracts this ascription and argues for a date of composition slightly before the edition of 1603.[1] A second attributes it to Robert Semple and thinks it was written about 1568.[2] A third is of the "notion . . . that the Scottish 'Philotus,' though not printed until 1603, may at an early date have been derived by its author from some authority, to which, perhaps, Riche also resorted" for the plot of his eighth tale, "Phylotus and Emelia."[3] A fourth is "inclined to accept the suggestion of Riche's editor . . . that Riche's story and the comedy alike go back to some lost common source."[4] In the opinion of a fifth the play is founded on the story, but he fails to explain how he arrived at his opinion.[5] A sixth, judging from the vocabulary of the play, believes that it cannot be much earlier than 1600.[6] And the most recent editor ventures no positive answers to the questions of source and date, declaring merely that "clearer evidence as to the immediate source of *Philotus* . . . would help further to define the date limits."[7]

Yet evidence could scarcely be clearer, or more abundant, than that which proves the dependence of the play on Rich's "Phylotus." The playwright follows the plot of Rich's story closely, making only one change in the order of the multifarious scenes as Rich presents them.[8] Besides, the drama abounds in words, phrases, and sometimes whole speeches manifestly inspired by Rich's language. The dramatist's way with Rich's words may usually be described as something halfway between paraphrasing and verbatim repetition. But regardless of the

III, 1–63; J. Sibbald, *Chronicle of Scottish Poetry* (Edinburgh, 1802), III, 398–440; *Philotus*, ed. D. Irving, Bannatyne Club (Edinburgh, 1835); and *Philotus*, ed. A. J. Mill, Scottish Text Society (Edinburgh, 1933).

[1] See Pinkerton, I, xxi.

[2] See Sibbald, III, 397.

[3] See Collier's edition of the *Farewell*, p. ix.

[4] See G. C. Moore Smith, "Riche's Story 'Of Phylotus and Emilia,'" *MLR*, V (1910), 343.

[5] See Irving, p. viii. He seems to have arrived at the correct conclusion on the basis of a mistaken inference—that Rich's "Phylotus" belonged to the "author's original stock."

[6] Sir William Craigie, whose opinion is quoted by Mill, p. 86.

[7] Mill, p. 86.

[8] In the tale the marriage of Phylotus and Phylerno is followed immediately by their fight to decide who shall be master of the household. Then comes Flanius' conjuration. In the comedy, however, his big scene directly succeeds the marriage and precedes the conflict. Why the author made this transposition is not clear, as either order could have been made dramatically expedient. "The Argument" of the play prefixed to the edition of 1612 follows the order of the tale instead of the play. See Mill, p. 99.

terms one may choose to describe the method, there is never any doubt that the borrower wrote with one eye on Rich's page. Since Rich tapped at least a dozen sources for the plot to which the dramatist faithfully adheres and for the language which he repeatedly echoes, any theory except that the comedy is based on the tale is plainly untenable.[1]

Not content with ransacking "Phylotus," the playwright also resorts to the first, sixth, and seventh stories—and probably to the second, third, and fifth, to which the play contains interesting and apparently significant resemblances.[2] Thus to make wholesale use of one of a collection of eight tales and then to turn for further material certainly to three, and probably to six, other selections in the same volume is a procedure that is almost unprecedented. In borrowing from the sixth story the dramatist displays considerable ingenuity, transforming the panderess who vainly practices her art on the redoubtable Agatha into the "Macrell" of the comedy, and supplying her with dialogue cleverly wrought out of a debate which Emelia has with herself in the story.[3] His use of Rich's first tale, however, is more ill-advised than ingenious. In "Sappho" Valeria elopes not only without her father's permission but in the face of his express opposition, gets caught, and consequently suffers the unreasonable, melodramatic fulminations of a father intent on having her killed. In "Phylotus" Emelia's sins provoke her father to a stern but sensible lecture. Unfortunately, the dramatist prefers the fulminations in "Sappho" to the more moderate scolding in "Phylotus."[4] As a result, the verbal punishment of his heroine fails to fit her crime.

In ascertaining the sources of *Philotus*, one necessarily arrives at a date before which it could not have been written—1581, when the *Farewell* first appeared. Knowing the origins of the comedy does little, however, to solve the problem of authorship. On September 20, 1581, the Glasgow civic authorities granted to one Robert Semple in Dumbarton the sum of £13. 6*s*. 8*d*. for "outsetting of the pastyme to the Kingis Majestie."[5] This minute engenders some tantalizing possibilities—that

[1] For the sources of "Phylotus" see below, pp. 349 f. Parallels between Rich's and the dramatist's plots and language, too copious to be specified here, are noted in my commentary, pp. 323–31.

[2] See the notes on 59. 9, 61. 32, 62. 4 f., 62. 30, 74. 11–13, 99. 11 f., 129. 17 f., 151. 2–17, 152. 2–11, 178. 11–14.

[3] See the notes on 151. 2–17, 152. 2–11, 184. 29–185. 9.

[4] See the notes on 62. 4 f., 62. 30.

[5] *Glasgow Burgh Records*, I, 469 (quoted by Mill, p. 85).

the "pastyme" mentioned was *Philotus*; that the beneficiary of the grant was the same Robert Semple (1530?–95) who was a captain participating (on the side of the English) in the siege of Edinburgh in 1573,[1] a campaign celebrated by Rich as one of the great triumphs of Sir William Drury;[2] that Semple and Rich, both captains and admirers of Drury, knew each other professionally; and that Semple, attracted by Rich's publication of 1581, lost no time in deriving a comedy from it. But of course all these notions are merely possibilities.

Though the identity of the author must remain unproved, he produced a comedy of exceptional interest to students of Scottish literature, the drama, and Elizabethan fiction. Among the plays drawn from the *Farewell*, only Shakespeare's *Twelfth Night* has inspired so great a mass of critical comment. However much *Philotus* may leave to be desired as literature, and however few people it may have amused if it was produced on the stage, it has already provided and, one suspects, will continue to provide scholars with an uncommon amount of entertainment.

E *Tugend- und Liebesstreit* (performed 1608, published 1677)

About a century after Rich fashioned them, those doughty characters Apolonius and Silla were still flourishing so far afield as Schloss Bevern in Germany.[3] There, on October 30, 1677, still young, still in love, and still bearing the names Rich gave them, they pursued their wonted careers on the stage in an English traveling company's

[1] For some account of Semple (or Sempill) the author and soldier see *The Sempill Ballates*, ed. T. G. Stevenson (Edinburgh, 1877), p. vii; A. J. Mill, *Mediæval Plays in Scotland* (Edinburgh, 1927), p. 192 n.; and the article on Robert Sempill in *DNB*.

[2] In "An Epitaph vpon the death of syr William Drury" (1580) Rich writes (my italics):

> "And Brute hath blowne, what glory he hath gaynde,
> In Scotish Land, *where they themselues can tell*,
> In Edenbrough he wan there Mayden tower,
> By fyrst assault, perforce the scotishe power."

See *The Paradise of Dainty Devices*, ed. H. E. Rollins (Cambridge, Mass., 1927), pp. 123, 266 f. Since Semple was among the Scots who could and did tell of the siege, the italicized clause may allude to his ballad "The Sege of the Castel of Edinburgh" (*The Sempill Ballates*, pp. 177–88).

[3] See E. Herz, *Englische Schauspieler und englisches Schauspiel* (Hamburg and Leipzig, 1903), p. 121.

performance of a comedy entitled *Tugend- und Liebesstreit*. According to the scholarly consensus, earlier versions of the comedy were enacted at Graz in 1608, at Dresden in 1626, and at Güstrow between 1654 and 1663.[1] "What is so remarkable about the play," asserts Anders, "is the fact that *Riche's* 'Apolonius and Silla' is the *unmistakeable* source of this German drama." With this opinion the other commentators on *Tugend* agree, though none can believe that it (or *Twelfth Night* either) came directly from the tale. They prefer to postulate a no longer extant English comedy which was based on "Apolonius" and which in turn inspired *Tugend* and *Twelfth Night*.[2]

It may not be fruitful to join in the various attempts to reconstruct the hypothetical lost English play. Instead, one may rest content with observing that the parallels between *Tugend* and "Apolonius" itself are appreciable. The Apolonius and Silla of the comedy not only retain the names of Rich's hero and heroine but suffer essentially the same tribulations. As for the minor characters, Silla's brother, Silvio, becomes her brother Silvius in the play, and, as Creizenach notes (p. 57), "Silla's maid [in *Tugend*] . . . is without doubt patterned after the servant Pedro in Riche." Incidentally, to this maid, who is called Petrona, seems to have passed (circuitously or not) the name of a character, the Duchess of Petrona, in Rich's first tale. Regardless of what route Rich's personages took in their journey from the pages of the *Farewell* to Germany, they fared tolerably well out of England. As seventeenth-century German plays go, *Tugend* is not unattractive.[3]

[1] See Herz, p. 122; W. Creizenach, *Die Schauspiele der englischen Komödianten* (Berlin and Stuttgart, 1889), pp. 58, 65; and H. R. D. Anders, *Shakespeare's Books* (Berlin, 1904), p. 69. Creizenach prints *Tugend*, pp. 71–124.

[2] See Creizenach, p. 58, Herz, p. 121, and Anders, p. 69.

[3] It is rather more attractive than two cognate German plays, the *Comoedia genandt dass wohl gesprochene Uhrtheil eynes weiblichen Studenten oder der Jud von Venedig* (dating in its present form from the second half of the seventeenth century) and *Die getreue Sklavin Doris* (acted in Munich between 1681 and 1685). According to Herz (pp. 84, 121), the first act and part of the second of *Dass wohl gesprochene Uhrtheil* "depend closely upon" the posited lost English dramatization of Rich's "Apolonius," and *Die getreue Sklavin* possibly stems from the same source. The parallels between the tale and these comedies are so general, however, that the three should in my opinion be considered no more closely related than cousins thrice removed. Those who care to make their own comparisons may find *Dass wohl gesprochene Uhrtheil* printed by J. Meissner, *Die englischen Comoedianten zur Zeit Shakespeares in Oesterreich* (Vienna, 1884), pp. 131–89, and *Die getreue Sklavin* lengthily summarized by C. Heine, *Das Schauspiel der deutschen Wanderbühne* (Halle, 1889), pp. 75–79.

F *Love Tricks* (licensed 1625, published 1631)

C. R. Baskervill first demonstrated that James Shirley borrowed the plot of his earliest comedy, *Love Tricks, or the School of Complement*, from Rich's "Phylotus," and R. S. Forsythe has supplied a thorough, lengthy analysis of Shirley's considerable indebtedness to Rich.[1] Despite his extensive use of Rich's plot, unlike the author of *Philotus*, Shirley obviously did not find the language in "Phylotus" irresistible. But verbal echoes of the story occasionally creep into Shirley's comedy, and, since these have hitherto escaped attention, they are quoted in my notes, as are several apparently significant verbal parallels between *Love Tricks* and Rich's first and fifth tales.[2]

Except for Shakespeare, Shirley was probably the most distinguished dramatist who availed himself of the *Farewell*. His use of "Phylotus" was intelligent, and *Love Tricks* is, by and large, an attractive comedy.

G *A Fine Companion* (1633)

"Phylotus," which seems to have been the most popular of Rich's tales with dramatists, inspired still another comedy, a weird piece entitled *A Fine Companion*, by Shakerley Marmion (1603–39). Of this mysterious literary figure little is known except that his plays were popular in the society surrounding Charles I. *A Fine Companion* was acted both at court and at the theater in Salisbury Court, where, one hopes, it induced applause instead of the bewilderment into which it plunges the twentieth-century reader.

Since I agree wholeheartedly with Sir Sidney Lee's judgment that Marmion's plays are "confused and deficient in plot,"[3] I shall be content to say merely that the action of *A Fine Companion* concerns Littlegood, a covetous father who tries to marry his two daughters to two wealthy suitors (one of them old, like Rich's Phylotus), and that the daughters thwart him by selecting and eventually marrying husbands of their own

[1] See Baskervill, "The Source of the Main Plot of Shirley's *Love Tricks*," *MLN*, XXIV (1909), 100 f., and Forsythe, *The Relations of Shirley's Plays to the Elizabethan Drama* (New York, 1914), pp. 117–36, 147–49.

[2] See the notes on 31. 19 f., 40. 24 f., 129. 35–38, 185. 28–30, 188. 25–30, 192. 36–38, 195. 38–196. 2, 202. 34–36.

[3] See the article on Marmion in *DNB*.

choice. The plot is thus roughly parallel to that of "Phylotus." Yet one must look further for conclusive evidence that Marmion knew the *Farewell.*

To begin with, Littlegood christened his daughters Valeria and Æmilia, after the heroines of Rich's "Sappho" and "Phylotus"; and Aurelio, the name of Valeria's sweetheart, may stem from the Aurelianus of "Sappho." Moreover, Marmion's characters often take part in scenes that are strikingly similar to episodes in "Phylotus," and they occasionally use language clearly reminiscent of Rich's. The passages from the comedy proving Marmion's dependence on "Phylotus" may be consulted in the notes.[1]

These passages will also show that Marmion produced some far from vapid dialogue, and that he was even able to turn out very creditable blank verse. It is a pity that he did not incur a larger debt to Rich by making more extensive use of the plot of "Phylotus." For the authors of *The Weakest* and *How a Man May Chuse*, not to mention Shakespeare and Shirley, had demonstrated long before Marmion's time what effective dramatic material the stories in the *Farewell* could prove to be in the hands of a skilful playwright.

[1] See those on 183. 13–30, 184. 7–13, 197. 16–21. For a possible reminiscence of Rich's "Apolonius" in *A Fine Companion*, see the note on 81. 6–8.

THE *FAREWELL* AND SHAKESPEARE

One editor of Shakespeare pronounces Rich's "Apolonius and Silla" a "coarse, repulsive novel" and expresses the (vain) hope that Shakespeare never read it because "his hours were more precious to us than those of any poet who ever lived; it would be grievous to think that he wasted even half a one over *Apolonius and Silla*."[1] But in his tastes Shakespeare was Elizabethan, not Victorian, and more apt to be amused than repulsed by the "coarse, unrefined atmosphere" which in the Victorian critic's opinion the *Farewell* exudes. Shakespeare was a busy, astute searcher for plots in Painter's *Palace* and other works of fiction, and in his search he was not one to overlook an Elizabethan best-seller like Rich's *Farewell.* In fact, if a theory to be examined presently is correct, he was the first of the long procession of dramatists to explore Rich's collection, and he emerged with at least part of a plot as early as 1597 or 1598.

Though he did not treat Rich with the respect he accorded Holinshed or North, the *Farewell* seems to have been as estimable in his judgment as, say, "Giletta of Narbonne" or *Rosalynde.* There is evidence that certain Elizabethans laughed at the *Farewell* (for reasons not envisaged by its author) but read it. Shakespeare may have laughed too. One can imagine a worse fate for a group of short stories than to be laughed at, read—and used by William Shakespeare.

A *Twelfth Night*

Despite the Victorian hope quoted above, Shakespeare conferred immortality on Rich and his *Farewell* by borrowing most of the plot of *Twelfth Night* from Rich's second tale and a bit from the fifth as well. Presumably the first to notice the connection between the comedy and "Apolonius" was the antiquary Octavius Gilchrist. He shared his discovery with Edmond Malone "in a very modest and respectful letter" in 1806, and Malone adopted the discoverer's opinion in the matter.[2]

[1] For these and other adverse comments on the story, see the *New Variorum Twelfth Night*, ed. H. H. Furness (Philadelphia, 1901), pp. xvii, 327.

[2] See *The Plays and Poems of William Shakespeare*, ed. Edmond Malone and James Boswell (London, 1821), XI, 321.

Both were anticipated in print by J. P. Collier in 1820.[1] Since that date, agreement that Shakespeare employed "Apolonius" has been all but unanimous. Since the relationship of *Twelfth Night* to its main source has been diligently studied time and time again, one may forbear to restudy it here, though the verbal parallels between the play and the story, including a few not detected before, appear in the notes.

Because Shakespeare knew "Apolonius," it has very often been reprinted, while the rest of the *Farewell* has suffered neglect. Few have read all Rich's stories from beginning to end, and fewer still have read them through with Shakespeare in mind. One of the latest to do so was W. A. Neilson, and the result of his reading fifty years ago was the discovery that an episode in "Two Brethren," Rich's fifth tale, inspired Malvolio's incarceration in the dark room.[2] One editor of *Twelfth Night* ends his consideration of the sources of the comedy with the sigh, "After all, for our relief, no one has yet found Shakespeare a debtor to anyone for Malvolio."[3] Perhaps not; but he was indebted to Rich for Malvolio's most hilarious predicament—and possibly for his yellow stockings and for Sir Toby's sink-a-pace as well.[4]

B *The Merry Wives of Windsor*

Another scholar who persisted beyond Rich's rather prolix first story observed that the tale which inspired Malvolio's humiliation in the dark room also displays remarkable similarities to *The Merry Wives of Windsor*.[5] In her study of Rich's fifth tale and the comedy Mrs. Bruce considers the six fabliaux (not counting Rich's) usually cited as analogues to *The Merry Wives*, shows how each of the six corresponds to the play, indicates numerous details which are common to Shakespeare and Rich but absent from the six, and asserts that in "certain points, though not in all, Riche's tale is nearer to Shakespeare's play than are any of the other stories." Indeed, only "Riche's tale . . . presents the particular combination of elements which reappears in certain portions of Fal-

[1] In *The Poetical Decameron* (London, 1820), II, 133–63.

[2] See the *Atlantic Monthly*, LXXXIX (1902), 717 f.

[3] See *Twelfth Night*, ed. Sir Arthur Quiller-Couch (Cambridge, 1930), p. xiv.

[4] See the notes on 5. 12–16. 12, 146. 37, 208. 26.

[5] Dorothy H. Bruce, "*The Merry Wives* and Two Brethren," *SP*, XXXIX (1942), 265–78.

staff's story, and nowhere else." After commenting on Rich's "patchwork procedure" in putting his tales together,[1] she suggests that instead of collecting "details from half a dozen tales" and from them devising a plot which "happened to correspond closely to Riche's version," Shakespeare "remembered and used Riche's 'fift historie.'" She concludes that Shakespeare and Rich "have enough in common to establish strong evidence of Shakespeare's knowledge" of "Two Brethren." In support of her arguments she presents abundant parallels in plot and language.[2]

There is little to add to her observations except that the action of both the play and the novel occurs in England, a locale not common in sixteenth-century drama or fiction. Though *Cymbeline* is set partly in Britain, *The Merry Wives* is the only one of Shakespeare's sixteen comedies in which English characters admittedly bustle about in an Elizabethan English town. "Two Brethren" is also an exception to the rule that Rich and his fellow-novelists preferred to follow. The action of seven of the eight tales in the *Farewell* takes place in exotic surroundings. Only the heroine of Rich's fifth tale holds court in England.

Also worth noting are two speeches in *The Merry Wives* in which Shakespeare seemed to glance at Rich. Into the busy mouth of Mistress Quickly he put the words of a brief passage from the *Farewell* which was so notorious that it was unquestionably quoted and requoted by Rich's contemporaries. As a result of the notoriety, Rich came to be known to certain Elizabethans as "honest Barnaby," so that the very mention of the words *honest* and *honesty* may have directed the minds of some to the captain.[3] In 1598, the year to which most scholars assign *The Merry Wives*, honest Rich published *A Martiall Conference . . . Newly Translated out of Essex* [Rich's home county] *into English*.[4] The title may explain a bit of Pistol's fustian. When Falstaff boasts of Mistress Ford's "leer of invitation," his brag elicits from Pistol the remark, "He hath studied her well and translated her well—out of honesty into English."[5]

[1] For the many sources of "Two Brethren," see below, pp. 342–46.

[2] These, plus a few others that I have been able to supply, are noticed throughout the notes, pp. 290–306.

[3] For discussion of the passage and Rich's sobriquet see below, pp. liv–lviii.

[4] Only the title-page in the British Museum (Harleian 5900, fol. 38) is now known.

[5] I. iii. 54 f. If this is a timely allusion to Rich and his work, it helps confirm 1598 as the proper date for *The Merry Wives* in its present form.

But to those who are comparing "Two Brethren" and *The Merry Wives*, the most impressive speeches in the play are the ones which seem to echo Rich's very words.[1] In the light of these speeches alone some might consider Mrs. Bruce's conclusion too modest. After studying the array of parallels, verbal and other, which she detects, many may conclude that Rich's story is not merely a striking analogue to the comedy but a source for it. If so, then the *Farewell* was grist to the miraculous mill first in 1598, about two years before Rich's "Apolonius" (after some exceeding fine grinding) yielded *Twelfth Night*, and Shakespeare exploited the dramatic potentialities of the *Farewell* earlier than any other known playwright.

"Two Brethren," the most fetching of Rich's tales, deserves any attention Shakespeare may have paid it. It is almost as amusing a fabliau as *The Merry Wives* is a play. The personages of the tale move on a comic level as high—or, rather, as deliciously low—as the one Falstaff lards. After a perusal of their deeds, most readers will allow, I think, that whatever time Shakespeare consumed in reading Rich's fifth tale was time well spent.

C *Othello*

In the notes to the present edition appear scores of quotations from twenty-nine plays by Shakespeare which passages in the *Farewell* illuminate in one way or another. No sensible man would pretend that Shakespeare borrowed from Rich every idea or phrase thus illuminated. But like the parallels between *Twelfth Night* and "Apolonius" and *The Merry Wives* and "Two Brethren," those between *Othello* and Rich's first two stories are sufficiently abundant and close to deserve treatment here, especially since Shakespeare clearly demonstrated his knowledge of Rich's second tale in *Twelfth Night*. Whether the series of similarities between *Othello* and the stories amounts to proof that Shakespeare drew from Rich certain incidents for one of his greatest tragedies each reader may decide for himself. In my opinion the similarities are, at the least, too interesting to be overlooked.

They are especially numerous in the first act and the first scene of the second act, where Shakespeare departs widely from his principal source,

[1] See particularly the note on 140. 18–141. 25.

Cinthio's account of the Moor and Disdemona (*Gli Hecatommithi*, Decade III, Novel 7). According to Cinthio, the Moor "embarked on board the galley with his wife and all his troops, and setting sail, they pursued their voyage, and with a perfectly tranquil sea arrived safely at Cyprus."[1] The "perfectly tranquil sea" is a far cry from the "desperate tempest" which scatters Othello's ships and destroys the Turkish fleet.

Othello's maritime trials are foreshadowed in Rich's second tale. Here Apolonius' fleet is "deseuered" by a "tempest whiche sodainly fell," and the hero manages to reach Cyprus, where he is "worthily receiued by Pontus Duke and gouernour of the same Ile" (68. 14–17). In Cinthio, incidentally, there is no mention of a governor who might have suggested Shakespeare's character Montano, the governor of Cyprus who is to be relieved by Othello, and who awaits the arrival of the seafarers in Act II, Scene 1.

The parallels between the first act of *Othello* and "Sappho Duke of Mantona," Rich's first tale, are more plentiful and on the whole more remarkable. Shakespeare's plot usually corresponds to Rich's in precisely those details which Cinthio lacks. In the *novella* a peaceful changing of the troops at Cyprus rather than an imminent invasion by the Turks prompts the Signoria, the ruling body of Venice (no duke appears), to put the Moor in charge of the relieving forces. Though the Moor has proved his martial valor and enjoys the esteem of the Signoria, Cinthio does not specify that he has won his reputation in campaigns against the Turks or that he is of unique military value to Venice. His courtship of Disdemona is not described. Disdemona's parents try to persuade her to choose another husband, but she and the Moor marry and live happily for some time in Venice. There is no elopement and consequently no pursuit, apprehension, and accusation by an enraged father and no trial of the bridegroom. To this relatively peaceful and leisurely beginning Shakespeare's feverish and violent first act presents a conspicuous contrast.

Rich and Shakespeare, on the other hand, share the following details. A Christian ruler who must meet alarming threats from invading Turks organizes a campaign (49. 25–51. 18; I. iii). As general of the expeditionary forces the ruler, a duke, appoints a leader famous for his

[1] J. E. Taylor's translation, *New Variorum Othello*, ed. H. H. Furness (Philadelphia, 1886), p. 378.

victories against the Turks and indispensable to the government in the military crisis (24. 3–7, 50. 13–18, 51. 17 f.; I. i. 148–54, ii. 17–34, iii. 48 f., iii. 222–26). After a clandestine courtship (45. 13–18; I. i. 166) a couple elopes and is pursued by the angry, revenge-bent father of the bride (46. 23–27; I. i. 176–83). Apprehending his son-in-law, the father accuses him of stealing the daughter and demands justice (53. 13–21; I. ii. 62–75, iii. 60). Much is made of a trial scene before the reigning duke, who appoints the father, a man of power and influence, judge of his own case (54. 11 f., 59. 15–63. 18; I. iii. 65–70). The accused man admits the elopement (59. 16–18; I. iii. 77–79), and the presiding duke and the spectators at the trial accord their sympathy to the defendant (53. 22–24, 59. 19–21; I. iii. 73). The duke addresses the father in the son-in-law's behalf (59. 25–35; I. iii. 171–75) and summons the daughter to give her testimony (54. 5–9, 59. 13 f.; I. iii. 120), which is designed to exonerate her husband.

If these not inconsiderable resemblances between the tragedy and Rich's stories are due to something more than coincidence, then Shakespeare made use of the second tale for *Twelfth Night* about 1600 and again for *Othello* about 1604, when he gleaned from "Apolonius" a few details which had been of no use to him in the comedy and from "Sappho" much matter which was serviceable in his first act. And, if so, Shakespeare's selection from the *Farewell* (it goes without saying) was brilliant and purposeful: on the stage a grieved, outraged, pursuing father is a more gripping spectacle than quietly disapproving parents, especially when he catches up with the runaways; trial scenes are always good theater; a military crisis which threatens to separate bride and groom and sends the hero packing on the very night of his elopement, apprehension, trial, and acquittal induces rather more excitement than a routine changing of the guard; and there is much to be said, dramatically, for a furious tempest which tears the hero's ship from the rest of his fleet and allows him, after anxious and suspenseful moments, to arrive safe in his bride's arms at Cyprus.

THE RECEPTION OF THE *FAREWELL*

If the Worshipful Company of the Stationers of London had compiled a list of best-selling works of fiction after 1581, Rich's *Farewell* would unquestionably have appeared on it. The signs that his stories enjoyed long and great popularity are various and unmistakable. By setting Rich's folk upon the stage again and again, the authors of the plays just dealt with paid the *Farewell* the sincerest of compliments, and at the same time provided the clearest of indications that it was attractive to Elizabethans and Jacobeans.

Ordinary readers were apparently as devoted to Rich's folk as were the playwrights—sufficiently devoted, that is, to read out of existence all but (1) a single copy of the first edition, 1581, which may have survived in fine condition only because it reposed (unread, one suspects) for who knows how many years in the austere library of Thomas Tanner (1674–1734), bishop of St. Asaph, from whom it went directly to the Bodleian Library; (2) two imperfect copies of the second edition, 1583, both of which narrowly escaped being read to pieces, having been handled until what is left of them is ragged, tattered, and torn; (3) a single imperfect copy of the third edition, 1594, which may owe its survival partly to the stout neighbor it is stalwartly bound with; and (4) two copies of the fourth edition, 1606. The dates show that the demand for the book was spirited enough to exhaust the first edition in two years and long-lived enough to justify a fourth edition twenty-five years after the first. It is no wonder that, as one bibliographer observes, Rich "appears to have been the favourite author" of Robert Walley, the lucky publisher of the first two editions.[1]

In the sixteenth century crowned heads joined commoners in reading the works of Walley's favorite. "Your Souldiour," wrote Rich in dedicating to Elizabeth *A Path-way to Military Practise* (1587), "hauing receiued so manie gratious wordes for other of his writinges, the which it hath pleased your Maiesty so fauorably to vouchsafe, is . . . incouraged, now once againe to betake him to his Penne." Of the "other of his writinges" the *Farewell* was the most celebrated and far likelier

[1] T. F. Dibdin, *Typographical Antiquities* (London, 1819), IV, 279.

to have inclined Her Majesty to graciousness than, say, the nearly interminable two parts of Rich's *Don Simonides* (1581, 1584).

If her "gratious wordes" could be recovered, it would be amusing to contrast them with the blast Rich's collection provoked from James VI of Scotland. Rich's masterpiece, it seems, was also known—too well known—in royal circles in Edinburgh. With one of the most charming sections in the book (which he knew in the third edition) the King was "not well pleased"; in fact, he was so much displeased that on June 18, 1595, the English diplomatic attaché in Edinburgh nervously relayed the royal reaction to London.[1] To King James himself, then, the *Farewell* can scarcely be said to have been pleasing. Yet the very fact that it had somehow made its way to Scotland and there swum into the monarch's ken is, I suppose, a tribute to its vitality. Besides, who can be sure that other readers in Edinburgh did not share the English public's opinion of the tales rather than James's? At least one Scot was so enthralled with them that he rifled them and turned his loot into a comedy.[2]

Rich even earned honorable mention from an Elizabethan critic who could be as dour as King James. In *Pierces Supererogation* (1593) Gabriel Harvey surrounds the author of the *Farewell* with highly reputable company and, indeed, allows him to lead the trio apparently intended to represent the fine art of fiction-writing in England:

> Our late writers are, as they are: and albeit they will not suffer me to ballance them with the honorable Autors of the Romanes, Grecians, and Hebrues, yet I will craue no pardon of the highest, to do the simplest no wrong. In Grafton, Holinshed, and Stowe; in Heywood, Tusser, and Gowge; in Gascoigne, Churchyarde, and Floide; in Ritch, Whetstone, and Munday; in Stanyhurst, Fraunce, and Watson; in Kiffin, Warner, and Daniell; in an hundred such vulgar writers, many things are commendable, diuers things notable, some things excellent.[3]

Praise from Caesar.

By far the most entertaining evidence that the *Farewell* enjoyed wide renown is to be found in contemporary quotations of a certain phrase from Rich's prefatory section addressed "To the right courteous gentle-

[1] See below, p. lxxi. [2] See above, pp. xl–xliii.

[3] *The Works of Gabriel Harvey*, ed. A. B. Grosart (London, 1884), II, 290.

women, bothe of Englande and Irelande." After teasing the ladies unmercifully, Rich concludes with the saucy and ambiguous remark, "And thus (gentlewomen) wishyng to you all, what your selues doe beste like of," and signs himself, with a mock solemnity worthy of Falstaff, "Yours in the waie of honestie Barnabe Riche" (8. 13 f.). Since *honesty* often meant *chastity* to Elizabethans, the phrase doubtless afforded Rich's contemporaries considerable merriment on semantic grounds alone. In the first quotation of it I have been able to discover, however, the merry is mixed with the sinister.

The source of that quote was one Michael Moody, who involved himself in the Stafford–Des Trappes plot of 1586 to assassinate the Queen, served as an informer probably responsible to Sir Francis Walsingham and after his death to Sir Thomas Heneage, and engaged in intrigues so complicated that "as Government agent [he] was despatching information to [Robert] Poley on the one side, and as pseudo-conspirator was sending pro-recusant intelligence to James Typpinge on the other: by the very same despatches!"[1]

Despite his deviousness, in the communications which he sent out from the shadowy world of the secret service a far from grim humor shines. In one bit of cryptic information to Sir Thomas Heneage he took leave of the vice-chamberlain with what appears to be a snatch from a celebrated song (and with a flippancy) that may have failed to amuse that dignitary: "Vale, 20 of the merry month of May, 1595."[2] While being examined on January 11, 1586, by Sir Christopher Hatton about his part in the Stafford–Des Trappes plot, he revealed a code devised by himself and a fellow-spy: "He sayeth, about the Tyme of his comynge out of *France*, it was agreed between him and *Lyllye*, that in such Letters conteyning any Secrets, which passed between them, this Examinat should be named *Quinty*, and *Lillye* to be named *Ascham*."[3] At this revelation how could his examiners have forborne to smile?

What could be expected next of an intelligencer who quoted a popular lyric to the vice-chamberlain and wrested the venerable names of two great rhetoricians (Quinty presumably being an irreverent

[1] Ethel Seaton, "Marlowe, Poley, and the Tippings," *RES*, V (1929), 282.

[2] HMC, *Salisbury MSS*, V, 214. Compare Nicholas Breton's "In the merry month of May."

[3] *A Collection of State Papers Left by . . . Lord Burghley*, ed. W. Murdin (London, 1759), p. 578.

abbreviation of Quintilian) into such contexts? Next, as a matter of fact, it was Rich's turn to serve as an alias. Witness the testimony in April (?), 1591, of one Robert Rutkin, who probably "served as what in modern espionage is known as a 'letter-box,' or 'cover address,' receiving and forwarding reports from the spy [Moody] and instructions to him":[1]

> Robert Rutkin broker saieth that the party who wrote the lettres vnto him by the name of Bar[naby] Riche is Michaell Moody who liveth either at Brussels or Antwerpe.... The said Rutkin saieth that his neighboure mencioned in the lettere is one Robt Poolye and that he deliuereth him letteres for Sir Thomas Henneage & sendeth letters to him from Sir Thomas Henneage. Sometime hee [Moody] writeth as hee doeth now (yours in the waye of honestie qd Bar Riche) but most commonly he writeth M. M.[2]

The correspondents of Moody-Quinty-Rich-M. M. were fortunate to be plied not only with the latest intelligence from abroad but also with aliases drawn from the world of letters and learning and with quotations of a popular song and *Riche His Farewell to Militarie Profession.*

The first to notice Rich's famous phrase in print, so far as I know, was Thomas Nashe, never one to overlook a chance to generate mirth, innocent or not, at the expense of a fellow-author. In dedicating *Have with You to Saffron-Walden* (1596) to Richard Lichfield, the Cambridge barber, he writes, "A rich spirit, quoth a? nay then, a spirit in the way of honestie too: loe, this is to bee read in nothing but in *Barnabe Riches* workes. Spend but a quarter so much time in mumping vppon *Gabrielisme* [as you have spent on Rich's works?], and Ile be bound . . . thou wilt not anie longer sneakingly come forth with a rich spirit."[3] Miraculous Barnaby, to receive (more or less) honorable mention from both Master Nashe and Dr. Harvey.

The author of the comedy *The Weakest Goeth to the Wall* (1600) also did Rich honor by borrowing the plot of the first story in the *Farewell* for his play, by naming one of his characters Barnaby, apparently after

[1] John Bakeless, *The Tragicall History of Christopher Marlowe* (Cambridge, Mass., 1942), I, 178.

[2] For the transcriptions of these excerpts (PRO, State Papers Domestic 12/238/140/ fol. 271), I am obliged to Leslie Hotson. Other parts of Rutkin's deposition are quoted by F. S. Boas, *Christopher Marlowe* (Oxford, 1940), p. 267, and Bakeless, I, 178. Note that the recorder of the deposition duly enclosed the quotation from the *Farewell* in parentheses, the Elizabethan equivalent of quotation marks.

[3] *The Works of Thomas Nashe*, ed. R. B. McKerrow (London, 1904), III, 16 f.

the author of his source, and by broadcasting Rich's famous valedictory from the stage.[1] Hoping to remain incognito, the hero of the drama, Duke Lodowick, offers a bribe to Barnaby Bunch, a tailor who provides most of the low comedy in the piece, to keep his identity a secret. In reply Barnaby refuses to exact a price for his silence and magnanimously proposes himself as a servant to the impoverished duke and his family: "Ye shall commaund me to serue you, your wife, and your daughter in the way of honestie, like honest *Barnabie*."[2] This bit of whimsy may have been the playwright's quaint way of acknowledging his debt to Rich. But did the dramatist also expect his audience to recognize the phrase and be excited to laughter by the fillip at honest Barnaby? One presumes so. Otherwise Bunch's speech would have struck his hearers as being meaningless patter.

It is possible that Shakespeare also paid his respects to honest Rich in much the same way as the author of *The Weakest Goeth to the Wall*. One scholar has recently advanced convincing arguments that the fifth story in the *Farewell* is a source of *The Merry Wives of Windsor*.[3] In the light of these arguments two passages in the comedy merit special scrutiny. In one speech which has never been satisfactorily glossed Shakespeare may allude to the fanciful title of a book by Rich, as we have already observed.[4] In the other, a far subtler comic character than Barnaby Bunch repeats the very words of Rich's valediction to the ladies of England and Ireland: prattling, malapropizing, and making ten words do the work of two as is her wont, Mistress Quickly says, "I had myself twenty angels given me this morning; but I defy all angels (in any such sort, as they say) but in the way of honesty" (II. ii. 72–75). And so Rich may deserve to take his place in the illustrious company of my old lad of the castle and Cousin Garmombles.

However one may choose to explain Mistress Quickly's babbling of the phrase, its use in Moody's dispatches before April (?), 1591, in Nashe's *Have with You* (1596), and in *The Weakest* (1600), suggests that it was more or less celebrated for at least a decade and breeds the suspicion that there are still other quotations of it not yet detected. That Rich remained ignorant of the celebrity which his words gained is most

[1] For the relationship of the comedy and the tale see above, pp. xxxviii f.

[2] *The Weakest*, ed. Sir Walter Greg, Malone Society Reprints (Oxford, 1912), lines 499 f. And see the note on 4. 15 f.

[3] See above, pp. xlviii–l.

[4] See above, p. xlix.

doubtful. "Yours in the way of honesty" probably had something to do with the title of another of his best-sellers, *The Honestie of This Age* (1614, 1615, 1616), and certainly had a great deal to do with a remark in *Faultes Faults, and Nothing Else but Faultes* (1606), where Rich says (sig. C2v), tongue in cheek, "This olde protestation, *Yours, in the way of honestie*, is little cared for: euerie Gull was woont to haue it at his tongues end, but now it is forgotten." Honest Barnaby was too pessimistic.

Long after every gull had ceased to quote the old protestation, the sort of humor which it represents and which pervades the *Farewell* attracted admirers of whom Rich could never have dreamed. After reading through such Elizabethan novels as *Euphues* and the *Arcadia*, not to mention H. C.'s *The Forrest of Fancy* and John Grange's *The Golden Aphroditis*, modern critics habitually fall with glad cries upon Rich's stories. A few samples of the critical rhapsodies will suffice.

One editor pronounces the *Farewell* "a landmark in Elizabethan short-story writing" and reprints Rich's second tale "on its merits, which are great. . . . The story is delightful in its circumstantial romantic incidents, and the characterization of Silla is charming in its psychological realism." He concludes: "Rich's contributions to the Elizabethan short story are romantic charm, gaiety and lightness of touch, good vivid dialogue, directness and ease."[1]

Though one may be unable to agree entirely with another critic who believes it to be "plain that the author's sole interest lies in the telling of his stories with as few external embellishments or encumbrances as possible," it is nevertheless gratifying to learn that, in the opinion of an authority on Continental as well as English fiction, "Few works of the English Renaissance show to the same extent [as the *Farewell*] the reserve and detachment characteristic of the Italian *novellieri*."[2]

The author of a history of the short story in English apparently considers no praise too high for "merry Barnabe Riche" and his *Farewell*, "one of the pleasantest story-books of the period." Rich's narrative, he asserts, is

neither burdened with digressions, as with Whetstone and Gascoigne, nor

[1] *Elizabethan Tales*, ed. E. J. O'Brien (London, 1937), pp. 23 f. For a Victorian critic's dissenting opinion of "Apolonius and Silla" see above, p. xlvii.

[2] René Pruvost *Matteo Bandello and Elizabethan Fiction* (Paris, 1937), p. 110.

overfraught, as in Fenton, with warning tragedies. The humor is of the gayest . . . and he comes to the charge merrily, with a constant rallying and a bantering flattery. . . . There is a suggestion of Chaucer about him, and not a little of the poet's merry humor appears in certain *fabliau*-like stories of this collection, while the comparative infrequency of oratorical love-speeches, the rapidity of movement, good dialogue and monologue, give an impression of ease and lightness wanting in most of the serious "histories" [by Gascoigne, Painter, Fenton, and Whetstone]. . . .

The stories themselves are diverse in character. . . . Some are condensed romances, . . . others admirably compact *novelle* . . . and all are primed with the spirit of the renaissance. . . . [Their] variegated narrative is carried on with much of the color and realistic detail of the later comedy, and shows what an Englishman could do when he was trying to be neither preacher, nor grand stylist. Read . . . "Of two brethren and their wives" . . . and see how much lively humor and true observation, and how little affectation is to be found there.

Indeed, under Riche's lighter fingering, some of the renaissance peculiarities of narrative lose their odious qualities. A lengthy declamation is not unpalatable when sauced with wit . . . and a long declaration of love not tedious if humorous as well. "You might do much," we feel like saying [to Rich] with Olivia, in the play whose plot was one of his own stories.[1]

More encomiums could be cited to show that other present-day readers have found as much delight in the *Farewell* as the Elizabethans, and for much the same reasons. The sixteenth century, the twentieth century: other times, other manners—but happily the same tastes, so far as Rich's stories are concerned. It is time, however, that each reader be invited to peruse the tales and validate or reject the judgments of critics ancient and modern for himself. The *Farewell* is his to use, though only, of course, in the way of honesty.

[1] H. S. Canby, *The Short Story in English* (New York, 1932), pp. 127–29.

EDITIONS OF THE *FAREWELL*

A *First Edition*, 1581

Title page: See facsimile, p. 1.

Collation: 4°, sigs. a⁴, B–Y⁴, Aa–Dd⁴, Ee², without page or folio numbers. [a1] title, verso blank. a2 "To the right courteous gentlewo-/ *men.*" Ital. with B.L. and Rom. R.T. "The Epistle/Dedicatorie." B1 "To the noble Souldiours bothe/ *of Englande and Irelande.* Ital. with Rom. R.T. "*The Epistle/ to the noble Souldiours.*" C2 "*To the Readers in generall.*" B.L. with Ital. [C2v] "W. I. Gentleman in/ *praise of the Auctor.* Rom. with Ital. C3 "Baptiste Starre in praise/ *of the Austhor.*" Ital. with Rom. [C3v] "The Printer to the Reader." Rom. with Ital. [C4] "Sappho Duke of/ Mantona." R.T. "Sappho Duke/ of Mantona." [I1v] "Of Apolonius and Silla." R.T. "Of Apolonius/ and Silla." M1 "Of Nicander and Lucilla." R.T. "Of Nicander/ and Lucilla." [O1v] "Of Fineo and Fiamma." R.T. "Of Fineo/ and Fiamma." [P4v] "Of two Bretheren/ *and their wiues.*" R.T. "Of twoo brethren/ and their wiues." [T2v] "Of Gonsales and his vertu-/ *ous wife Agatha.*" R.T. "Of Gonzales/ and his wife Agatha." [X3v] "Of Aramanthus/ *borne a Leper.*" R.T. "Of Aramanthus." [Aa2v] "Of Phylotus and Emelia." R.T. "Of Phylotus/ and Emelia." Every story, "Sappho" through "Phylotus," is in B.L. with Ital. and Rom. [Dd2v] "The Conclusion." B.L. with Rom. R.T. "The Conclusion."

Running titles: Irregularities are as follows: normally "Sappho Duke" appears on the versos C4v–H4v, but "Sappho Duke." appears on C4v. Normally "Of twoo brethren" appears on the versos Q1v–T1v, but "Of two Bretheren" appears on R1v, R2v, R3v, R4v, and T1v. Normally "Of Aramanthus." appears on X4—Aa2, rectos and versos, but "Of Aramanthns." appears on Y1 and "Of Aramanthus" on Aa1v. Normally "and Emelia." appears on the rectos Aa3–Dd2, but "ann Emelia." appears on Bb1 and Bb2. Normally "Of Phylotus." appears on the versos Aa3v–Dd1v, but "Of Phylotus" appears on Aa3v, Aa4v, Cc1v, Cc2v, and Cc4v.

Catchwords: The following do not agree with the words which they indicate: *verie* (B2) for *very*, [*bun-*]*gler* (B3) for [*bun-*]*gler.*, *summon* (D4v) for *sommon*, *This* (E2) for *The*, *Obliga-* (H1) for *obligation*, *coniur-*

yng (I3) for *coniuring*, *bothe* (L1) for *both*, *birthe* (M1) for *birth*, *housband* (N3) for *housbande*, [*Trum*]*pettes* (N4v) for [*Trum*]*petts*, *him* (P1v) for *hym*, *To* (Dd4v) for *The*.

Signatures: In B.L. except all the signed leaves in a, B, and C, and M3, O1, T2, X3, and Aa2, which are in Ital.; a1 and fourth leaves unsigned. J, U, W, and Z do not appear as signatures.

Printer and publisher: Despite the assertion on the title page "Imprinted at London, by Robart Walley" (1. 14 f.), Walley was the publisher, not the printer of *A*. Actually John Kingston printed it, as abundant typographical evidence indicates.[1] Apparently a member of the Grocers' Company but never of the Stationers' Company, Kingston nevertheless kept two presses, according to a list compiled in May, 1583.[2] For Walley he also printed the second edition of the *Farewell* (1583) and the two parts of Rich's *Don Simonides* (1581, 1584). Besides the first and second editions of the *Farewell* and the two installments of *Don Simonides*, Walley published Rich's *The True Report of a Late Practise Enterprised by a Papist* (1582) and *A Path-way to Military Practise* (1587), in all a rather impressive number of volumes by a single author —impressive enough to lead one bibliographer to remark that Rich seems to have been the favorite author, "upon whose publications Robert Walley speculated."[3] By the time the *Farewell* had run to a second edition, Walley probably regarded works by Rich less as speculations than as steady money-makers.

Copy: The unique copy in the Bodleian Library (Tanner 213) was in the collection of Thomas Tanner (1674–1734), bishop of St. Asaph.[4] This celebrated antiquary and divine willed to the Bodleian his

[1] The ornamental border on the title page of *A* Kingston used from 1563 till 1584. See R. B. McKerrow and F. S. Ferguson, *Title-Page Borders Used in England & Scotland 1485–1640* (London, 1932), No. 117, p. 102, and plate. The border with the positions of Moses and his tables and David and his harp reversed adorns the title page of Rich's *Don Simonides*, printed by Kingston for Walley in 1581. Compare also the ornamental initial *G* at 3. 6 with that on sig. H3 of Wilson's *The Art of Rhetoric* (1563), "Imprinted at London, by Jhon Kingston," and the initial *T* at 22. 2 with that on sig. K2v of Leonardo Fioravanti's *Compendium of the Rational Secrets*, "Imprinted at London by Jhon Kyngston, for George Pen, and I. H. 1582."

[2] E. G. Duff, *A Century of the English Book Trade* (London, 1905), p. 86; Edward Arber, *A Transcript of the Registers of the Company of Stationers of London*, I (1875), 248.

[3] T. F. Dibdin, *Typographical Antiquities* (London, 1819), IV, 279.

[4] The *Farewell* may not have been a volume of which Tanner was proud, since he fails to mention it in the account of "Rych [Barnabas] ordinum ductor" in his *Bibliotheca Britannico-Hibernica* (London, 1748).

nabe Riche Ge
tleman

...ui me diuitem esse quam vocari.

Imprinted at London, by
Robart Walley.
1583.

manuscripts and whatever printed books not already in the library the curators might select. En route from Norwich to Oxford, the barge containing the episcopal library sank at the Bensington lock near Wallingford. In the *DNB* article on Tanner, W. P. Courtney says, with what must be stunning understatement, that over nine hundred volumes "were submerged for twenty hours, and the effects are still visible." If this copy was among the nine hundred, it somehow escaped undamaged, for the text is nearly perfect. The very slight imperfections in it (a few letters are illegible or hard to read at the thirty-fifth line, pages 193–98) seem due to a minor stain or to foxing. Like the whole of the Tanner collection, *A* is bound in late eighteenth- or early nineteenth-century calf with a Greek acanthus pattern stamped on the outer edges. Bound with *A* are the second part of Rich's *Don Simonides* (1584) and Roger Bayne's *The Praise of Solitarinesse* (1577). Bishop Tanner evidently gave his copy of *A* little wear: it is unusually well preserved, especially in comparison with Malone's copy of the 1606 edition, also in the Bodleian.[1]

B *Second Edition*, 1583

Title page: See facsimile, p. lxii.

Collation: As in *A*, except that the following phrases in *B* differ from the corresponding phrases in *A* in minor details of capitalization, spelling, type, linear arrangement, or punctuation: a2 "To the right courteous Gentlewo-/ *men*." [C2v] "W. I. Gentelman, in/ *praise of the Author*." C3 "Baptiste Starre in praise/ *of the Aucthour*." [C3v] "The Printer to the/ *Reader*." Ital. with Rom. [P4v] "Of twoo Bretheren/ *and their wiues*." R.T. "Of two Brethren/ and their wiues." [X3v] "Of Aramanthus./ *borne a Leper*.

Running titles: Irregularities are as follows: "to the noble Souldiours." appears on B2 and C1, while "to the noble soldiours." appears on B3 and B4. Normally "of Mantona." appears on the rectos D1–I1, but "of Mantona" appears on D3, D4, F3, and G3. Normally "and Silla." appears on the rectos I2–L4, but on I2, the second page of "Apolonius," "of Mantona." appears, apparently carried over from the preceding story. Normally "and Lucilla." appears on the rectos M2–O1, but "and

[1] For information about the binding and state of preservation, I am indebted to my friend F. L. Beaty.

Luilla." appears on N2. "Of two Brethren" appears on Q1v, Q3v, R1v, R3v, and T1v, "Of two brethren" on Q2v, Q4v, R2v, and R4v, and "Of twoo brethren" on S1v, S2v, S3v, and S4v. Normally "Of Aramanthus." appears on X4–Aa2, rectos and versos, but "Of Aramanthus" appears on Y1v and Y2v. "Of Phylotus" appears on Aa3v, Aa4v, Cc1v, Cc2v, Cc3v, and Cc4v, "Of Philotus" on Bb1v, Bb2v, Bb3v, Bb4v, and Dd1v.

Catchwords: The following do not agree with the words which they indicate: *verie* (B2) for *very*, *Emperour* (C4) for *Emperor*, *bashful-* (F1v) for *bashfulnesse*, *his* (H1) for *obligation*, *him* (H4v) for *hymself*, *almighty* (L2) for *almightie*, *housband* (N3) for *housbande*, *himself* (O2v) for *hymself*, *him* (S1v) for *hym*, *easily* (S3) for *easilie*, *began* (S4) for *beganne*, *pointed* (T4v) for *poincted*, *doubt* (Y2) for *doubte*, *To* (Dd4v) for *The*.

Signatures: In B.L. except all the signed leaves in a, B, and C, and M2, M3, O1, T2, X3, and Aa2, which are in Ital.; a1 and fourth leaves unsigned. J, U, W, and Z do not appear as signatures. The B.L. *E* of E1 is broken so that it appears at a glance to be a B.L. *C*.

Copies: Only two are known, and they are both in the Folger Shakespeare Library, Washington, D.C. One of these, bound in old rough limp vellum manuscript, Folger acquired on November 17, 1933, from Maggs Bros. for £12. 12*s*.[1] Maggs bought it at a Sotheby sale on March 17, 1930, for £4. 10*s*.[2] Though badly torn and held together with mending tape, most of the lower half of the title page of this copy, with the imprint, survives. Otherwise the date of the second edition would be hard to guess since the title page of the other copy of *B* is lost. A small tear in the middle of K3–K3v has rendered half a dozen letters illegible. Partially lost through shaving, wear, or tear are the running titles on a2v, a3, a3v, B1v, M2, M2v, Aa4, and Aa4v. Several words of the text in the first few lines of Bb3–Dd2v are lost because the top outer corner of each of these signatures has been torn or worn away. The bottom outer corner of Dd2v has been torn away, and with it the first two words of the last eight lines of the text. Thus of "The Conclusion," which occupied Dd2v–Ee2, only a portion of the first leaf survives.

The imperfections in the second Folger copy—which is bound in

[1] Maggs Bros. catalogue no. 590 (1933), lot 232, pp. 82 f.

[2] *Book-Prices Current*, 1930. Sotheby's sale catalogue for March 17, 1930, contains a description of the copy (lot 66) but no hint of its former owners.

brown sheep—are so numerous that only the chief ones may be specified. The title page and all the prefatory sections a1–C1 are lost. Only portions of "To the Readers in generall" and the commendatory verses survive. Most of Aa2 and Ee1v have been torn away, and about half of Aa3. But the copy is of very great value to an editor, for its imperfections seldom coincide with those of the other copy, and it consequently supplies part of the text that would otherwise be irrecoverable. It contains, for example, most of the text of the delightful "Conclusion," which is missing from the other Folger copy.

The earliest traceable owner of the second Folger copy was Charles Kirkpatrick Sharpe (1781?–1851), the Scottish antiquary and artist, whose name is written in ink on the front pastedown. The copy appeared at a Sotheby auction of the Christie-Miller collection, June 14, 1920,[1] but when Christie-Miller acquired it or whether he had it directly from Sharpe I have been unable to discover. At the Sotheby sale a London bookseller, Maurice Jonas, bought it in a lot of three, "sold not subject to return."[2] From Jonas, Folger purchased the Sharpe copy in October, 1921, for £400.

C *Third Edition*, 1594

Title page: See facsimile, p. lxvi.

Collation: 4°, sigs. A–X⁴, without page or folio numbers. [A1] title, verso blank. A2 "*To the right curteous Gentlewomen.*" Ital. with Rom. R.T. "The Epistle Dedicatorie." [A3v] "*To the noble Souldiours both of England*/ and Ireland. Rom. with Ital. R.T. "The Epistle/ to the noble Souldiers." B2 "To the Readers in generall." B.L. with Rom. [B2v] "W. I. Gentleman, in praise/ *of the Authour.*" Rom. with Ital. B3 "Baptist Starre, in praise of/ the Authour." Ital. with Rom. [B3v] "*The Printer to the Reader.*" Rom. with Ital. [B4] "Sappho Duke of/ Mantona." R.T. "Sappho Duke/ of Mantona." G2 "Of Apollonius and

[1] *Catalogue of... Early English Tales, Novels, and Romances... from... Britwell Court*, lot 53, p. 9. This catalogue dates the copy "? 1581," but *The Britwell Handlist* (London, 1933), II, 824, calls it "1581. Imperfect." Pasted to the fly leaf opposite sig. C2 (the first surviving in the copy) is a photographic facsimile of the title page of *A*, clipped from *Rich's "Apolonius & Silla,"* ed. Morton Luce (London, 1912).

[2] The lot included a fragment of the second book of *Primaleon of Greece* (1596) and Part I of *Bellianis of Greece* (1683). The price Jonas paid for the lot is not revealed in *Book-Prices Current*, 1920, or *Book Auction Records*, 1919–20.

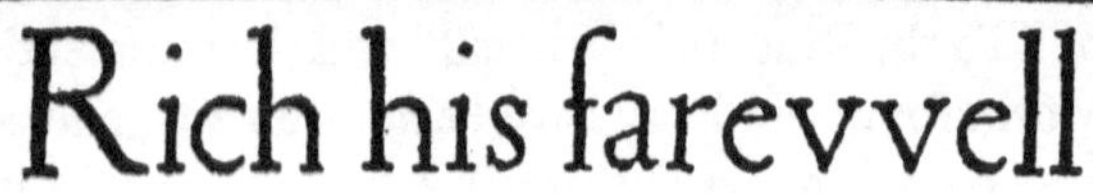

Rich his farevvell

to *Militarie*
profeſsion.

Containing very pleaſant Diſ-
courſes, fitte for a peaceable
time.

Gathered together for the on-
lie delight of the courteous Gen-
tlewomen , both of England and Ireland for whoſe onelie pleaſure they were
collected together, and vnto whom they
are directed and dedicated by
BARNABE RICH
Gentleman.

Malui me diuitem eſſe quàm vocari.

Imprinted at London by
V. S. for Thomas Adams, dwelling
in Paules Churchyard at the
ſigne of the white
Lion.

1594.

Silla." R.T. "Of Apollonius/ and Silla." [14] "Of Nicander and Lucilla." R.T. "Of Nicander/ and Lucilla." L3 "Of Fineo and Fiamma." R.T. "Of Fineo/ and Fiamma." N1 "Of two brethren and their/ *wiues.*" R.T. "Of two brethren/ and their wiues." Q1 "Of Gonsales and his vertuous/ *wife Agatha.*" R.T. "Of Gonsales/ and his wife Agatha." [R4v] "Of Aramanthus, borne/ *a Leper.*" R.T. "Of Aramanthus." [T2v] "Of Phylotus and Emelia." R.T. "Of Phylotus/ and Emelia." Every story, "Sappho" through "Phylotus," is in B.L. with Rom. and Ital.

Running titles: Irregularities are as follows: normally "Of Apollonius" appears on the versos G2v–I2v, but "Of Apollonius." appears on G3v and H4v. Normally "Of Nicander" appears on the versos I4v–L2v, but "Of Nicander." appears on I4v and K2v. Normally "and their wiues." appears on the rectos N2–Q1, but "and their wiues" appears on N3, N4, O3, and O4. Normally "Of Gonsales" appears on the versos Q1v–R4v, but "Gonsales" appears on Q2v and Q4v.

Catchwords: The following do not agree with the words which they indicate: *hou* (C2v) for *thou*, *gouer* (G2v) for *gouernour*, *woman* (G3) for *women*, *things* (G4) for *thinges*, *imploied* (H4v) for *employed*, *law* (V2v) for *lawe*, *thinke* (X2) for *think*.

Signatures: In B.L. except on A2, A3, B3, K1, L3, N1, and Q1, which are in Ital., and on B1 and B2, which are in Rom. A1 and fourth leaves unsigned. The *R* on R1 is misprinted *K*. J, U, and W do not appear as signatures. Several leaves signed Y no doubt originally appeared in *C* and contained the suppressed Conclusion.

Printer and publisher: On October 12, 1591, Thomas Adams, the publisher of *C*, entered in the Stationers' Register sixteen works "for his copies by assignement from master Robert walley," including "Rych*is farewel*."[1] It was in good company, for among the authors represented in the transaction were Josephus, Aesop, Solomon, Cato, Grafton, Rastell, Webbe, and Spenser. Some indication of the value of the *Farewell* to the publisher may be provided by the fact that it was listed by title in an entry which continues, "and all other the said Robert walleis bookes and balletes whatsoeuer. All which bookes. yt is agreed shalbe printed by John Charlwood for the said Thomas Adams: as often as

[1] Arber, II, 596. The sixteen also included the two parts of Rich's *Don Simonides* (1581, 1584) and "Rych*ys* [*Path-way to*] *military practis.*"

they shalbe printed And the said Charlwood to be as reasonable for the workmanship as other men would." Charlewood had no opportunity to display his reasonableness in reprinting the *Farewell*, for he died in 1593,[1] and *C* was printed for Adams by Valentine Simmes. Rich's works seem to have been even more popular with Adams than they had been with Walley. In addition to *C* and the fourth edition of the *Farewell* (1606), Adams published the following by Rich: *The Adventures of Brusanus* (1592), *Greenes Newes* (1593), *A New Description of Ireland* (1610), *A Catholicke Conference* (1612), *A True and a Kinde Excuse* (1612), *Opinion Diefied* (1613), three editions of *The Honestie of This Age* (1614, 1615, 1616), and *My Ladies Looking Glasse* (1616).

Revisions: There appear to be few irregularities in the printing of *A* and *B*. A study of the spelling, punctuation, and style of the considerable amount of prose Rich left in manuscript[2] indicates that the compositor of *A* seldom departed significantly from what Rich actually wrote. And *B* is a faithful, often page-for-page reprint of *A*. *C*, on the other hand, though clearly a reprint of *B*, contains evidence that Rich's text fell into the hands of a reviser some time between 1583 and 1594.

He must be called reviser rather than corrector because, even if one excepts from consideration the hundreds of changes in punctuation and spelling which could represent the compositor's efforts to standardize and modernize, there are still scores of what appear to be deliberate attempts to improve or refine by verbal additions, subtractions, substitutions, and rearrangements. To do this reviser justice, one is bound to admit that in a few passages he modified the text of *B* for what would be judged the better by any standards. As a rule, however, his changes make one think of an eager, overcareful young pedant attacking, red pencil in hand, his first set of freshman themes.

He was extremely anxious, for example, to tidy up any passages which contain misplaced modifiers or faulty parallelism (to use the terms now current among grammarians). In a dozen passages he repaired a lack of agreement between subject and verb. Another grammatical impropriety

[1] His last entry in the Stationers' Register was dated January 29, 1593. He was dead before September 8, 1593, when his widow, Alice, recorded an entry (Arber, II, 625, 635).

[2] Among the manuscripts now available in modern editions are several letters and reports (1592, 1604), ed. E. M. Hinton, *Ireland through Tudor Eyes* (Philadelphia, 1935), pp. 86–88, 93–99; "Remembrances of the State of Ireland" (1612), ed. C. L. Falkiner, *Proceedings of the Royal Irish Academy*, XXVI (1906), 125–42; and "The Anothomy of Ireland" (1615), ed. Hinton, *PMLA*, LV (1940), 81–101.

to which he invariably reacted is the loosely used participial construction that Rich sprinkled with interesting abandon throughout the *Farewell* and other works.

For many revisions, however, no satisfactory explanation can be advanced. The reviser was as apt to supply an archaism as to replace one. With matters of style he was continually busy. Where Rich enlivened his prose with the racy, informal, colloquial, and idiomatic, the reviser preferred the stiff and formal. Clichés appeared in *C* where there were none in *B*, some of them suggesting the legal mind at work. Once finickingness even prompted the reviser to introduce a manifest absurdity into the text upon which he was operating.[1] On the whole, he may be indicted for aimlessness, inconsistency, capriciousness, poor judgment, perverseness, and pedantry.

The identity of the reviser is a mystery. The very nature of the revisions seems to rule out Rich himself as a possibility. In none of the more than two dozen works by him, including the holograph manuscripts still in existence, is there a scrap of evidence that he was able to cope with the niceties of grammar, syntax, and diction. On the contrary, the very kinds of cheerful solecisms that roused the reviser to action recur abundantly everywhere in Rich's writings.

It is also difficult to imagine that Valentine Simmes or Thomas Adams, the printer and publisher of *C*, went carefully through a copy of *B*, introducing revision after revision. Presumably both these men of business were, like their fellows, more interested in convenience and economy than in refinements of style. Some bumptious, overzealous corrector at the press possibly deserves the blame for tampering with *B*. But unless more evidence is discovered, the precise identity of the culprit who laid a heavy, impertinent hand on Rich's text must remain unknown.

Almost as puzzling as his identity is the question why the revisions were deemed necessary or desirable. A partial answer to the question may lie in three of Rich's earliest works. The prefatory sections of these teem with self-deprecations and abject apologies for the author's "lack of knowledge," "simplicitie," "abylitie . . . far insufficient," "base and

[1] Examples of each kind of revision are quoted in an article (upon which this section is based) by T. M. Cranfill, "Barnaby Rich: An Elizabethan Reviser at Work," *SP*, XLVI (1949), 411–18. For a list of verbal variants in *C* see below, pp. 213–24.

barren style," "homely maner of inditing," and "ignorance in the knowledge of wryting."[1] To regard such phrases from Rich as altogether insincere, perfunctory, or conventional is unwise because there is evidence, both historical and literary, that they contain much truth. In a commendatory poem to Rich's *Don Simonides* (1581) Thomas Lodge wrote:

> Good *Riche* a wiseman hardly can denye,
> But that your Booke by me ill mended is. . . .
>
> Some errours yet, if any suche there bee,
> Your willyng mynde, maie quicklie them subdue.

Though the lines prove that somebody besides Rich took his humbly acknowledged deficiencies as a writer seriously and even tried to remedy them, they do not indicate Lodge as the reviser of *C*. *Don Simonides*, in fact, abounds with the very kinds of "errors" which received the attention of the reviser of *C*, "errors" which Lodge was evidently content to ignore. The Lodge-Rich relationship is described only so that the heavy-handed culprit whom we have earlier been belabouring may receive any justice due him: let it therefore be said in his defense, though he deserves little, that the text of the *Farewell* was not the first by Rich that, in the opinion of others doubtless far worthier than the reviser, required "mending" and received it.

Copy: The unique copy in the Folger Shakespeare Library is bound with another book by Rich, *The Adventures of Brusanus* (1592). The two works, both published by Thomas Adams, were stabbed together, probably in the print shop, and are covered with an old illuminated vellum manuscript. The only known copy of *C* is a large, clean, fine one. A small part of the text of seven lines is lost where sigs. T4–T4v are torn off at the bottom. Also missing is "The Conclusion," which began on sig. Y1 and probably ended on sig. Y3.[2] On the title page a name (possibly "John Thacken") was written in ink in an old hand and then scratched out. "Elizabeth Webb," ".3 June 1599," and an undecipherable phrase appear on the front flyleaf. On sig. A3, at the end

[1] These phrases, from the introductory matter of *A Right Exelent and Pleasaunt Dialogue* (1574), *Allarme to England* (1578), and *Don Simonides*, Part I (1581), are parts of rather extended apologies which are quoted in full by Cranfill, pp. 416 f.

[2] In large Roman type on sig. X4v, the last surviving in the copy, appears the catchword *The*, which pointed to "The Conclusion."

of Rich's section "To the right curteous Gentlewomen," someone wrote in a beautiful Elizabethan hand, "If my fortunes torment mee, / my hopes shall content mee."[1] Folger bought the copy from Bernard Quaritch, Ltd., in whose *Handlist* for February, 1923, it is described (lot 257) and priced at £400.

Possible censorship: *C* may have undergone censorship as well as revision. The only known copy is in such splendid condition that the missing "Conclusion," which occupied the final gathering, seems to have been neatly removed, not worn away. Its absence is perhaps explained by a communication from George Nicolson, acting English agent in Edinburgh while Robert Bowes, the English ambassador, was on leave. On June 18, 1595, Nicolson reported to Bowes:

> In the conclusion of a booke in England called Rich his farewell printed by V. S. for Tho. Adams at the signe of the white lyon in Paules churchyard 1594 such matter is noted as the *King* is not well pleased thereat; so as one grief comes in thend of another, it wold please the *King* some thinck that some order were taken there*with*. The *King* saies litle but thinkes more.[2]

Why James was "not well pleased" with the "matter" (205. 29–211. 23 in the present edition) the reader will have no difficulty in judging for himself.

Unfortunately there is no record to prove that "some order" was indeed "taken therewith" and the King accordingly pleased.[3] Printed and even verbal affronts to His Scottish Majesty sometimes spurred the English authorities to action.[4] But lacking evidence beyond the royal complaint itself and the absence of "The Conclusion" in a single copy of *C*, one must be content with surmises—and with one interesting reflection. If an order to suppress "The Conclusion" came thundering down after June 18, 1595, and after the popular *Farewell* had already

[1] The writer may have felt moved thus to translate into English Pistol's "Si fortuna me tormenta, spero contenta" by the tone of Rich's bantering section, which would have done credit to Shakespeare's ancient.

[2] Quoted in *Poems of Alexander Montgomerie*, ed. George Stevenson, Scottish Text Society (Edinburgh, 1910), p. lxiii n. See also *Calendar of the State Papers, Relating to Scotland, 1509–1603*, p. 683.

[3] Bowes's reply to Nicolson's letter has not survived, the Stationers' Register is mute on the subject, and (most frustrating of all) the records of the Privy Council for the months in 1595 during which the order, if any, would presumably have been issued are lost.

[4] For examples, see T. M. Cranfill, "Barnaby Rich and King James," *ELH*, XVI (1949), 69 f.

Rich his Farewell
to Militarie profession:
Conteining very pleasant discourses fit for a peaceable time.
Gathered together for the onely delight of the courteous Gentlewomen, both of England and Ireland,
for whose onely pleasure they were
collected together, and vnto
whom they are directed
and dedicated.
Newly augmented.
By *Barnabe Riche*
Gentleman.

Malui me diuitem esse quam vocari.

Imprinted at London by *G.E.*
for *Thomas Adams*.
1606.

gone through the editions of 1581 and 1583, then much of the damage the book could supposedly wreak on James's royal dignity and honor had already been wrought.

D *Fourth Edition*, 1606

Title page: See facsimile, p. lxxii.

Collation: 4°, sigs. A–Y⁴, without page or folio numbers. [A1] title, verso blank. A2 "To the right curteous Gentlewomen." Ital. with Rom. R.T. "The Epistle Dedicatorie." [A3v] "To the noble Souldiours both of Eng-/ land and Ireland." Rom. with Ital. R.T. "The Epistle/ to the noble Souldiers." B2 "To the Readers in generall." B.L. with Rom. and Ital. [B2v] "W. I. Gentleman in/ *praise of the Author.*" Rom. with Ital. B3 "Baptiste Starre in praise/ *of the Author.*" Ital. with Rom. [B3v] "The Printer to the Reader." Rom. [B4] "Sappho Duke of/ Mantona." R.T. "Sappho Duke/ of Mantona." [G2v] "Of Apolonius and Silla." R.T. "Of Apolonius/ and Silla." [I4v] "Of Nicander and Lucilla." R.T. "Of Nicander/ and Lucilla." [L3v] "Of Fineo and Fiamma." R.T. "Of Fineo/ and Fiamma." [N1v] "Of two Bretheren/ *and their wiues.*" R.T. "Of two brethren/ and their wiues." Q2 "Of Gonsales and his vertuous/ *wife Agatha.*" R.T. "Of Gonsales/ and his wife Agatha." [S1v] "Of Aramanthus borne/ a Leper." R.T. "Of Aramanthus." [T3v] "Of Phylotus and Emelia." R.T. "Of Phylotus/ and Emelia." Y2 "The Conclusion." B.L. with Rom. R.T. "The Conclusion." Every story, "Sappho" through "Phylotus," is in B.L. with Rom. and Ital.

Running titles: Irregularities are as follows: "to the noble Souldiours." appears on A4, but "to the noble Souldiers." on B1 and B2. Normally "Of Apolonius" appears on the versos G3v–I3v, but "Of Apolonins." appears on G3v, "Sappho Duke" on G4v, and "Of Apolonius." on I3v. Normally "and Silla." appears on the rectos G3–I4, but "Of Mantona." appears on G3 and I1. Normally "Of two brethren" appears on the versos N1v–Q1v, but "Of two Brethren" appears on O1v, O2v, and O3v, and "Of two Bretheren" on O4v and Q1v. Normally "and their wiues." appears on the rectos N3–Q1, but "and their wiues" appears on P1 and P2. Normally "Of Aramanthus." appears on S1v–T3, but "Of Aramanthus" appears on S3v and S4v.

Catchwords: The following do not agree with the words which they indicate: *Galliard* (B4v) for *Galliarde*, [*think-*]*ing* (C2) for [*think-*]*yng*, [*Mo-*]*narchie* (E1) for [*Mo-*]*narchy*, *shippes* (G3) for *Shippes*, [*counte-*] *naunces* (H1v) for [*counte-*]*nances*, *my* (H4v) for *of*, *breasts* (I3) for *breastes*, *Genoua* (L3v) for *Gauona* (properly *Sauona*), *pleasure* (M1) for *sure*, *remedy* (N2) for *remedie*, *Law* (N4v) for *Lawe*, *beganne* (Q2v) for *began*, *bounde* (R3) for *bound*, *saie* (R4) for *say*, *tormentes* (T1v) for *torments*, *fellow* (V2v) for *fellowe*, *if* (X1) for *it*, *Phylerno* (X3) for *Philerno*. S4v lacks a catchword.

Signatures: In B.L. except on A2, A3, B2, B3, G2, and K2, which are in Ital., and on B1, which is in Rom. A1 and fourth leaves unsigned. J, U, W, and Z do not appear as signatures.

Revisions: Rich's charming story of the devil who possesses the King of Scotland (205. 29–211. 23 in the present edition) provoked from James VI of Scotland a bitter complaint in 1595, as we have seen. How James I of England would have reacted to the same tale in 1606 we can never be sure because somebody treated it to a meticulous revision before it reappeared in *D*. Here the Turk and Constantinople everywhere replace the King of Scotland and Edinburgh (see facsimile, pp. lxxvi–lxxvii). Before *D* came out, another and much shorter section (16. 18–17. 3) also received attention. In *A*, *B*, and *C* this section contains a list of the principal enemies of Britain, including "The Scottes [who are inimical] by custome." In *D*, however, the latter vanish from the unholy roster.[1]

Rich himself was probably the discreet reviser of *D*. Such changes as "depart our Grandseigniour the Turke" from "departe the Kyng of Scots" (210. 28)—in fact, the whole revision in general—would seem to lie beyond the powers or the duties of corrector, printer, or publisher. Furthermore, the substitution of the Turk for the King of Scotland, of Constantinople for Edinburgh, seems to point clearly to Rich, who had a special affinity for Turks. The fourth tale in the *Farewell* contains a reference to the Turk and his seraglio (113. 9). The hero of the first story has won his fame by defeating Turks and refurbishes his unjustly tarnished reputation by conquering them anew. The hero of the second

[1] The passages in *D* containing the most significant departures from *A*, pp. 209–11, are reproduced below, pp. lxxvi f. For other verbal variants from *A* in *D* see below, pp. 213–24.

spends a year fighting the Turks, and most of the action occurs in Constantinople.

The "greate Turke" himself is a leading character in the seventh, much of which revolves around his successful attempt to conquer a fortified Christian city and his conversion to Christianity. Incidentally, this lost sheep in Rich's source, a story by Belleforest, is Hadding, the notorious Scandinavian-Norman berserker; but in his place Rich prefers, significantly, the Turk, though in other details he is content to follow Belleforest. Finally, on the list of England's enemies from which the Scots disappear in *D* the Turk remains in a place of signal honor between the pope and the devil. If Rich set about to replace the King of Scotland as the devil's victim, then, what more natural choice for him to make than the Turk? There is plenty of evidence, moreover, that Rich was in London in 1606 and therefore available for furnishing the much-needed revisions.[1]

Composition: Rich's claim to the revisions in *D* is further reinforced by a peculiarity in the composition of this edition. Except for the first gathering, all of *D* was set up from a copy of *A*—from a revised copy of *A*, in all probability. It would be hard to explain why any besides Rich among the men interested in the publication of *D* would have been likely to own a copy of *A* so late as 1606. Thomas Adams, who published *D* as well as *C*, acquired his rights to the *Farewell* from Robert Walley on October 12, 1591;[2] and *C*, as one might expect, was printed from *B*. Normally, of course, *D* would have been set up from *C*. As a matter of fact, the normal course was pursued at the outset of the composition: sigs. A1–A4v, the first gathering of *D*, are a paginal reprint of *C*. Then, from the top of sig. B1, at the beginning of the second gathering, *D* is unquestionably printed from *A*.

I am at a loss to account with complete satisfaction for this peculiarity. Unless one assumes that the needed revisions somehow prompted the printer to abandon *C* and turn to *A*, no reasonable motive for the abandonment can be posited. If *D*'s departure from *C* and reliance on *A* had begun on sig. B1v instead of on B1, the problem would have

[1] His *Faultes* was registered in January, 1606; he was involved in legal actions in London in February and July, 1606; and from London he addressed a petition to Cecil in the same year. See T. M. Cranfill and Dorothy H. Bruce, *Barnaby Rich: A Short Biography* (Austin, Texas, 1953), pp. 100, 116 f.

[2] See above, p. lxvii.

The Conclusion.

The poore Gentlewoman not able to speake one worde for weeping, at the last bursting out into these tearmes, if (quoth she) I had made my choise of a husband worthy of my selfe, I should neuer haue giuen him cause thus to wonder at me, nor my selfe haue had occasion to complaine for such a trifle, for that I might haue done, as other women doe, and haue followed euery fashion, and euery new deuise, without either grudging, or restraint of my desire, I should not then haue bin inioyned to such a kinde of silence, but I might haue made my husband priuie to my wantes, I should not then haue bin kept like Ione of the Countrey, in a tire of the olde fashion deuised a moneth agoe.

While Mistres Mildred was proceeding in these speeches or such other like, the Deuil her husband was strooke in such a dumpe, that not able any longer to indure her talke, he not onely auoided himselfe from her presence, but also deuised with speede to flie the Countrey, and comming to Douer, thinking to crosse the Seas, finding shipping ready, he toke his course and gat him to Rome, neuer staying till hee came to Constantinople, where the Turke kept his Court, and nowe forgetting all humanitie which he had learned before in England, he began againe a fresh to play the deuill, and so possessed the Tuke himselfe, which such straunge and vnacquainted passiōs, that by the coniecture of Phisitions, and other learned men that were then assembled together, to iudge the Tukes diseases, they all concluded that it must needes bee some Feend of hell, that so disturbed their Soueraigne, wherevpon Proclamations were presently sent forth, that whosoeuer could giue releefe, should haue a thousand crownes by the yeere, so long as he did liue. The desire of these crownes, caused many to attempt the matter, but the furie of the deuill was such, that no man could preuaile.

Nowe it fortuned that Persinus, the Father of Mistres Mildred, at this present to bee at Constantinople, who by constraint of some extreamitie, was now compelled to practise Phisicke, wherein he had some pretie sight, but there withall so good successe, that who but Persinus the English Phisition, had all the name through the whole Turkish Empire. The fame of this Phisition came to the hearing of the Turke, who sending for Persinus, began to debate with him of the straungnesse of his fites, proffering large sommes of money if he could finde a remedie. To whom Persinus aunswered, that it passed farre his skill: the Turke notwithstanding, would not giue ouer, but intreated Persinus to take in hand the cure, which when hee still denied, did thinke it rather proceeded of stubbornesse, then for want of experience, wherefore he began to threaten him, swearing that if he would not accomplish his request, it should cost him his life.

Persinus seeing him selfe so hardly bestede, was contented to trie some parte of his cunning: and the next day when the Turke was in his fitte, he was brought in, to see the maner howe it helde him. Whom the deuill perceiuyng to come in at the dore, speaking to Persinus, he saied in this manner.

My Father Persinus, I am glad I see you here, but what wind hath driuen you hether to this place.

P. Why what art thou (quoth Persinus) that callest me thy Father.

B. Marie (quoth the Deuill) I am Balthaser, that was once married to your daughter, indeede a deuill of hel, though you neuer knew it before, whō your daughter

wearied

The Conclusion.

wearied so much with her new fashions, as I had rather be in hell, then married to such a wife.

And arte thou then Balthaser (quoth Persinus) why then I pray thee good son depart our Grandseigniour the Turke, for he hath threatned me for thy cause, to take away my life.

Marry (quoth Balthaser) euen so I would haue it, it were some part of acquittance, for your daughters kindnesse towards me,

Persinus seeing the disposition of the Deuill, thought it not good to deale any farther with him at that present, but afterward when the Turke was come to himselfe, he requested of him but respite for one moneth, and against the day that he should then take him in hand againe, he deuised with the Turke, that all the Ordnaunce in the Towne might be shot off, all the Belles in the Towne might be rong, and that all the Trumpets, Drummes, and all manner of other instruments might altogether sound, about the court and lodging of the Turke.

These things being accordingly prepared, and the day come that was assigned, Persinus being with the Turke at the beginning of his fit, according as it was appointed, the Ordnaunce was shot off, the Belles began to ring, Musitions played on euery side, at which sodaine noise, the Deuill beganne to wonder, and calling to Persinus he said: why how now father, what meaneth all this noise? Why (quoth Persinus) doest thou not know the meaning, then I perceiue Deuils do not know all: but because thou must be acquainted with it, I will tell thee afore hand. The last time I talked with thee thou toldest me thou hadst married my daughter, and thy tokens were so true, that I am sure thou doest not lie, for which cause knowing where thy biding is, I haue sent for her to the Towne, and this noise that thou hearest, is her welcome to the Court.

And is my wife then come hether to seeke me out? (quoth the Deuill) then I shall be sure to be troubled with new fashions: nay then farewell Constantinople, for I had rather goe to hell: and thus leauing the Turke he departed his way.

Now to conclude, if a silly woman were able to weary the Deuill, that troubled him with new fashions but once in a moneth, I thinke God himselfe will be wearied with the outrages of men, that are visited with new fangles at the least once in a day: I can no more, but wish that Gentlemen leauing such superficiall follies, would rather indeauour themselues in other exercises that might be much more beneficiall to their countrey, and a great deale better to their owne reputation, and thus an ende.

FINIS.

been less knotty. One could then reasonably suppose that the setting up of *D* from *C*, commencing according to custom, had innocently proceeded through the first gathering, through page one of the second gathering, and perhaps through a few lines of page two—until the compositor or the corrector encountered on line 10, sig. B1v of *C*, nestled hair-raisingly among the foes of England, the four words which disappear in *D*, "the Scottes by custome."

The wisdom of interrupting the press until a revised text could be fetched from the author would have been obvious, one could argue. But, as the facts stand, why B1 is set up from *A*, not from *C*, must remain unexplained. The likeliest guess is that the objectionable passage on B1v was somehow discovered before the second gathering was set up at all. If B1 had been set up from *C* before the discovery, few bibliographers could explain why it was necessary to scrap the page and reset it from *A*.

Since thought is free, other theories to explain the oddity in *D*, none of them very likely, could be advanced. Perhaps James's complaint about *C* had long before 1606 filtered through the strata of English officialism to Thomas Adams' ears. In order to keep them, he may have requested revisions from Rich and proceeded with the printing of the first gathering of *D* from *C* while Rich was busy revising a copy of *A*. Or perhaps the printer set up *D* from an imperfect copy of *A* and supplied the missing text from *C*. If so, however, the text in his copy of *A* would have had to be missing from the title page to the middle of line 17 in the middle of sig. B3v.

Copies: Of the two known, one, formerly Edmond Malone's, is now in the Bodleian Library (Malone 613), the other in the Folger Shakespeare Library.[1] Malone enriched his copy with many notes in his own hand, some on leaves which had been inserted and some on the margins themselves.[2] Though the paper of the copy is badly discolored and the volume is generally in poor condition, it does not suffer from the slight textual imperfections of the other survivor. The Malone copy is bound in eighteenth-century marble boards with half-calf on the corners. It

[1] One leaf (B3–B3v) of a third copy is preserved in the British Museum (Harleian MS. 5995, fol. 366). On it appear "Baptiste Starre in praise/ *of the Author*" and "The Printer to the Reader."

[2] For a sample of his illuminating comments, see above, p. xxiii.

has been rebacked, and there is lettering up the spine. It contains no marks of ownership besides Malone's.[1]

The Folger copy, bound in red morocco with gilt line borders and gilt edges by Francis Bedford, has been remargined, and the title page within a woodcut border has been cut around and inlaid. A few letters at the lower outer corner of the leaf A2–A2v, which has been torn and mended, are lost. Six letters on D1v missed in printing. The first traceable owner of the copy was J. B. Inglis, from whom it passed on June 16, 1826, to H. G. Bohn for £10. 10*s*.[2] It next appeared on June 13, 1859, at the sale of the library of J. O. Halliwell-Phillipps, who probably had it from Bohn and who wrote on the front flyleaf, "I know of only one other perfect copy" (i.e. Malone's?).[3] At the Halliwell-Phillipps auction, T. Thorpe, probably acting as agent for S. R. Christie-Miller, bought the copy for £17.[4] Quaritch, the next owner, acquired the copy at the Britwell sale, June 15, 1920, for £90, and sold it the same year to John L. Clawson for $375.[5] A. S. W. Rosenbach purchased it for Folger for $1,050 at the Clawson sale on May 24, 1926.[6]

E *Collier's Edition*, 1846

Eight Novels Employed by English Dramatic Poets of the Reign of Queen Elizabeth. Originally Published by Barnaby Riche in the Year 1581, and Reprinted from a Copy of That Date in the Bodleian Library. London: Printed for the Shakespeare Society. 1846. (8°)

In the preface to this reprint of *A*, Collier is careful (p. xv) to "warn

[1] For information about the binding and condition of the copy, I am indebted to my friend F. L. Beaty.

[2] See Sotheby's *Catalogue of . . . the Library of a Gentleman* (London, 1826), lot 1329, p. 83. The price and the name of the purchaser are written in a copy of the catalogue at the Huntington Library.

[3] Rich enjoys a place of honor on the title page of Sotheby's catalogue of the Halliwell-Phillipps sale: *A Catalogue of Rare & Curious Books . . . Including Some Choice Editions of the Works of Shakespeare, Robert Greene, Barnaby Rich, and Others.* The copy of *D* was sold (lot 338, p. 35) in the midst of twelve Shakespeare quartos (lots 332–37, 339–45).

[4] The price and the name of the purchaser are written in a copy of the catalogue in the Library of Congress. On Thorpe, bookseller and librarian at Britwell Court, see S. De Ricci, *English Collectors of Books & Manuscripts* (New York, 1930), pp. 105, 108.

[5] Sotheby's *Catalogue of . . . Early English Tales, Novels, and Romances . . . from . . . Britwell Court*, lot 256, p. 33; *Book Auction Records*, 1919–20.

[6] *The Splendid Elizabethan & Early Stuart Library of Mr. John L. Clawson*, Anderson Galleries, lot 671; *American Book-Prices Current*, 1926.

the reader against the misprints of the original edition: some of these we have corrected, because they were obvious, while others we have allowed to remain, because it may, possibly, be a question whether they do not contain the true reading: in such cases we have not allowed ourselves to take any liberty with the text." Despite this profession of editorial conservatism, he allows himself liberties that seem unjustifiable by twentieth-century editorial standards.

Throughout his reprint Collier changes both the punctuation and the paragraphing of *A* in an effort to make them conform with modern, or rather Victorian, practices—some of which are themselves now outmoded. He fails to be consistent in these changes. On one page, for instance, he may elevate a lower-case letter to a capital and on the next reverse the procedure. Part of Rich's direct discourse he encloses in quotation marks, while part he fails so to distinguish. Words which he adds to *A* sometimes appear in square brackets, sometimes not. He also undertakes, like the reviser of *C*, to correct Rich's grammar as well as his punctuation. Hence the verbal alterations in *C* and *E* very often coincide.[1]

Apart from deliberate deviations from *A*, Collier also introduces into the text many errors, some typographical, some caused by misreading or miscopying. Errors in his own transcription of *A* may account for his claim (p. xv) that he has altered "'thrast,' as it is absurdly given in the copy of 1581," to "thrall" and "'change,' as it is misprinted in the old edition," to "charge." But actually in *A* the readings are already "thrall" (92. 13) and "charge" (92. 22). Consequently, one must either suppose that "thrast" and "change" are errors which understandably crept into Collier's transcription or entertain the less charitable theory that he invented these imaginary misprints in order to magnify his own editorial acumen by seeming to apprehend and correct them.

Unnecessary or ill-advised though many of his departures from *A* may now appear, some of his emendations are sound, perspicacious, and useful to a modern editor.[2] Collier deserves thanks for providing even an unreliable text of the *Farewell*. Without his reprint one of the most popular of Elizabethan works might have remained unknown except to those with access to the six copies which are all that survive

[1] See the verbal variants listed below, pp. 213–24.

[2] See, for example, the notes on 63. 8, 73. 33, 97. 32, 155. 33 f., 179. 23.

of the early editions. To casual readers unconcerned with the sacrosanctity of Elizabethan texts but interested only in Rich's highly readable stories, Collier's edition is still of value. But it leaves much to be desired by students who want to know Rich's work in the form in which he left it and Elizabethans read it.

F *The Present Edition*

In the facsimile reproduction of *A* which forms the text of the present edition, page and line numbers have been inserted for convenience in reference. In my notes (pp. 286 f., 327, below) the few letters which are lost or scarcely legible at 113. 26–31, 114. 27–29, 195. 35, and 196. 35 are supplied from the text of *B*. Most of the misprints against which Collier warned his readers will not greatly disturb students of Elizabethan prose, but typographical errors which might possibly prove troublesome are dealt with in the notes.

Attention is also called there to about three dozen passages in which the punctuation may be seriously misleading to those not initiated into the mysteries of Rich's own brand of pointing. If one may judge from the considerable amount of prose Rich left in manuscript, he was habitually careless in distinguishing between commas and periods, as a sample from his holographic report to King James will show:

> But for thos physytyons that do not thynke it necessary that the Idolatry of *Irelande* shuld be Impugned. but that the cuntry shuld styll remayne, to be the place of *Rende vous*, for traytors. for Idolators. for papystes. for runegates. for fugytyves, that fly out of *England* out of *Spayne* . . . wher all thes may have lyberty to conspyre. to compacte, to practyse, agaynst the state. agaynst the kynge. & agaynst *God* hym self, and that *Irelande* shuld styll remayne, to be a nurssery of treason. of rebellyon. of incevylyte. of Impyete. & of all maner of inormyte: God blysse me from such physytyans.[1]

When confronted with similar punctuation in the manuscript of *A*, the compositor, I believe, forgot from time to time that Rich's periods did not invariably signalize the end of a sentence, consequently neglected to change some to commas, and began the next word with a capital. Such a procedure would account for "sentences" like the following: "And because I haue been somethyng tedious in my first discourse,

[1] "The Anothomy of Ireland" (1615), ed. E. M. Hinton, *PMLA*, LV (1940), 84.

offending your pacient eares, with the hearyng of a circumstaunce ouer long. From hence forthe, that whiche I minde to write, shall bee doen with . . . celeritie" (67. 28–31).

It is sometimes possible to obviate one other kind of textual difficulty in *A*. *A* has its share of evidently corrupt or confusing passages, but the proper readings for these are not necessarily irrecoverable. Rich was so inveterate and usually so faithful a borrower that after consulting the source of a difficult passage one may be able to recommend a clarifying change in punctuation, suggest a revised word order, or even supply a missing word. In *A*, for instance, one reads the mystifying declaration, "The first thing that was to bee considered in mariage was the dowrie, and the woman" (90. 5 f.). A glance at its source dispels the mystery: "Ne' matrimonii era prima da considerare la quantità della dote, e *poi* la donna."[1] The reading in *A* should obviously be, "The first thing that was to bee considered in mariage was the dowrie, and *then* the woman."

In the notes other changes of this sort are suggested. Yet in a text 211 pages long the passages which invite emendation do not seem overly numerous. Despite the vagaries in punctuation, *A* is in my opinion an interesting and reliable text as Elizabethan texts go and is certainly a more faithful reflection of Rich's intentions than any other version of the *Farewell* available.

[1] Giraldi Cinthio, *Gli Hecatommithi*, reprinted in *Raccolta di novellieri italiani* (Torino, 1853), II, 317. The italics are mine.

Riche his Farewell to Militarie profession (1581)

¶ Riche his Farewell
to Militarie profession: conteinyng verie pleasaunt discourses fit
for a peaceable tyme: Gathered together for the onely delight of the courteous Gentlewomen, bothe of Englande and Irelande, for whose onely
pleasure thei were collected together,
And unto whom thei are directed
and dedicated by Barnabe
Riche Gentle-
man.

Malui me diuitem esse quā vocari.

¶ *Imprinted at London, by*
Robart VValley.
1581.

¶ To the right courteous gentlewomen, bothe of Englande and Irelande, Barnabe Riche wisheth all thynges thei should haue appertainyng to their honour, estimation, and all other their honest delightes.

Entlewomen (I am sure there are many (but especially of suche as beste knowe me) that wil not a-little wonder to see suche alteration in me, that hauyng spent my yonger daies in the warres emongest men, and vowed my self onely vnto Mars: Should now in my riper yeares, desire to liue in peace emongst women, and to consecrate my self wholy vnto Venus. But yet the wiser sorte can verie well consider, that the older we waxe, the riper our witte, and the longer we liue, the better we can conceiue of thynges, appertainyng to our owne profites, though harebrained youth ouerhaled me for a tyme, that I knewe not bale from blisse. Yet wisedome now hath warned me, that I well knowe Cheese from Chalke, I see now it is leſſe painfull to ſollowe a Fiddle in a gentlewomans chamber: then to marche after a Drumme in the feeld. And more ſounde ſleapyng vnder a ſilken Canapie cloaſe by a freend, then vnder a buſhe in the open feelde, within a mile of our foe. And nothyng ſo daungerous to be wounded with the luryng looke of our beloued Miſtres: as with the crewell ſhotte of our hatefull enemie, the one poſſeſt with a pitifull harte, to helpe where ſhe hath hurte: the other with a deadly hate, to kill where thei might ſaue.

Experience now hath taught me, that to bee of Mars his crewe, there is nothyng but paine, trauaill, tormoill, diſquiet, colde, hunger, thriſte, penurie, badde lodging, worſe fare, vnquiet ſlepe, with a number of other calamities that haps I knowe not how. And when a Souldier hath thus ſerued in many a bloudie broile, a flappe with a Foxe taile ſhall bee his beſte reward: for I ſee no better recompence that any of theim can gette. Now contrary to bee of Venus bande, there is pleaſure, ſporte, ioye, ſolace, mirthe, peace, quiet reſte, daintie fare, with a thouſande other delites, ſuche as I can not rehearſe. And a man hauyng ſerued but a reaſonable tyme, maie ſometymes take a taste at his Mistres lippes for his better recompence.

But now (gentlewomen) as I haue vowed my self to bee at your dispositions, so I knowe not how to frame my self to your contentations, when I consider, with how many commendable qualities he ought to bee endued, that should bee welcomed into your blessed companies: I finde in my self no one maner of exercise, that might giue me the least hope to win your good likinges.

As firste for Dauncyng, although I like the Measures verie well, yet I could neuer treade them a right, nor to vse measure in any thyng that I went aboute, although I desired to performe all thynges by line and by leauell, what so euer I tooke in hande.

Our Galliardes are so curious, that thei are not for my daunsyng, for thei are so full of trickes and tournes, that he whiche hath no more but the plaine Sinquepace, is no better accoumpted of then a verie bongler, and for my part, thei might assone teache me to make a Capricornus, as a Capre in the right kinde that it should bee.

For a Ieigge my heeles are too heauie: And these braules are so busie, that I loue not to beate *my braines about them.*

A Rounde is too giddie a daunce for my diet, for let the dauncers runne about with as muche ſpeede as thei maie: yet are thei neuer a whit the ner to the ende of their courſe, vnleſſe with often tourning thei hap to catch a fall. And ſo thei ende the daunce with ſhame, that was begonne but in ſporte.

Theſe Hornepipes I haue hated from my verie youth: and I knowe there are many other that loues them as euill as I.

Thus you maie perceiue that there is no daũce but either I like not of theim, or thei like not of me, ſo that I can daunce neither.

There reſteth then, if I could plaie of any Inſtrumente, or that I had any ſight in ſonge, whereby I might delight your daintie eares, (Gentlewomen) by ſweete plaiyng or ſainyng ſome pretie Dities. But to the firſte my fingers would neuer be brought in frame: for the ſeconde my mouthe is ſo vnpleaſaunt, either to ſyng, or to faigne, as would rather breede your loathyng then your liking.

VVhy yet if I could diſcourſe pleaſauntly to driue awaie the tyme, with amourous deuiſes,

Dedicatorie.

or that my conceipte would serue me, either to propone pretie questions, or to giue readie aunsweres: with a number of other delightes, to long to be rehearsed, there were some comfort, that I might bee alowed of emongst you. But my capacitie is so grosse, my wittes bee so blunt, and all my other sences are so dulle: that I am sure you would soner condemne me for a Dunce, then confirme me for a Disciple, fit to whisper a tall in a Gentlewomans eare.

But yet I truste (Gentlewomen) when you shall perceiue the zeale, that I beare to my newe profession: although you will not presently admit me to the Pulpit, yet you will not denaie me, to be one of your Parishe. VVhere if it please you but to place me in the bodie of the Churche, you shall finde my deuotion as muche as he that kneles next the Chauncell doore.

And here (Gentlewomen) the better to manifest, the farther regarde of my duetie: I haue presented you with a fewe rough hewen Histories. Yet I dare vndertake so warely polished, that there is nothyng let slipp, that might breede offence to your modest myndes.

I haue made bolde to publishe theim vnder your

your ſauecundites, and I truſt it ſhall nothyng at all offende you: My laſt requeſt is, that at your pleaſures you will peruſe theim, and with your fauours you will defende them, whiche if I maie perceiue, not to bee miſliked of emongeſt you, my encouragement will bee ſuche, that I truſt within a verie ſhorte ſpace, you ſhall ſee me growe from a yong Punie, to a ſufficient Scholer. And thus (gentlewomen) wiſhyng to you all, what your ſelues doe beſte like of, I humbly take my leaue.

Yours in the waie of honeſtie
Barnabe Riche.

To the noble Souldiours bothe of Englande and Irelande, Barnabe Riche wisheth as to hym self.

There is an old prouerbe (Noble Souldiours) & thus it foloweth: It is better to be happie thē wise, but what it is to bee happie how should I discipher, who neuer in my life could yet attaine to any happe at all that was good, and yet I haue had Souldiours lucke and speede as well as the reste of my profession. And with wisedome I will not meddle, I neuer came where it grewe, but this I dare boldly affirme (& the experience of the present tyme doeth make daiely proofe) that wit standes by in a thredbare coate, where folly sometyme sittes in a Veluet goune, and how often is it seen that vice shall be aduaunced, where vertue is little or naught at all regarded, small deserte shall highly bee preferred, where well doyng shall goe vnrewarded, and flatterie shall be welcomed for a guest of greate accompt, where plaine Tom tell troth shall be thrust out of doores by the shoulders: and to speake a plaine truthe in deede, doe ye not see, Pipers, Parasites, Fidlers, Dauncers, Plaiers, Iesters, and suche others, better esteemed and made of, and greater beneuolence vsed towarde them, then to any others that indeuours them selues to the moste commendable qualities.

Then seeyng the abuse of this present age is suche, that follies are better esteemed then matters of greater waight.

I haue ſtept on to the Stage amongſt the reſte, contented to plaie a part, and I haue gathered together this ſmall volume of Hiſtories, all treatyng (ſir reuerence of you) of loue.

I remember that in my laſt booke intituled the Allarum to Englande, I promiſed to take in hande ſome other thyng, but beleeue me, it was not this that I ment, for I pretended then to haue followed on, and where I ended with the decaie of Marciall diſcipline, ſo I ment to haue begun againe with the Diſcipline of Warre, and with all to haue ſet forthe the orders of ſondrie battailles, and the maner of Skirmiges, with many plattes of fortification: but eſpecially thoſe of the lowe Countries, as Delfte, Delftes Hauen, Roterdame, Leiden, the Breylle, bothe the hedde and the Towne Gorcoum, Gouldſluce, Maaſelandeſluce, the Crympe, with diuerſe others worthie the peruſyng, for ſuche as haue not ſeen them. But I ſee the tyme ſerues not for any ſuche thyng to bee accoumpted of. And therefore to fitte the tyme the better, I haue putte forthe theſe louyng Hiſtories, the whiche I did write in Irelande at a vacant tyme, before the commyng ouer of Iames Fitz Morice: And it pleaſed me the better to doe it, onely to keepe my ſelf from Idelneſſe, and yet thei ſaie, it were better to be Idle then ill occupied. But I truſte I ſhall pleaſe Gentlewomen, and that is all the gaine that I looke for. And herein I doe but followe the courſe of the worlde. For many now adaies goe aboute by as great deuiſe as maie bee, how thei might become women theimſelues. How many Gentlemen ſhall you ſee at this preſent daie, that I dare vndertake, in the wearyng of their apparell, in the ſettyng of their Ruffes, and the freſelyng of their heire, are more new fangeled and fooliſhe, then any curtiſan of Venice.

And I beſeche you (Gentlemen) giue me leaue to tell you a tale, that comes euen now in my mynde: the matter is not worthe the hearyng, but yet very ſtraunge vnto me at the firſt.

It was my fortune at my laſt beyng at London, to walke through the Strande towardes Weſtminſter, where I mett one came ridyng towardes me, on a footeclothe Nagge, apparailed in a Frenche Ruffe, a Frenche Cloake, a Frenche Hoſe, and in his hande a greate fanne of Feathers, bearyng them vp (verie womanly) againſt the ſide of his face: And for that I had neuer ſeen any man weare theim before that daie, I beganne to thinke it vnpoſsible, that there might a manne bee founde ſo fooliſhe, as to make hym ſelf a ſcorne to the worlde, to weare ſo womaniſh a toye. But rather thought it had been ſome ſhameleſſe woman, that had diſguiſed her ſelf like a manne, in our Hoſe, and our Cloakes: for our Dublettes, Gounes, Cappes, and Hattes thei had got long agoe.

But by this tyme he was come ſome thyng nire me, and I might ſee he had a bearde, whereby I was aſſured that he ſhould haue been a manne, whereat I beganne to muſe with my ſelf, whether his ſimplicitie were more to be pitied, or his follie more to be laughed at. For in myne opinion it is as fonde a ſight to ſee a manne with ſuche a bable in his hande, as to ſee a woman ride through the ſtreate with a launce in hers.

And as he paſſed by me, I ſawe three followyng that were his meinie, and taking the hindermoſte by the arme, I asked hym what Gentlewoman his maiſter was: but the fellowe not vnderſtandyng my meanyng, tolde me his maiſters name, and ſo departed.

I beganne then to muſe with my ſelf, to what ende that fanne of Feathers ſerued, for it could not bee to defende the Sunne from the burnyng of his beautie, for it was in the beginnyng of Februarie, when the heate of the Sunne maie bee *very well indured.*

Now if it were to defende the winde, or the coldnesse of the aire, my thinke a Frenche hoode had been a great deale better, for that had been bothe gentlewoman like, and beyng close pinde doune aboute his eares, would haue kepte his hedde a greate deale warmer. And then a Frenche hoode on his hedde, a Frenche Ruffe aboute his necke, a Frenche Cloake on his backe, and a paire of Frenche Hose on his legges had been right. A la mode de Fraunce: & this had bin somethyng sutable to his witte.

But I thinke he did it rather to please Gentlewomen, and the better to shewe what honor he bare theim, would weare one of the greatest vanities that long to their sexe. And to this ende (Gentlemen) I haue tolde you my tale, that you might perceiue the sundrie meanes we vse, and all to please women. I see it is the pathe that all desires to pace, and sure I would wishe my frendes to tread the same trace. For what is he that is wise, whiche desires to be a Souldiour: Mars his Court, is full of bale. Venus is full of blisse. And my good componions and fellowe Souldiours, if you will followe myne aduise, laie aside your weapons, hang vp your armours by the walles, and learne an other while (for your better aduauncementes) to Pipe, to Feddle, to Syng, to Daunce, to lye to forge, to flatter, to cary tales, to set Ruffe, or to dooe any thyng that your appetites beste serues vnto, and that is better fittyng for the tyme. This is the onely meane that is best for a man to bryng hym self in credite: Otherwise, I knowe not whiche waies a man might bende hym self, either to gett gaine or good report.

For first the Militarie profession, by meanes whereof menne were aduaunced to the greatest renowne, is now become of so slender estimation, that there is no accompt nei-

ther

ther made of it, nor any that ſhall profeſſe it.

To become a Courtier, there is as little gaines to be gotten, for Liberalitie, who was wont to be a principall officer, as well in the Court as in the Countrey, by whoſe meanes wel doyng could neuer go vnrewarded. Is tourned Iacke out to office, and others appoincted to haue the cuſtodie of hym to hold him ſhort, that he range no more abroad, ſo that no mā can ſpeake with hym. And thei ſaie, the poore Gentleman, is ſo fleeſt from tyme to tyme, by theſe that bee his keepers, that he hath nothing to giue that is good but it falls to their ſhares.

To become a Student in the Lawe, there are ſuche a number of theim already, that me thinkes it is not poſsible, that one of theim ſhould honeſtly thriue by an other. And ſome will ſaie that one Lawyer, and one Goſhauke, were enough in one Shire. But of my conſcience, there are more Lawyers in ſome one Shire in Englande, with Attorneis, Solicitours, or as thei are termed brokers of cauſes, or Pettie foggers: then there are Goſhaukes in all Norwaie.

To become a Marchaunt, trafique is ſo dead, by meanes of theſe foraine broiles, that vnleſſe a man would be a theefe to his Countrey to ſteale out prohibited wares, there were ſmall gaines to be gotten.

To become a Farmer, Landes be ſo racked at ſuche a rate, that a manne ſhould but toyle all the daies of his life, to paie his Landlordes rent.

But what occupation or handy craft, might a man then followe to make hym ſelf riche: when euery Science dependes vpon newe fangled faſhions. For he that to daie is accompted for the fineſt workeman, within one moneth, ſome newe found fellowe comes out with ſome newe found faſhion: and then he beares the priſe, and the firſt accompted but a ban-

gler. And within an other moneth after, the ſecond ſhall be ſerued with the ſame ſauce: and thus there is no Artificer that can hold his credite long.

Suche is the miſerable condition of this our preſent tyme, this is the courſe of the worlde: but eſpecially here in Englande. Where there is noman thought to be wiſe, but he that is wealthy: where no man is thought to ſpeake a truth, but ſuche as can lie, flatter, and diſſemble. Where there is no aduiſe allowed for good, but ſuche as tendeth more for gaine then for glorie. And what pinchyng for a penie, that ſhould be ſpent in our Countries defence? How prodigall for a pound, to be ſpent vpon vanities & idle deuiſes? What ſmall recompence to Souldiours, that fightes with foes for their Countries quiet? How liberall to Lawyers, that ſettes frendes at defiaunce, and diſquietes a whole Common wealthe? What faunyng vppon hym whom Fortune doeth aduaunce? What frounyng on hym whom ſhe hath brought lowe? What little care of the poore, and ſuche as be in want? What feaſtyng of the riche, and ſuche as be wealthy? What ſumptuous houſes built by men of meane eſtate? What little hoſpitalitie kept from high and lowe degree.

And here I can not but ſpeake of the bountie of that noble Gentleman ſir Chriſtofer Hatton, my verie good Maiſter and vpholder: who hauyng builded a houſe in Northhampton Shire, called by the name of Holdenby. Whiche houſe for the brauerie of the buildynges, for the ſtatelineſſe of the châbers, for the riche furniture of the Lodginges, for the conueighance of the offices, and for all other neceſſaries appertenent to a Pallas of pleaſure: Is thought by theſe that haue iudgement, to be incomparable, and to haue no felowe in Englande, that is out of her Maieſties handes, and although this houſe is not yet fully finiſhed, and is but a newe

erection,

erection, yet it differeth farre from the workes that are vsed now a daies in many places. I meane where the houses are builte with a greate number of Chimneis, and yet the smoke comes forthe but at one onely tunnell. This house is not built on that maner, for as it hath sundrie Chimneis, so thei cast forthe seuerall smokes: and suche worthie porte, and daiely hospitalitie kepte, that although the owner hym self vseth not to come there once in twoo yeares, yet I dare vndertake, there is daiely prouision to be founde conuenient, to entertaine any noble manne with his whole traine, that should hap to call in of a sodaine. And how many Gentlemen and straungers, that comes but to see the house, are there daiely welcomed, feasted, and well lodged. From whence should he come, be he riche, bee he poore, that should not there bee entertained, if it please hym to call in. To bee short, Holdenby *giueth daiely relief to suche as bee in wante, for the space of sixe or seuen miles compasse.*

Peraduenture those that be enuious, will thinke this tale nothyng appertinent to the matter, that I was in hand with all, but I trust my offence is the lesse, considering I haue spoken but a truthe: and doe wishe that euery other man were able to saie as muche for his maister, and so an ende.

And now where I lefte of I was tellyng, what Pride, *what* Coueteousnesse, *what* Whooredome, *what* Glotonie, *what* Blasphemie, *what* Riot, *what* Excesse, *what* Dronkennesse, *what* Swearyng, *what* Briberie, *what* Extortiō, *what* Vsurie, *what* Oppression, *what* Deceipte, *what* Forgerie, *what vice in generall, is daiely entertained, and practized in* Englande. *And although it hath pleased God by wonderfull signes and miracles, to forewarne vs of his wrathe, and call vs to repentaunce, yet you see the worlde runneth forewardes, & keepeth his wonted course, without any remorse*

of

of conſcience,neither making ſigne,nor proffer to amende. But like as we ſee an old ſore beyng once ouer run,will not be cured with any moderate medicine,but muſt be eaten with corſiues till it comes to the quicke: and like as wee ſaie,one poiſon muſt bee a meane,to expell an other. So what ſhould wee otherwiſe thinke of our ſelues, but if wee bee growne to ſuche extreamitie, as no gentill admonition will ſerue to reclaime vs: what other thyng ſhould we looke for,but a miſchief to be the Medicine:God will not ſuffer that vice ſhall alwaies floriſhe,he will ſurely roote it out at the laſte. And how long hath he alredy borne with vs in our wickedneſſe? And what reformation is there had emongeſt vs? vnleſſe it be to go from euill to worſe. But if we did duely conſider, how mercifully he hath ſtill dealt with vs, how fauourably he hath preſerued vs? and how wonderfully he hath defended vs? I thinke we ſhould not be(altogether) ſo vnthankefull as we ſhewe our ſelues to bee. For who knoweth not what an eye ſore,this little Ile of Englande,hath been to the whole worlde,and how long haue we liued(as it were)in contempt of ſuche Countries as be our nexte neighbours, who ſtill enueighyng our quiet and happie gouernment:haue practized by as many deuiſes as thei could,to bring vs into their owne predicament,had it not been the onely prouidence of GOD that preſerued vs.Or what freendſhip might we yet hope to finde at any of their hands: if their oportunitie would ſerue them to be reuenged of the diſpite,which long agoe thei had conceiued againſt vs.Firſt the Frenche hath euer been our enemies by Nature.The Scottes by cuſtome.The Spanyardes for Religion.The Duche although we haue ſtoode them in greate ſteade,and holpe thē at many a pinche:yet I could buye as muche freendſhipp as thei doe all owe vs,for a barrell of Engliſhe Beere.If we ſhould goe any further,then wee

come

come to the Pope, the Turke, and the Deuill, & what frendſhip thei beare vs, I thinke euery one can Imagine.

And here we might conſider how wonderfully God hath wrought on our behalfes, and with all humbleneſſe of harte, giue hym daiely thankes, for his benefites beſtowed vpon vs, but moſte of all, and eſpecially, for our moſte gracious and Soueraigne Ladie Queene Elizabeth, who from tyme to time he hath ſo mightily preſerued, to be the verie inſtrumente of his mercie, and louyng kindneſſe towardes vs: and for whoſe ſake (no doubt) he hath forborne vs in his diſpleaſure, as many tymes he did the children of Iſraell, at the requeſt of his ſeruaunt Moyſes.

Firſt how was ſhe aſſaulted in her ſiſters tyme, by theſe rauenyng Wolues, that daiely ſought her death: for thei all ſtoode in doubt, that ſhe ſhould bee that Iudith, which ſhould cut of proude Holofernes his hedde. And it pleaſed God to bryng it euen ſo to paſſe: not onely defendyng her from their crueltie and rage, but raiſed her vp (in deede) to the vtter ſubuerſion of thoſe bloudie Butchers, and to the greate comfort of vs all, that were in bondage, and ſubiect to tyrannie.

Not onely ſetting vs free, frō thoſe deteſtable enormities, that ſo coroſiued our cōſciences, but made open waie & paſſage, for the worde of God freely to be publiſhed (I thinke) to our owne deſtruction, that ſo vnworthely receiue it. Vppon this, how many mightie enemies proteſted againſt her, and what harme haue any of them been able to doe her. And how many treaſons and priuie conſpiracies (ſith that tyme) hath been practiſed by our peltyng Papiſtes againſt her. But God hath reuealed and brought them to light.

Let vs therefore praie vnto GOD, that he would ſo lengthen her daies, that we might ſtill enioye ſo gracious a Princes, long to gouerne and reigne ouer vs. And that from tyme to tyme,he would ſo directe her Noble Counſaill, in all their meetynges and conſultations,as maie redounde to his glorie, to the benefite of their Countrey, and to their owne immortall fame.

Let vs likewiſe praie, that God would roote ſuche couetuous hartes out of Englande, that for the ſparyng of a penie for the preſent tyme: care not to let ſlippe ſuche matter, as maie coſte many a pounde here after this.

Now laſtly,and as Mariners vſe to ſyng at the Sea,God ſaue my Mate and me alſo: And GOD ſende all Souldiours that hath honeſtly ſerued their Countrey, better conſideration then of long tyme thei haue had.

And thus noble Souldiours and Gentlemen all, I haue heeld you with a long Sermon,neither can I tell how my preachyng will bee allowed of: I craue no more,but wiſhe you all better Fortune then I knowe the preſent tyme will afforde you, and ſo will reſt at your diſpoſition.

Barnabe Riche.

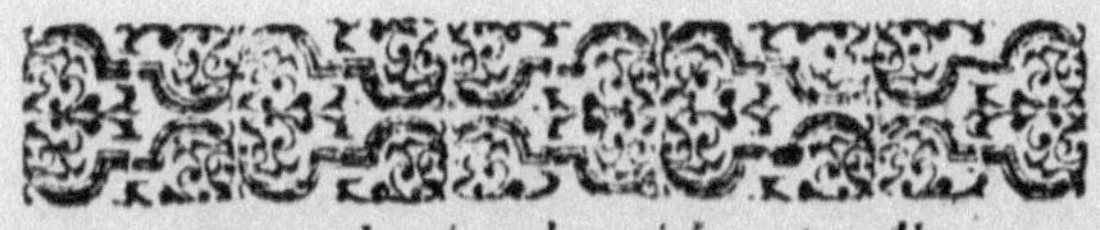

¶ To the Readers in generall.

I Assure thee (gentle reader) whē I first tooke in hande to write these discourses, I meante nothyng lesse then to put theim in print, but write theim at the request of some of my dearest frēdes, sometymes for their disporte, to serue their priuate vse. And now againe by greate importunitie, I am forsed to sende thē al to the Printer. The Histories (altogether) are eight in nūber, whereof, the first, the seconde, the fift, the seuenth and eight, are tales that are but forged onely for delight, neither credible to be beleued, nor hurtfull to be perused. The third, ẏ fourth, and the sixt: are Italiā Histories, written likewise for pleasure by maister L. B. And here gētill reader, I must instauntly intreate thee, that if thou findest any wordes or tearmes, seimyng more vndecent, then peraduenture thou wilte like of: thinke that I haue set them doune, as more apropriate to expresse the matter thei intreate of, then either for want of iudgement or good maners. Trustyng that as I haue written them in Jest, so thou wilt read them but to make thy self merie. I wishe thei might as well please thee in the reading, as thei displease me in puttyng them forthe. I bid thee hartely farewell.

Barnabe Riche.

C.ii. W.I.

VV.I.Gentleman in *praiſe of the Auctor.*

WHo ſeekes by Ladie fame to reape renoune,
Muſt aske conſent of worthie vertues grace:
To her belonges the ſtaulement of the croune,
She yeeldes all thoſe their iuſt deſerued place.
As tred her path and runne her royall race:
Suche Riche rewardes to eache, ſhe yeeldes eache where
As might become this worthie Riche to weare.

The painfull man that tilles his grounde, reapes frute,
Eache merrit hath his meede, paine hath his hire:
Deſerte requires that fame ſhould not ſtande mute,
Where wiſedome doeth to vertues waies aſpire,
The hope of gaine doeth ſet mens hartes on fire,
Then yeeld hym thankes, that erſt hath vndertooke,
For thy delight to penne this little booke.

Let *Momus* mates chat on, in their diſpight,
Let wranglers wreake and wreſt the worſt thei maie:
The wiſeſt ſorte will iudge and take delight,
Though ianglyng iayes that knowe not what thei ſaie:
Will oftentymes their witleſſe wittes bewraie,
Yet Riche ſhall reape, what he by right hath wonne,
Deſerued praiſe for that whiche here is doen.

Finis. q. VV.I. Gent.

Baptiſte Starre in praiſe of the Auſthor.

IF due deſerte ſhould reape rewarde,
Or worthie merrit, guerdon haue:
Why ſhould not Riche preſſe forth hym ſelf,
The louely laurell croune to craue:
Whoſe life in fielde that wonne hym praiſe,
He leades at home in Pallas waies.

Skorne not then Zoylus his good happe,
That can his will ſubdue and tame:
But trie to treade his path whereby,
Thou maieſt thy life with vertue frame:
Alowe his paine, and penne to wright,
Who naught pretendes but thy deligth.

Loe he who wonted was in fielde,
To meete his furious foe in face:
Hath ſcalde Parnaſſus hill where he,
Attendes Mineru' her noble grace.
And there his penne doeth plaie his parte,
As did els where his ſhielde and darte.

Finis. q. B. S.

The Printer to the Reader.

THE fragrant Roſe can make no choyſe,
 Who ſhall vpon hym light:
The ſpraulyng Spider turnes to gaule,
 The Bee to honey right.

So fares it with this booke, whoſe leaues
 Are open ſpred to thee:
Make choiſe good Reader of the beſt,
 Sucke honey with the Bee.

Miſconſter not eache merrie phraiſe,
 Deeme not the worſt of it:
Whiche is not pende to doe thee hurte,
 But recreate thy wit.

And for ſuche faultes as ſcaped haue
 The preſſe, whereof thers ſtore:
Reproue the Printer for his haſte,
 Blame not the booke therefore.

But as by mirth tis meant to moue,
 Thy mynde to ſome delight:
Rewarde his paine with praiſe, whiche did
 Theſe pleaſaunt Stories wright.

FINIS.

The

Sappho Duke of Mantona.

The argument of the firste Historie.

¶Sappho, *Duke of* Mantona *hauyng long tyme serued* Claudius *the Emperour, by whose magnanimitie, & Martiall prowest, sundrie victories were achiued against the Turke, was by false imposition banished, hym self,* Messilina *his wife,* Aurelianus *his sonne, with* Phylene *his daughter, in whiche banishement thei susteined sundrie conflictes of Fortune, but in the ende, restored againe to their former estate and dignitie.*

HE one of the greatest vertues that worldlie men can expresse in the commō behauiour of this life, is neither to ware proude by prosperitie, nor to fall into dispaire by aduersitie, for Fortune hauyng a free will to come and goe, when, and where she listeth: the wise mā ought not to be sorie when he looseth her, nor to reioyce whē he holdeth her, for that the valiant man looseth no reputation, whē that Fortune faileth hym, but is the lesse esteemed of, if he want discretion to beare her mutabilities, the whiche for the most part is altogether uncertain now promisyng good, now performyng ill, now liftyng up to the tip of the highest dignitie, now throwyng doune to the pit of perpetuall infamie: now aduauncing aloft those that be unworthie, now throwing downe the climmers up into extreame aduersitie: suche are the giftes and graces of Fortune, to haue no better thing more certaine in them, then to be for the moste parte in all thynges uncertaine, as the sequell of this Historie shall more better describe, and followeth in this manner.

There was sometymes remaynyng in the Courte of the Emperor

Emperor Claudius, a noble Duke whose name was Sappho Duke of Mantona, who as well, through his owne magnanimitie and valiaunce, as otherwise through his greate policie and experience in Marciall affaires, had atchiued many notable victories, in the behalfe of the Emperour againste the Turke, whiche made hym bothe famous to the worlde, and feared of his enemies, but moste entirely beloued of the Emperour Claudius: But the warres beeyng once finished and brought to an ende, so that the Empire remained in tranquilitie and peace: Souldiors were forgotten, Captaines were not cared for, suche as had profered them selues to fight for the saftie of their Countrey, were now shaken of, and suche were preferred in their romes, as had any facultie in them tendyng to pleasure and delight, as Dauncers, Pipers, Fidlers, Minstreles, Singers, Parisites, Flatterers, Iesters, Rimers, Talebearers, Newes cariers, Loue makers, suche as can deuise to please women, with newe fangles, straunge fasshions, by praisyng of their beauties, when sometymes it is scarce worthie, by commendyng of their manifolde vertues, when God knowes thei haue fewe or none at all. But see I praie you how farre my wittes beginne to square, I pretended but to penne certaine pleasaunt discourses, for the onely pleasure of Gentilwomen, and euen at the very first entrie, I am falne from a reasonable tale to a railyng rage, as it may seeme. But I praie you Gentilwomen beare with my weakenesse, and as the Preacher in the Pulpit, when he is out of his Texte, will saie for excuse: Good people, though this bee somethyng degressyng from my matter, yet it maie very well serue at this present: Take this I praie you for my excuse in like case.

And now to my purpose where I lefte of before, this noble Duke Sappho, had no skill in Courting trade: his head which had been accustomed to beare the loftie Helme, had now quite forgotten to weare the wauering Plumes, readie to blowe awaie with euery winde. His bodie moste inured to weare a coate of steele, could not be brought in fasshion with this queint and nice araie. His necke he thought more fitly to paise the trustie targe, then to bee hanged with Gemmes or Chaines

of

of golde: his fingers commonlie practiſed to graſpe the ſworde or launce, could not bee brought in frame to ſtrike the Virginall or Lute: His voice ſerued hym better to cheare his Souldiers in the feeld, then either to faine or ſyng ditties in a ladies Chamber: His tongue had more uſed to ſpeake ſimplie and plaine, then to diſſemble with his freend, or to flatter with his foe: His legges had better ſkill to marche after dubbe a dubbe a dubbe, then to mince it with a Minion, tracyng a Pauion or Galliarde uppon the Ruſhes: what ſhould I ſaie farther, this noble Duke had no maner of ſkill in Carpet trade: But thus it fell out that Paraſites and Flatterers, hauyng once entered credite with the Emperour (as ſurely it is almoſte a common infirmitie, aſwell emongeſt Princes, as other ſuperiour officers, to bee ſeduced by Flatterers, Pickthankes, and Talebearers) this noble Emperour likewiſe, by the inſtigation of ſuche as were aboute hym, who perceiuyng the Duke to bee none of their flattryng fraternitie, and enueighyng the greate reputation wherein the Emperour helde hym, had ſo incenſed the Emperour againſte hym, that now his likyng was conuerted into loathyng, and his greate loue tourned to a more hate, that in the ende the poore Duke was brought to anſwere unto many forged articles ſurmiſed againſt hym, who neither in conſideration of his former ſeruice dooen for his Countery, neither in reſpecte of the innocencie of his cauſe, could otherwiſe bee diſpenſed withall, then to bee baniſhed into exile, hym ſelf, Meſilina his wife, Aurelianus his ſoonne, with Phylene his daughter: And although the common ſorte of people helde hym in greate honour, and muche lamented his caſe, yet it could not bee holpen, but the Emperours decree openly pronounced, muſt needes take place.

I beſeche you gentilwomen, yet to comfort your ſelues, I knowe your gentill hartes, can not endure to heare of ſuche ungentill partes, but theſe are but the frumpes of ordinarie Fortune, not priuate to Duke Sappho alone, but common to all menne that bee of the like profeſſion, for what happened better to the moſte noble Captaines of the worlde, or what other recompence receiued either Cæſar, Scipio, Hanniball, or many other like, who hauyng honoured their countries, with sondrie triumphes, and many notable victories, when the warres were ended, and that there was no more neede of theim, finished their daies in suche pitifull plight, as I will keepe to my self, because right courteous Gentilwomen, I rather desire to drawe you into delightes, then to droune you in dumphes, by reuealyng of suche vnnaturall factes, as I knowe your gentle Natures is not able to digest.

Thus you haue heard how this noble Duke, with his wife and children, by sentence from the Emperoure, were banished from out their natiue Countrey, as also from any other Realmes, Cities, tounes, or territories, beyng within the Emperours Dominions. There resteth now for the Duke to make suche poore prouision for his furnishing, as his habilitie might any waies serue hym, the whiche GOD knoweth, fell out so meane and skante, as it scarcely serueth hym to defraie his charges, to carrie hym from out those places, from whence he was prohibited: and takyng his course towardes the partes of Macedonia, after a long and wearie iourney, he arriued at a toune called Tariffa, where beyng lodged in a meane and simple house, his money now beyng at the laste caste, wherewith to beare his charges, his poore wife and children altogether wearied, with their long and troublesome trauaill, and hym self all ashamed to bee knowne what he was. Now it fell out, that the Hoste of the house many tymes bewyng, and castyng his eyes vpō the Duchesse of Messilina, who notwithstandyng she dissembled her estate and degree, cōtented to leaue her honourable dignitie, and to perticipate suche equall fortune with her housebande and children, as their hard happes had conducted them vnto, yet her beautie (whiche could not bee blemished with meane and homely garmentes, had so entangled her arrant Hoste, that he could not be merrie when he was out of her sweete sight, and now though he perceiued his ghest beganne to ware slacke in his paiement, and not able to disburse for his ordinarie expences, yet for the loue he bare to his wife, he was contented to chalke vp the charges behinde the doore, hopyng in the ende to haue cleared the scores to his better content, and

as

as tyme and conuenience might serue him, he spared not to let the Duchesse vnderstande his greate likyng towardes her, assuryng her that the courtesie that he vsed towardes her housebande, was onely for her sake, and that if he were assured his good will might bee acceptable in her sight, she might assure her self of suche a freend of hym, as would be as carefull of her as her housebande, to whom she was married.

This Ladie now hauyng well pondered the woordes of her amourous Hoste, who would not thinke but that she was muche perplexed in her mynde, that she who had been borne of honourable Parentage, Espoused to a noble Duke, whose dignitie in tymes paste, surmounted all the rest, whose trainyng vp had euer been emongst those of the highest degree, and now that her honourable estate, was not onely eclipsed by crooked Destinie, but also to haue her Chastitie assailed, by suche a simple coisterell, whom she durste not so sharpely shake of, as her harte would very well haue serued, for that she knewe the Duke her housebande was runne in his debt, neither could she tell by what meanes he was able to discharge it, she was therfore constrained with faire speeches, to shift hym of from time to tyme, the whiche the knaue perceiuyng very well, beganne to thinke with hym self, that it was but her housebandes presence, that hindered hym of his purpose, and therefore determined to finde a present remedie.

And now commyng to his ghest, beganne to recken with hym, and to call hym to accoumpt for the charges wherein he was behinde, tellyng hym, that at that verie instaunte, he had occasion to occupie money, whiche made hym not onely to seeke vp suche small sommes as were due vnto hym, but also to trie his freendes otherwise to serue his tourne, and that helping him now at his present neede, he might then begin againe a newe score, and would beare with him a muche lenger time.

The poore Duke then inforced to seeke out an old Salue for an newe Sore, whiche is to paie when he was not able to paie, with verie courteous speeches, desired his Hoste to beare with his inabilitie, assuryng him that when time should serue, he would so throughlie recompence hym, as he should haue cause to holde hym well contented.

But what praiers maie preuaile, where pitie is cleane exiled, or what gentlenesse is to be looked for, to come from suche an vngentle chorle, whose mynde was onely sette vpon Rape and Rauine, who had premeditated before the drifte (whiche as he presupposed) was now sorted out as he looked for.

Wherefore (as it were) halfe in a furie, he vttered forthe these woordes: My freende content your self, and take this for a resolute aunswere, the money whiche now resteth in your handes, although I might verie ill forbeare it, as my case standeth, yet for that it is not myne ease, to runne into any farther charges, without a better assuraunce, then either woordes or promises, I am notwithstanding contented to beare with you for that whiche is alreadie paste, myndyng from this daie forwardes to giue no further credite, and for that you are altogether a straunger, vnto me vnknowne, bothe what you are, from whence you come, whether you will, and where I should finde you, I purpose therefore for my better securitie, and the rather to come by that you alreadie doe owe me, to keepe your wife in paune, whom I knowe is so dearely beloued vnto you, that for her sake I shall the sooner heare from you againe, otherwise I knowe not where to inquire after you, nor how to come by that is my due, whiche I am not well able to forbeare, neither doe I mynde clearely to lose.

The poore afflicted Duke, hauyng neuer falne before into cutthrotes handes, perswaded in deede that the tenour of this Varlettes woordes, and the keepyng of his wife tended to no other ende, but for his better assuraunce to come by his money, was constrained to make a vertue of necessitie, and was so muche the better pleased, for that his wife might stil remain free from farther trauaile, and thinkyng in tyme to settle hym self, and to recouer his wife and children about hym: with this resolution he began to relate vnto his wife, with what salutations his gentle hoste had greeted hym withall, desiryng her to comfort her self for a season, assuryng to doe his best indeuour, and to set vp his sailes to the prosperous gales of Fortune.

This good Ladie, hearyng her housebandes discourse vncertaine

certaine

certaine what to doe, wepte bitterly, as well for greef to looſe his preſence, as for that ſhe ſhould bee lefte in the houſe of the arrant knaue her Hoſte, but like a wiſe Ladie, hearyng the alleadged reaſons of her Lorde and houſebande, did thinke it not for the beſte, to encreaſe his old ſorowe with a newe greef, contented her ſelf, vtteryng theſe woordes.

Deare houſebande, knowyng all that you haue ſaied to be verie iuſte and true, I am contented for a certain tyme to force my will, in hope that hereafter we maie liue together, ioiyng our ſelues in the companie of our children, and this I would deſire you, that ſo often as you can by conueniente and truſtie meſſengers, to ſende me worde and intelligence of your health and eſtate, becauſe the ſame ſhould bryng greater contentation vnto me, then the welfare of myne owne ſelf.

This ſaied, ſhe imbracyng hym verie louyngly, and he kiſſyng her with greate ſorrowe and greefe, tooke his leaue, and badde his Ladie and ſpouſe hartely farewell, leauyng with her Phylene her deare daughter.

Thus hym ſelf with Aurelianus his little ſonne, departed from Taryffa, towardes the famous citie of Cayre, and as thei paſſed through a Wilderneſſe, hauyng loſte their waie, wanderyng twoo or three daies without any maner of foode, ſauyng Hippes, Hawes, and Slowes, ſuche as thei could gather in the deſert, the poore child beyng ouer come with faintneſſe, not longer able to trauaile, beganne to complaine to his afflicted father, deſiryng hym to ſitte doune to reſte hym ſelf a tyme, the wofull Father tormented in his mynde, to ſee his poore diſtreſſed child, ſatte hym doune vnder a tree, where after a while, recountyng to hym ſelf his ſonderie misfortunes, beyng oppreſſed and wearied with trauaile, he fell into a ſound ſleape, the Childe after he had a while reſted hymſelf, leauyng his Father a ſleape, beganne to ſeeke about for ſomethyng to ſlake his hũger, and as he was ſtraiyng thus about the wooddes, it fortuned the Duke of Vaſconia, hauyng loſte his companie in the purſute of a Stagge, where he had been a huntyng and as he was croſſyng the nexte waie to goe to the Citie of Meſſyna, where he helde his Courte, hauyng in his companie but the Lorde of Sura, with three of fower seruyng menne; he fortuned to espie the child runnyng in the bushes all alone, and callyng the child vnto hym, he saied, alas my little boye, what makest thou in this place, art thou here alone, or how camest thou hether I praie thee tell me. Forsothe Godfather (ꝗ the child) I came hether with my Father, who lyes a sleape here by, and I was seekyng somethyng to eate, for by my troth I am so a hongered, that I could eate worse meate then a peece of a rosted Pigge, and that with all my harte.

The Duke greately pleasuryng to heare the pretie aunswere of the Childe, replied in this wise: How saiest thou my little knaue, wilt thou bee my boye and dwell with me, and I will giue thee good meate thy beallie full, how saiest thou wilt thou goe with me.

Yea forsooth Godfather (ꝗ the Childe) on that condition you will giue me roste meate enough, I will goe with you, for I thinke I did not eate my beallie full of roste meate, this moneth and more.

The Duke then commaunded one of his menne to take vp the Child, whom he carried awaie with hym, and now perceiuyng it to be bothe well fauoured, quicke witted, and very apt to learnyng, he brought it vp sat choole, where he proued not onely wise and learned, but also in many other exercises, conuenient and fitte for Gentlemen, he commonly excelled euery other man, and thus leauyng hym at Schoole, I will conuert my tale to his wofull Father, who when he was awaked, and missed his pretie soonne, began to prie aboute in euery bushe, sekyng and callyng, what Aurelianus, Aurelianus, where bee you Aurelianus: But in the ende when he could no where finde hym, thinkyng assuredly that he had been deuoured by some wilde beaste, beganne with pitifull exclamation to crie out. O Fortune, Fortune more then fickle, who in a moment hoiste a man vp to the highest degree, and by and by, in lesse space then in the twincklyng of an eye, she throweth hym doune againe so lowe, as more miserie is prepared for him in one daie, then she aduaunced hym in an hundred yeres, whiche I now proue, and haue experience in my self, and so muche the more, the greater

is

is my greef, who haue been nourished delicately emongest my freendes, maintained still in moste prosperous estate, hopyng for the full perfection of my felicities, by Marriyng a Noble Dame, with whom I pretended to spende the residue of my life, accordyng to the scope and lotte appointed by the almightie God, but now beholde all my enterprises bee quite pluckte backe, and my purposes tourned cleane topse torue, in suche wise, that from honourable estate, I am driuen to wander like a vacabonde, driuen from Poste to Piller, from Countrie to coūtrie, from Region, to Region, to sequestrate my self from emongest my freendes, without any assured place where to make my abode. Oh froward fate, how canst thou bee so hard harted, and voide of pitie, still to prosecute thy cruell pursute, first to depriue me of my honourable dignities, then to banishe me from emongest my louyng freendes, thirdlie to separate me from Messilina, my well beloued wife, more deare vnto me then the balles of my vnhappie eyes, and not yet contented, but now to bereue me of my sweete infant, my onely hope of comforte in my olde age. O Death Death, the ende of all sorrowes, and the beginner of felicities, now make sharpe thy Darte, and giue no longer delaye of life, dispatche, dispatche at once, the moste infortunate manne that liues this daie on pearth: for what auailes my life, if in the gulfe of sorow & greef I drounde the pleasures of the same: But ah I see right well, thou preseruest the same of purpose, but to delight in my grœues, and to triumphe ouer my aduersities. And here withall the brinishe teares so streamed doune his cheekes, that he was not farther able to speake one woorde, but runnyng vp and doune the woodes, sighyng and sobbyng in greate anguishe of mynde, and his bodie muche infeebled for want of foode and sustenaunce. He fortuned to meete certaine labouryng menne, that dwelte in a poore Village not farre from the place, who perceiuyng by his geasture, that he was passionated in his thoughtes, thei beganne with suche courtesie, as thei had learned in the Countrie, to demaunde the occasion of his greef.

But he knowing verie well, how farre thei were vnable to minister releef to the leaste of his afflictions, could render no

other

other aunswere, then piteous sighes and subbes: but the poore Pesauntes, when thei had better beheld the talnesse of his stature, the seemelinesse of his countenaunce, and the comelinesse of his personage, were greatlie mooued with compassion towardes hym, and with suche badde eloquence as their skill would permit, beganne to perswade hym to walke with them to their Cabbins, where he might refreshe hymself, with suche homely Junckettes, as was prouided for their owne suppers. The Duke contented to yeelde to their requestes, walked along with them, where he remained all the night verie pensiue and heauie in his harte, and beganne to thinke with hym self, that there was no more hope left for him to heare of his sonne, and therefore beganne to imagine, how he might render some releef to his poore wife and daughter, whom he had left as you before haue heard.

Now there was dwellyng harde by the place, a noble man that was Lorde of the Village, who hauyng intelligence of this distressed straunger, caused hym to bee sente for, before whom when the Duke was presented, after many questions debated betweene theim, the noble manne demaunded of the Duke what Countrey manne he was, and how he had been trained vp, and then if he could bee contented to plaie the Seruyngman, and would bee carefull and diligent in his maisters affaires, that then, he would bée contented to receiue hym into his seruice, and would rewarde hym accordyngly, as he was able to deserue.

The Duke all ashamed to bée knowne what he was, reuerently made aunswere, that he was borne in the Countrey of Achaia: and that he had been trained vp in seruice with sonderie noble menne, and would bée very well contented to doe his best indeuour, to serue him with the beste seruice he could doe.

Thus the poore Duke became a seruyng man, whom we will leaue with his maister, and returne to his wife, who was lefte in Hursters handelyng (as you haue heard) remained in the house with this Verlette, who sought by sondrie assaies, to satisfie his villanous luste, and like an experte Souldier when he commeth to besiege a holde, first sendeth his Herauldes to summon sommon the Forte, proferyng many large conditions, if thei will quietly surrender, but if defiaunce be made, then presently he placeth his Batterie, thunderyng forthe his Canon shot against the walles, whiche if thei bee so well Rampered, that there will no breache bee made, yet he ceaseth not with giftes and bribes to corrupte the Warders, not caryng how he conquereth so he maie haue the spoyle.

This vilaine in likewise, sought first with piteous sighes, whiche saust with sugred woordes, did serue in steede of Harauldes, to perswade her to yeeld vp the keyes of the fortresse, that with peaceable entrie, he might take possessiõ at his pleasure: but beeyng by her repulsed, and the Flagge of defiaunce displaied vpon the Bulworke, then with thunderyng threates he thinketh to make his Batterie, proferyng to caste her into prison, for the debt whiche was owyng hym for her housbande and her self. Other whiles againe he would tempte her, and trie her with giftes, thinkyng that for the necessitie she was driuen into, she would haue made sale of that, whiche she preferred before her owne life.

This noble Dame, perceiuyng her self so hardly beset on euery side, fearyng in the ende, the Verlet should woorke her some greater despight, so enforced her self, with Phylene her little daughter to fall to worke, that with weauyng and knittyng of laces, and otherwise with their needles, thei had gained so muche money, as she was able to set her self free, from out a knaues debt. And thinkyng with her self, that her housbande had remained about the Citie of Cayre, to the whiche he purposed to iourney when he departed from her: she determined with all conuenient speede to repaire thether, as well to comforte her self with the companie of her Lorde and housbande, as otherwise with her yearnynges to helpe to releue hym, but for that she had vnderstandyng that the passage by lande, was not onely troublesome, but also very inconuenient for her to trauaile, by reason it laie through woodes and desertes, she gate inteligence of a small Barke that was bound thether by Sea, whiche onely staied but for a winde to serue her turne; here vpon she discharged her self from the Towne of Taryffa, and when wether serued, agreyng with the Maister for her passage, her self with her daughter repaired abord the Barke, which beyng put to Sea, was forced by the extremitie of a contrary winde, to put them selues romer for the safetie of their liues, to a cleane contrary place. And where thei ment to haue sailed to the Citie of Cayre, thei were now arriued at the Citie of Cherona, where the Ladie commyng a shore, she ioyed nothyng so muche in the narrowe escape she had made with life, by reason of the tempest, as she sorrowed for beyng so farre driuen from her housbande, whose fellowshippe she more desired, then either wealthe or worldly treasure. But for asmuche as both her self and her daughter, were very euill at ease, and greatly infeebeled with sicknesse at the Sea, and bad liyng in the Shippe, she determined to make her abode still at Cherona, till she might conuaie letters to Taryffa, that should certifie her housbande of all that had happened.

In the meane tyme, her housbande hauyng receiued some small beneuolence of his Lorde and Maister, who had conceiued some good likyng of hym, by reason of the skill that he had in the ridyng of Horse, very desirouse to render his wife some portion of his good fortunes, who had bin so long tyme partaker of his euill happes, crauyng leaue of his Lorde for a tyme, came to Taryffa, where when he missed his wife, whose letters were not yet come from Cherona, and therefore could get no intelligence, but that she was gone to Cayre, of purpose to seeke hym: in a greate perplexitie he traueiled towardes Cayre, where makyng greate inquirie could learne nothyng of her, from thence he posted from place to place, from Citie to Citie, from Towne to Towne, but beyng neuer the neare his purpose, he then began to double his dolours, and with bitter wordes to curse the celestiall Signes, and Planets, which raigned at the daie of his Natiuitie, and howre of his birthe, contented to yeeld hym self a captiue to mishappe, and to surrender hym self a subiecte to Fortunes frowarde frumpes.

Beyng thus turmoyled with greate anguishe of mynde, wanderyng to and fro, he was brought so lowe and bare, that he he was readie to begge an almes from doore to doore, and cōmyng to a poore countrey Village, his penurie was suche, that he was glad to become a seruaunt to hym that was the Sexten of the Parishe, whom he had not serued long, but the old Sexten his maister died, and for that he had now learned to ryng Belles, and had some cunnyng in the keepyng of a Clocke: the Parishoners were contented to place hym in his Maisters rome, the Duke thinkyng hym self more then thrise happie to gett so greate preferment, thanked Ladie Fortune that had so freendly dealt with hym, resoluyng hym self to cōtinue the office while he liued, but Fortune findyng hym so thankfull for a little, dealte more freendly with hym, as after you shall heare.

But I will firste declare how it happened with his soonne Aurelianus, who was taken vp in the woodes by the Duke of Vasconya, as before you haue heard.

But here I muste firste remember you, that the Duke chaunged his name from Aurelianus to Siluanus, whiche name he gaue hym of purpose, for that he was founde in the woodes.

Siluanus now hauyng been trained vp at Schoole, was come to mannes estate, and besides that he had the knoweledge of good letters, he was comely in his personage, and of verie good proportion, and in all maner of actiuities, appertainyng to a gentilman, he exceeded euery other that was in the Courte, besides in his demeamours he was so courteous and gentill, that he gained the good will and likyng, bothe of one and other, but especially of the Duke hym self, who alowed hym suche large expenses, whereby to maintaine hym self as braue as the beste.

Now this noble Duke hauyng no other children but one onely daughter, whose name was Valerya, in whom it seemed that bothe Vertue and Beautie had helde some greate contention, who should beare awaie the prise, for although that in beautie and good grace she exceeded euery other Dame, yet her vertues and good conditions surmounted more her beautie, then the finest golde surmounteth Leade or drosse.

The Ladie now hauyng heard greate reporte of the nobleneſſe of Siluanus, who was ſuſpected to bee but ſome poore mannes ſonne, by reaſon he was founde in the woodes, beganne yet to beare hym very good countenaunce, whiche at the firſt proceeded but of the noble Nature, whiche euer was accuſtomed to bee fauourable to ſuche, in whom was founde any worthie deſarte: but as the fiſhe whiche by little and little ſucketh vpon the baite, till at the length ſhe ſwalloweth doune the hooke, whereby ſhe hangeth faſte, not able to free her ſelf, ſo this Ladie Valerya, contemplatyng her ſelf many tymes to beholde that yong gentilman Siluanus, was ſo farre intangeled with his ſweete and pleaſaunt countenaunce, that now perforce her will, ſhe was conſtrained to yeelde to Loue, and feelyng her ſelf inſnared, and bereued of former freedome, beyng by her ſelf alone, ſhe began to complaine as followeth.

Alas (ſaieth ſhe) is it poſſible, that now force perforce my mynde ſhould bee ſo altered, that ſtraiyng from the boundes and limites of vowed Chaſtitie: I ſhould now become amourous, and ſubiect to a certaine vnacquainted luſte, frō whence commeth this alteration? or how happeneth this vnaccuſtomed hewe? ah Loue Loue, how haſte thou tormented me, and taken awaie the healthe and ſoundneſſe of my mynde, it behoueth me to ſhewe my ſelf, as iſſued forthe of the noble houſe of Vaſconya, and with the greater care I ought to take heede, how I degenerate from the noble blood whereof I am deſcended, rather then to ſette my mynde on a fondlyng vnknowen, vnto whom peraduenture if I diſcouer my fondneſſe, will not let to mocke me for my labour, and for all the beautie or nobleneſſe of my birthe, will make me his teſtyng ſtocke, and ſolace hym ſelf with the fondneſſe of my conceiptes. But ſtaie ſtaie vnhappie tongue, that thundereth forthe ſuche hatefull wordes againſt my beloued Siluanus. Oh thriſe accurſed wenche that can ſo vngently conceiue againſt hym, that in all his demeanours, doeth ſhewe hym ſelf as noble as the beſte, but of what metall are either Monarche, Kyng or Keiſer framed of, otherwiſe then of naturall, and common yearth, whereof other menne doe come? Or what maketh theſe differences, whiche

whiche by ſottiſhe opinion we conceiue, either of gentle or vngentle, otherwiſe then the ſhewe of vertue and good conditions. Then the partie whom I loue, is both vertuous, valiant, ſage, of good grace, learned and wiſe. Vaunte thee then Valeria, that thou likeſt no inferiour fondlyng, vnworthie of thy loue, but a worthie gentilman, indued with noble qualities, in whom bothe Heauen and Nature haue forgotten nothyng, to make hym equall to them that marche in formoſte ranke: It is Siluanus whom I loue, and of hym I pretende to make a lawfull houſbande, for otherwiſe I deteſt to leade the filthie life of lawleſſe luſte, but thus the bonde of mariage beeyng made, I maie loue and liue without offence of conſcience, neither ſhall I doe any blotte or blemiſhe to the greatneſſe of my houſe. But if any be ſo ſcrupulous, as to thinke by marriyng of hym, I ſhould deminiſhe myne honour: It is the thing that I dooe leaſte eſteeme, for what is honour worthe, where the mynde is voide of contentation, and where the harte is bereued of his cheefeſt deſire, the bodie remaineth reſtleſſe, and the mynde is neuer in quiet. Siluanus therefore ſhalbee my loyall houſbande, meanyng therby neither to offende God nor mã.

And now from hence forwardes, ſhe deuiſed with her ſelf, how to make her loue knowne to Siluanus, not ſparyng when ſhe was out of his preſence, before all men to praiſe his greate perfections, wherewith he was enriched, and in his owne preſence ſhe vſed ſuche louyng countenaunce towardes hym, that although Siluanus were but yong, and had neuer been trained vp in the Schoole of Loue, yet he perceiued verie well, that thoſe frendly glances were ſent hym of good likyng, and thoſe louyng countenaunces were grounded of good will, and albeit, he ſawe the inequalitie and difference betweene them both, ſhe beeyng ſorted out of royall race, and hym ſelf altogether ignorant of his owne eſtate, and from whence he was ſprong, yet beyng now ledde by Loue, whoſe lawes haue no reſpecte either to eſtate or dignitie, he determined to followe his Fortune, and to ſerue her, whiche ſo louyngly ſhewed her ſelf, to requite hym with the like, and the more he called to mynde the diuine beautie of his Ladie, her graces, wiſedome, behauiour, and curtesie, so muche the more increased his desire, fortifiyng him self against all mishappes, and perilles that might succede, and began to debate with hym self in this maner.

How is it possible that I should be so foolishe, to despise a dutie so rare and preciouse, and to set light by that whiche the noblest would pursue, with all reuerence and indeuour, I am not the first, that hath obtained the loue of a Ladie: no no, I see she loueth me, and shall not I requite it by yeeldyng loue againe, if I were so voide of humanitie and good nature, besides I might worke myne owne ouerthrowe, in seemyng to dispise so noble a Ladie, so the Goddes would not let to minister reuenge, as thei did vpon Narcissus. But ah silly wretche that I am, what folly is this that I haue now premeditated, with the perill of myne honour, and the hazarde of my life: see see how farre my affections begin to straie, through the hot assaultes of foolishe fantasie, inraged with an appetite risyng on vaine hope, what madnesse on me to thinke that Valerya will so muche forget the greatnesse of her house, or yet imbase her self in respect of me poore silly soule: but what if she would be contented, either in respecte of mariage, or otherwise in respecte of good will, to surrender her self to satisfie my request, how muche were I the neare my purpose, alas nothyng at all, the first, I knowe should be denaide me by the Duke her father, and as for any other curtesie, although I knowe it bee farre frō her thought, yet surely myne owne conscience would not suffer me, to proffer so greate villanie to so noble a Ladie, neither the reuerence and duetie whiche I owe to her father would permitte me, to requite his gentilnesse towardes me with so greate an iniurie. Cease therefore Siluanus, subdue thy sensualitie, that by vanquishyng thy self, thou maist set open the gate to fame, who with her Trompe of euerlastyng glorie, she maie aduaunce thee renowmed to all posteritie.

But alas, shall I then giue ouer to loue my Ladie Valerya, reason willes me so to doe, but loue hath so blinded all my sences, that reason giueth no maner of light, what helpe haue I then hereafter to hope for, alas I knowe no one, and therefore be content. Here withall he staied his trauaile, resoluyng

with

which hym self to conquere his affections , and keepyng in his Chamber takyng pen and ynck, he sate hym doune and wrote these verses followyng.

No shame I trust, to cease from former ill,
Nor to reuert, the leudnesse of the mynde:
Whiche hath bin trainde, and so misled by will,
To breake the boundes, whiche reason had assyngde.
I now forsake, the farmer tyme I spent,
And sory am, for that I was miswent.

But blynde forecast, was he that made me swarue,
Affection fond, was lurer of my lust:
My fancie fixte, desire did make me serue,
Vaine hope was he, that trained all my trust:
Good likyng then, so dasled had my sight,
And dimnde myne eyes, that reason gaue no light.

O sugred swete, that trainde me to this trap,
I sawe the baite, where hooke late hidden fast:
I well perceiude, the drift of my mishap.
I kenwe the bit, would breede my bane at last.
But what for this, for sweete I swallowed all,
Whose taste I finde, more bitter now then gall.

But loe the fruites, that grewe by fonde desire,
I seeke to shunne, that pleased best my mynde:
I sterue for colde, yet faine would quenche the fire,
And glad to loose, that fainest I would finde.
In one self thyng, I finde both baall and blisse,
But this is straunge, I like no life but this.

When he had thus penned these verses , he committed them to memorie, and the next daie beyng in the companie of certaine Gentlemen and Gentlewomen in the Court, takyng a Lute , whereon he could plaie very well, and hauyng likewise good knowledge in his song, and therwithall a very plea-

saunt

faint voyce, he began to sing this dittie before mentioned, in the middest whereof came in the yong Ladie Valerya, wherewith Siluanus staied his song, but she ioynyng her self to the cõpanie, seyng the sainct that secretly shrined in her thought, she had vowed her greatest deuotion vnto, desired Siluanus at her request, to begin his song againe, Siluanus, makyng the matter nothyng nyce, was pleased very well to satisfie her request, and takyng the Lute began his song, to the whiche the Ladie gaue intentiue eare, from the beginnyng to the endyng, and perceiuing the song to be made in some extreame passion forced by loue, she demaunded of Siluanus who had penned those verses, who aunswered, thei were of his owne pennyng, and so lately doen that he could not forget theim: the Ladie then thinkyng Siluanus to be in loue with some other Gentlewoman, departed very speedily, as though some sodaine motion had happened to her mynde, and commyng to her Chamber, shuttyng fast the doore, she began to saie as followeth.

How muche am I vnfortunate aboue all other women, that beyng a Ladie of suche bloud as I am, and yet am happened into so straunge a miserie, that in maner with myne owne mouth, I haue made request to him, whiche rather with all humilitie, ought to profer me his seruice, & yet am scornefully reiected, and an other like to catche the birdes, whilest I doe but beate the bushe. Oh Siluanus Siluanus, deemest thou me no better worthe, then so lightly to reiecte my proffered loue, and shall an other that is muche lesse worthie, beare awaie the sweete fruite of my desired hope, and shall possesse without deserte, the glorie due to a firme and faithfull frende: No no, I can not thinke thee so ingrate, and my harte foretelleth me, that it is impossible my Siluanus should wander so farre from equitie, but that he is able to discerne of colours, and will not requite me with wrong for right, I am sure not to be deceiued in my loue, I knowe he loueth me, but that he dareth not to disclose the same, fearyng I should refuse hym, and cast hym of with shame, I will not let therfore with myne owne mouth to bewraie the same vnto hym, and to manifest my good will, wherby my chast & honest amitie once knowne

vnto

vnto hym, vertue her self maie knitte the knotte betweene vs, whiche can not chuse but bryng forthe the fruites of true and perfect freendship.

And shall I then beeyng a Ladie of suche degree, bee constrained to sew, where euery other woman of the meanest reputation, bee ordinarily required, and that with the importunate instance of their suters, I shall then be noted of boldnesse, and bee thought to straie too farre from the limites and boundes of modestie, and to make a greater showe of lightnesse, then is properly looked for in vs ẏ be of ẏ feminine gēder, but what strictnesse is this prescribed to our sexe, that wee should bee bereued of our libertie, and so absolutely condemned of lightnesse in seeking to satisfie our lawfull and honest desires, with what crampe bee wee tempered withall more then menne, whereby wee should bee able to withstande the forces of the fleshe, or of power to resiste the concupiscenses whiche Nature it self hath assigned, wee bee tearmed to bee the weaker vesselles, and yet thei would haue vs more puissaunte, then either Samson, or Hercules, if manne and woman bee made of one mettall, it must needes followe by consequence, wee bee subiect to like infirmitie, from whence commeth then this freedome, that menne maie aske what thei desire of vs, bee it neuer so leude, and wee maie not craue any thing of them, that tendeth to good and honest pretence: It is termed to bee but a mannes parte that seeketh our dishonour, by leude and lawlesse luste, but to a woman it is imputed for lightnesse, to firme her lawfull likyng, with pure and loyall loue, if menne will haue preheminence to dooe euill, why should wee bee reproued for doyng well.

Whereuppon stande I then amazed with these fonde opinions, my loue is not vnlawfull, neither before God nor man, I loue Siluanus, whom I will take for my housebande, for otherwise to loue hym, my harte dooeth not intende, therefore without any farther respite or delaye, I will make my loue knowne vnto hym, and the bande of Mariage once confirmed betweene vs, shall couer the fault whiche menne would deme, neither shall my mynde bee altered, either by the sugred perswasion of freendes, neither terrified with any threates, that maie bee thundered forthe by parentes blusteryng wrathe, I am not so farre ouerwhelmed with Pride, that in respecte for the greatnesse of my parentage, I should despise a gentleman indued more with vertue then with riches, though there bee some that be of this condition, that thei will soner preferre the greatnesse of birthe, then the greatnesse of vertue, the aboundance of wealthe, then the aboundance of witte, the perfection of beautie, then the perfection of the minde, but I am out of the nomber of those women, whiche care more to haue their housbandes purses well lined with money, whereby thei maie bee maintained in their brauerie, or sometymes fixe their fancie vpon some yongman, that is of goodlie personage, although voide of vertue, qualitie, and good conditions, that ought to garnishe a gentleman, and doeth more beautifie and enriche hym, then either the bare shewe of beautie, or any other giftes of Fortune, but I cannot emploie my loue vppon transitorie treasure, when the riches of the mynde is cleane taken awaie: no no, it shall better content me to se a meane gentleman beloued and praised of euery one for his vertues, then to marie a miser possessed with all the goodes of the worlde, hated and ill spoken of for his vices. Feare not then *Valeria*, to followe thy determination, and to put in proofe what thou hast pretended.

Here withall staiyng her self, she beganne to practise the meane, in what maner she might bewraie her loue to *Siluanus* seekyng for occasion and tyme meete for her purpose, and although there remained in her, a certaine naturall shamefastnesse, wher with maidens are commonlie accompanied, which for a tyme did close her mouthe, and made her to deferre the tyme of her desolued mynde, yet in the ende throughlie perswaded in her intent, she sent one of her maidens, willyng *Siluanus* to come and speake with her, aboute certaine affaires that she had to imploye hym: The maide hauyng finished her message, there could neuer more ioyfull newes happen to *Siluanus*, who entryng the chamber of *Valeria*, with tremblyng harte after he had dooen his reuerence, with greate feare and bashefulnesse saied, for that I vnderstande your Ladiship hath to employe me aboute certaine affaires, I shall thinke my self the moste happiest man in the worlde, if my trauaile and diligence, might any waies doe you seruice, bee it that therein I should offer or sacrifice myne honour or life, crauyng no greater benefite for the satisfaction of all my contentations, receiued in this worlde, then to serue, obeye, and honour you, so long as my life doeth laste.

The Ladie nowe, all rauished with ioye and contentation, perceiuyng by his chaunge of colour, the fault proceaded of vehemente loue, takyng hym aside into a windowe, Loue had so closed vp her mouthe, that she knewe not how to beginne her tale, her mynde was so troubled, her wittes so farre out of course, that her tongue failed to doe his office, in suche wise that she was not able to speake one onely woorde.

He likewise perplexed with the like Feuer, was now astonied to see the alteration of his Ladie.

Thus these twoo louers, like twoo sencelesse Images, stoode still beholdyng eche other, without any maner of moouyng, in the ende the Ladie takyng courage in her self, with a tremblyng voyce, ioyned with a maidenlike shamefastnesse, began to saie as followeth.

Beyng assured (my Siluanus) of your discretion and wisedome, whiche Nature hath not onely indued you withall, but art hath also accomplished, what Nature beganne to woorke, I will therefore make no doubte at all, to lette you knowe the hidden secretes of my harte, neither will I goe aboute with circumstaunce to colour my woordes, but beyng well perswaded, that when you shall bothe heare and fauour my speeches, and therewithall sounde the deapth of my deuises, you will easily coniecture, that my enterprises be none other then iuste, and that my alledged reasons, are grounded of good pretence, I thinke sithence your ariuall here in the Court of the Duke my father, you haue not seene me in any behauiour, otherwise then vertue doeth permitte, nor in any my demeanours exceadyng the boundes of modestie, otherwise then becommeth a maiden of my callyng, beyng descended of so worthie a stocke, but if this be a faulte that beyng prouoked by the purenesse of my harte, and fidelitie of my good will, who to keepe the same inuiolable, doe voluntarilie offer my self to the honest disposition of your iudgemente, as it shall please you to conceiue of me, I haue then committed a faulte in likyng you too well, but I trust nothyng at all offended God, who knoweth the innocencie of my crime. Thinke not Siluanus, that I am the freend of Fortune, and practise pleasure alone without vertue, for it is modestie that commaundeth me, and honestie is the guide of my conceiptes, swearyng and protestyng by the Almightie God, that neuer manne shall touche Valerya, excepte it bee in Mariage, and he that otherwise would assaile me, I haue a harte that shall encourage my handes to Sacrifice my life. And now Siluanus, if you will not thinke me more prodigall of my present, then your fancie will serue you to take in good parte, beholde, it is you that I haue chosen for my spouse and loyall housebande. And although I had determined to dissemble that, whiche now I haue laied open vnto you, yet reposyng my self in your vertue and honestie, I truste I shall not haue cause to repent me, for any thyng that I haue either saied or doen.

Siluanus whiche all this while hearyng this heauenly harmonie, with full assuraunce of that he moste wished for, albeit he sawe no possibilitie, how to bryng to passe this desired mariage, yet determined not to refuse so greate a preferment, beyng so francke and liberally offered, aunswered in this maner.

I knowe not Madame, with what humilitie and reuerence I might receiue, and accept this your greate bountie and noblenesse, so graciouslie offered vnto me, I dooe acknowledge my condition and state too base, and that my Loue maie bee thought to presume too farre beyonde the boundes of order, consideryng that my ignobilitie and birthe, are no meete matches for suche a peerelesse Princes, yet this I dare boldlie affirme, that if loue and entire affection borne to your Ladiship, might serue to coūteruaill that defect, whiche by place of birth the Destinies haue denaied me, I dare vndertake I should as well deserue to bee receiued, as he that is lineallie descended from the greatest Monarchie of the worlde. The whiche loue if till this tyme I haue delaied to open, I beseeche you Madame, to impute it to the greatnesse of your estate, and to the duetie of my callyng, but now for as muche as by your owne motion, grace, courtesie, and greate liberalitie the same is proferred, and that of your owne bountie, it pleaseth you to accept me for yours: I humblie beseche you, not to dispose of me as of a housebande, but as of one whiche bothe is, and shall bee your seruaunt for euer. Thus saied, he takyng her by the hand, kissed it with greate deuotion, his tongue and wittes were so rapt and tied: As the Ladie perfectly perceiued this alteratiō, and seeyng it to proceade of loue, replied on this maner.

Then my Siluanus, there nedeth at this present no farther circumstaunce, but for that I am well assured, there are some that will bee offended with my choice, but especiallie the Duke my father, who will conceiue some greate displeasure against me: there resteth then that this our contracte bee kept verie secret, vntill it please God to appoint the tyme, that the rest of our determinations, maie without daunger be consummate and accomplished. In the meane tyme, trustyng that your desire is godlie, and that the freendshipp you pretende to beare me, is founded vpon vertue, and to be concluded by mariage, receiue me for your spouse and lawfull wife, you shall haue suche part in me, as without any regard to the obedience and duetie that I owe to my Parentes I am yours, beeyng readie and dispose to obeye you, so farre as my honour maie permit me.

These twoo louers now grounding them selues, the one in the others fidelitie, could not so cunnyngly dissemble and cloke their affections, but that it was easily perceiued by their secret glaunces, and countenaunces conueighed from the one to the other (and as wee haue a Prouerbe) (it is ill haultyng before a creeple) so there were many about the court, that were so well studied in the schoole of Loue, that thei were able to haue commenced maisters of arte, and could easily coniecture frō whēce those rowlyng lookes did proceade, that beeyng now assured of that whiche before was but suspected, the brute was spread about the Courte, of the loue that was betweene Siluanus and

Valeria, that in the ende it came to the Duke her fathers eare, who takyng the matter verie greeuouslie, that his daughter to whom the inheritaunce of the Dukedome remained after his decease, should so meanely bestowe her loue of a fondlyng founde in the woodes. And myndyng to finde a remedie for the matter, willed Siluanus that in paine of his life, within twentie daies he should departe the Courte, and neuer after to bee seen within the iurisdictions of the Dukedome of Valconia.

Valeria now hauyng intelligence what had happened, had no leasure to vexe or moleste her self, when tyme rather required a speedie remedie, for the incountryng of those misshapps, deuised with Siluanus to conueigh her self awaie, contented rather to liue in the fellowship of an honest louyng housebande, with whom she should hold faithfull and loyall companie, with what estate and Fortune so euer it might please GOD to appoincte, then to liue without hym, beautified with the graces and foolishe names of honour and preheminence.

Siluanus, contented to satisfie her desire, with the hazarde of his life, yeelded to her request, and before the twentie daies were expired, so cleanely conueighed hym self and Valeria awaie, that when thei were missyng, the Duke wist not which waies to sende after theim. Wherefore in a greate furie, he spared not to sende out greate companies, whiche postyng euery waie, made enquirie and searche after theim, but all in vaine: for Siluanus had so disguised hym self and Valeria, that without any maner of trouble, thei quietly passed the Countrey, and hauyng freede theim selues from out the daunger of the Duke, desiryng that the daie of their Mariage might now bee preferred, the whiche by mutuall consent, was presently determined, and by greate Fortune (or rather conduction by the prouidence of GOD) thei happened to arriue in the Countrey Village, where Duke Sappho that was father to Siluanus, had remained all this while Sexten of the Parishe. In this Village, because it was a place free from resort, whereby thei might remaine unknowne, and in the better safetie, thei purposed aswell to celebrate their Mariage, as for a tyme to make their aboade, till matters were better quieted, and that

thei

thei might at leisure resolue, what course were beste for theim to take. Siluanus now hauyng conferred with the Prieste, the Mariage daie was appoincted, where the poore Belrynger takyng the vewe of this newe married couple, fell in a greate likyng of Siluanus, not for that he knewe hym to be his sonne, for thereof he could haue no maner of suspition, aswell for that he demed he had been deuoured in the woodes, by some wilde beaste, as also because his name was chaunged, but whether it were by the instigation or secresie of Nature, or otherwise by the will and pleasure of God, to bryng to passe that, whiche afterwardes happened in effecte, this poore Sexten I saie, lead by the secret motion of his owne affections, proffered Siluanus that if his seruice might any waies stande hym in steede (for that he was a straunger in the place) he should vse hym in any respecte, and should finde hym readie to stande hym in suche steade, as his poore abilitie might any waies permit.

Siluanus in like case hauyng forgotten his Father, beeyng separated from hym in his infancie, yet nothyng despisyng his freendly offer, craued his helpe for the hieryng of a Chamber, for some reasonable rent, till tyme that he might better prouide for hym self. The Sexten verie glad that he had so good oportunitie to pleasure hym, brought hym with his wife to his owne house, where he lodged hym in the beste roome that he had, profferyng not onely his house, but all that was in it to be at their disposition and pleasure. This newe Married couple, now gladdyng and sportyng them selues, with all suche swete imbracementes, as thei can better describe, whiche haue been possessed with the like delightes: but as some will saie, it is the mannes parte to be first wearied in those Veneriall sportes, so Siluanus hauyng now well feasted hym self, with that sweete repaste, had leisure to bethinke hym of his owne estate: began inwardly to growe into greate sorrowe and heauinesse, not so muche for hym self, as for his wife, who for his sake had disposest her self from so greate honour, abandonyng her freendes, contented to yeeld her self a thrall to Fortune.

These cogitations did so nippe hym, that he could not so well dissemble his greef, but that his wife perceiued some dis-

quietnesse

quietnesse in his mynde, and therefore verie greeuouslie she demaunded of hym, to shewe her the cause of his discontentment, whiche by outward appearaunce, seemed inwardlie so muche to molest hym.

Siluanus hearyng his Ladies requeste, aunswered in this wise, my deare wife, the sweetest companion that euer manne did possesse, for so muche as you so earnestly desire to vnderstande, what it is that so muche withdraweth my delightes, I will not let to bewraie the truthe, whiche is this, when I consider with my self, of your present estate and condition, who from the tippe and height of dignitie, haue not spared for my sake to surrender your self, to become a subiect to all mishaps, besieged on euery side, with the future assaultes or ordinarie Fortune: It maketh me therefore to haue the greater care, by what meanes I might endeuour my self, to maintaine and continue your estate, though not accordyng to your worthinesse and callyng, yet accordyng to your well contentmente and likyng. And herevpon conceiuyng in my hedde diuerse imaginations, no meanes but one in my fancie seemeth beste, whiche is, that I goe to the Courte of the Emperour Claudius, who at this present is leadyng a greate bande, to encoūter the Turke, at whose handes I doubte not, but to receiue some good entertainment, and besides the honour and reputation, I maie gaine by good deserte, I maie likewise reape suche liuyng and good likyng of the Emperour, that in despight of Fortunes teethe, wee maie liue hereafter a quiet and honourable life, to our greate ioye and comforte. But when I did consider the beloued companie of you deare wife, I feared to bewraie that, whiche now I haue disclosed, not knoweyng in what parte you would take it, that I should so sodainly departe. Loe here the cause of my disquietnesse, whiche you desire so instantly to knowe.

The Ladie whiche was wise, perceiuyng the greate loue that her housebande did beare her, when he had staied hym self from talke, with glad and merrie countenaunce, aunswered in this wise.

Ah Siluanus, the exampler of all vertue and gentlenesse,

let

let death and fortune doe what thei list, for I compt myselfe more then satisfied of all that is past, by the onely enioying of your presence, contentyng my self to bee a partaker of your misfortunes, and haue no doubt but that I can so moderat my affections, that duryng my life, I will rest better contented with that which your abilitie wil permit be it neuer so meane, then otherwise to bee honoured with names and titles of nobilitie in Princely state or porte hauing not your presence. Disquiet not your self therefore, but perseuer in your determination, and that sorowe which shall assaile me by reason of your absence, I will sweten and lenefie with cõtentation to se your commendable desire appeased: and the pleasaunt memorie of your valiaunt factes shall beguile my pensiue thoughtes, hauyng that our nexte meetyng shall bee more ioyfull and glad, then this our partyng shall be either heauie or sad.

The Ladies aunswere did wonderfully quiet the mynde of Siluanus, and callyng his hoste the Sexten vnto hym, whõ he had made partaker of his determinations, he departed, leauyng his wife suche money and Jewelles as thei had remainyng: and commyng to the Courte of the Emperour Claudius, he was very well entertained, and the rather for that the Emperour had greate neede of menne to supply his armie, whiche had sustained sondrie conflictes, and diuers ouerthrowes, for the Turke did wonderfully incroche vpon the Emperour, and had taken sondrie Cities, Townes, and Castelles from hym, and was like still euery daie more to preuaile then other, that now the Emperour beganne to repent hym, of the slender accoumpte he had made of Souldiours in the tyme of peace, for that he had too fewe that were sufficient to serue him in his warres: For in steede of Experience, Valiaunce, and Policie (whiche three ought to be gouernours, commaunders and cheef officers in a Campe) he was glad to preferre Vaineglorie, Foolishehardinesse, and Rashenesse: Simple sottes that were more fitter to waite in Gentlewomans chambers, then to be made Captaines, or leaders in the warres.

The Emperour now standyng in greate distresse for wãt of menne, for those that he had made greatest accoumpt of in the tyme of peace, were now able to stande him in no steede in the tyme of warres: and those that had braued it vp and doune the Courte in the newe cuttes, straunge fashions, their haire friseled, lookyng with suche grisly and terrible countenaunces, enough to make a wiseman beleeue thei were cleane out of their wittes, now in the tyme of warres, were glad to runne vnder a Gentlewomans Farthyngall to hide them.

The Emperour (I saie) beeyng thus perplexed, called to his remembraunce the iniurie that he had doen Sappho, whō he had banished onely to satisfie the willes of those that were aboute hym, whiche he knewe did hate hym more of spight, then for any occasion the Duke had giuen. Without any farther delaie therefore, the Emperour sent sondrie messengers into euery parte of Christendome to make inquirie, that who so euer could finde the Duke, should bee worthily recompenced, and those Proclamations were spread through euery Region, in Citie, Towne, and Village. In so muche that in this Parishe where the Duke remained Sexten (as you haue heard) the Priest made inquirie on Sondaie in the Churche, as the custome is) that where as aboute fourteene or fifteene yeares sithence, the Duke of Mantona was banished by the Emperour, whiche was procured rather by enuie, then for any deserte, as now it was proued, who so euer therefore could giue any intelligence of the same Duke, should bee verie liberally recompensed by the Emperour.

The Sexten now hearyng these newes, did thinke it more better to liue still in his Sextens rome, where he remained without enuie, then to become againe the Duke of Mantona, subiecte to the spite of hatefull persones. But callyng to his mynde his wife and daughter, which he thought remained yet a liue (although he knewe not where) and for the greate loue that he bare to Siluanus, whose wife remained in his house (as you heard) seeyng that Fortune offered hym so good oportunitie to pleasure them, onely for their sakes, resolued hym self to goe to the Emperour. But firste comfortyng his geste Valerya, whom for a tyme he should leaue in his house, onely with suche seruauntes as her self had aboute her: he tolde her

that

that he was well assured where to finde this Duke, that was so muche inquired after, and that he doubted not, (if it were but in respecte of his good newes) he should worke Siluanus, her housbande into some credite with the Duke, who might likewise procure his better preferment with the Emperour.

And thus the Sexten departed, and with all conuenience came to the Courte of the Emperour, to whom when he had made hym self knowne, he was moste honourably receiued, and great ioye and gladnesse was made throughout the whole Courte: the Emperour now in consideration of the iniurie he had doen hym, did not onely restore hym to his former name and dignitie, but also aduaunced hym in honour and estimation, to be preferred before all other next vnto hym self.

Thus after many benefites receiued of the Emperour, the Duke prepared hym self, accompanied with many his frendes, to goe to the Emperours Campe, of the whiche he was made Generall, where he knewe well how to behaue himself, and giuyng out newe ordinaūces, he appointed certaine suche as he hym self knewe worthie, and gaue them charge, emongest the reste, seeyng Siluanus who all this while remained in the Campe, whom the Duke did very well knowe, although Siluanus, did little suspecte that a poore Sexton of a Parishe, should become a General to an Emperours armie. The duke perceiuyng hym self to bee vnknowne to Siluanus, was contented so to remaine for a tyme, but yet desirous to see what was in hym, he gaue hym the leadyng of certaine horsemen, with the whiche Siluanus serued so valiauntly, and there withall had so happie successe, that euery manne extolled vp to the heauens, the worthinesse of Siluanus. This pleased the Duke passyng well, and the Duke hauyng now sondrie tymes incountred with the power of the Turkes, and had giuen them many ouerthrowes, he was now preparyng a greate force, for the recouerie of the Citie of Cayoe, the whiche the Turkes had taken before from the Emperour. And callyng Siluanus vnto hym, he saied: GOD graunt yong Gentleman, that your ende agree with your good beginnyng, then makyng Siluanus to kneele he dubbed him knight, and made him

Colonell of twentie enſignes.

Siluanus after he had dooen his reuerence, thanked the Duke of the honour and fauour, whiche it had pleaſed hym to dooe hym, promiſyng to dooe ſo well in tyme to come, as he ſhould not bee deceiued in his conceiued opinion, whereof he gaue aſſured teſtimonie at the aſſaute that was giuen to the Citie before mentioned, where he behaued hym ſelf ſo valiantly, as he was the firſt that mounted vpon the walles, and by his dexteritie and inuincible force, made waie to the Souldiours in the breache, whereby thei entered and tooke the citie, killyng and driuyng out their enemies before theim. In many ſuche like attemptes Siluanus ſtill ſhewed hym ſelf ſo noble and valiaunt, that his praiſe and renowme was ſounded in euery place.

The Duke now hauyng recouered againe all ſuche cities, Townes, and other Fortes, whiche the Turke had before taken from the Emperour, and there with all had baniſhed the Turkes from out the boundes, and borders of the Empire, and a League agreed vpon betweene the Emperour and the Turke. The Armie beeyng broken vp, and Souldiours diſcharged, euery manne well recompenſed for his ſeruice, accordyng as he had deſerued. Siluanus likewiſe, who by his worthineſſe, hauyng not onely made himſelf famous to the world, but alſo had well lined his purſe with good ſtore of golde, bethinkyng hym now of his faire Ladie, came to the Duke to haue take his leaue, but the Duke myndyng now to performe the good that he ment to Siluanus, was reſolued in his minde, that Siluanus with his wife ſhould bee his geſtes, as well at Mantona where he was Duke, as thei had been before, where he was but a Sexten, ſaied to Siluanus as followeth.

Sir knight, what haſte is this, that you would ſo ſodainly withdrawe your ſelf from out my companie, belike you haue ſome faire wife, to whom you make ſuche ſpeede to be gone, but ſir content your ſelf to beare me companie to the Emperours Courte, where I doubt not but you ſhall receiue ſome better recompence for your ſeruice ſo happely begunne, for it is not requiſite, but that the vertue of valiaunce, ought to bee

rewarded

rewarded and cherished by Princes, that he aided in their necessitie, with the diligence of suche vertuous and noble gentilmen as your self. Siluanus greatly comforted with these wordes of the Duke, was well pleased to waite vpon hym: Thus thei tooke their iourney towardes the great Citie of Chirona, whiche was in the uttermoste borders of the Emperours dominions, there the Duke purposed to staie a while, to recreate hym self with the rest of his companie.

Now it fortuned that the valiaunt actes, and hautie enterprises of Siluanus were so renowmed and spredde, that the same therefore came to the eares of the Duke of Vasconya, that was father to Valerya the wife of Siluanus, who with all possible speede made suche haste, that he came to Cherona, where he founde Siluanus in the companie of the Duke of Mantona, to whom turnyng hym self, he saied as followeth.

Sir Duke the onely hope that I haue, that you will not let to extende Justice vpon the mischeeuous and vngratious actes of wicked menne, doth let me at this instant, to forbeare with myne owne handes, to auenge the wrong that I assure my self, to haue receiued of this traitour Siluanus.

The companie were wonderfully abashed with these wordes, but especially the Duke of Mantona, who loued Siluanus more dearly then any other.

But the other goyng still forwardes in his tale saied, if the hartebreake that afflicteth the soule of a wofull father, whose house is made desolate by loosyng his child, by the mischiuous inticementes of a Theefe, if this president I saie, moue you not to minister suche speedie reuenge, as the Lawe doeth prescribe, I suppose that all impunitie of vice and sinne hath place on your behalf. And there with al staiyng his talke, but yet by his gesture and countenaunce so inraged, that he seemed like a man that were besides hym self.

The Duke of Mantona now perceiuyng the matter, that Valerya was the daughter of the Duke of Vasconya, whom he supposed to haue been of some meane birthe and parentage was wonderfully sorie for Siluanus, whose facte by the Lawe deserued death, and seyng the Duke in suche a furie, he wiste not by what meanes to worke Siluanus safetie, for to intreate the Duke he thought it but vaine, and to bryng Siluanus to aunswere the facte, he knew the Lawe would condemne him, and therefore knowyng where Valerya did remaine, whom he knewe did loue Siluanus as her owne life, and thinkyng that her teares might lenifie and soften the hardened harte of the Duke her father. He therefore priuely sent for her, to bee brought immediatly to the Citie of Cherona, in the meane tyme he committed Siluanus into safe custodie, and desired the Duke at his request to staie hymself a while, and he should haue suche Iustice on Siluanus, as hymself would require.

Matters beeyng thus pacified for a while, I will in like case lette them rest for a tyme, and will now discourse how it befell to the Dutches Messilina, with her daughter Phylene.

You haue heard before how by cōstraint of weather at the Sea, thei were driuen to this Citie of Cherona, where the Duke now remained, and at her first commyng, fallyng to her worke as before she had doen at Taryffa, a riche Marchaunt that dwelte in the Towne, takyng the viewe of this newe come workewoman, fell into so greate a likyng with her, that onely to haue accesse to come into her companie, he bestowed more money in cloathe to make hym shirtes and handcarchifes in one weeke, then he was able to weare out in three yeares after, whiche he put to her to make, whereby he became somethyng well acquainted with her, but to the ende that she might thinke her self somethyng the better beholdyng vnto hym, he proffered her a more conuenient house then that she was in, whiche he would furnishe with all maner of householde stuffe for a reasonable rent. She beeyng very glad of so good an offer, became his Tenaunt. The Marchaunt now perceiuyng his tyme did so well serue hym, without any greate circumstaunce, declared vnto her the greate good will he bare her, but Messilina so delaied hym with suche wise and reasonable aunswers, that from tyme to tyme the Marchant hymself could not importunatly craue that whiche with suche modestie, she so honestly denaied hym.

Now there laie in this Citie of Cherona, the olde Dut-

ches

ches of Petrona, who hauyng inteligence of Messilina to be so good a woorke woman, she sent for her, to whom she put sendrie parcelles of woorke, whiche she so well finished to the likyng of the Dutches, that from tyme to tyme she still plide her with the like, whereby Messilia, with her daughter Phylene, had continuall recourse to the Pallas of the Dutches, where Arabianus the onely sonne of the Dutches of Petrona (and inheritour of the dukedome, but that he was vnder age) did marke and behold the beautie and good grace of this yong Seamester Phylene, was so clogged & fettered in the bandes of loue, that all other thoughtes seemed lothsome vnto hym, and euery other ioye displeasaunt, in respecte of the pleasure that he suffered, by thinkyng of his faire Phylene, wherefore baityng hymself with hope, and tickled onely by loue, he determined what soeuer happened to loue her.

Whiche beyng perceiued by his mother, she began very sharpely to rate hym, blamyng hym that would so indiscretly place his loue, not waiyng his estate and birthe, as come of Princely race, and now would make hym self a fable to the worlde, to like of suche a one so farre vnworthie his degree.

Arabianus fallyng doune vpon his knees, moste humbly desired his mother to beare with all that was paste, and although it were truthe that she had saied, that he deemed her for her birthe to be vnworthie his degree, yet she deserued for her beautie to be compared to the greatest dame, and brauest minion els where. And whereas other girles by artificiall meanes and trumperies, doe inforce that whiche the heauens haue denaied them, yet Phylene had no other ornament then that whiche Nature had inlarged in her: and otherwise for her vertue, wisedome, and modestie, he knewe it to be suche by reporte of many, as she might bee a Lanterne to the greatest Dame that liued.

Notwithstandyng Madam, for so muche as you doe take my facte in so ill parte, consideryng the reuerence, that I owe to the place whiche you holde on my behaulf, and the duetie and obedience that God will and hath commaunded, that children should beare to those that haue begotten and borne them:

if

if it please you to pardon me of this that is past, I protest that from hence foorthe, I will bee more wise and better aduised, how I enter into any thing that might turne to any suche consequence, or any maner of waies to offende you.

The Dutches knowyng all to be true that her sonne had saied, very well pleased with his speeches, remained satisfied, thinkyng in her mynde in deede, that if Phylene had bin the daughter but of some meane Gentleman, her sonne should neuer haue sought farther for a wife.

From this tyme forwardes, although Arabianus by the perswasion of his mother, had vowed to reuolt and let slip the loue that he bare to Phylene, yet he could not so clearely loose his likyng, but that he did manifest some parte of his good will, by giftes and good countenaunces whiche still he bestowed vpon Phylene, causing his mother likewise to bestowe many liberall rewardes vpon Messilina, thus the mother and the daughter perceiued them selues a thousande tymes beholdyng to the olde Dutches and her sonne.

In this meane space the Marchaunt before mentioned had buried his wife, and knowyng no other but that Messilina his Tenaunte had bin a widowe, he began now a freshe sute, and with greate importunitie requested her in the waie of mariage, and so hardly he laied vnto her, that Messilina not knowyng otherwise how to rid hym, confessed vnto hym that she had a housbande aliue and therefore might not marie.

The Marchaunt thinkyng these to bee but delaies to shift hym of, came to this pointe, that if hereafter he could proue her by her owne confession to bee a widowe, that then before witnesse she would take hym for her lawfull housbande, and till that tyme he would no farther trouble her till he had made his profe, she beyng glad to be at rest, thinkyng that he should woorke very wisely to make her confesse her self to bee a widowe, agreed to his request, and witnesse was had in the matter. The Marchaunt now lettyng his matter rest a tyme for his better purpose, in the ende commyng vnto her, he tolde her, that although she were so discourteous to forsake his frendshippe in euery respecte, first in the waie of good fellowshippe, and after in the waie of Marriage, whereby he was driuen to goe ſeeke farther, but now hauyng founde a wife in the Countrey, to whom he was aſſured, and ment preſently to be married, yet for the olde freedſhippe that he bare her, conſideryng that he would preſently remaine in the Countrey altogether, and forſake the Citie, therefore for her better ſecuritie and aſſuraunce of her dwellyng, he would make her a Leaſe of the houſe that ſhe dwelte in, for one and twentie yeres, if it might doe her any pleaſure, without paiyng any penie Income.

Meſsilina giuyng hym greate thankes, tooke his offer verie courteouſlie, and the Leaſe was put to makyng, which the Marchaunt ſigned and deliuered, and here withall deſired her ſingle Obligation, for the performaunce of ſome ſmall rente, were it neuer ſo little, that ſhe might acknowledge hym to bee her Landlorde, the whiche ſhe neuer denaied to giue.

The Obligation was made in this maner. Knowe all men by this preſentes, that I Meſsilina widowe, and ſo forthe with wordes in maner and forme of euery Obligation. This Obligatiō thus made, was ſigned and deliuered by Meſsilina to the Marchaunte, who had now gotten that ſo long he had ſought for, and by vertue of this Obligation, craued Meſsilina to bee his wiſe, ſhe denaiyng his demaunde, but what could that preuaile, when he had her owne hande and ſeale to ſhewe, whereby ſhe confeſſed her ſelf a widowe, and then by her owne agrement (as you haue heard before) ſhe muſt yeeld her ſelf to be his wiſe.

This matter was long in fendyng and prouyng, in ſo muche that the Duke beyng now in the toune, miniſtryng of iuſtice to ſuche as would craue it, the Marchaunt brought the matter before the Duke, who hearyng the maner of the bargaine, and ſo many witneſſes to affirme theſame, gaue Sentence that the Marchaunte ought in deede to haue her. But Meſsilina fallyng at the feete of the Duke, deſiryng him with teares to deferre his iudgement: the Duke now taking better vewe of the woman, knowyng her bothe by her voyce, and alſo by lookyng well on her face, perceiued aſſuredly that it was his owne wiſe, he called againe to the Marchaunte to ſee his obligation, whiche when he had receiued, he said in this maner.

Maister Marchaunt, this Obligation whiche you haue deliuered me, now I haue perused with better aduise, I finde it to bee neither sufficient nor lawfull, for this woman that you would make a widowe, without doubte is Maried, and hath a housebande, now she beyng vnder couert barne, your Obligation is vnpleadable, and I knowe not whō you should blame, whether your self, or the Seriuener. And here withall beeyng replete with greate ioye and gladnesse, takyng his wife vp in his armes very louyngly imbraced her, he saied.

Ah my deare and louyng wife, how muche am I bounde, to render innumerable thankes to the almightie GOD, that when all hope was paste, haue yet againe recoured my greatest hope and comforte. Messilina likewise perceiuyng her Lorde and Housebande, claspyng her handes about his necke, was not able to speake a woorde for ioye and contentation: the companie that stoode by amased to see this sodaine happe, were likewise verie ioyfull to see this freendly meetyng. The Marchaunt seyng how he had been deceiued, tare his Obligation, and departed all ashamed. The Duke now desirous to see his daughter Phylene, caused her mother to sende for her, who not knowyng her father otherwise then by reporte, fell doune on her knees to craue his blessyng: The Duke takyng her vp, kissyng her with fatherlie affection, could not staie his teares, in remembryng her brother Aurelianus, whom he deemed to be dedde.

These newes were sodainly spred throughout the Citie of Cherona, in so muche that Arabianus, hauyng now intelligence, that Philene was the daughter of the noble Duke Sappho, certifiyng his mother the truthe whiche he had learned, without any greate deliberation, bothe the mother and the sonne commyng to visite the Duke and his companie, where thei were very well welcomed, but especially to Messilina, to whom the olde Duches and her Soonne bothe had been verie bountifull: And when a while thei had passed the time with pleasaunt discourses of all that had passed, the Duchesse of Perona craued Philene in Mariage for her Sonne. The Duke beyng

beyng made priuie to the matter, knowyng Arabianus to bee come of greate discent, and to bee indued with large and faire possessions, seyng hym likewise to bee a toward yong gentleman, would not stande against it, but referred the matter to his daughters likyng. Philene who had been greatly bounde to the courtesie of the yong Duke, and had receiued many giftes and good turnes at his handes, would not doe as a nomber of these nise Dames, that will many tymes make daintie of that thei would fainest come by, gaue her free consent. There was then no more to do, but to prepare for the mariage, which was presently solemnized with greate pompe and glorie.

By this Valeria (whom as you haue heard before the duke had sent for) was come to Cherona, who was priuely lodged by the dukes commaundment in a priuie place. The daie now beyng come, that Siluanus was brought to his aunswere, he could not denaie the facte where with he was charged, but that he had stolne Valeria from her father, by whiche confession the Lawe condemned hym to dye. There were many that knewe the noblenesse of Siluanus, that began to entreate the Duke of Vasconia to remit the facte, but all in vaine, for the more thei entreated, the more he hastened to see execution.

The Duke of Mantona seyng his greate obstinacie, did thinke it hye tyme to finde a remedie for Siluanus, if it might bee, therefore he saied, sir Duke, were it possible that this condemned manne, who is like (so farre as I can see) to beare the whole blame, and yet might bee enticed to this facte by your daughters meanes, or at the leaste, your daughter muste bee halfe partner of this faulte, and yeelded with her good will to come awaie, for otherwise it had been vnpossible for hym, to haue brought her from out your Courte, whiche if it bee true, if you will needes see Iustice so duely executed in the one, I can not see how your daughter can goe quite, but must bee as well partaker of the punishement, as she was in the facte, by yeeldyng her consent.

The Duke of Vasconia aunswered, as it is the office and duetie of euery good Iusticer, to knowe the valour and difference, betweene vertue and vice, to the ende that all vertuous actes maie bee honoured, and the contrary chastised and punished: otherwise he is not worthy the name of a righteous iudge but of a cruell and traiterous Tyraunt, wherefore sir Duke, you sittyng here in the place of Iustice, to minister equitie and right, to euery one that calleth. Then I desire that I maie haue the Lawe extended vppon this wretche Siluanus, as for my daughter that you speake of, as I knowe not where she is, so I doe not desire to learne what is become of her, but this I protest, that if euer I maie finde her, rather then she should escape vnpunished, I will not let with myne owne handes to do execution vpon her, accordyng to her demerites, and the filthinesse of her facte: from henceforthe denouncyng her to bee any child of myne, and make no better accoumpt of her, otherwise then to bee a filthie strompet, vnworthy of me her father, or to chalenge her descent from suche a stocke.

The Duke of Mantona was now troubled worse then before, for where as he had some hope, that the humble sute of Valeria should somethyng haue mooued her father to compassion, he now thought that her sight would rather increase his rage and furie: Againe he thought, that to bryng her into his presence, if he continued in one moode, he might woorke Valeria so greate preiudice, as he would be hartely sorie to see. Yet thinkyng with hym self, that it was impossible, that a Father should be so voyde of good Nature, to see the vtter ruine of his childe without any remorse: He caused Valeria to bee sent for, who beeyng conducted to the place, seeyng her Father and the reste of the companie, she beganne to coniecture that all was not well. But when Siluanus sawe his Valeria, wondering by what meanes she was brought to so euill a banquett, remembryng what woordes her father before had protested, he began with a piteous voice to crie out.

O my deare beloued wife, the onely cause of my ioye and quiete, what euill Fortune hath conducted thee to this place, what froward Faates haue forced thee, that thou shouldest be made a companion of my misshappes. O fraile and inconstant Fortune, how hast thou fronted my honest desires, with suche crooked spight, that where I couet the countenaunce of greatest

test credite, there I am forced to hazard the losse of life and all, what cooked aspecte hath gouerned my proceadynges, that the hoped tyme I spente in this Warlike seruice, should thus conclude with his contrary, and I forced as it were by Faate to followe the vnhappie euent of the same, wherein I doe confesse my Predestinate follies. But suche are the sonderie dealynges of this life, as those that tende their steppes to monsterous mountaines, doe sometyme scarce conclude with meane Moole hilles, the sondrie conflictes of Fortune, maskyng my hope with a shewe of happie reward, hath not onely wracked me, but it threateneth the sequell of worse successe: That in steade of happie and quiet life, my daies shalbe a bridged with moste shamefull and vile Death. O Valeria, Valeria, the ioye and comforte of my life, I shall no more see that incomparable beautie of thyne, whiche darkeneth and obscureth the Rayes and Beames of the Sunne.

Then tournyng hymself to the Duke of Vasconia, he said, I moste humbly beseche your grace, to haue compassion vpon me, not for that I would consume my life in your displeasure, I make offer of the same to your mercifull will and dispositiō, choosyng rather to dye, and to leaue your grace satisfied and contented, then to liue a happie life, your Princely minde displeased, and albeit, the right good intente and vnstained conscience is free from faute, yet the iudgemente of menne hath farther relation to the exteriour apperaunce, then to vertues force. Is it a synne to Marrie, is it a faulte to flye and auoyde the synne of whoredome? What Lawes bee these then, where the marriage bedde and ioyned Matrimonie, is pursued with like seueritie, as Murther, Thefte, Adultrie. But seyng the fault of this mishap, to a rise by my predestinate euill lucke, I moste humbly beseche you, to mitigate your rage, and to conceiue no sinister opinion of this your worthie daughter, whose smallest greef, is my double paine, as for my self I am well pleased with my misfortune, cōtented to sacrifice my life, onely to receiue your cleare acquitaunce for my offence, and will make satisfaction with the price of my blood.

The Duke of Vacsonia bendyng his browes, aunswered:

No traitour no, it is not thy life that shall appease my furie, but I will so coole the whorishe heate of your Minion, for whom you seeme so muche to pleade, that I will make her an example to all others, for dooyng of an acte so detestable. But what abuse haue thei comitted vnder the title of Marriage, thinkyng without remorse of conscience, by that meanes to continue their mischeef, and their promise and faithe, that was made vnder a Bushe, muste serue for a cloake and visarde for their moste filthie whoredome. But what if their Marriage were concluded, and confirmed by God hymself? Is Siluanus a manne worthy to bee alied or mingled with the royall blood of the house of Valconia, no no. I vowe I will neuer take sound nor restfull slepe, vntill I haue dispatched that infamous facte from our blood, and that villaine whoremonger with his trull be vsed accordyng to their desertes.

Valeria now knowyng how matters were sorted out, and hearyng this cruell Sentence pronounced by her Father, fell doune vppon her knees, and bitterly criyng out, she saied: My deare father, moste humbly I beseche you, sithe no other thing maie appease your Ire, then the life of the offender, let not this gentleman abide the penaunce of that, whiche he neuer committed, be reuenged on me, by whom the faulte (if a womans faithe to her housebande, maie be termed a fault) is doen. And lette this vnfortunate gentleman departe, who God knowes is innocente of any other crime, then what he was brought into onely by my prouocation. And as she was aboute to haue proceded farther in her talke, her father interrupted her, saiyng.

Haue you founde your tongue now pretie peate, then wee must haue an Almon for Parrat: How durst thou strompette chalenge me to bee thy Father? That without regarde, either of my renowme, or of the honour of my house, thou art contente to bee abandoned from this noble estate, and to become a fugitiue and a straunger, to followe a rooge vp and doune the Countrey, no Minion no, thinke not that any Feminine flatterie, shall staie me from doyng thee to Death, nor your darlyng that standes by you, shall escape with his life, verely beleeuyng that in tyme it shall bee knowne, what profite the

worlde

worlde shall gaine, by purgyng the same of suche an infected plague: And I dooe hope besides this, that in tyme to come, menne shall praise this deede of myne, who for preseruyng the honour of my house, haue chosen rather to dooe to death twoo offendours, then to leaue the one of them aliue, as lesse faultie or giltlesse then the other.

Valeria once againe fallyng frustrate before her Father, saied: I moste humbly beseche you, for that all other comforte is denaied me, that I maie craue this onely grace at your handes, for the laste good that euer I hope to receiue, whiche is, that you beeyng thus greeuouslie offended with me, dooe vengeaunce at your pleasure vppon her, who willingly yeeldeth her self to the death, with the effusion of her blood, to satisfie your Ire, graunte onely that Siluanus, who is innocente and free from fault maie goe quite.

But her father no longer able for anger to heare her speake, crieth out to the Duke to haste the execution, the Duke of Mantona, whose harte did bleede in his beallie for sorrowe, perceiuyng it follie to delaye longer tyme, gaue Sentence of death, and present execution to bee made, although he tooke so greate sorrowe for theim, as if his daughter Philene should haue borne them companie: but he was not able to helpe it, the lawes and ordinaunces of the Countrey would not otherwise permit. And thinking to take his laste farewell of Siluanus, he saied, O Siluanus the glorie and honour of all yong gentlemen that euer were, that bee now, or shall be hereafter this, whose vertue, valiaunce, and worthie exploites, doe glister emongst the multitude, as the Sunne beames doe vpon the [illegible] of the yearth: Oh that thy harde Fortune should conduct thee to suche distresse, that onely by thyne owne valiaunce and prowesse, hast escaped so many daungers, emongst thy thronged enemies, and now thy ruine and ouerthrowe should bee thus wrought, amiddest thy assured frendes, that knowes not how to helpe it. What heapes of cares hath besieged me on euery side: To thinke that I should craue thy companie, whereby thou art brought into the midst of so greate mischeef, which otherwise mightest haue escaped this mishappe, and the Valeria

leria would God thy vnfortunate hoste, whiche departed from thee, thinkyng to dooe thy housebande pleasure, had remained with thee a poore Sexten still, till this present daie.

The reste of the companie that stood by, hearyng the duke to make so greate lamentation, was likewise striken into a maruailous greef and sorowe, in so muche that euery one that durste speake, cried to the Duke of Vasconia for pardon, and that he would remitte the offence, and what pitie it were, if he should seeke the death of so noble a Gentleman as Siluanus, had shewed hym self to bee: But the Duke perseueryng still in one mynde, asked theim, with what face thei could make request for a verlet of no reputation, whom he had founde in the woodes, and brought hym vp to that estate he was come to, not knowyng who was his father, but by seemyng some poore Countrey cloune, and forgettyng hym self from whence he sprong, neglectyng so many benefites, which he had bestowed vpon hym, would enter into those thynges, so farre vnseemely and exceadyng his degree.

The Duke of Mantona, giuyng good eare to this tale, remembryng his Soonne Aurelianus, whom he had loste in the woodes aboute those partes, questioned with the Duke, of the tyme, and what apparell the child had on at that present, who in all thinges shewed a trothe as it was: he demaunded farther how he knewe his name to be Siluanus, or whether he had any other name, yes (q the Duke of Vasconia) his name he saied was Aurelianus, whiche my self changed to Siluanus, because I founde hym in the woodes.

Here withall without any farther staie, the Duke of Mantona runnyng hastely vppon Siluanus, imbrasyng hym in his armes, criyng: O my soonne, my soonne, and with this sodain ioye, the teares trickled doune his cheekes so fast, that he was not farther able to speake one woorde.

The Duke of Vasconia muche amazed to see this sight, but a greate deale more gladde, that Siluanus had founde out suche a father, and now nothyng at all offēded with his daughters choyce, came likewise with chearfull countenaunce, and imbrased Siluanus, desiryng bothe the Duke his Father, and hymself

hymself to forgiue what was past, and takyng Valerya by the hande, he deliuered her to Siluanus, promisyng hym for her dowrie 40000. Franckes in golde presently to be paied, and after his descease to remaine for his inheritour.

Siluanus better pleased with Valerya her self, then with al the rest that was promised, gaue hym greate thankes, and so did the Duke his father.

All the companie were replenished with the greatest ioye that might be, to see this sodaine sight, and thus thei departed to the Pallas where the Duke kepte his abode, where Siluanus was welcomed, to his mother, to his sister, to Arabianus, and to all the rest, where there was greate feastyng and triumph, and a bonde of euerlastyng amitie betwene the houses of the Duke of Mantona, the Duke of Vasconya, and the Duke of Petrona, and after a whyle thei had feasted and sported them selues, thei rode altogether in companie to the Emperours Courte, who receiued them with so greate honour as he could deuise, and makyng hym self a partaker of their mirthe, wonderyng to here the hole discourse how thynges had happened, when after a while he had feasted them, and shewed them as greate pleasures as might be deuised, he bestowed of them al large and bountifull giftes, but especially of the two yong Ladies Valerya and Phylene, and this agreyng amongest them selues, to meete once a yeare at the least to sporte and make them selues merrie, for this season thei departed, euery one where it lyked them beste.

Of Apolonius and Silla.

The argument of the second Historie.

¶ Apolonius *Duke, hauyng spent a yeres seruice in the warres against the Turke, returnyng homward with his companie by sea, was driuen by force of weather to the Ile of* Cypres, *where he was well receiued by* Pontus *gouernour of the same Ile, with whom* Silla *daughter to* Pontus, *fell so straungely in loue, that after* Apolonius *was departed to Constantinople,* Silla *with one man followed, and commyng to Constantinople, she serued* Apolonius, *in the habite of a manne, and after many prety accidentes fallyng out, she was knowne to* Apolonius, *who in requitall of her loue maried her.*

here is no child that is borne into this wretched worlde, but before it doeth sucke the mothers Milke, it taketh first a soope of the Cupp of errour, which maketh vs when we come to riper yeres, not onely to enter into actions of iniurie, but many tymes to straie from that is right and reason, but in all other thinges, wherein wee shewe our selues to bee moste droonken with this poisoned Cuppe, it is in our actions of Loue, for the louer is so estranged frō that is right, and wandereth so wide from the boundes of reason, that he is not able to deeme white from blacke, good from badde, vertue from vice: but onely led by the apetite of his owne affections, and groundyng them on the foolishnesse of his owne fancies, will so settle his likyng, on such a one, as either by desert or vnworthinesse, will merite rather to be loathed then loued.

If

If a question might be asked, what is the ground in dede of reasonable loue, whereby the knot is knit, of true and perfect freendship: I thinke those that be wise would aunswere: Deserte, that is, where the partie beloued, dooeth requite vs with the like, for otherwise, if the bare shewe of beautie, or the comelinesse of personage, might bee sufficient to confirme vs in our loue. Those that bee accustomed to goe to Faires and Markettes, might sometymes fall into loue with twentie in a daie: Desert must then bee (of force) the grounde of reasonable loue, for to loue them that hate vs, to followe them that flie from vs, to faune on them that froune on vs, to currie fauour with theim that disdaine vs, to bee glad to please theim that care not how thei offende vs: who will not confesse this to be an erronious loue, neither grounded vppon witte nor reason. Wherfore right curteous gentilwomen, if it please you with pacience to peruse this Historie following, you shall se Dame Errour so plaie her parte, with a Leishe of Louers, a male and twoo femalles, as shall woorke a wonder to your wise iudgement, in notyng the effecte of their amorous deuises and conclusions of their actions. The firste neclectyng the loue of a noble Dame, yong, beautifull, and faire, (who onely for his good will, plaied the parte of a seruing manne, contented to abide any maner of paine onely to behold him. He again setting his loue of a Dame that despisyng hym, (beeyng a noble Duke) gaue her self to a seruyng manne (as she had thought) but it otherwise fell out, as the substance of this tale shall better discribe. And because I haue been somethyng tedious in my first discourse, offending your pacient eares, with the hearyng of a circumstaunce ouer long. From hence forthe, that whiche I minde to write, shall bee doen with suche celeritie, as the matter that I pretende to penne, maie in any wise permit me, and thus followeth the Historie.

During the tyme that the famous Citie of Constantinople, remained in the handes of the Christians, emongst many other noble menne, that kepte their abidyng in that florishing Citie, there was one whose name was Apolonius, a worthie Duke, who beyng but a verie yong man, and euen then newe come to his possessions whiche were verie greate, leuied a mightie bande of menne, at his owne proper charges, with whom he serued againste the Turke, duryng the space of one whole yere, in whiche tyme although it were very shorte, this yong Duke so behaued hym self, as well by prowesse and valiaunce shewed with his owne handes, as otherwise, by his wisedome and liberalitie, vsed towardes his Souldiors, that all the worlde was filled with the fame of this noble Duke. When he had thus spent one yeares seruice, he caused his Trompet to sounde a retraite, and gatheryng his companie together, and imbarkyng theim selues he sette saile, holdyng his course towardes Constantinople: but beeyng vppon the Sea, by the extreamitie of a tempest whiche sodainly fell, his fleete was deseuered some one waie, and some an other, but he hym self recouered the Ile of Cypres, where he was worthily receiued by Pontus Duke and gouernour of the same Ile, with whom he lodged, while his Shippes were newe repairyng.

This Pontus that was Lorde and gouernour of this famous Ile, was an auncient Duke, and had twoo children, a soonne and a daughter, his sonne was named Siluio, of whom hereafter we shall haue further occasion to speake, but at this instant he was in the partes of Africa, seruyng in the warres.

The daughter her name was Silla, whose beautie was so perelesse, that she had the soueraintie emongest all other Dames, aswell for her beautie as for the noblenesse of her birthe. This Silla hauing heard of the worthinesse of Apolonius, this yong Duke, who besides his beautie and good graces, had a certaine naturall allurement, that beeyng now in his companie in her fathers Courte, she was so strangely attached with the loue of Apolonius, that there was nothyng might content her but his presence and sweete sight, and although she sawe no maner of hope, to attaine to that she moste desired: Knowyng Apolonius to be but a geaste, and readie to take the benefite of the next Winde, and to departe into a straunge Countrey, whereby she was bereued of all possibilitie euer to see hym againe, and therefore striued with her self to leaue her

fondenesse,

fondenesse, but all in vaine it would not bee, but like the foule whiche is once Limed, the more she striueth, the faster she tieth her self. So Silla was now constrained perforce her will to yeeld to loue, wherefore from tyme to tyme, she vsed so greate familiaritie with hym, as her honour might well permitte, and fedde him with suche amourous baites, as the modestie of a maide, could reasonably afforde, whiche when she perceiued, did take but small effecte, feelyng her self so muche out raged with the extreamitie of her passion, by the onely countenaunce that she bestowed vppon Apolonius, it might haue been well perceiued, that the verie eyes pleaded vnto hym for pitie and remorse. But Apolonius commyng but lately from out the feelde, from the chasyng of his enemies, and his furie not yet throughly desolued, nor purged from his stomacke, gaue no regarde to those amourous entisementes, whiche by reason of his youth, he had not been acquainted with all. But his minde ranne more to heare his Pilotes, bryng newes of a merie winde, to serue his turne to Constantinople, whiche in the ende came very prosperously: and giuyng Duke Pontus hartie thankes for his greate entertainment, takyng his leaue of hym self, and the Ladie Silla his daughter, departed with his companie, and with a happie gaale arriued at his desired porte: Gentlewomen accordyng to my promise, I will heare for breuities sake, omit to make repetition of the long and dolorous discourse recorded by Silla, for this sodaine departure of her Apolonius, knowyng you to bee as tenderly harted as Silla her self, whereby you maie the better coniecture the furie of her Feuer.

But Silla the further that she sawe her self bereued of all hope, euer any more to see her beloued Apolonius, so muche the more contagious were her passions, and made the greater speede to execute that she had premeditated in her mynde, whiche was this: Emongest many seruauntes that did attend vppon her, there was one whose name was Pedro, who had a long tyme waited vpon her in her Chamber, wherby she was well assured of his fidelitie and trust: to that Pedro, therefore she bewraied first the feruencie of her loue borne to Apolonius,

 coniuryng

coniuring him in the name of the Goddes of Loue her self, and bindyng hym by the duetie that a Seruaunte ought to haue, that tendereth his Mistresse safetie and good likyng, and desiryng hym with teares tricklyng doune her cheekes, that he would giue his consent to aide and assiste her, in that she had determined, whiche was for that she was fully resolued to goe to Constantinople, where she might againe take the vewe of her beloued Apolonius, that he accordyng to the trust she had reposed in hym, would not refuse to giue his consent, secretly to conuaie her from out her fathers Courte, accordyng as she should giue hym direction, and also to make hym self pertaker of her iourney, and to waite vpon her, till she had seen the ende of her determination.

Pedro perceiuyng with what vehemencie his Ladie and Mistresse had made request vnto hym, albeeit he sawe many perilles and doubtes, dependyng in her pretence notwithstandyng, gaue his consent to be at her disposition, promisyng her to further her with his beste aduice, and to be readie to obeye whatsoeuer she would please to commaunde him. The match beyng thus agreed vpon, and all thynges prepared in a readinesse for their departure: It happened there was a Gallie of Constantinople, readie to departe, whiche Pedro vnderstandyng came to the Captaine, desiryng him to haue passage for hym self, and for a poore maide that was his sister, whiche were bounde to Constantinople vppon certaine vrgent affaires, to whiche request, the Captaine graunted, willyng hym to prepare aborde with all speede, because the winde serued hym presently to departe.

Pedro now commyng to his Mistres, and tellyng her how he had handeled the matter with the Captaine: she likyng verie well of the deuise, disguisyng her self into verie simple atyre, stole awaie from out her fathers Court, and came with Pedro, whom now she calleth brother aboarde the Galleye, where all thynges beyng in readinesse, and the winde seruyng verie well, thei launched forthe with their Ores, and set saile, when thei were at the Sea, the Captaine of the Galleye takyng the vewe of Silla, perceiuyng her singular beautie, he

was

was better pleased in beholdyng of her face, then in takyng the height either of the Sunne or Starre, and thinkyng her by the homelinesse of her apparell, to be but some simple maiden, callyng her into his Cabin, he beganne to breake with her after the Sea fashion, desiryng her to vse his owne Cabin for her better ease: and duryng the tyme that she remained at the Sea, she should not want a bedde, and then wisperyng softly in her eare he saied, that for want of a bedfellow, he hym self would supplie that rome. Silla not beyng acquainted with any suche talke, blusshed for shame, but made hym no aunswere at all, my Captaine feelyng suche a bickeryng within him self, the like whereof he had neuer indured vpon the Sea: was like to bee taken prisoner aboard his owne Shippe, and forced to yeeld hym self a captiue without any Cannon shot, wherefore to salue all sores, and thinkyng it the readiest waie to speed, he began to breake with Silla in the waie of mariage, tellyng her how happie a voiage she had made, to fall into the likyng of suche a one as hym self was, who was able to keepe and maintaine her like a gentilwoman, and for her sake would likewise take her brother into his fellowship, whom he would by some meanes prefarre in suche sorte, that bothe of theim should haue good cause to thinke theim selues thrise happie, she to light of suche a housbande, and he to light of suche a brother. But Silla nothyng pleased with these prefermentes, desired hym to cease his talke, for that she did thynke her self in deede to bee too vnworthie suche a one as he was, neither was she minded yet to marrie, and therefore desired hym to fixe his fancie vppon some that were better worthie then her self was, and that could better like of his curtesie then she could doe, the Captaine seeyng hym self thus refused, beyng in a greate chafe, he saied as followeth.

Then seeyng you make so little accompte of my curtesie, proffered to one that is so farre vnworthie of it, from henceforthe I will vse the office of my authoritie, you shall knowe that I am the Captaine of this Shippe, and haue power to commaunde and dispose of thynges at my pleasure, and seyng you haue so scornfully reiected me to be your loiall housbande,

I

I will now take you by force, and vse you at my will, and so long as it shall please me, will kepe you for myne owne store, there shall be no man able to defende you, nor yet to perswade me from that I haue determined. Silla with these wordes beyng stroke into a greate feare, did thinke it now too late, to rewe her rashe attempte, determyned rather to dye with her owne handes, then to suffer her self to be abused in suche sorte, therefore she moste humbly desired the Captaine so muche as he could to saue her credite, and seyng that she must needes be at his will and disposition, that for that present he would depart, and suffer her till night, when in the darke he might take his pleasure, without any maner of suspition to the residue of his companie. The Captaine thinkyng now the goole to be more then half wonne, was contented so farre to satisfie her request, and departed out leauyng her alone in his Cabin.

Silla, beyng alone by her self, drue out her knife readie to strike her self to the harte, and fallyng vpon her knees, desired God to receiue her soule, as an acceptable sacrifice for her follies, whiche she had so wilfully committed, crauyng pardon for her sinnes, and so forthe continuyng a long and pitifull reconciliation to GOD, in the middest whereof there sodainly fell a wonderfull storme, the terrour whereof was suche, that there was no man but did thinke the Seas would presently haue swallowed them, the Billowes so sodainly arose with the rage of the winde, that thei were all glad to fall to heauing out of water, for otherwise their feeble Gallie had neuer bin able to haue brooked the Seas, this storme continued all that daie and the next night, and thei beeyng driuen to put romer before the winde to keepe the Gallie a hed the Billowe, were driuen vppon the maine shore, where the Gallie brake all to peeces, there was euery man prouidyng to saue his own life, some gat vpon Hatches, Boordes, and Caskes, and were driuen with the waues to and fro, but the greatest nomber were drouned, amongst the whiche Pedro was one, but Silla her self beyng in the Caben as you haue heard, tooke holde of a Cheste that was the Captaines, the whiche by the onely prouidence of GOD brought her safe to the shore, the whiche

when

when she had recouered, not knowyng what was become of Pedro her manne, she deemed that bothe he and all the rest had been drouned, for that she sawe no bodie vppon the shore but her self, wherefore, when she had a while made greate lamentations, complainyng her mishappes, she beganne in the ende to comforte her self with the hope, that she had to see her Apolonius, and found suche meanes that she brake open the Chest that brought her to lande, wherin she found good store of coine, and sondrie sutes of apparell that were the captaines, and now to preuent a nomber of iniuries, that might bee proffered to a woman that was lefte in her case, she determined to leaue her owne apparell, and to sort her self into some of those sutes, that beyng taken for a man, she might passe through the Countrie in the better safetie, & as she changed her apparell, she thought it likewise conuenient to change her name, wherefore not readily happenyng of any other, she called her self Siluio, by the name of her owne brother, whom you haue heard spoken of before.

In this maner she trauailed to Constantinople, where she inquired out the Palace of the Duke Apolonius, and thinking her self now to be bothe fitte and able to plaie the seruyngman, she presented her self to the duke, crauyng his seruice, the duke verie willyng to giue succour vnto strangers, perceiuyng him to bee a proper smogue yong man, gaue hym entertainment: Silla thought her self now more then satisfied, for all the casualties that had happened vnto her in her iourney, that she might at her pleasure take but the vew of the Duke Apolonius, and aboue the reste of his seruauntes was verie diligent and attendaunt vppon hym, the whiche the Duke perceiuyng, beganne likewise to growe into good likyng with the diligence of his man, and therefore made hym one of his Chamber, who but Siluio then was moste neate aboute hym, in helpyng of hym to make hym readie in a mornyng, in the settyng of his ruffes, in the keepyng of his Chamber, Siluio pleased his maister so well, that aboue all the reste of his seruauntes aboute hym, he had the greatest credite, and the Duke put him moste in trust.

At this verie instaunt, there was remainyng in the Citie a

noble Dame a widowe, whoſe houſebande was but lately deceaſed, one of the nobleſt men that were in the partes of Grecia, who left his Lady and wife large poſſeſſions and greate liuinges. This Ladies name was called Iulina, who beſides the aboundance of her wealth, and the greatneſſe of her reuenues, had likewiſe the ſoueraigntie of all the Dames of Conſtantinople for her beautie. To this Ladie Iulina, Apolonius became an earneſt ſuter, and accordyng to the maner of wooers, beſides faire wordes, ſorrowfull ſighes, and piteous countenaunces, there muſt bee ſendyng of louyng letters, Chaines, Braceletes, Brouches, Rynges, Tablets, Gemmes, Iuels and preſentes I knowe not what: So my Duke, who in the tyme that he remained in the Ile of Cypres, had no ſkill at all in the arte of Loue, although it were more then half proffered vnto hym, was now become a ſcholler in Loues Schoole, and had alreadie learned his firſt leſſon, that is, to ſpeake pitifully, to looke ruthfully, to promiſe largely, to ſerue diligently, and to pleaſe carefully: Now he was learnyng his ſeconde leſſon, that is to reward liberally, to giue bountifully, to preſent willyngly, and to write louyngly. Thus Apolonius was ſo buſied in his newe ſtudie, that I warrant you there was no man that could chalenge hym for playing the truant, he followed his profeſſion with ſo good a will: And who muſt bee the meſſenger to carrie the tokens and loue letters, to the Ladie Iulina, but Siluio his manne, in hym the Duke repoſed his onely confidence, to goe betwene hym and his Ladie.

Now gentilwomen, doe you thinke there could haue been a greater torment deuiſed, wherewith to afflicte the harte of Silla, then her ſelf to bee made the inſtrumente to worke her owne miſhapp, and to plaie the Atturney in a cauſe, that made ſo muche againſte her ſelf. But Silla altogether deſirous to pleaſe her maiſter, cared nothyng at all to offende her ſelf, followed his buſineſſe with ſo good a will, as if it had been in her owne preferment.

Iulina now hauyng many tymes, taken the gaze of this yong youth Siluio, perceiuyng hym to bee of ſuche excellente perfecte grace, was ſo intangeled with the often ſight of this

ſweete

sweete temptation, that she fell into as greate a likyng with the man, as the maister was with her self: And on a tyme Siluio beyng sent from his maister, with a message to the Ladie Iulina, as he beganne very earnestly to solicet in his maisters behalfe, Iulina interruptyng hym in his tale, saied: Siluio it is enough that you haue saied for your maister, from henceforthe either speake for your self, or saie nothyng at all. Silla abashed to heare these wordes, began in her minde to accuse the blindnesse of Loue, that Iulina neglectyng the good will of so noble a Duke, would preferre her loue vnto suche a one, as Nature it self had denaied to recompence her likyng.

And now for a tyme, leauyng matters dependyng as you haue heard, it fell out that the right Siluio in deede (whom you haue heard spoken of before, the brother of Silla,) was come to his Fathers Courte into the Ile of Cypres, where vnderstanding, that his sister was departed, in maner as you haue heard coniectured, that the very occasion did proceade of some liking had betwene Pedro her man (that was missyng with her) and her self, but Siluio who loued his sister, as dearly as his owne life, and the rather for that as she was his naturall sister, bothe by Father and Mother, so the one of theim was so like the other, in countenaunce and fauour, that there was no man able to descerne the one from the other by their faces, sauyng by their apparell the one beyng a man, the other a woman.

Siluio therefore vowed to his Father, not onely to seeke out his sister Silla, but also to reuenge the villanie, whiche he conceiued in Pedro, for the carriyng awaie of his sister, and thus departyng, hauyng trauailed through many Cities and Tounes, without hearyng any maner of newes, of those he wente to seeke for, at the laste he arriued at Constantinople, where as he was walkyng in an euenyng for his owne recreation, on a pleasaunte greene yarde, without the walles of the Citie, he fortuned to meete with the Ladie Iulina, who likewise had been abroad to take the aire, and as she sodainly caste her eyes vppon Siluio, thinkyng hym to bee her olde acquaintaunce, by reason thei were so like one an other, as you haue heard before, saied vnto hym, sir Siluio, if your haste be not the greater, I praie you let me haue a little talke with you, seyng I haue so luckely mette you in this place.

Siluio wonderyng to heare hym self so rightlie named, beeyng but a straunger, not of aboue twoo daies continuaunce in the Citie, verie courteouslie came towardes her, desirous to heare what she would saie.

Iulina commaundyng her traine somthyng to stande backe, saied as followeth. Seyng my good will and frendly loue, hath been the onely cause to make me so prodigall to offer, that I see is so lightly reiected, it maketh me to thinke, that men bee of this condition, rather to desire those thynges, whiche thei can not come by, then to esteeme or value of that, whiche bothe largely and liberallie is offered vnto theim, but if the liberalitie of my proffer, hath made to seme lesse the value of the thing that I ment to present, it is but in your owne conceipt, consideryng how many noble men there hath been here before, and be yet at this present, whiche hath bothe serued, sued, and moste humbly intreated, to attaine to that, whiche to you of my self, I haue freely offred, and I perceiue is dispised, or at the least verie lightly regarded.

Siluio wonderyng at these woordes, but more amazed that she could so rightlie call hym by his name, could not tell what to make of her speeches, assuryng hym self that she was deceiued, and did mistake hym, did thinke notwithstandyng, it had been a poincte of greate simplicitie, if he should forsake that, whiche Fortune had so fauourably proffered vnto hym, perceiuyng by her traine, that she was some Ladie of greate honour, and vewyng the perfection of her beautie, and the excellencie of her grace and countenaunce, did thinke it vnpossible that she should be despised, and therefore aunswered thus.

Madame, if before this tyme, I haue seemed to forgett my self, in neglectyng your courtesie, whiche so liberally you haue ment vnto me: please it you to pardon what is paste, and from this daie forewardes, Siluio remaineth readie prest to make suche reasonable amendes, as his abilitie maie any waies permit, or as it shall please you to commaunde.

Iulina the gladdest woman that might bee, to heare these ioyfull

ioyfull newes, saied: Then my Siluio see you faile not to Morowe at night to Suppe with me at my owne house, where I will discourse farther with you, what amendes you shall make me, to whiche request Siluio gaue his glad consente, and thus thei departed verie well pleased. And as Iulina did thinke the tyme verie long, till she had reapte the fruite of her desire: So Siluio he wishte for Haruest, before Corne could growe, thinkyng the tyme as long, till he sawe how matters would fall out, but not knowyng what Ladie she might bee, he presently (before Iulina was out of sight) demaunded of one that was walkyng by what she was, and how she was called, who satisfied Siluio in euery pointe, and also in what parte of the toune her house did stande, whereby he might enquire it out.

Siluio thus departing to his lodging, passed the night with verie vnquiet sleapes, and the nexte Mornyng his mynde ran so muche of his Supper, that he neuer cared, neither for his Breakfast nor Dinner, and the daie to his seemyng passed awaie so slowlie, that he had thought the statlie Steedes had been tired, that drawe the Chariot of the Sunne, or els some other Iosua had commaunded them againe to stande, and wished that Phaeton had been there with a whippe.

Iulina on the other side, she had thought the Clocke setter had plaied the knaue, the daie came no faster forewardes, but sixe a clocke beeyng once stroken, recouered comforte to bothe parties: and Siluio hastenyng hymself to the Pallace of Iulina, where by her he was frendly welcomed, and a sumpteous supper beeyng made readie, furnished with sondrie sortes of delicate dishes, thei satte them doune, passyng the Supper tyme with amarous lokes, louyng countenaunces, and secret glaūces conueighed from the one to the other, whiche did better satisfie them, then the feedyng of their daintie dishes.

Supper tyme beeyng thus spent, Iulina did thinke it verie vnfitly, if she should tourne Siluio to goe seeke his lodgyng in an euenyng, desired hym therefore, that he would take a bedde in her house for that Night, and bryngyng hym vp into a faire Chamber, that was verie richely furnished, she founde suche meanes, that when all the reste of her houshholde seruauntes were a bedde and quiet, she came her self to beare Siluio companie, where concludyng vppon conditions, that were in question betweene them, thei passed the night with suche ioye and contentation, as might in that conuenient tyme be wished for, but onely that Iulina, feedyng too muche of some one dishe aboue the reste, receiued a surfet, whereof she could not bee cured in fourtie wekes after, a naturall inclination in all women whiche are subiecte to longyng, and want the reason to vse a moderation in their diet: but the mornyng approchyng, Iulina tooke her leaue, and cõueighed her self into her owne chamber, and when it was faire daie light, Siluano makyng hym self readie, departed likewise about his affaires in the toune, debatyng with hymself how thynges had happened, beyng well assured that Iulina had mistaken hym, and therefore for feare of further euilles, determined to come no more there, but tooke his iourney towardes other places in the partes of Grecia, to see if he could learne any tidynges of his sister Silla.

The duke Apolonius hauyng made a long sute, and neuer a whit the nerer of his purpose, came to Iulina to craue her direct aunswere, either to accept of hym, and of suche conditions as he proffered vnto her, or els to giue hym his laste farewell.

Iulina, as you haue heard, had taken an earnest penie of an other, whom he had thought had been Siluio the Dukes man, was at a controuersie in her self, what she might doe, one while she thought, seyng her occasion serued so fitt, to craue the Dukes good will, for the mariyng of his manne, then againe, she could not tell what displeasure the Duke would conceiue, in that she should seeme to preferre his man before hym self, did thinke it therefore beste to conceale the matter, till she might speake with Siluio, to vse his opiniõ how these matters should be handled, and hereupon resoluyng her self, desiryng the duke to pardon her speeches, saied as followeth.

Sir Duke, for that from this tyme forwardes I am no longer of my self, hauyng giuen my full power and authoritie ouer to an other, whose wife I now remaine by faithfull vowe and promise: And albeeit, I knowe the worlde will wonder, when thei shall vnderstande the fondnesse of my choice, yet I

trust

truſt you your ſelf will nothyng deſlike with me, ſithe I haue ment no other thing, then the ſatiſfiyng of myne owne contentation and likyng.

The Duke hearyng theſe wordes, aunſwered: Madam, I muſt then content my ſelf, although againſt my wil, hauing the Lawe in your owne handes, to like of whom you liſte, and to make choiſe where it pleaſeth you.

Iulina giuyng the Duke greate thankes, that would content himſelf with ſuche pacience, deſired hym likewiſe, to giue his free conſent and good will, to the partie whom ſhe had choſen to be her houſebande.

Naie ſurely Madam (q the Duke) I will neuer giue my conſent, that any other man ſhall enioye you then my ſelf, I haue made too greate accompt of you, then ſo lightly to paſſe you awaie with my good will: But ſeeyng it lieth not in me to let you, hauyng (as you ſaie) made your owne choiſe, ſo from hence forwardes I leaue you to your owne likyng, alwaies willyng you well, and thus will take my leaue.

The Duke departed towardes his owne houſe verie ſorrowfull, that Iulina had thus ſerued hym, but in the meane ſpace that the Duke had remained in the houſe of Iulina, ſome of his ſeruantes fell into talke and conference, with the ſeruantes of Iulina, where debatyng betwene them, of the likelihood of the Mariage, betweene the Duke and the Ladie, one of the ſeruantes of Iulina ſaied: that he neuer ſawe his Ladie and miſtres, vſe ſo good countenaunce to the Duke hym ſelf, as ſhe had doen to Siluio his manne, and began to report with what familiaritie and courteſie, ſhe had receiued hym, feaſted hym, and lodged hym, and that in his opinion, Siluio was like to ſpeede before the Duke, or any other that were ſuters.

This tale was quickly brought to the Duke hymſelf, who makyng better enquirie in the matter, founde it to be true that was reported, and better conſideryng of the wordes, whiche Iulina had vſed towardes hymſelf, was verie well aſſured that it could bee no other then his owne manne, that had thruſt his Noſe ſo farre out of ioynte, wherefore without any further reſpect, cauſed hym to be thruſt into a Dongeon, where he was kept

kept prisoner, in a verie pitifull plight.

Poore Siluio, hauyng gotte intelligence by some of his fellowes, what was the cause that the Duke his Maister did beare suche displeasure vnto hym, deuised all the meanes he could, as well by meditation by his fellowes, as otherwise by petitions, and supplications to the Duke, that he would suspende his Iudgemente, till perfecte proofe were had in the matter, and then if any maner of thyng did fall out againste hym, wherby the Duke had cause to take any greef, he would confesse hym self worthie not onely of imprisonmente, but also of moste vile and shamefull death: with these pititions he daiely plied the Duke, but all in vaine, for the duke thought he had made so good proofe, that he was throughlie confirmed in his opinion against his man.

But the Ladie Iulina, wonderyng what made Siluio, that he was so slacke in his visitation, and why he absented hym self so long from her presence, beganne to thinke that all was not well, but in the ende, perceiuyng no decoction of her former surfette, receiued as you haue heard, and findyng in her self, an vnwonted swellyng in her bellie, assuryng her self to bee with child, fearyng to become quite banckroute of her honour, did thinke it more then tyme to seke out a Father, and made suche secret searche, and diligent enquirie, that she learned the truthe how Siluio was kepte in prison, by the Duke his Maister, and myndyng to finde a present remedie, as well for the loue she bare to Siluio, as for the maintainaunce of her credite and estimation, she speedily hasted to the Pallace of the Duke, to whom she saied as followeth.

Sir Duke, it maie bee that you will thinke my commyng to your house in this sorte, doeth somethyng passe the limites of modestie, the whiche I protest before GOD, proceadeth of this desire, that the worlde should knowe, how iustly I seke meanes to maintaine my honour, but to the ende I seeme not tedious with prolixitie of woordes, nor to vse other then direct circumstaunces, knowe sir, that the loue I beare to my onely beloued Siluio, whom I doe esteeme more then all the Iewells in the worlde, whose personage I regard more then my

my

my owne life, is the onely cause of my attempted iourney, beseching you, that all the whole displeasure, whiche I vnderstand you haue conceiued against hym, maie be imputed vnto my charge, and that it would please you louingly to deale with him, whom of my self I haue chosen rather for the satisfaction of mine honest likyng, then for the vaine preheminences or honourable dignities looked after by ambicious myndes.

The Duke hauing heard this discourse, caused Siluio presently to be sent for, and to be brought before hym, to whom he saied: Had it not been sufficient for thee, when I had reposed my self in thy fidelitie, and the trustinesse of thy seruice, that thou shouldest so traiterously deale with me, but since ẏ tyme haste not spared, still to abuse me with so many forgeries, and periured protestations, not onely hatefull vnto me, whose simplicitie thou thinkest to bee suche, that by the plotte of thy pleasaunt tongue, thou wouldest make me beleeue a manifest vntrothe, but moste habominable bee thy doynges in the presence and sight of God, that hast not spared to blaspheme his holy name, by callyng hym to bee a witnesse to maintaine thy leasynges, and so detestably wouldest forsweare thy self, in a matter that is so openly knowne.

Poore Siluio whose innocencie was suche, ẏ he might lawfully sweare, seing Iulina to be there in place, aunswered thus.

Moste noble Duke, well vnderstandyng your conceiued greefe, moste humbly I beseche you paciently to heare my excuse, not myndyng thereby to aggrauate or heape vp youre wrathe and displeasure, protestyng before God, that there is nothyng in the worlde, whiche I regarde so muche, or doo esteeme so deare, as your good grace and fauour, but desirous that your grace should know my innocencie, and to cleare my self of suche impositions, wherewith I knowe I am wrongfully accused, whiche as I vnderstande should be in the practisyng of the Ladie Iulina, who standeth here in place, whose acquitaunce for my better discharge, now I moste humbly craue, protestyng before the almightie God, that neither in thought, worde, nor deede, I haue not otherwise vsed my self, then accordyng to the bonde and duetie of a seruaunte, that is both willyng & desirous, to further his Maisters sutes, which if I haue otherwise saied then that is true, you Madame Iulina, who can verie well deside the depthes of all this doubte, I moste humblie beseche you to certifie a trothe, if I haue in any thyng missaied, or haue other wise spokē then is right and iust.

Iulina hauyng heard this discourse whiche Siluio had made, perceiuyng that he stoode in greate awe of the Dukes displeasure, aunswered thus: Thinke not my Siluio, that my commyng hither is to accuse you of any misdemeanour towardes your Maister, so I dooe not denaie, but in all suche Imbassages wherein towardes me you haue been imploied, you haue vsed the office of a faithfull and trustie messenger, neither am I ashamed to confesse, that the first daie that mine eyes did beholde, the singuler behauiour, the notable curtesie, and other innumerable giftes wherwith my Siluio is endued, but that beyonde all measure my harte was so inflamed, that impossible it was for me, to quenche the feruente loue, or extinguishe the least parte of my conceiued torment, before I had bewraied the same vnto hym, and of my owne motion, craued his promised faithe and loialtie of marriage, and now is the tyme to manifest the same vnto the worlde, whiche hath been doen before God, and betwene our selues: knowyng that it is not needefull, to keepe secret that, whiche is neither euill doen, nor hurtfull to any persone, therefore (as I saied before) Siluio is my housbande by plited faithe, whom I hope to obtaine without offence, or displeasure of any one, trustyng that there is no manne, that will so farre forget hym self, as to restraine that, whiche God hath left at libertie for euery wight, or that will seeke by crueltie, to force Ladies to marrie otherwise, then accordyng to their owne likyng. Feare not then my Siluio to keepe your faith and promise, whiche you haue made vnto me, and as for the reste: I doubte not thynges will so fall out, as you shall haue no maner af cause to complaine.

Siluio amased to heare these wordes, for that Iulina by her speeche, semed to confirme that, whiche he moste of all desired to bee quite of, saied: Who would haue thought that a Ladie of so greate honour and reputation, would her self bee

the

the Embassadour, of a thyng so preiudiciall, and vncomely for her estate, what plighted promises be these whiche bee spoken of: Altogether ignoraunt vnto me, whiche if it bee otherwise then I haue saied, you Sacred Goddes consume me straight with flashyng flames of fire. But what wordes might I vse to giue credite to the truthe, and innocencie of my cause? Ah Madame Iulina, I desire no other testimonie, then your owne honestie and vertue, thinkyng that you will not so muche blemishe the brightnesse of your honour, knowyng that a womā is or should be, the Image of curtesie, continencie, and shamfastnesse, from the whiche so sone as she stoopeth, and leaueth the office of her duetie and modestie, besides the degraduation of her honour, she thrusteth her self into the pitte of perpetuall infamie, and as I can not thinke you would so farre forgette your self, by the refusall of a noble Duke, to dimme the light of your renowne and glorie, whiche hetherto you haue maintained, emongest the beste and noblest Ladies, by suche a one as I knowe my self to bee, too farre vnworthie your degree and callyng, so moste hūbly I beseche you to confesse a trothe, whereto tendeth those vowes and promises you speake of, whiche speeches bee so obscure vnto me, as I knowe not for my life how I might vnderstande them.

Iulina somethyng nipped with these speeches saied, and what is the matter that now you make so little accoumpte of your Iulina, that beyng my housbande in deede, haue the face to denaie me, to whom thou art contracted by so many solemne othes: what arte thou ashamed to haue me to thy wife? how muche oughtest thou rather to be ashamed to breake thy promised faithe, and to haue despised the holie and dreadfull name of GOD, but that tyme constraineth me to laye open that, whiche shame rather willeth I should dissemble and keepe secret, beholde me then here Siluio whom thou haste gotten with childe, who if thou bee of suche honestie, as I trust for all this I shall finde then the thyng is doen without preiudice, or any hurte to my conscience, consideryng that by the professed faithe, thou diddest accoumpt me for thy wife, and I receiued thee for my spouse and loyall housbande, swearyng by the

 almightie

almightie God, that no other then you haue made the cōquest and triumphe of my chastitie, whereof I craue no other witnesse then your self, and mine owne conscience.

I praie you Gentilwomen, was not this a foule ouersight of Iulina, that would so precisely sweare so greate an othe, that she was gotten with childe by one, that was altogether vnfurnishte with implementes for suche a tourne. For Gods loue take heede, and let this bee an example to you, when you be with childe, how you sweare who is the Father, before you haue had good proofe and knowledge of the partie, for men be so subtill and full of sleight, that God knoweth a woman may quickly be deceiued.

But now to returne to our Siluio, who hearyng an othe sworne so deuinely that he had gotten a woman with childe, was like to beleeue that it had bin true in very deede, but remembryng his owne impediment, thought it impossible that he should committe suche an acte, and therefore half in a chafe, he saied. What lawe is able to restraine the foolishe indiscretion of a woman, that yeeldeth her self to her owne desires, what shame is able to bridle or withdrawe her from her mynd and madnesse, or with what snaffell is it possible to holde her backe, from the execution of her filthinesse, but what abhomination is this, that a Ladie of suche a house should so forget the greatnesse of her estate, the aliaunce whereof she is descended, the nobilitie of her deceased housbande, and maketh no conscience to shame and slaunder her self, with suche a one as I am, beyng so farre vnfit and vnsemely for her degree, but how horrible is it to heare the name of God so defaced, that wee make no more acompt, but for the maintenaunce of our mischifes, we feare no whit at all to forsweare his holy name, as though he were not in all his dealinges moste righteous true and iuste, and will not onely laie open our leasinges to the worlde, but will likewise punishe the same with moste sharpe and bitter scourges.

Iulina, not able to indure hym to proceede any farther in his Sermon, was alreadie surprised with a vehement greefe, began bitterly to crie out vtteryng these speeches followyng.

Alas

Alas, is it poſſible that the ſoueraigne iuſtice of God, can abide a miſchiefe ſo greate and curſed, why maie I not now ſuffer death, rather then the infamie whiche I ſee to wander before myne eyes. Oh happie and more then right happie had I bin, if inconſtant fortune had not deuiſed this treaſon wherein I am ſurpriſed and caught, am I thus become to be intangled with ſnares, and in the handes of hym, who inioiyng the ſpoyles of my honour, will openly depriue me of my fame, by makyng me a common fable to al poſteritie in tyme to come, ah Traitour and diſcourtious wretche, is this the recompence of the honeſt and firme amitie which I haue borne thee, wherin haue I deſerued this diſcourteſie, by louing thee more then thou art able to deſerue, is it I arrant theefe is it I, vppon whom thou thinkeſt to worke thy miſchiues, doeſt thou think me no better worthe, but that thou maieſt prodigally waſte my honour at thy pleaſure, dideſt thou dare to aduenture vppon me, hauing thy conſcience wounded with ſo deadly a treaſon: ah vnhappie and aboue all other moſt vnhappie, that haue ſo charely preſerued myne honour, and now am made a praie to ſatiſfie a yong mans luſt, that hath coueted nothyng but the ſpoyle of my chaſtitie and good name.

Here withall the teares ſo guſhed doune her cheekes, that ſhe was not able to open her mouth to vſe any farther ſpeeche.

The Duke who ſtoode by all this while, and heard this whole diſcourſe, was wonderfully moued with compaſſion towardes Iulina, knowyng that from her infancie ſhe had euer ſo honourably vſed her ſelf, that there was no man able to detect her of any miſdemeanour, otherwiſe then beſeemed a Ladie of her eſtate, wherefore beyng fully reſolued that Siluio his man had committed this villanie againſt her, in a greate furie drawyng his Rapier he ſaied vnto Siluio.

How canſt thou (arrant theefe) ſhewe thy ſelf ſo cruell and careleſſe to ſuche as doe thee honour, haſt thou ſo little regard of ſuche a noble Ladie, as humbleth her ſelf to ſuche a villaine as thou art, who without any reſpecte either of her renowne or noble eſtate, canſt be content to ſeeke the wracke and vtter ruine of her honour, but frame thy ſelf to make ſuch ſatiſfaction as she requireth, although I knowe vnworthie wretche, that thou art not able to make her the least parte of amendes, or I sweare by god, that thou shalt not escape the death which I will minister to thee with my owne handes, and therefore aduise thee well what thou doest.

Siluio hauyng heard this sharpe sentence, fell doune on his knees before the Duke crauyng for mercie, desiryng that he might be suffered to speake with the Ladie Iulina aparte, promising to satisfie her, accordyng to her owne contentation.

Well (q the Duke) I take thy worde, and there with all I aduise thee that thou performe thy promis, or otherwise I protest before God, I will make thee suche an example to the worlde, that all Traitours shall tremble for feare, how they doe seeke the dishonouryng of Ladies.

But now Iulina had conceiued so greate greefe againste Siluio, that there was muche a doe, to perswade her to talke with hym, but remembryng her owne case, desirous to heare what excuse he could make, in the ende she agreed, and beyng brought into a place seuerally by them selues, Siluio beganne with a piteous voice to saie as followeth.

I knowe not Madame, of whom I might make complaine, whether of you or of my self, or rather of Fortune, whiche hath conducted and brought vs both into so greate aduersitie, I see that you receiue greate wrong, and I am condemned againste all right, you in perill to abide the brute of spightfull tongues, and I in daunger to loose the thing that I moste desire: and although I could alledge many reasons to proue my saiynges true, yet I referre my self, to the experience and bountie of your minde. And here with all loosing his garmentes doune to his stomacke, and shewed Iulina his breastes and pretie teates, surmountyng farre the whitenesse of Snowe it self, saiyng: Loe Madame, behold here the partie whom you haue chalenged to bee the father of your childe, see I am a woman the daughter of a noble Duke, who onely for the loue of him, whom you so lightly haue shaken of, haue forsaken my father, abandoned my Countreie, and in maner as you see am become a seruing man, satisfiyng my self, but with the

the

the onely sight of my Apolonius, and now Madame, if my passion were not vehement, & my tormentes without comparison, I would wish that my fained greefes might be laughed to scorne, & my desēbled paines to be rewarded with floutes. But my loue beyng pure, my trauaile continuall, & my greefes endlesse, I trust Madame you will not onely excuse me of crime, but also pitie my destresse, the which I protest I would still haue kept secrete, if my fortune would so haue permitted.

Iulina, did now thinke her self to be in a worse case then euer she was before, for now she knewe not whō to chalenge to be the father of her child, wherfore, when she had told the duke the very certantie of the discourse, which Siluio had made vnto her, she departed to her owne house, with suche greefe and sorrowe, that she purposed neuer to come out of her owne doores againe aliue, to be a wonder and mocking stocke to ẏ worlde.

But ẏ Duke more amased, to heare this strāge discourse of Siluio came vnto him, whō when he had vewed with better consideratiō, perceiued in deede that it was Silla the daughter of Duke Pontus, and imbrasing her in his armes, he saied.

Oh the braunche of all vertue, and the flowre of curtesie it self, pardon me I besiche you of all suche discourtesies, as I haue ignorantlie committed towardes you: desiring you that without farther memorie of auncient greefes, you will accept of me, who is more ioyful and better contented with your presence, then if the whole worlde were at my commaundement. Where hath there euer been founde suche liberalitie in a Louer, whiche hauyng been trained vp and nourished emongest the delicacies and banquettes of the Courte, accompanied with traines of many faire and noble ladies liuing in pleasure, and in the middest of delightes, would so prodigallie aduenture your self, neither fearing mishapps, nor misliking to take suche paines, as I knowe you haue not been accustomed vnto. O liberalitie neuer heard of before! O facte that can neuer bee sufficiently rewarded! O true Loue moste pure and vnfained: here with all sendyng for the moste artificiall workmen, he prouided for her sondrie sutes of sumpteous apparell, and the Marriage daie appointed, whiche was celebrated with

with greate triumphe, through the whole Citie of Constantinople, euery one praising the noblenesse of the Duke, but so many as did behold the excellent beautie of Silla, gaue her the praise aboue all the rest of the Ladies in the troupe.

The matter seemed so wonderfull and straunge, that the brute was spreade throughout all the partes of Gretia, in so muche that it came to the hearyng of Siluio, who as you haue heard, remained in those partes to enquire of his sister, he beyng the gladdest manne in the worlde, hasted to Constantinople, where commyng to his sister he was ioyfullie receiued, and moste louynglie welcomed, and entertained of the Duke his brother in Lawe. After he had remained there twoo or three daies, the duke reuealed vnto Siluio, the whole discourse how it happened, betweene his sister and the Ladie Iulina, and how his sister was chalenged, for gettyng a woman with childe: Siluio blushyng with these woordes, was striken with greate remorse to make Iulina amendes, vnderstanding her to bee a noble Ladie, and was lefte defamed to the worlde through his default, he therefore bewraied the whole circumstaunce to the Duke, whereof the Duke beyng verie ioyfull, immediatlie repaired with Siluio to the house of Iulina, whom thei found in her chamber, in great lamentation & mournyng. To whom the Duke saied, take courage Madam for beholde here a gentilman, that will not sticke, bothe to father your child and to take you for his wife, no inferiour persone, but the sonne and heire of a noble Duke, worthie of your estate and dignitie.

Iulina seyng Siluio in place, did know very well that he was the father of her childe, and was so rauished with ioye, that she knewe not whether she were awake, or in some dreame. Siluio imbracyng her in his armes, crauyng forgiuenesse of all that past: concluded with her the mariage daie, which was presently accomplished with greate ioye, and contentation to all parties: And thus Siluio hauyng attained a noble wife, and Silla his sister her desired housebande, thei passed the residue of their daies with suche delight, as those that haue accomplished the perfection of their felicities.

FINIS.

¶The

Of Nicander and Lucila.

The argument of the third Historie.

¶ Lucilla, *a yong maiden endued with singuler beautie, for want of a conuenient dowrie, was restrained frō mariyng her beloued* Nicander, *in the ende, through the greate magnificence of the courteous yong prince* Don Hercules, *the onely sonne and heire of* Alfonso *duke of Farrara, she was releeued with the somme of 2000. crounes, the which money beyng receiued by the father of* Nicander, *the mariage was performed, to the greate contentation of the noble yong Prince, but especially to the twoo yong Louers* Nicander *and* Lucilla.

N the tyme that Alfonso firste of that name, and third duke of Ferrara gouerned that State, there was in the Citie of Ferrara, a gentle younge Gentlewoman named Lucilla, borne of a noble Familie, but by the frowardnesse of blinde Fortune, reduced to greater pouertie, then her vertues did deserue: whose beautie appeared to be suche, in the prime and flower of her yeres, as it filled with maruaile, all those that caste their eyes vpon her. Of this gentlewoman was feruently enamoured, a gallant yong gentleman, whose name was Nicander, and in like sorte borne of noble blood: and desired nothyng more, then to bee ioyned with her in Matrimonie. But she beyng as it is saied poore, though of noble parentage, and endued with singular vertues: The father of the yong gentleman disdained her, who (as for the moste part, we see old men, naturally enclined to couetise) regardyng rather the wealth that their daughters in lawe, are to bryng into their families, then either

birth, vertue, or giftes of the minde, could in nowise be perswaded, or intreated to content his sonne in that behalfe, and to suffer hym to enioye his Loue, by takyng her to wife: alledgyng that the first thyng that was to bee considered in mariage was the dowrie, and the woman. For that the vertues of the wome͂ doe not enriche the houses wherein thei came (saied he) but the qualitie of goodes and wealthe, that thei brought with them.

The coueteous disposition of the father of Nicander, was cause that these twoo yong folke languished in miserable loue: For although their flames were of equall force and heate, yet the yong gentlewoman beyng of a verie honest minde, nor the yong gentleman, neuer thinking vpon any other meanes then honestly to enioye his desire, without touche or breache of her honor: and the obstinate wilfulnesse of the old man beyng cast, as a barre or blocke, betweene the vnitie and concorde of their twoo mindes: thei liued in greate torment, eche consumyng, and as it were meltyng awaie with desire, for loue of eche other. Whilest their mutuall loue continued in this sorte eche daie, with lesse hope then other, through the obstinacie of th'old carle, it happened that Don Hercules the Dukes onely sonne and heire, beyng then in the freshest tyme of his youth, passing by the streate where this gentlewoman dwelt, sawe her standyng in her doore, apparailed in white, whiche kinde of attire encreased greatly her naturall beautie. And consideryng somwhat curiously, the comelinesse and excellencie of her personage, together with her perfection of beautie, he receiued with suche force into his imagination, the firste impression of theim bothe, that from thence forward her liuely Image semed continually to be before his eyes: by the consideration whereof he grewe by degrees, to conceiue so vehement a desire, to enioye the singularitie whiche he sawe in her, that he thought it impossible for hym to liue, if he did not attaine it.

And ofte tymes discoursyng to hym self thereof, he would saie, what iniurie hath Fortune doen vnto this faire gentlewoman, that as Nature hath been liberall in bestowyng of beautie vpon her, meete for any greate Princes, she hath not likewise caused her to bee borne of some Kyng or mightie Prince:

whiche

whiche if she were, I would neuer cease till I had founde the meanes to gett her to bee my wife, and so enioye her as myne owne, with the safetie of her honour, and with the satisfaction and contentment of my Father.

But in the ende, although he sawe her degree to bee farre vnequall to his, to wishe, or to procure any suche matche: Yet ceased he not by all the meanes he could, to win her good will, and now by one deuise, and now by an other to induce her to loue hym, and to yeelde to his feruent desire. But all in vaine. For where many others would haue taken it for a great good Fortune, that suche a Prince should haue fallen in Loue with them, Lucilla consideryng the basenesse of her degree, in respecte of the high estate of her newe Louer, reputed it to bee a greate mishappe vnto her, as she that considered, that she could not nourishe or entertaine any suche loue, but with the harme and preiudice of her honour. Besides that, she feared least that Nicander should once perceiue, that this yong Prince haunted after that haunte, he would forsake her, for feare of farther displeasure, wherefore to auoide bothe inconueniences, whereas till then, she was wont to shewe her self sometyme at the dore, sometyme at the Windowes, she now retired her self in suche sort, that she could neuer be seen but on the Sondaies and Holie daies, as she went to a little Churche nere adioinyng to the house. Wherefore Nicãder not a little meruailyng, and greatly troubled in spirite, fearyng that Lucilla (waueryng as women vse to doe) had forsaken hym, and turned her affection elswhere: as one full of gelousie and greef, for fault of better cõforte, he would watche his tymes, and followe her to that Churche: there to feede his fancie with a looke or twoo, whiche yet amid his miserie, he semed to esteeme as a releef, without the whiche he could not liue. Finally, not beyng able to endure those tormentes, that this absence and straungenesse of his ladie caused hym to feele, he sent vnto her a conuenient messenger with a letter, conteinyng this effecte.

The birde whiche long hath liued in pleasant feeld,
Esteemes nowhit his cage of wreathed golde:

Of Nicander

The du'ced note, wherewith he pearst the Skie,
For greef of mynde, he can not then vnfolde,
Yet liues he still but better were to die,
More worse then death, euen suche a life haue I.

The Turtle true, of his deceased mate,
Bewailes the want, he reakes no more of blisse:
The swellyng Swanne, doeth hardly brooke the place,
When he his beste, beloued birde doeth misse.
Suche is my ioye Nicander *needes must die,*
Lucilla *doeth his wonted presence flie.*

How can I liue, that double death possesse,
How should I ioye, that drenched am in thrall:
What foode maie feede, or beare a pleasaunt taste,
Where as the harte, lies bathed still in gall,
If this be life, then life bee farre from me,
And welcome death, to set Nicander *free.*

What cause my deare, hath thy Nicander *wrought,*
That makes thee eshunne in whom thou shouldst delight:
What moues thy mynde to mewe thee vp so close,
And keepe thee from, thi beste beloued sight.
If I offended haue, then charge me when and how,
Nicander *shall hym cleare, or to thy mercie bowe.*

If no offence, but fonde conceipt hath taken holde,
Condempne hym not, that shewes his giltlesse hande:
Who hetherto hath neuer ment the thyng,
That iustly might against your honour stande.
If giltie I, I aske no other grace,
Giue dome of death, and doe my sute deface.

I saie no more, but as I doe deserue,
So shewe the fruite, of my deserued hire:
Seeme not so straunge, vnto thy faithfull frende,
Whose absence sets my scorchyng harte on fire.
But as my loue, to thee no tongue can tell,

Esteeme

Esteeme the like of me, and so farewell.

Thyne owne Nicander.

The yong gentlewoman who had fixed all her thoughtes, and setled all the contentmentes of her harte, onely vpon Nicander, neither desiryng any thyng in the worlde, so muche as to please and content hym: felte an intollerable perplexitie of minde, in that she sawe hym greeue thus, at her late straungenesse, and yet thought it better that he should complaine, then come by any knowledge of the loue, that Don Hercules did beare her, wherefore hidyng from hym the matter, replied in this sorte.

The birde whiche is restrainde,
Of former hartes delight:
I must confesse, twixt life and death,
Doeth alwaie combate fight.

So doeth the harte compelled,
By heste of parentes will:
Obaye for feare, yet forst by loue,
Continues constant still.

No absence by consent,
My deare Nicander *I:*
Haue wrought to worke thy wo, from thee,
Like Cressed *falce to flie.*

Ne shall I liue to lothe,
What maie content thy minde:
Hap life or death, as true as steele,
Thou shalt Lucilla *finde.*

Thy eares shall neuer heare,
Nor eyes shall neuer see:
That any wight shall reape the fruite,
Whiche planted was for thee.

Then frame thy self my deare,

To take against thy will:
Our absence in good part till tyme,
Maie better happe fulfill.

And there withall receiue,
This pledge to cure thy paine:
My harte is thyne, preserue it well,
Till we twoe meete againe.

Euer thyne Lucilla.

This sweete aunswere, mitigated not a little the moode of the yong gentleman, and so he framed him selfe the best he could to tollerate the absence of his Lucilla. On the other side Don Hercules, who in like maner founde hym self depriued, of the sight of that yong Ladie, whom he loued extremely, was very muche discontented, and perceiuyng that neither messages, nor faire offers, with large giftes sent vnto her, whereof neuer any were accepted, could once moue her to shewe her self courteous vnto hym, of so muche as a looke, and considering the pouertie, wherein her mother liued, now in her latter yeres, beganne to imagine that it would be muche easier for him, by offeryng her liberally where withall to Marrie her daughter, to perswade her to yeeld her into his handes, then to wynne the yong gentlewoman to his desires.

Wherefore hauyng sent a fit persone to Lucillas mother, to let her vnderstande, that if she would be cōtent, that the yong Prince might enioye her daughter, he would giue her suche a dowrie in recompence of his pleasure, that no Gentleman of what degree soeuer, should for her pouertie refuse to take her to wife: whereas if she refused that good offer, she should therby be constrained through necessitie, either to bestowe her vpō some Artificer or craftes man, or if she would needes Marrie her to a gentleman, she must giue her to some suche as was so poore, as that she should liue all the daies of her life in wāt and miserie. The whiche in effect would be nothyng els, but to bee cruell towardes her owne daughter, in barring that good hap whiche

whiche he did offer, besides the fauour that he should be able to shewe, in furtheryng her Mariage to bothe their endlesse comfortes. The mother beyng often sollicited, and summoned to this effecte: and on the one side punished with pouertie, and on the other charged with yeres, bothe whiche pressed her verie muche, after diuers discourses made to and fro with her self, lastly she saied. And where to ought I to haue regarde, but to the wealthe and profite of my daughter, whiche bothe she shall reape aboundauntly, if by the giuyng her self vnto this yong Prince, he doeth bestowe vpon her that dowrie, whiche he hath promised. And although in doyng thereof, there be some touch and spotte to my daughters honour and myne, yet shall it bee so recompensed with the benefite of her dowrie, that the profite will be greater then the harme. And if therein be any offence, the blame thereof is not to be imputed vnto me, but vnto my euill Fortune, that hath brought me into this miserable necessitie. Besides that my daughter beyng now alreadie eightene yeres of age, and of moste singular beautie, and my self alreadie so olde, that from daie to daie, I maie looke to goe to my graue, I might happen to dye, and leaue her without any gouernement, or ouersight, and she stirred with those appetites, where to yonge folkes are enclined, through the frailtie of her sexe, and the pouertie wherein I shall leaue her, be brought to yeelde her self vnto the handes of some suche one, as would not haue due regard vnto her calling, but bring her vnto the spoile.

And after these and suche like discourses, sondrie times had with her self: finally, she sent hym worde that if it would please hym, she would gladly speake with hym her self: whiche he hauyng vnderstoode, caused her to be brought one euenyng, into a place where thei twoo alone might talke, and there hauyng giuen her opportunitie to saie what she would, thus she began.

Sir, the weapons where with necessitie, and my pouertie hath assaulted me, haue been so sharpe and so pearcyng, that although I haue endeuored all the waies I could deuise, to resist and defende my self frō them, yet in th'ende I haue been forced to yeld, as vanquished and ouercome, and cōstrained to do that with my daughter, as to thinke of it onely I am so abashed,

that

that I dare not for shame lifte vp myne eyes, to beholde you. But for asmuche as no other thyng hath perswaded me thereunto, but the desire whiche I haue to get her a dowrie, wherewith I maie afterward bestowe her honestly, I beseche you to be content, to extende your liberalitie in suche sort, as she maie haue ẏ large dowrie, which it hath pleased you to promise me.

Thereof I assure you (saied the Prince) and larger to then hath been spoken of to you besides: And also I will minister suche releefe vnto you for your owne state, that you shall haue cause to giue me thankes for the same. Then replied the olde gentlewoman and saied: Since that you perceiue (sir) that no desire to make Marchaundize of my daughter, but extreame pouertie, whereunto my froward Fortune hath brought me, doeth driue me to this exigent. I doe likewise besech you, that you will come vnto my daughter, at suche tyme as I shall deuise moste conuenient, with as muche regard vnto her credite as maie be possible. I will therein be ruled wholie by you (answered the yong Prince) and looke in what sorte you will appoint me to come, so shall it be.

The firste thyng then sir (q she) that I thinke requisite, is that you come alone without any companie, when I shall assigne you the tyme, so that the thyng rest secret betweene you and me, and my daughter, and no occasion be giuen to publishe it, whereby my daughter might leese her good name.

This courteous yong Prince was there withall well content, and that beyng concluded and agreed vpon, she saied further, I knowe (sir) the honestie of my daughter to bee suche, that if I should open my lippes vnto her, of any suche matter, she would not onely reiecte any perswasion, that I might vse vnto her, but also ridde her self out of my house. And therefore leaste that should happen, and to the ende that you maie haue your desire, and she haue a dowrie, wherewith she maie be maried, if not withall the honour that the state and callyng, wherein she was borne doeth require, yet with the leaste harme that maie be possible, since my hard happe is suche, and that my pouertie doeth so constraine me: I haue determined to doe herein as you shall heare.

My

My daughter useth to lye in a lowe Chamber neare unto the streate doore of my house, in the whiche Chamber I my self in like sorte am wont to lye, whensoeuer we two remaine alone in the house, as often tymes we doe: and commonly I rising early in the mornyng about such businesse as I haue, doe leaue my daughter in bed, where she slepeth some tymes two howres or three after that I am gone. To morowe mornyng therefore will I rise and leaue her alone in that Chamber, and will set open the streate doore, so as you shall not neede but to pushe at it, and the chamber dore likewise. You shall come very early as we haue concluded all alone, and entryng into the Chamber, there shall you finde my daughter, and abide with her as long as it shall please your self. But I doe once againe (sir) beseche you as I haue doen before, that the matter maie passe secrete, and not to bee imparted to any other then to us three, to the ende, that where I suffer my self to be led through necessitie to doe that which I doe, and with an entent to place my daughter in mariage, by the meane of that dowrie whiche you doe giue her, the case beyng knowne, we reape not eternall shame and infamie.

At this deuise the yong Prince paused a while, thinking it straunge that he should goe to a yong maide, that not onely was unwillyng, but also not so muche as made priuie of his commyng, did what he could to refuse that meane, and to perswade the mother to deuise some better. But at the last seyng none other could be founde more fitte for the purpose, beyng pricked forwarde with the vehemencie of that appetite, whiche loue had stirred up in him, consideryng him self to be a Prince, and a gallant yong gentilman, and that he should be alone with his loue, thought that it should not be harde for hym to winne her to his will: and so content to doe as the olde gentilwoman had deuised. And beyng parted eache from other, he began to attende the commyng of the nexte mornyng and all that night, which seemed longer unto him then a hole yeare, he laie with his thoughtes and imaginations in the armes of his Lucilla. As sone as the daie began to peepe, Don Hercules all alone as he had promised to the mother, went to the house of his Ladie, and findyng the doores open accordyng to promise, entered into the Chamber wherein Lucilla laie, and hauyng barred the doore, approched nere the bedde wherein she laie.

It was in the Moneth of Julie, whiche season in that Countrie is extreame hotte: by reason whereof Lucilla tumblyng from one side of the bedde vnto the other, had rolled of all the clothes wherewith she had been couered: so as she had lefte her self all naked, and in that sorte he found her, with Coralles about her necke and her armes, whiche with the difference of their ruddie couler did sette out and beautifie greatly the excellent fairenesse of her white bodie. She laie a slepe vpon her backe, with her handes cast ouer her hedde, (as for the moste parte yong women are wont to dooe): so that forthwith the yong Prince discouered her frō toppe to toe: and consideryng with a greedie eye all her whole bodie, not onely he commended her to hym self so naked, as he had doen whilest she was apparailed, but also did so singularlie well like her in that state, that he thought he saw rather some diuine thing, or some Goddesse come doune from Heauen, to heape hym with happinesse, then a mortall creature: And beganne to allowe and commende his owne iudgemente, in that he had placed his loue vppon so excellente and rare a peece. And therewith bowyng doune hym self to giue her a kisse, and so to awaken her. Beholde she opened her eyes, whiche right well resembled twoo faire shinyng Starres. And where she was vsed to see none other bodie in that Chamber but her mother when she waked, now seyng this yong Prince standyng thus ouer her, and findyng her self in that sorte all naked, she gaue a greate skritche, and saied.

Out alas sir (for she knewe hym straight waie) what euill happe hath brought you hither at this tyme? And in so saiyng as one wonderfullie ashamed to bee seene in that plight, she wrapped about her one of the sheetes, and began with a loude voice to call her mother.

But perceiuing that her mother would not heare, and that she called in vaine, she began to imagine that she was consentyng vnto his commyng thether, and lamentyng with teares that

that

that trickled downe her cheekes, like droppes of dewe hanging vppon Roses, in a Maie mornyng, she saied: Alas now I see my mother also hath betraied me. Whiche thyng the yong Prince vnderstandyng, saied vnto her. Trouble not your self, nor greeue not (faire Damsell) at my commyng hether, but rather reioyce, that your singuler beautie, hath so enflamed me, as one in a maner forgettyng my estate, haue beene contented to come hether all alone, as a priuate manne to enioye your companie, if it will please you to accepte my good will, whiche though a thousande other Dames of this Citie, dooe wishe and would bee glad of, yet haue I deemed none of them worthie thereof but your self. And seeyng your mother, who hath that power ouer you, that in reason she ought to haue ouer her childe, and knoweth beste what is for your good and commoditie, doeth consent herevnto: you (in my iudgement) are not but to shewe your self in like sorte content. For in giuyng your self to me, you doe not abase or caste your self away vpon any vilde persone: but shewe your self courteous vnto a Prince, whom your beautie hath made thrall: and in whom you shall finde nothyng but gratefull courtesie, to your benefite and satisfaction.

And with these and other like wordes stretched forthe his hande towarde her breastes, that were like two little balles of Iuorie, and drawyng nere her to kisse her, she with her hande thrustyng hym modestly backe, saied thus.

Sir I beseche you, by the Princely nobilitie that is in you, and by that loue which you say you beare me, that it wil please you, not to force me, or to seeke at my hands any thing against my will: and that since my mother, who ought to haue beene the cheef defender of mine honestie, hath abandoned and forsaken me, you will yet of your courtesie vouchsafe, to giue me the hearyng of a fewe wordes, whiche the speciall care I haue of mine honour doeth force me to expresse.

The courteous yong Prince at this request, staied hym self proceadyng any further: and not beeyng desirous to haue her, but with her owne good will, stoode still to heare what it was that Lucilla would saie vnto hym: yet euer hoping, with faire meanes to winne her at the laſte. And ſhe weepyng verie tenderly, beganne to ſaie vnto hym in this ſorte.

I am verie ſorie (moſte noble Prince quod ſhe) that Fortune hath been ſo muche myne enemie, that ſhe hath made me a woman, farre vnworthie and vnmeete for you: For that you beyng ſo greate a Prince as you are, and I ſo meane a gentlewoman: I ſee ſo greate a ſpace and diſtaunce betweene your high eſtate, and my lowe degree, that betweene vs there can bee no portion, or conuenient equalitie: For the whiche cauſe (ſir) I conſideryng myne owne eſtate, and not myndyng to exceade my callyng, haue a good while ſince choſen Nicander to be my louer, who in reſpect of his bloud, though he bee richer then I, is no whitte nor more noblie borne then my ſelf am. By reaſon of whiche conformitie of bloud and birthe, our loue is likewiſe growne to bee equall, and equall the deſire in vs bothe, he to haue me to his wife, and I to haue hym for my houſbande. But the couetouſneſſe (let it be lawfull for me to ſaie ſo) of his father is ſuche, that although he knoweth me to be a gentilwoman borne, yet becauſe I am not of that wealth as to bryng hym ſo greate a dowrie, as his riches perchaunce require, he deſpiſeth me, and will not yeeld by any perſwaſion his good will and conſent, that wee maie matche together accordyng to our deſire. Neuertheleſſe (ſir) I conſideryng how feruently this yong Gentleman loueth me, and that alreadie we are in mynd vnited and knitte together, with conſent, faith and loue, doe yet beleeue aſſuredly, that GOD of his ſpeciall goodneſſe and fauour, will graunt vs his aſſured grace, that we maie one daie bee ioyned together in the holie ſtate of Matrimonie. Which thyng if it ſhould happen and come to paſſe, I not hauyng any thyng els to bryng with me for my dowrie but my virginitie, am determined and fully reſolued (by Gods help) to giue it vnto hym, as pure and vnſpotted as I brought it from my mothers wombe. And if my vnhappie chaūce and Fortune be ſuch, as that I can not haue Nicander to my houſbande, I haue concluded with my ſelf (by the grace of God) neuer to couple my ſelf to any man liuyng: but to giue and vowe me wholie vnto almightie GOD, and in his ſeruice to ſpende

my

my daies a virgine, in continual Fastyng and Praier. Therefore (moste excellent Prince) if Honestie, if Justice, if Religion, haue that power and force in your noble mynde, whiche in reason thei ought to haue, I doe beseche you, and for that loues sake that you saie you beare me, that you will preserue and kepe unstained my honestie, and that it would please you with the sounde discourse of reason, to temper that feruent appetite whiche hath brought you hether, to the preiudice and breache of my honestie and credit. In doyng whereof you shall shewe your self to be, in deede that noble Prince that the highnesse of your birthe and bloud doeth promise you should be, whereas if you should force and violate me a Uirgine, and a weake maiden without defence, there could thereof ensue nought els to me but dishonor and reproche, and withall small praise would it be unto your excellencie, when it shall be saied that you had ouercome a simple Damsel. And here being interrupted with sobbes and teares exceedyng for the greefe of her minde, casting doune her eyes for shame and sorow, she helde her peace, attending what her hap and the goodnesse of the Prince should dispose of her, in whose courtesie she had reposed all her hope and confidence.

This yong Prince understanding the honest desire of Lucilla, first praised her greatly to hymself for the chastnes of her minde, and beyng moued with the magnanimitie of his noble minde, though he were pricked with the sharpest darte of the blind boyes quiuer, and that his ardent appetite did still stirre hym to the accomplishment of his desire, yet conquering him self with reason, he turned all the loue whiche erst he bare unto this young Ladie, into compassion of her estate, and thus he saied unto her. The vertue and honestie of thy mynde faire Damsell doe require, that I should make no lesse accompt of thine honour, then if I were come hether to no other entent, then to defende it against any other that should goe aboute to staine or spot it. Therefore not onely thou needest not to feare any violence at my handes, but also maiest hope that I will not faile to further this thy chast purpose, so that thou maiest enioye that yong Gentleman whiche thou hast chosen for thy

 housband,

housbande, with all the honour and satisfaction that appertaineth to the honestie of thy minde. And therfore, since nothing els doeth let thee from the gettyng of him but the pouertie of thy state, whereunto thy frowarde Fortune hath vnworthily brought thee: I will my self supplie in that behalf, that wherein she hath failed, and correcte with my liberalitie, the iniurie that she hath doen thee. And hauyng so saied, he hymself opened the doore and called her mother, who had gotten her self into a Chamber, and there sate bewailyng the miserie of her state, whereby she had bin driuen in suche sorte to prepare a dowrie for her daughter.

She beyng come he saied vnto her. Gentlewoman, if erst I came hether as a louer vnto your daughter, now I will departe and leaue her as if I were her brother, leauyng her honour no lesse safe and vntouched then I founde it, for so deserueth her vertue that I should deale with her. And forasmuch, as I perceiue she is in loue with a yong Gentleman whom I well knowe, and is in my opinion very worthie of it, and that he in like sorte is in loue with her, and that onely the want of a reasonable dowrie is the cause that she cã not become his wife as she desireth. I am content to bestowe vpon her for her contentment, that summe for her dowrie whiche I had purposed to haue giuen her in recompence of my contentation, to the ende that this her honest desire maie haue that effecte, whiche is moste conuenient to so greate and well grounded an affection, and that her greate honestie and vertue doe deserue. Therfore sende you this daie vnto my Treasorer, and he shall forthwith disburse vnto you 2000. poundes, which shalbe the dowrie of this your gentle and honest daughter.

And turnyng hym self towarde the yong Gentlewoman, he said vnto her. And as for you faire Damsell (q he) I craue nothyng els now at your handes, but that you keepe this faith of yours, wherewith you are lincked vnto your louer inuiolate and vnspotted, euen as I doe leaue you inuiolate and vnspotted in your mothers handes. How greate the ioye of the mother was, when she sawe the honestie of her daughter (as it were) resaued out of this yong Princes handes, by the force of

her

her owne vertue, maie better be imagined then expressed with wordes. But aboue all ioyes, the ioye of Lucilla exceded all other: when she vnderstoode that through the magnificence and liberalitie of the noble yong Prince, she was to haue her Nicander for her housbande.

And tournyng her eyes full of modestie towardes him she saied, I could not (Sir) haue had any more certaine and infallible token of your loue towarde me, then that whiche now of your greate courtesie and bountie you haue shewed me: whiche I acknowledge to bee so greate, that I am bounde to yeeld your excellencie my moste humble and infinite thankes. But for asmuche as wordes doe faile me wherewith I might doe it, I must beseche you, that it maie reste in your discrete Iudgement, to consider how muche I confesse my self to bee your debter, when woordes dooe faile me, to yeeld you at the least thankes for so greate a benefite. This onely will I saie vnto your grace, that the remembraunce of so noble an acte shall neuer weare out of my minde: and that I will so long as I liue, praie vnto almightie GOD, so to preserue and maintaine your noble persone, as you of your goodnesse haue saued mine honestie: And so to graunt you the accomplishement of all your noble desires, as you haue offered me to make me cōtent of mine, by hauyng my Nicander to bee my housbande: Unto whom, aswell because I haue euer been so disposed, as for that it hath pleased your excellencie to commaunde me, I will alwaies keepe sounde and vnstained that faithe, whiche through your courtesie shall ioyne me to him in mariage.

The Damsell seemed vnto the Prince at that instaunt to bee in maner greater then she was in deede, when she once stoode assured of the saueguarde of her honestie: and delighting no lesse in the excellencie of her minde, then he had before doen in the beautie of her bodie, he departed from her.

And hauyng caused the two thousande pounde to be paied vnto her mother as he had promised: he went vnto the Duke his father, and tolde hym all that had passed betweene Lucilla and hym: the maner whereof liked so well the Duke, that he concluded with hym self, that all the vertues that euer had

been

been before that tyme in his progenitours, would bee moste excellently ioyned in hym.

This yong Prince required his father, to sende for Nicanders father, and to perswade hym to agree, that his soonne might matche with Lucilla since that she was prouided, and furnished with so reasonable a dowrie: which thyng the Duke did with a very good will, for that he knewe that if his sonne should haue taken in hande, to perswade the old manne to any suche matter, it might haue stirred some suspition in his head, why the Prince should so dooe: And hauyng sent for hym accordyngly, when he was come, the Duke after some familier speeches of course and curtesie, tolde hym he was desirous that his soonne Nicander should take Lucilla to be his wife, who aswell for her birthe, as for the rare giftes of her mynde, (as he had learned) was worthie to be wife to any great lorde. The old Gentleman aunswered, that although she had those vertues and giftes whiche he spake of, and were verie well borne, yet had she not any dowrie conuenient, or agreeable to his wealthe, wherby she might be true to bee matched with his sonne. Yes Marie said the Duke, for I my self because I would not haue so greate vertue as is in her, to bee oppressed by Fortunes spight, haue bestowed upon her twoo thousande pounde to serue for her dowrie.

The old manne hearyng of suche a somme, was very wel content to dooe as the Duke would haue hym, and the nexte daie through the liberalitie of the Prince, the mariage was concluded and knitte up, whiche had so long been delaied and hindered by the couetousnesse of the olde manne, and the pouertie of Lucilla, with the infinite ioye and contentment of the twoo yong louers, who had long wished and desired that happie daie.

What vertue, or what continence of Alexander, or of Scipio maie be compared to this? Scipio abstained from the yong Gentlewoman whiche was presented unto hym in Spaine, Alexander from Darius his daughter. But it was verie easie for either of theim so to dooe: Aswell because thei were in the furie of warre, and the soundes of Drummes and Trum-

pettes:

pētis: as for that those women were of a strange Nation, and enemies unto them, and neuer before that tyme seen of any of them, muche lesse desired. Whereas this yonge Prince, who euen bathyng as it were in blisse, liuyng at his ease and pleasure, in the flowre of his youthe, and in the heate of his amourous flames, had a yong gentlewoman of a rare beautie, not of straunge Nation, or any other wise to be hated, but extremely beloued, in his handes, and voluntarily yeelded, and committed unto hym by her owne Mother: and yet not onely tempered hym self, and refrained to defile her chast and honest bodie, but also bestowed liberally her dowrie uppon her, to the ende that an other might enioye her, and bee her housebande, whom she had chosen to loue and like of: did without all question farre exceade all humaine courtesie, in so Noble and so vertuous an acte. Whereby he made apparant, that although he were pricked forward, with the sharpe spurres of Loue, and his sensuall appetite, yet was he of that highnesse of courage, and of that constancie of minde, that he was able not onely to cōquere him self, but also to subdue the forces of loue, whereunto bothe mortall mennes valour doeth commōly yeeld, and the very power of the Goddes themselues (if we shal beleeue the Fables of the auncient writers) hath shewed it self often tymes inferiour.

And thus this honeste Damsell Lucilla, by the meanes of her Chastitie, the vertue and excellencie whereof, did winne and maister the harte of that yonge Prince, muche more then the perfection of her bodily beautie had dooen before, obtained the thyng she moste desired and ioyed in, whiche was to haue Nicander to her housebande. With whom she liued euer after in greate contentment and happinesse: still nourishyng with kinde and louyng demeanour eche to other, that feruent affection whiche from their first acquaintaunce, had taken full possession of bothe their liberties.

FINIS.

Of Fineo and Fiamma.

The argument of the iiij. Historie.

¶ The harde aduenture of Fineo, *with his beloued* Fiamma, *who after sondrie conflictes of Fortune, were in the ende solde as slaues to the Kyng of* Tunise, *who seyng their perfecte loue caused them to be Maried, and after honouryng theim with sondrie presentes, sent them home to* Sauona, *where by their Parentes and freendes, thei were ioyfully receiued.*

IN Genoua, one of the fairest and moste famous Cities of Italie, there was sometyme a yong gentlewoman of excellent beautie called Fiamma, that was in Loue with a yong Gentleman of Sauona (a Citie Subiecte vnto the State of Genoua, and distaunte from thence aboute thirtie miles) whose name was Fineo, and their Loue beyng mutuall, and tendyng to no other ende, then to be linked and ioyned together by Marriage, thei would not long haue staied, to bryng their honest desires to a good ende and conclusion, had not the Father of the gentlewoman refused his consente, and shewed hym self contrary to this their loue and good will. For he misliking with the matche, either for that he purposed to place her better, or because he would not haue her married to any man, that should carry her out of Genoua, did ofte tymes chide and reprehende his daughter, for castyng her affection vppon that yong Gentleman, that was a straunger vnto theim, and in effecte but a subiecte, though he were bothe of bloud and riches equall vnto them.

But for all that the father could doe, or any other of her frendes,

des, the fire whiche loue had kindled in this yong couples breastes, slaked no whit at all, but still encreased, bothe hopyng in the ende, to winne her freendes good will, and attaine the fruites of their desired loue. This yong damsell had to her brother a stout and valiant yong gẽtleman, who being offended greatly, that Fineo should continue his loue towarde his sister, and followe the pursute of that, whiche he knewe well enough her freendes were vnwillyng to yeeld vnto: had caused hym to bee spoken vnto, and to bee warned that he should desiste and leaue to sollicite her: but he for all that ceased not, but continued his suite. Wherfore this brother of hers determined, to make him leaue of, by force and dint of sworde. For although there were at that tyme a very straight lawe in the Citie, that no manne should weare his sworde, and paine of death appointed for him that should hurte any man with any weapon: Yet bothe these gentlemen weare their swordes, for that thei bothe had charge of souldiers, that laye then in garrison for defence of the Citie.

And hauyng one daie mette Fineo in the streate alone, and hymself beyng very well accompanied with other gentlemen, he beganne to giue hym euill language: And beeyng a gentleman of greate courage, and though he were a stranger there, not beyng able to endure to be iniured in wordes, saied to him boldely and roundely againe, that if thei twoo were alone, he durst not vse those speeches vnto hym, for he would well giue hym to vnderstande, that he was no man to take wrong at his handes, and that tyme and occasion would serue one daie (he doubted not to make hym knowe that he had offended one that would beare no Coales. Wherevppon his aduersarie hauyng drawne forthe his sworde, whilest he was yet speakyng, ran feercely vpon hym, thinkyng to haue striken hym: But Fineo also a verie lustie gentleman and quicke of eye, and nimble of hande, drewe out his sworde, and not onely warded the blowe of his enemie, but also hurte hym, though but lightly in the hand. Forthwith thei that were with the yong gentlewomans brother, enuironed hym, and tooke hym prisoner, and deliuered hym into the handes of the Magistrate, or cheef Officer of the citie. And the penaltie being suche, as is before mentioned, for hurtyng of any man within the Citie, and especially a gentleman, Fineo was condemned to lose his heade.

Neuerthelesse, he beyng verie well freended, and supported by many principall gentlemen of the citie, thei laboured so muche for hym, that thei obteined that he should not be beheded: But that his penaltie should bee conuerted vnto an other punishement, verie little better if it were no worse. For hauyng bounde hym faste hande and foote, thei laied hym in a small boate, and in verie stormie weather, set him in the maine sea, and there left him to the rule and gouernment of Fortune, and to the disposition of GOD, and mercie of the waues and windes. The boate was a long while beaten and tossed, by the rage and furie of the Seas, and poore Fineo vnder diuerse and sondrie stormes and shapes, had before his eyes a thousande tymes the presence of Death. Yet in that fearfull and mortall perill, he ceased not to call vppon the name of his deare Fiamma and in that extremitie and imminent daunger, did he yet in maner glorifie hym self, and thinke hym self happie, that he should ende his life for the loue of his Ladie.

Whiles he was thus tossed and tormented, still lookyng for none other but present death, the Tempest began to cease, and the storme and rage of Seas to bee asswaged. When loe he discouered a Fregate of Moores that went a roauyng, and were then newe gone abrode, to spie whether the storme which was then past, had not happely prepared for theim, some occasion of gaine and bootie. These Moores had no soner discouered this little Boate, thus fleetyng at all auentures, but hopyng to finde therein some prey for their profite, thei made towarde it: And hauyng at the bordyng thereof, founde Fineo bounde hande and foote, and perceiuyng by his countenaunce and apparell, that he was no very base person, thei vntied him, and sette hym in their Fregate as a slaue to rowe, vntill suche tyme as thei should determine further what to doe with hym: who although that seruitude and captiuitie were greeuous vnto hym, yet consideryng with hym self, that it was better for hym to be in the power of men, though thei were Infidels, then in the power of Seas and windes: he comforted hymself, that

that yet if he liued, he might still hope through the goodnesse of GOD, one daie to be so happie, as to enioye his Ladie and Loue: He framed hym self to beare with pacient minde, that heauie yoke of his captiuitie.

Fiamma hauyng vnderstoode the vnfortunate accidente happened to her Louer, beleeuyng certainly that he was dead, and that she should neuer see hym againe. Wherefore she her self resoluyng that she would no longer liue, gaue her self to deuise what kinde of death she were best to chuse, and in doubt thereof she passed some fewe daies, dissemblyng still in the house her sorowe and greef, with a merie and chearfull countenance, as though she had cleane forgotten, and not once remembred her louer Fineo. But in the ende, after long debatyng with her self, she resolued to dye the same kinde of death, and to make that ende, whiche she imagined Fineo had doen.

There was an other gentleman of the Citie, who was no lesse enamoured of this gentlewoman, then Fineo was: Who supposyng that now since she sawe there was no remedie, for her to recouer her louer, whom bothe she and all the Citie accompted certainly to be dedde: he might perchaunce by sute obtaine her good will, and so procure her to bee his wife, with the consente of her freendes. And therefore not long after the mischaunce of Fineo, he caused her father to bee dealt withall for the bestowyng of his daughter vpon hym: And the Father beyng willing enough to agree thereunto, and hauing questioned with his daughter thereupon, and findyng her to giue sober and obedient aunswere with fewe wordes, presupposyng that she was willyng to doe as he would haue her, made promise of her vnto this yong gentleman, and agreed vppon the dowrie, and all other circumstaunces necessarie, for the couplyng of twoo suche persones together.

The night that went before the daie appoincted for their Marriage. Fiamma callyng vnto her a Moore that was slaue in her Fathers house, and had the keepyng of a small Boate of the gentlemans, wherein when he liste to disport hym self, he was wont to take the aire vpon the sea, in tyme of faire weather, and to goe to their houses of pleasure, wherof that coaste is verie plentifull, and theim of exceadyng beautie. Whiche Moore had lived so many yeres in that thraldome, that he was now become so olde as she thought, she needed not to feare any force or violence at his handes, she beganne to perswade hym, to put on a desire to deliuer hymself out of Captiuitie, so as he might liue the reste of his yeares in libertie and at his ease: whereunto findyng hym readie and willyng, if the meanes or occasion were offered him, she gaue hym in hand a good round somme of money, which she had laied together, and made him promise to carrie her into the sea in the Boate, whereof he had the custodie, and afterwardes to doe that whatsoeuer it were, that she should commaunde hym.

This wicked and faithlesse Moore, seyng hymself not onely to purchase his libertie, but also make so greate a gaine of readie money, that he was not like at any tyme after, to liue in wante or pouertie, was onely thankefull in his mynde towarde the yonge Gentlewoman, but straight waie beganne to purpose and to deuise, to make a greater gaine of her owne persone, by carriyng her unto the Kyng of Tunise, and sellyng of her unto hym at a verie high prise. And with this entention, the mischeeuous knaue assured her, that he would doe in all pointes, as she would haue hym. Wherefore when all the reste of the house were in their firste sleape, the Damsell with this wretched Moore, went out of her fathers house, & gat her into the boate, and the weather beyng verie faire, the knaue began to rowe and make saile along the coast, towarde Ligorno from whiche by breake of the daie, thei were not verie farre. When this yong gentlewoman, sawe that she was now so far from home, that she needed not to feare to bee driuen backe againe to Genoua, she willed the Moore to rowe to the shore & to lande himself, and then to shoue of the boate againe: for that her determination was so to dye, swallowed up with the waues of the sea, as she supposed her Fineo to haue bien. But the wicked knaue, who had a farther fetche in his hed and thoughtes farre differed from the Gentlewomans, made her beleeue that thei were yet nere unto Genoua and aduised her to bee content, that thei might goe somewhat farther, to the ende that

her

her father if he sent after them, might not ouertake them.

Neverthelesse, she hauyng often tymes vrged hym to doe as she erste bad hym, and he still protracted the tyme, and shifting her offe with one tale or an other: she began to suspect his drift. The mornyng therefore beeyng well spent, she made as though she would haue looked ouer the Boate side, into the water, or haue washed her handes in the Sea, and on the sodaine would haue caste her self ouer boarde. But the craftie Moore suspectyng her entent, caught holde of her aboute the middle, and not onely held her from throwyng her self into the Sea, but also bounde her faste hande and foote, and whereas she of her curtesie had bothe set hym at libertie, and liberallie bestowed good store of wealth vpon hym, he as a treacherous Infidell bereued her of her libertie, makyng her an vnfortunate slaue vnder his disposition, and beyng moued with a greedie couetous mynde, thought that too little whiche she had giuen him, and therefore determined (as is afore saied) to sell her persone, and to encrease his goodes by that meanes.

The desolate Damsell, when she sawe her self so vsed by that villaine, full of woe and greef, ceased not to rebuke the vilde Caitiue, that little regarded her speeches, the breache of his faithe and promise, and blamyng her self for trustyng of hym, and then repented when it was too late, that she had not obeyed her Father, and followed the aduise of her frendes, she began to curse her Destinie and her cruell Fortune, and to crie out vppon the Heauens, that had made her become the vnfortunatest yong woman that euer loued man.

And whilest she was thus lamentyng her hard happe, and the Moore as faste as he could with his Owres labouryng to speede his voiage: A little Foiste or Galley of Moores, that were prollyng vp and doune the Coaste, hauyng espied the small Boate, drewe nere vnto it, and boorded it. And hauyng founde this yong gentlewoman beeyng bounde therein, thei would haue taken her awaie: but the old knaue offeryng to resiste them, and to keepe her out of their handes, thei tooke her awaie from hym perforce, and woundyng hym very sore. And asked of her in their language, from whence she came, and what she

she was: But she not vnderstandyng theim, could make theim no aunswere, but onely with teares and weepyng, make them to vnderstande, that she was a wofull and vnfortunate Damsell. But the olde Moore feelyng hym self wounded to death, before he died tolde theim, bothe of what place and parentage she was, and laied before them by plaine reason, how greate a bootie thei might accoumpte thei had made that Mornyng, if thei did carrie her vnto the kyng of Tunise (as he had thought to haue doen) and sell her vnto hym. He beyng dedde, thei dispoiled hym, and tooke from hym all that, whiche Fiamma had giuen, and so he hauyng thought by treacherie, and breakyng of his faithe, to make greate gaine, loste bothe his life and all that, whiche he had gotten of the vnaduised, and euill counselled yong gentlewoman. And hauyng placed her in their Foist, and comforted her aswell as thei could, thei tooke their waie straight toward Tunise.

It fortuned that the other Fregate of Moores, that had founde and taken Fineo (as is alreadie saied before) met with this other Foiste or Gallie, wherein Fiamma was, and assaulted it, and hauyng fought together a good while (for that the other resisted, and defended them selues stoutly) in fine, the Fregate wherin Finio was (who in the encounter and duryng the fight, had shewed greate valour emong the reste) ouercame the other, and tooke from them all that thei had: so that Fiamma and Fineo were bothe now together, in the compasse of one smal vessell. And although in that extremitie of bothe their euill fortunes, it was a greate comfort for these twoo Louers to see one the other, and that bothe longed and desired extremely, to embrace eche other, and to tell the one to the other their accidentes, and vnfortunate aduentures. Neuerthelesse Fineo made signes to Fiamma, that in nowise she should take knowledge, or acquaintaunce of hym, and accordyngly she dissembled and made no shewe, but as one had neuer seen hym.

Fineo for the valour and courage, whiche he had shewed in the battaile, was deliuered of his chaines, and muche made of emong the Moores, vntill suche tyme as thei had conducted bothe hym and her (as thei did verie shortly after) vnto the

kyng

kyng of Tunise. Who hauyng seen and considered Fineo, and understoode by the Pirates, that his comelie personage was accompanied with greate valour, brought him, and tooke him to his service in good place nere his owne persone. And beyng moued with the beautie of the yong Gentilwoman, bargained for her likewise, for a greate somme of money, and caused her to be put in the Cube, whiche is a place where he keepeth his Concubines (as the Turke doeth his in his Serraglio) emong a greate many of other women, and esteemed her verie much for that the Rouers (who had learned of those other that thei ouercame) all that whiche the olde Moore had declared unto them, of her callyng and condition, did assure him that she was a Gentlewoman, borne of a noble familie in Genoua.

Fineo by his service and discret behauiour, became in short tyme verie deare unto the Kyng, so that in lesse then the space of one whole yeare, the Kyng of speciall trust gaue hym the charge of the gate of the Cube, whiche office the Kynges of Tunise are neuer wont to giue, but unto suche as are in singular fauour aboute them: In the whiche Fineo to his greate contentment, had the commoditie daiely to see his Fiamma, and she had no lesse comforte and satisfaction to beholde and looke upon hym, whiche oportunitie thei enioyed and handeled so discreetly, that thei neuer gaue any cause of suspition to any persone of their feruent good will and affection.

The manner and custome of the Kyng was, to cause his women to come unto him, and to lie with them by order, as thei had been bought or come to his handes: By reason of whiche custome, for that there were very many bought before the commyng thether of Fiamma, there was alreadie a whole yeare and a halfe welnie paste after her sale, and yet her turne was not come to be called for. But remainyng now but three others to be brought unto the kyng before her, Fineo consideryng to his intollerable greefe, that she was ere it were long to be likewise called for, beganne to be tormented with incredible passion and anguishe of mynde: and his woe encreased tenne thousand folde, by feare and imagination whiche he conceiued, that she being aboue all the Kynges Concubines farre the fairest, when he had once enioyed her, he would take her to be one of his wiues, whiche feare did no whitte lesse torment and afflicte Fiamma, then it did her Louer.

Whilest bothe these yong Louers liued in this sorte, there chaunced to arriue at Tunise a Shippe of Sauona, with certaine Marchauntes of that Citie: who seeyng Fineo there and knowyng hym, were wonderfully amarueiled findyng hym aliue, for that he had been lamented at Sauona of all his freendes for dedde. Fineo likewise knowyng those Marchauntes, and hauyng auctoritie and meanes to pleasure them in the Court, welcomed them, and made muche of them in freendly sorte: and demaundyng of the state and welfare of his father and brother and other fre͂des, thei certified hym that thei were all well, and that when thei should vnderstande that he was aliue and in so good a case, thei would be very ioyfull, and think them selues happie if thei might hope to see hym once come againe, as thei doubted not but one daie he would and might.

These Marchantes hauyng dispatched their businesse departed thence, and by theim Fineo wrote letters to his father, and to his brother, certifiyng them of his beyng in Tunise, and how that Fiamma was with hym, and that he desired to deliuer hym self out of bondage, and her with hym: whiche thyng he thought he might easily bryng to passe, if his brother would come thither, and with all describe vnto them a plot, whiche he had cast for the execution of his entent and desire.

Thei beyng returned safe vn[illegible] Sauona, deliuered [illegible]ters vnto the father and brother of Fineo, who with the r[illegible] of his freendes, and in effecte all the whole Citie, were ve[illegible] glad that his Fortune had not bee[illegible] altogether so froward t[illegible]ward hym, as thei had supposed.

And his brother accordyng to his instructions, prepared a verie pretie Fregat, verie well appointed and furnished with Marchaundize, emong whiche there were many trifles, and thynges of price meete for Ladies and Gentlewomen, And beyng arriued therewith at Tunise, Fineo brought them vnto the kyng, whom thei presented with some thynges of small price, whiche were very gratefull and acceptable vnto

him,

hym, and emong other speeches thei saied, that thei had abord many pretie thynges for Dames and Ladies, whiche thyng the kyng vnderstandyng, cōmaunded Fineo that the chefest of them might be brought into the Cube, to shewe suche thinges as thei had vnto his Concubines: By whiche occasion he gatte that oportunitie whiche he looked for, to conferre and deale more priuatly with thē without suspition, and to giue the better order for the accomplishment of asmuch as he had deuised.

Fineo and his brother therfore beyng come into the Cube, shewed forthe emong those women, suche wares as they had brought to please their fancies, and gaue vnto theim all some one trifle or an other, as a gentle present to the firste, and the brother of Fineo presented Fiamma emong the reste, with a very faire Purse richely embrodered with golde and Pearle, in the whiche there was enclosed a letter, written by Fineo, by the contentes whereof she might vnderstande at large, al that whiche he did wishe and would haue her to doe, to make their escape together, and to ridde them selues out of that thraldome and captiuitie. Assone as the twoo brethren had doen that thei came for and were departed, Fiamma by their maner gatheryng, that the gift of that purse conteined some misterie, withdrewe her self into a secrete place, and hauyng opened it, she founde therein the letter, whiche when she had redde, she thanked almightie God, that of his goodnesse had shewed her the waie to deliuer her self out of captiuitie, and from becomming dishonestly the Concubine of an Infidell kyng.

And when this appointed daie for the performing of their purpose was come: Fiamma in the night when all was silent, and others slept, came to a windowe barred with Iron, where Fineo and his brother were attendyng for her: who with certaine Instrumentes which thei had brought for that purpose, brake and wrested the grate of the window, and takyng her awaie with them, thei gotte her into their Barque, and hoissed saile, and directed their course with a merie winde toward the coaste of Italie, whiche serued theim verie faire all that night long, and the moste parte of the nexte daie. In the mornyng Fiamma beyng missed and Fineo likewise, the kyng (was aduertised of their eskape) who perceiuyng the Marchauntes to be gone also, rested assured that it was a sette match made for the stealyng of Fiamma awaie. And beyng full of rage and despight towardes them all, he caused certaine Galleis and other light vesselles to be armed in all haste, and to be sent after thē, giuyng straight charge and commissiō to his Captaines, that either thei should bryng Fineo and the Damsell, with the cheef of the Marchauntes aliue vnto hym, because he would cause them all three to be buried aliue: Or that if thei could not get thē aliue, thei should bring their three heddes for that he would haue them be set ouer the Gate, for an example and a terrour to all others.

But before those Galleis and other vesselles could bee in a readinesse to departe, Fortune not hauyng yet her fill of persecutyng and afflictyng these two poore Louers, caused a contrarie winde, with an extreame storme and tempest to arise, by force whereof the vessell wherein thei were, was not without greate daunger driuen backe againe to Tunise, with so muche greefe and sorrowe of all them that were in it, as they maie imagine that knowe the crueltie and barbarousnesse of that people. But in the beginnyng of the storme, the brother of Fineo dispairyng of his life, as he that was assured either to be drouned by rage of the winde and Seas, or els to die in torment if he retourned into the handes of those Infidels, gat him self into his Cockboate, and therein hazarded his life: and after muche adoe, and a thousande perilles of present death, recouered the coaste of Italie at the last, and retourned home to Sauona full of woe, with heauie tidynges declaryng vnto his father, that either the Fregate would be lost, or els driuen backe againe to Tunise, where he was well assured that bothe his brother and the yong Damsell his Louer, should bee murthered in moste cruell maner.

At whiche dolefull newes, the father, as if he had seene his sonne lye dedde before hym, beganne to weepe and lamente, complainyng of his harde Destinie that caused hym to liue so long, or reserued hym to see those cruell and bitter daies.

Fineo seeyng hym self brought to so harde an exigent, for that

that their vessell was now driuen backe nere vnto Tunise, and knowyng that he should feele the smarte of his faulte, and the kynges anger in sharpest maner and sorte: beyng determined to liue no longer, & to preuent the crueltie of the kyng drewe out his sworde, and would therewith haue stroken hym self to death. But Fiamma catchyng hym by the arme: Alas Fineo (q she) what shall become of me if you bee dead? Shall I remaine behinde to endure the cruell tormentes, that I knowe this Infidell hath prepared for me? Yet rather since that death must needes deliuer vs of our misfortunes, before you execute vppon your self this your determination, ridde me out of the worlde, and deliuer me from the paines, whiche alreadie I feele in my imagination, wherewith I assure my self thei will bryng me to a shamefull death. And with these wordes offeryng her breast vnto him, she requested him to strike her with his sworde. But Fineo bad her bee of good comforte, for your beautie (my Fiamma said he) beeyng so singular as it is, I knowe will saue you, and therefore you neede not feare, and I alone should bee the manne that thei would plague, and torment to death for vs bothe, and therefore (my deare) suffer me to dye before, and content thy self to liue, and vouchsafe sometyme to remember thy vnfortunate Fineo when he is dedde.

Whilest thei were thus talkyng and debatyng whiche should firste dye, the people whiche the Kyng had sent out to apprehende them, came and bourded their Fregate, and tooke them bothe, whom thei bound in chaines, and brought on land to the presence of the king. Who assone as he beheld the beautie of Fiamma, felte his former wrathe and crueltie entended to relent, and in muche milder maner then the two Captiues hoped or looked for, he saied vnto her: Tell me what moued you, I praie you faire Damsell to runne awaie, and flie from me, at whose handes you had no cause to looke for any other entreatie, then louyng and freendlie? Fiamma who in that yere and a half that she had been in the Cube, had learned the language indifferently well, made aunswere vnto hym. That no cause or meanyng to flee from hym, but her earnest desire to enioye Fineo, whom she had loued and chosen for her hous-hande many yeares before, had forced her to doe that whiche she had doen: And herewith she told him the beginning of their acquaintaunce and loue, and how many perilles and daungers thei had run through, still hopyng one daie to come vnto that happie houre, wherein their troubles should haue an ende, and that thei might bee honestlie vnited and enioye one an other: And finallie, castyng her self doune at his feete, with aboundaunce of teares, she besought hym with all humilitie to pardone her, if she had offended him, and withal to forgiue Fineo, since that long and faithful loue, had made them to procure the accomplishement of their desires.

The teares of Fiamma and the onelie name of Loue were of suche force and vertue in the harte of the kyng, though he were barbarous and cruell of Nature, that the Ire and hatred whiche he had conceiued against thē before, was then conuerted and changed into pitie and cōpassion of their misfortunes, and where before he had appoincted a cruell death to bee their punishments, he now determined to ouercome with his courtesie, the frowardnesse of their peruerse Fortune: and to make them, after so many perilles and dangers contented and happie, and to see an end at last of their miseries, by making them to enioye their long hoped for desires. Wherfore hauyng caused them to bee bothe forthwith vnbounde, he tooke from his owne finger a merueilous faire and precious Rubie, and giuing it vnto Fineo, he saied vnto him: since your Fortune hath bin suche that after so many strange aduentures, and through suche daungers you are fallen into my handes, I for my parte will not be he that will extinguishe, or quenche the flames of so feruent and constaunte Loue, or vnloose or dissolue the bandes where with your hartes bee bounde and knitte together. And therefore Fineo, I doe not onely pardon you bothe, but also I will haue thee before thou departe hence to wedde this Damsell with this ryng, and to take her for thy wife, and that she henceforth enioye thee for euer as her housbande, it is not to be demaunded whether the two louers, (who looked for none other of the kynges courtesies then death) were glad to heare hym vse those speeches yea or no. But bothe beeyng fallen on

their

their knees, and in humbleſt maner hauing yeelded their thankes vnto his Maieſtie. Fineo in his preſence wedded Fiamma and tooke her for his wife, to the vnſpeakable ioye and contentation of bothe their hartes and myndes. And the Kyng to honour their mariage, cauſed a ſumptuous feaſte to be prepared with no leſſe charge and aboundaunce of all thinges, then if he had married a daughter of his owne to ſome greate Lorde or chiefe man of that Countrey.

And after certaine daies, the two yong maried louers beyng deſirous to retourne into their owne Countrey, he gaue them very riche and coſtly preſentes, and ſent them honourably accompanied home to Sauona: whoſe ariuall was no leſſe marueilous then ioyful to the father and brother of Fineo, and to all the Citie, thei hauyng been aſſuredly eſteemed and accompted as deade. Afterwards thei ſent to Genoua to Fiammas father and brother, certifiyng of al that had happened, who then perſwading them ſelues that God and Nature had created thoſe two yong folke, to bee matched and ioyned together in Wedlocke, were well contented with that whiche thei ſaw was Gods will ſhould be. And beeyng gone both to Sauona, the father embraced and accepted Fineo for his ſonne in lawe, and the brother for his brother in lawe. And the two yong Louers liued euer after in greate happeneſſe and felicitie, giuyng by this ſucceſſe of their harde Fortune, an aſſured argument and a notable example, whereby we maie learne, that though froward Fortune doe for a while, croſſe and moleſt the deſires and trauailes of men, yet in the ende ſhe can not let, but that of neceſſitie thoſe thinges muſt come to paſſe, whiche GOD by his diuine prouidence wherewith he ruleth the whole world, hath appointed ſhal take effecte.

FINIS.

¶*The*

Of two Bretheren
and their wiues.

The argument of the fift Historie.

¶ *Two brothers making choyse of their wiues, the one chouse for beautie, the other for riches, it happened vnto them after thei were married, the one of their wiues proued to bee of light disposition, the other a common scolde, in what maner thei liued with their housbandes, and how in the ende the first became to liue orderly and well, but the other could be brought by no deuise, to any reason or good maner.*

Gentlewomen, before I will proceede any farther in this Historie, I must desire you to arme your selues with patience in readyng hereof, that if you finde any thing that might breede offence to your modeste myndes, take it in this sorte, that I haue written it onely to make you merrie, and not to sette you a snarryng or grudgyng against me, for although I meane to present you with a Chapter of knauerie, yet it shall be passable, and suche as you maie very well permit, and the matter that I minde to wright is vpon this question, whither a man were better to bee maried to a wise Harlot, or to a foolishe ouerthwart and brauling woman, this question I know will seeme very doubtful vnto some, and yet in my opinion very easie to bee aunswered, and to speake my mynde without dissimulation of bothe those euilles, I thinke the first is least, and therfore is to be chosen, and herein I could alledge for my better proofe, an example of the auncient Romaines, who in all their gouernmentes were moste wise & politique, amongst

whom

whom the infirmite of the firste was borne withall, because it proceaded of the frailtie of the fleshe, but the outrage of the second was euer condemned, for that it did abounde frō a wicked and mischeuous mynde. And in common reason, it is not lesse noisome for a man, to liue accompanied with a wife, who although she will some tyme flie out, can so wisely dissemble with her housebande, that he shall neuer so muche as suspecte her, whereby he shall receiue no discontentment in his minde, then to be bedfellowe with Xantippa a cōmon scold, who dailye and hourely will be checkyng, tauntyng, and railyng at him, in suche sorte, that he shall thinke hym self moste blest and happie, when he is farthest from her companie, but for your better confirmation, I haue set forthe this historie of twoo brethren, the one of them married to a wenche, that could so cunnynglie behaue her self towardes hym, that he had thought she had beleued there had been no other God but himself, and yet by your leaue, she would take reason when it was proffered her, but what of that: the harte neuer greeues, what the eyes see not. The other was married to a dame, that from her nauill dounewarde was more chast and continent, but otherwise of her tong suche a deuill of helle, that the poore man her housebande could neuer enioye merrie daie nor houre, although he deuised many a prettie remedie, as by the readyng of the processe of this tale you shall better perceiue, whiche followeth in this sorte.

There was somtime remainyng in a famous Citie twoo brethren, the eldest (accordyng to the custome of the place) enioyed his fathers goodes and possessions after his death, whereby he was well able to liue, the yongest had neither landes nor liuynges, sauyng that his Father had trained hym vp in learnyng, whereby he was able to gouerne hymself, in all maner of companies where soeuer he became. These twoo brethren beyng wearie of their single liues, disposed them selues to mariage: The eldest beeyng of hymself well able to liue, sought a wife onely for her beautie, without any other respect either to her conditions or riches, and as the Prouerbe is (he that sekes shall finde) so in the ende he lighted on a Gentlewoman, called by the name of Mistres Dorithe, whose beautie in deede was verie excellent, and there withall had a passyng readie witte, Marie her trainyng vp had not been after the beste, nor worst maner, but as a man might saie, after the common sorte: this gentlewoman he Married, who could so well handle hym with kissynges, cullynges, and other amarous exercises, that her housebande thought hymself, the moste fortunate manne that liued, to light on suche a wife, although she cunnyngly armed his hedde with hornes, as after you shall heare.

The second brother left (as you haue heard) without maintenaunce or liuyng, sought for a wife onely to releue his want, and fortuned to hit of a widowe in deede with greate wealthe, but in conditions so ouerthwart, and so spitefull of her tongue, that the poore man had not been Married fullie out a moneth, but he more then a thousande tymes, cursed the priest that maried hym, the Sexten that opened the Churche doore when he went to bee married, yea, and his owne vnhappie legges that had carried his bodie to bee yoked to so greate a mischeef. But because I doe minde more orderly to tell you the maners of these twoo gentlewomen: I will firste beginne with Mistres Doritie, whose housebande after thei had been a while maried, fortuned to fall sicke, and then accordyng to that Countrey maner, a Doctor of Phisicke was presently sent for, who commyng many tymes to visite his pacient, began to beholde and contemplate the liuely beautie of this gentlewoman, and lent her many rowlyng looke, and secrete countenaunces, in suche sorte that Mistres Doritie beyng well practised in the Arte of Loue, and seyng Maister Doctor to be a man as sufficient, to content a gentlewoman in her Chamber that was whole, as to minister Medicines to those that were sicke, did not onely requite hym againe with looke for looke, but she yelded hym a large vsurie, and paied him more then fourtie in the hundred, Master Doctor who was likewise skilfull enough, could well perceiue whereto those lookes did tende: Upon a tyme beyng alone in her companie, he saied vnto her as followeth.

Mistres Doritie, if the experience whiche I haue learned in Phisickes arte, might craue credite, and make my tale to bee the better beleeued, assure your self then that I minde to saie

saie nothyng, but that that shall bee to your owne behoofe, and the reason that makes me to enter into this discourse, is the pitie that I take to see so proper a gentlewoman as your self, should bee so deceiued in a housebande, who although you shall finde hym bothe honeste, gentle, and louyng, yea, and peraduenture maie contente you with suche rightes, as appertaine to the Marriage bedde, yet assure your self he shall neuer be able to get you with child, consideryng your Natures and complexitions be so farre different the one from the other, whereby you are like for euer to remaine without issue; and one of the greateste comfortes that maie happen vnto vs in this worlde, is to see our selues as it were regenerate and borne a newe in our children, and barrenesse in the auncient tyme, hath been accompted not onely infamous, but also moste hatefull emongst women, in so muche that Sara gaue her owne handmaide to her houseband, because she could not her self conceiue a child: but I would wishe women more witte then to followe Saras example. God defende thei should be so foolishe to giue their Maidens to their Housebandes, I woud wishe them rather them selues to take their menne, it hath been euer holden for the greater wisedome, rather to take then to giue, and sure thei shal finde it more for their owne profites, that if their housbandes want be suche, that he is not able to get a child, to take helpe of some other, that maie supplie his imperfections, but I truste I shall not neede to vse many perswasions, consideryng that euery wise woman will thinke, that I haue reason on my side: Thus Mistres Doritie, you haue heard the somme of my tale, protestyng, that if my seruice maie any waies stād you in steade, I am as readie to obeye, as he ouer whom you haue power to commaunde.

Mistres Doritie, who all this while had well pondered his woordes, knewe verie well how to whet Maister Doctor on, and the more to set his teeth on edge, aunswered hym thus: I perceiue Maister Doctor you are something pleasantly disposed, and hereafter when I shall finde my housbandes infirmitie to be suche as you haue saied, I meane to sende for you, desiryng you, that you would not be out of the waie, to helpe me when I haue neede.

The Doctour knewe not well how to vnderstande these wordes, whether thei were merily spoken, or otherwise in disdaine of his former talke, aunswered thus. Alas Mistres Doritie, pardon me if my woordes seeme any thyng offensiue vnto you, assuryng you that in this meane space, that I haue made my recourse to your housebande, (whose healthe by the sufferance of God, I haue now well restored) am my self falne into a Feuer so extreame, as neither Galen, Hypocrates, Auicen, Plinij, nor any other that euer gaue rules of Phisicke, could yet prescribe a Medicine for the malladie, or diet to suppresse the humour that feedes it: I shall not neede to vse longe circumstaunce in the matter, knowyng your wisedome to bee suche, that you can well conceiue the somme of all my greef, it is your beautie that is like to breede my bane, and hath alreadie driuen me into the greatest depth of daunger, vnlesse some plaintes of pitie maie preuaile, to yeelde remorse to hym, that vowes hymself to doe you seruice duryng life.

Mistres Doritie seyng the matter sorted out as she looked for, could tell well enough how to handle maister Doctor, and to make hym the more eger, she delaied hym of with doubtfull speeches, but yet fedde hym still with suche entisyng and pleasaunt countenaunces, that ministered greate hope of comfort to his desease, she aunswered thus.

And could you then finde in your harte (Maister Doctor) to deceiue your very freend of his deare and louyng wife, how can you offer hym so manifest an iniurie, to whom you are so lately linckt in so greate a league of freendship, as is betweene my housebande and your self, I can not thinke maister Doctor, that it is good will that hath caused you to moue this sute vnto me, but rather to see how I were disposed, or peraduẽture you vse these wordes for exercise sake, knowyng the fashion of you men to bee suche, as by praisyng of our beautie, you thinke to bryng vs into a fooles paradize, ꝧ we wil giue credite straight waie, that you loue vs so soone as you shall but tell vs the tale: but for my part (Maister Doctor) although I want wit to encoũter you with wordes, so likewise I want wil to beleue any thing

thing that you haue said, to be otherwise then wordes of course.

These speeches did ingender suche a nomber of swete and sowre alterations in Maister Doctor, that for his life he wiste not how to vnderstande them: one while thei were like to driue hym to dispaire: An other while thei somethyng quieted hym with hope, but in the ende determinyng to followe what he had begonne, he saied.

Swete mistres, moste humbly I desire you to accompt of me, not accordyng to my desertes, which as yet are none at all, but accordyng to the dutifull seruice, whiche hereafter I vowe faithfully to doe vnto you, and for the better testimonie of my wordes which (as you saie) seme to be of suche ordinary course, I desire no other credite maie bee giuen theim, then shall bee agreable to my deedes, when it shall please you to commaūde, but alas for the iniurie which you speake of, that I should offer to your housebande, who in deede I make accompt to bee my verie freende, what is he I praie you, that is able to prescribe lawes to loue? And as loue is without lawe, so it is without respect, either of freende or foe, father or brother, riche or poore, mightie or weake, vertuous or vicious: the exāples are so many & generall, that I should but waste the time to repeate thē. But (Mistres Doritie) I proteste the verie cause that maketh me to moue this mattter vnto you, is for no ill will that I bear to your housbande, but for the good wil I beare to your swete self, you maie vse your housbande as your housbande, and me as your freende, glad to stande at reuersion, when your housebande maie take his fill of the banket, and be glutted with more then enough: farther, if you make so greate accompte of your housbandes good likyng as you saie, what wiues be euer better beloued, or more made of by their housebandes, then those that haue discretion to helpe their frendes whē thei neede. But what sottishe opinion is this, whiche so many doeth holde, that thei thinke it so greate an iniurie for a man, to seke the wife of his freende, when he is attached by loue, whose arrest, neither Goddes nor men haue bin euer able to resist. But I praie you (Mistres Doritie) if I might aske you this question, would you not thinke your good will better bestowed vpō your housbandes freende then his foe, if you loue your housebande, I am sure you wil saie I haue reason, what should I longer trouble you then with circumstances: I knowe you are wise, and now I desire you for the good will that you beare to your housebande, to pitie me his freende, whom I trust you will restore with one drop of mercy, & the rather for your housbands sake.

Now thinke you gentlewomen, bee not these gentle perswasions to bee vsed by a Doctor, Marie he was no Doctor of Diuinitie, and therefore you neede not followe his doctrine, vnlesse you liste your selues, but this pitifull gentlewoman, seyng Maister Doctor at suche desperate poinctes, for feare of damning of her owne soule, that so deare a freende to her housbande as Maister Doctor was, should perishe and bee so wilfully caste awaie through her default, she receiued hym for her freend, and so I praie God giue them ioye.

But it fortuned afterwardes, this Gentlewoman to light into the companie of a Lawier, who perceiuyng this Dame to be of suche excellent beautie, ioynyng hymself some thing nere her, he saied: Gentlewoman, although I haue no skill in the arte of Paintyng, yet assure your self, your forme and passing beautie, is so surely engrauen and fixed in my mynde, that although your self were absent, I could drawe your perfect coũterfecte, sauyng that I thinke all the Apothecaries in this citie, were not able to furnishe me with colours, to make the perfecte distaine of the beautie in your face.

Mistres Doritie knowyng whereto these speeches pretended, aunswered: In deede sir, it should seeme you would proue a passyng Painter, that can so cunnyngly Painte forthe with wordes, that whiche I knowe is too farre vnworthie of so excellẽt a flourishe, as you would giue it, Mistres (q the Lawier) if I haue committed any offence, in these woordes whiche I haue spoken, it is in that I haue taken vpon me to praise your beautie, and not able to giue it suche due commendations, as I see it doeth deserue, the sight whereof doeth so captiuate my affections, and hath so creepled all my sences, that it hath caused me in maner to forgette my self, no maruaile then though my tongue doeth faile, and is not able to expresse the perfectiõ

of

of you, vnto whom with vowe of continuall seruice, I subiecte my life, liuyng, and libertie, if it please you to accept of it.

This Gentlewoman, that had yet but one freend to truste vppon, besides her housebande, beganne to thinke that store was no sore, and therefore determined not to forsake his frendlie offer, but firste she demaunded of hym of his facultie, and what trade of life he vsed, to whiche he aunswered, that he was a Gentleman appertainyng to the Lawe. It maie well bee so (q she) for I perceiue by your experience, that this is not the firste plea that you haue framed. And yet beleeue me (q the Lawier) I was neuer brought before to pleade at Beauties barre, but sithe my happe is suche, I humblie holde vp my handes, desiryng to be tried, by your courtesie and myne owne loialtie, contentyng my self to abide suche dome and iudgement, as it shall please you to appoincte, beeyng the cheef and Soueraigne Iudge your self, she replyng, saied: Seeyng you haue constituted me to giue Sentence at my pleasure, it is not the office of a good Iusticer, to bee parciall in his owne cause, and therefore this is the hope you shall looke for at my handes, that if hereafter in your deedes, I shall see as plaine proofe of perfecte good will, as your woordes by pretence importe likelyhood of earnest Loue, you shall finde me ready to render suche recompence, as shall fall out to your owne contentation and likyng: This comfortable aunswere, verie well pleased hym, and within a verie little space after, he so handeled the matter, that he had entered his action in her Common place. Thus what betweene Maister Doctor on the one side, who was still ministeryng of Phisicke vnto her, so long as there were any Drugges remainyng in his Storehouse, and the Lawier on the other side, who sufficiently enstructed her with his Lawe: thei vsed suche haunt vnto this gentlewomans companie, that the one beganne to growe suspicious on the other, and eche of theim desirous to haue her seuerall to hymself, beganne in the ende to enuaigh the one against the other: the Doctor against the Lawier, and the Lawier against the Doctor, and to tel her to her face what thei suspected, the one against the other. But Mistres Doritie beeyng very angrie with theim bothe, that

would

would so narrowlie looke into her doynges, did thinke it had been sufficient for reasonable men, that she had receiued them into her fauor, and as often as it had pleased them to come, she welcomed them as them selues did desire, and what can a man desire any more, then to drinke so often as he shalbe a thirste? But with faire speeches she contented them bothe for a tyme: but she thought in th'ende, to finde a remedy for that mischæf.

And thus it fell out, that a Souldiour, who was latelye retourned from the warres, I gesse aboute the same tyme, that Kyng Henry the fift was retourned, from the winnyng of Agincourt feelde: this Souldiour I saie, brauyng it out aboute the streates of the Citie (as commonly the custome of Souldiours is, to spend more in a moneth, then thei get in a yere) as he roomed to and fro, and fortuned to espie this blasyng starre lookyng out at a windowe, was sodainly stroken into a greate maze, to see this Lampe of light, then euer he had been in the feelde, to see the Ensignes of his enemies, and was so farre ouercharged with her loue: that but for feare to haue been marked by the passers by, he would haue stoode still gazyng and lookyng vppon her: but learnyng in the ende, that she was the Mistres of the house, he began to deuise how he might make her vnderstande the feruencie of his Loue, on whiche he determined to write vnto her: But then he knewe not how to beginne his Letter, because Souldiours are verie seldome accustomed to endite, especially any of these louyng lines: And to speake vnto her, he was likewise to learne how to vse his tearmes, neither wiste he how to come into her presence, but you shall see Fortune fauoured hym: For in an Euenyng as he passed through the streate, she was sittyng alone in her doore to take the aire, and commyng vnto her, not knowyng for his life how to begin his tale: In the ende, Mistres (q he) I praie you is your housebande within? No surely sir (q she) he is abroade in the Towne, but I knowe not where: And I would gladlie haue spoken with hym (q the Souldiour) if he had ben within: Beleeue me sir he is not within (q she) but if it please you to leaue your arrande with me, at his commyng home I will shew hym your minde. In faith Mistres (q the souldiour)

my

my arrande is not greate, I would but haue craued his helpe in chusyng me a wife, because I perceiue he hath some experience in the facultie, or els I think he could neuer haue chosen so well for hymself. If your arrande be no other then this (q Mistres Doritie) you maie at your owne leisure come and doe it your self, and as for my housebandes experience that you speake of, although peraduenture it bee not fittyng to your fancie, yet I am well assured that he hath made his choyse of suche a one, as he hymself very well liketh. I beleeue it well (q the Souldiour) and if without offence I might speake it, I sweare so God help me, I like his choise so wel, that I would thinke my self more then a thousand tymes happie, if I might be his halfe, or if my vnworthinesse deserued not so greate a portion, I would craue no more thē your self would willingly bestow on me, accordyngly as you should see me able to deserue it. Why sir (q Mistres Doritie) I doe not vnderstande whereunto your speeches doeth tende, neither what part you would haue me to giue you, when I haue alreadie bestowed of my housebande, bothe my hande, my harte, my minde, and good will. Alas Gentlewoman (q the Souldiour) these bee none of them that I would craue, there is yet an ouerplus whiche you haue not yet spoken of, whiche if you please to bestow of a Souldiour, I should think my self the happiest man aliue, whose loue and good likyng towardes you is suche, that I trust in tyme to come, your self will iudge me worthie, for my well deseruyng zeale, to haue deserued hire. Souldiours are seldome seene (q Mistres Doritie) to marche vnder the banner of Venus, but what so euer you bee, doe you thinke to ouerthrowe my vertues, with the assault of your wanton perswasions, or would you make me beleeue that you loue me as you saie, whē you haue no more respect to the hurt of my soule: Gentlewoman (q the Souldiour) I am not able to encounter you with wordes, because it hath not been my profession, nor traynyng vp, but if you doubte of my loue and good likyng. Please it you to make triall, commaunde any thyng that your self shall thinke requisite, whiche if I doe not performe to the vttermoste, then esteeme my loue in deede to be but feined, and where you thinke that I goe aboute to seeke the preiudice or hurte of your soule, beleeue me I neuer ment it.

Mistres Doritie, who had beene well acquainted before with many suiters, had neuer been apposed with such a rough hewen fellowe, that was so blunt and plaine, aswell in his gesture, as in his tearmes: Beganne to thinke with her self, that he might well bee a Souldiour, for she knewe that thei had little skill in the courting of Gentlewomen, yet she perceiued by his countenaunce, the vehemencie of the Loue he bare vnto her, and perceiuyng his plainesse, she beganne to thynke hym more fitter for her diet, then either Maister Doctor, or Maister Lawyer: that could not bee contented the one with the other, when she gaue them bothe so muche as thei could craue, and therefore thinkyng with her self, that to loose any longer tyme were but a poinct of follie, takyng the Souldiour by the hande, she ledde hym vp into a chamber, where other speeches were passed betweene them in secrete, whiche I could neuer yet vnderstande, and what thei did farther when thei were by themselues, gentlewomen I praie gesse you, but this I must aduertise you of, that before thei came forth of the chamber againe, the Souldiour had pleased Mistres Doritie so wel, that both Maister Doctor, & Maister Lawyer, were put quite out of conceipt, so that from that tyme forwards whē thei came of their visitation, the gentlewoman was not well at ease, or she had companie with her, or she was not at home, that thei could no more speake with her: which tourned them both into a wōderful agonie. The Doctor had thought she had forsaken hym for the loue of the Lawyer: The Lawyer he thought asmuche by the Doctor, that in the ende not knowing otherwise how to spitte out their venime against her, thei deuised eache of them a letter, whiche thei sent her. The first of these letters deliuered vnto her, came from the Doctor, whiche letter he left vnpoincted of purpose, because that in the readyng of it, it might bee poincted two waies, and made to seeme either to her praise or dispraise, but Mistres Doritie her self in the readyng of it, poincted it as I haue set it doune, and followeth in this sorte.

And who would haue thought mistres Doritie, that for the

louyng

louyng aduertisementes giuen you by your frende, you could so lightly haue shaken hym of, if I burdened you with any thyng that might seeme greeuous vnto you, thinke it was Loue that ledde me vnto it, for that I protest inwardly in my mynde, I neuer did esteeme you otherwise then for as honest a gentlewoman as liues this daie in Bridewell, I haue heard saie some haue been scourged more vpon euill will, then for any desertes whereof thei might iustly be accused, so if it be my happe to suffer vndeserued penaunce, I must impute it to my owne misfortune, but yet contrarie to my expectation, consideryng how I haue euer taken you to be giuen in your conditions to practise vnseemely, filthie, and detestable thynges: I knowe you haue euer abhorred to liue chastly, decently, and orderly: you haue euer been trained vp to be wanton, proude, and incontinent: you neuer tooke delight in that was good, honest, or commendable: you wholie gaue your self to leudenesse, luste, and lecherie: you were an open enemie to vertue: a frende to vice. What should I saie, I doe but waste the time in the settyng of you forth, and therefore will leaue you like as I founde you.

This letter brought Mistres Doritie into suche a furie when she had perused it, that she sware by no Beggers she would be so reuenged vpon the Doctor, that she would make hym a spectacle to all the Phisitions in the worlde, how they should abuse an honest Gentlewoman while thei liued. And in the middest of her Melancholie, her dearest freende the Souldiour happened to come in, whom she made partaker of all her secretes, shewyng him the letter whiche Maister Doctor had sent her: and as thei were deuisyng how to vse reuengemente, a messenger was knockyng at the doore, to deliuer a letter from the Lawyer, the tenure whereof followeth in this maner.

Maie this bee the rewarde of my true and faithfull Loue, whiche so firmely I haue borne thee? Or is this the delight of thy dalliaunce, whiche so many tymes thou haste vsed with me? So carelesslie to shake me of, as though I had committed some notable abuse, when in deede I haue loued thee a greate deale more, then I perceiue thou art worthie of. Oh feminine flatterie, O fained, fawnyng, O counterfect courtesie, O depe dissimulation: But what hope is otherwise to be looked for in these Rites of Cressides kinde. Or what constancie maie any man thinke to finde in a woman? No no, if a man maie generally speake of their sexe, you shall neuer finde them but counterfect in their courtesie, fained in their frendship, dissembling in their deedes, and in all their actions moste daungerous, for men to deale withall: For if she haue a faire face, it is euer matched with a cruell harte, their heauenly lookes with hellishe thoughtes: their modest countenaunces, with mercilesse myndes: thei haue witte, but it is in wiles: if thei loue, it is too vehement: when thei hate, it is to the death. But good God, with how many fopperies are thei accustomed to feede fooles, I meane suche as bee louemakers and suiters vnto theim, whom thei delaie with as many deuises, as thei be in number that seekes to serue them. Some thei lure with lookes, some thei practise with promises: some thei fœde with flattery: some thei delaie with daliance: some thei winde in with wiles: some thei keepe with kisses: some thei diet with dissimulation. One must weare her Gloue, an other must weare her Garter, an other must weare her Coulers: an other shall weare the spoile of as muche as she can gette from all the reste by cousonage, and yet to see how daintie these darlynges, wil seeme to those that be not acquainted with their customes, were able to dash a young man out of countenaunce: I warrant you, thei can make it more nice then wise: more coie then comely, more fine then honest. And to whō doe thei make the matter most daungerous, but to them that deserueth best to be rewarded: For where thei see a man that is drouned in affection towardes thē, ouer hym thei will triumph, and can tell how to ride the foole without a snaffle: one while thei will crosse hym with froward language, then againe comfort hym with some fained looke. Now she driues hym into desperation with frownyng face, by and by she baites hym againe with banquettes of vncertaine hope, suche is their euill nature (as I saie) that thei will shewe them selues moste squeamishe and daintie, to hym that loues

them

them moste entirely, and hym that seekes them least dishonestly, hym thei rewarde with their coldest courtesie. For better proofe, lette a man seeke to winne one of these tender peeces, that goes for a maide, honestly, and in the waie of Mariage, and I warrant you she will make the matter more coye and nice to hym that meanes good earnest, then to an other that comes but to trie and proue them. And what signes of shamefastnesse will thei seeme to make, when a man doeth but touch them: faining them selues to be too young, when (in deede) if thei once past ẏ age of fifteen yeres (if thei were not a feard of breedyng of bugges in their beallie) by their good willes they would neuer be without the companie of a man. Thus to conclude, their nature is openly to scorne all men, bee their loues neuer so honest, and secretly to refuse no manne be his lust neuer so leude. Full aptly did Salomon in his Prouerbes compare you to Wine, that can make vs so dronken with your deuises, that notwithstandyng we see the snares with our eyes, whiche you haue sette to entangle vs, wee can not shunne the baite, whiche wee knowe will breede our bane. Thus muche Mistres Doritie, I haue thought good to signifie vnto you, whose discourtisie at this tyme hath caused me so generally to enuaie against your whole sexe, not otherwise myndyng to accuse your self perticularly, knowing that if you should otherwise haue vsed me then you haue, you should haue degressed and swarued quite from your kinde, and so I leaue you.

Gentlewomen I beseche you forgiue me my fault, in the publishyng this infamous letter, I promise you I doe but signifie it accordyng to the copie, whiche this vnhappie Lawyer sent to Mistres Doritie, and when I had well considered the blasphemie that he had vsed against your sexe, I cutte my penne all to peeces, wherewith I did copie it out, and if it had not been for the hurtyng of my self, I promise you I would haue cutte and mangled my owne fingers, wherewith I held the penne while I was writyng of it: and trust me accordyng to my skill, I could well haue founde in my harte, to encountred hym with an aunswere in your defence, but then I was interrupted by an other as you shall well perceiue. For the

Souldiour, whiche you haue heard spoken of, that was remainyng with Mistres Dorithie, when he had perused this letter, was put into a wonderfull chafe, and in the middest of his furie he vttered these wordes,

Ah moste vile and blasphemous beast, what art thou that with suche exclamations, goest about to defame those, whom by all honest humanitie and manhood, we bee willed specially to loue, honour, and reuerence, what art thou? A man, a deuill or a subtill Lawyer, yea surelie, and so thou maiest well bee, and herein haste thou shewed thy self no whit at al to degresse from thy profession. For as at the firste the Lawes were constituted to minister Iustice, and to giue euery one his right, so now are thei made by the practise of a nomber of Pettie foggers, the instrumentes of all iniquitie and wrong. Euen so that worthie sexe whiche at the firste were giuen vnto man by the almightie God himself, to be his cheefest comfort and consolation. See here the practise of a wicked caitife, who with his eloquence would perswade vs, that thei were our greatest ruine and desolation: Ah wicked wretche that thou art, how thinkest thou to escape, thus to blowe forthe thy blasphemie, against those blessed ones, whom God hath perfited aboue all other creatures. For at their firste creation, thei were made of the moste beste and purified mettall of mane, where man hym self was framed but of slime and drosse: what reason then that beyng at the firste framed moste pure and perfecte creatures, but that thei should continue their firste perfection to the ende of the worlde. And like as at the firste thei were made more excellent then man, where should wee now seeke for grace, vertue, and goodnesse, but onely in the feminine sexe, accordyng to their singuler creation.

I trust this is so euident that there is no man able to denaie it, and enough to proue, that as women at the first were created moste perfecte, so they haue still remained the storehouse of all grace vertue and goodnesse, and that if there be any thing founde in vs men that is worthie of commendation, we are onely to giue thankes to women from whom wee receiue it, as beyng descended from out their entrailes: but with

how

how greate and manifolde miseries, should wee men bee daily afflicted, were it not for the comforte wee finde at womens handes, for besides that by their industrie we be netified, made mor clendly, and kept swete, who otherwise of our selues we should become to bee moste filthie and lothsome creatures, so at all tymes and seasons thei bee so necessarie and conuenient aboute vs, that it were impossible for vs to bee without their blessed companies. First, in our health thei content vs with their familiaritie, in our sicknesse thei cherish vs, in our mirth thei make it more abounde, in sorrowe their companie doeth beguile our pensiue thoughtes, in pleasure thei bee our cheefe delightes, in paine their presence bredeth comfort to our grief, in wealth what greater treasure then to enioye our beloued, in want what greater wealth then a louyng and faithfull wife, in peace we labour still to get their likyng, in warres thei make vs shewe our selues more valiaunt: but how is it possible that women should behaue themselues, but that there are some wil finde faught with them: first, if she be familiare, wee iudge her to be light, if she seeme any thing straunge in her conuersation, ah we saie she is a daungerous Dame, if merrie, wee thinke her to be naught, if sad, we saie she is more graue then honest, if she bee talkatiue, we saie she is a tatlyng houswife, if silent, we saie she is a sheepe, if clendly in her apparell, we saie she is proude, if plaine or homely, we saie she is a doudie or a slut, if thei denaie vs their curtesie when we sue vnto them, wee saie thei be cruell Tygers, Beares, and Bugges, if thei haue compassion of vs, we discredit them amongst our companions.

But see here the cunnyng of a Caitife, that would wreste the wordes of Salomon to the dispraise of women, because in his Prouerbes he compareth them to wine, but to interprete the words of Salomon by Salomon him self: in an other place of the same Prouerbes, he willeth Wine should bee giuen to comforte those that bee feeble and weake, now compare these places together and see what harme he hath doen to women, and in my opinion, he could not more aptly haue made a comparison, for as Wine is a comforte to those that are feeble and weake, so are women our greatest solace, both in sicknesse and

in

in health: but if any wil saie that wine maketh vs dronken, and from reasonable men to become more brute then beastes. I aunswere that the faught is not to be imputed to the wine, but to ye beastlinesse of him that taketh more then enough, for there is nothyng so precious for our behoofes, but by our own abuse we make it seeme most vile and lothsome, and thus graunting maister Lawyer his comparison to be true, he hath doen little hurt, sauyng he hath shewed hym self a diligent scholler to his Maister the Deuill, who is father of all lyes, in maintainyng so manifest a lye against suche harmelesse creatures.

There were many other speeches pronounced by this Souldiour in the behaulf of women, whiche I haue forgot to recite. But I pray gentle women how like you by this Souldiour, doe you not thynke hym worthie a Sargantes fee for his aunswere: in my opinion, you ought to loue Souldiours the better for his sake.

But to retourne to Mistres Doritie, those two letters had so vexed her, that there was nothing in her minde but how she might be reuenged. Her freende the Souldiour promised for her sake, that he would so cudgill bothe Maister Doctor, and the Lawier, that thei should not in one moueth after be able to lift their armes to their heds, sauyng he wist not how to get them into a place conuenient, for ye it was daungerous to deale with them in the open streates. Mistres Doritie giuyng hym twentie kisses for his courtesie, tolde him she would deuise to bryng them into some place where he might worke his will.

Presently after, Mistres Doritie sent for Maister Doctor, whom she knewe very well how to handle, and in a milde maner she began greatly to blame hym, that beyng wise as she knewe hym to be, would so rashly iudge of her, for that he might well know that there was some greate cause, that moued her to vse hym as she had doen, otherwise then he had coniectured: and thus with many other like speeches, she so smothed the matter with Maister Doctor, that she made hym beleeue her housbande had some suspition in their familiaritie, and that by his commaundement she had abstained his companie for a tyme, the which (Maister Doctor ꝗ she) I did for no

euill

euill will that I beare you, but for a tyme to bleare my housebandes eyes, thinkyng in the ende so to haue handled the matter, that we might haue continued our accustomed freendship without any maner of suspition: And then drawyng forthe the letter, whiche the Doctor had sent her (she saied) But see maister Doctor your good opinion conceiued in me, loe, here the reward that I haue for my courtesie bestowed of you, thus to raile and rage against me, as though I were the moste notable strumpet in a countrey.

The Doctour knowyng in what forme he had wright the Letter, and desirous againe to renue his late acquaintaunce, aunswered, that he neuer writte Letter vnto her, whereby he had giuen any occasion for her to take any greef. No haue? (quod Mistres Doritie) read you then heare your owne lines, takyng hym the Letter, whiche the Doctor as I told you before, had lefte vnpointed, and therefore in the readyng, he poincted it after this maner.

And who would haue thought (Mistres Doritie) that for the louyng aduertisementes giuen you by your freende, you could so lightly haue shaken hym of, if I burdeined you with any thing, that might seme greeuous vnto you, thinke it was loue that ledde me vnto it, for that I protest inwardlie in my minde, I did neuer esteeme you otherwise, then for as honest a gentlewoman as liues this daie. In Bridwell I haue heard saie, some haue been scourged more vpon euill will, then for any desertes whereof thei might iustly be accused: so if it be my hap to suffer vndeserued penaunce, I must impute it to mine owne misfortune, but yet contrarie to my expectation, consideryng how I haue euer taken you to be giuen in your conditions: to practise vnseemely, filthie, and detestable thinges, I knowe you haue euer abhorred: To liue chastlie, decentlie, and orderly, you haue euer bin trained vp: to be wantō, proude, and incontinent, you neuer tooke delight: in that was good, honest or commendable, you wholie gaue your self: to leudnesse, luste, and lecherie, you were an open enemie, to vertue a freende, to vice: what should I saie, I dooe but waste the tyme in the settyng of you foorthe, and therefore will leaue you like as I founde you.

I praie you Mistres Doritie (q the Doctor) where is this railyng and ragyng you speake of, I trust I haue written nothing that might discontent you. Mistres Doritie perceiuyng the knauerie of the Doctour, and seeyng the matter fell out so fitte for her purpose: first giuyng hym a freendly busse she said. Alas my deare freend, I confesse I haue trespassed in misconsteryng of your lines: But forgiue me I praie you, and now haue compassion of her, whose loue towarde you is suche, that it is impossible for me to liue, without your good likyng, and seyng that my housebandes Jelousie is so muche, that you can haue no longer accesse to my house, but it must needes come to his eare, by suche spie and watche as he hath laied, neither my self can goe abroade to any place, but I am dogged, and followed by suche as he hath appoincted: But now if your loue bee but halfe so muche towardes me, as I trust I haue deserued, and hereafter doe meane to requite. I haue alreadie deuised a meane, how for euer I might enioye my desired freend, without either lette or molestation of any one, seeme he neuer so muche to be offended at the matter.

The Doctor the gladdest man in the worlde to heare these newes, aunswered: And what is it then that should make you stagger, or doubt of the frēdship of your louyng Doctor, no not if thereby I should hazard the losse bothe of life and goodes.

Alas (q Mistres Doritie) God defende I should worke you so greate a preiudice, and I beseeche you vse no more suche speeches vnto me, that I should goe about to put you into any suche perill, the remembraunce whereof is more greuous vnto me, then if I had felte the force of a thousande deathes, and now behold my determination, and what I haue deuised: You haue a house not farre hence standyng in the feeldes, whiche you keepe for your solace, and recreation in the tyme of Sommer: To this house I haue deuised, how you maie so secretly conueigh me, that you maie there keepe me at your pleasure to your owne vse, and to my greate contentation, where I maie at pleasure enioye hym, more dearely beloued vnto me, then the baales of myne owne eyes. And here withall she gaue hym

an

an other Iudas kiſſe, that the Doctor deſired her of all friendeſhip, not to bee long in her determination, for that he was readie to followe her direction, when ſoeuer it would pleaſe her to commaunde: yea, if it were preſently he was readie.

Miſtres Doritie, who had driuen the matter to that paſſe ſhe looked for, ſaied: Naie Maiſter Doctour, there reſteth yet an other thyng, my houſebandes Ielouſie (as I tolde you) is ſuche, that there muſte bee greate circumſpection uſed, in the conueighyng of me awaie, and therefore giue eare to that I haue deuiſed: I haue in my houſe a certaine Male with ſtuffe, that is left with me to bee ſent by the Carriers into the Countrie, whereof my houſbande doeth knowe verie well, this ſtuffe I will cauſe to bee ſecretly taken forthe, and to bee ſent to the carriers truſt vp in ſome other thing, without any knowledge to any, ſauyng to my Maide, that ſhall worke this feate her ſelf, whoſe truſtineſſe I knowe to bee ſuche, as there is no ſuſpition to be had in the matter, the whiche when ſhe hath doen, ſhe ſhall truſſe vp me in the ſame Male, then ſee that you faile not to morowe in the Euenyng about eight of the Clocke, diſguiſed in a Porters weede, to come to my houſe to enquire for the ſame Male, whiche you ſhall ſaie, you will beare to the carriers, my Maide who ſhall of purpoſe bee readie to waite for your commyng at the houre, ſhall make no bones to deliuer you this Male, and thus without either doubte or Ielouſie of any one, you maie carrie me into the feeldes, where for your better eaſe you maie take me forthe, and diſguiſyng our ſelues wee maie walke together, to your houſe afore ſaied, where I maie remaine without any maner of ſuſpition, or knowledge to any, ſo long as it ſhall pleaſe your ſelf.

O moſte excellent deuiſe (q the Doctor) I haue this matter alreadie at my fingers endes, and I warrant you, you ſhal ſee me plaie the Porter ſo cunnyngly, that how many ſo euer I meete, there ſhall none of them be able to ſuſpect me: Thus with a fained kiſſe that ſhe againe beſtowed of hym, for that tyme thei departed.

Miſtres Doritie, in like maner ſent for the Lawier, whom ſhe handeled in like ſorte, as ſhe had doen the Doctor, makyng hym beleeue, that her housebandes Jelousie was suche, as she durst no more come in his companie: But of her self she loued hym so entirely, that she would hazard any thyng for his sake, and because he should the better beleeue it, to morrowe (q she) in the after noone, my housebande will be forthe of the dores, wherefore I praie you faile not aboute three of the Clocke, to come and visite me, when we shall haue leisure to disporte our selues, to our better contentation: many like enticyng wordes she vsed, whiche so perswaded the Lawier, then dreadyng no badde measure at all, he promised her not to faile, but he would keepe his hower: And thus departed verie ioyfull, that he had againe recouered his Mistres. And the nexte daie, euen as it had stroke three of the Clocke, he was knockyng at the doore of this Gentlewoman, who lookyng for his commyng, was readie to receiue hym, and vp thei goe together to a chamber, whiche she had appointed for the purpose: where for a tyme she dalied hym of with deuises: and sodainly her maide (accordyng as her Mistres had giuen her instructions) came hastely to the Chamber doore, callyng her Mistres, saiyng: that her maister was come in, and had asked for her: Mistres Doritie, who was not to learne to plaie her parte, seemed to be striken into a wonderfull feare, alas (q she to the Lawier) for the loue of God keepe your self secret for a tyme, that I maie goe doune and ridde hym awaie, if it be possible, and thus goyng her waie doune, she shuttes the doore after her.

The Lawier who was readie to beraie hym self for feare, crepte vnder the bedde, where she lefte hym alone the space of an hower, and then commyng vp into the chamber, and could not see hym, she beganne to muse what was become of hym, he hearyng one was come in at the Chamber doore, beganne to prie out vnder the beddes feete, and perceiuyng by the skirt of her Goune who it was, with a faint voice he saied: alas my deare what newes, is your housebande gone? Ah my louyng freende (q she) I was neuer so hardlie beset sith I was borne, my housebande is come home with three or fower of his freendes, whiche he mette withall in the Citie, and bee come out of the Countrey of purpose, to make merrie with hym, and here

thei

thei bee appoincted this night to Suppe, and hether bee come to their beddes, so long as thei remaine in the Citie, and this Chamber is appointed for twoo of them to lye in, that for my life I knowe not what shifte to make, nor how to conueigh you hence.

Alas (ꝙ the Lawier) then am I vtterlie vndooen, for the loue of GOD, deuise some meanes to conueigh me out of the house, for I would not remaine all night in this perplexitie, no not for all the golde in the worlde. Mistres Doritie makyng a little pause, sodainlie as though she had an inuention, but euen then come into her bedde, she saied.

I haue this onely remedie left, here is in the house a Male full of stuffe, whiche should this night be sent to the Carriers: my deuise is therefore to take forthe the stuffe, and laie it a side till somtyme the next weeke, when I will make shift to sende the stuffe awaie verie well, and you shall bee presently packed vp in this Male, whiche my maide shall doe while I am below with my housebande and his freendes, and so causyng a Porter to be sent for, he shall carrie you to your Chamber, or to any other place where it shall please your self, so that my housebande seeyng this Male goe forthe of doores, will thinke it is the stuffe, whiche he knoweth this night should be sent.

No better deuise in the worlde (ꝙ the Lawier) and let the Porter conueigh this Male to my Chamber, you knowe where, and deliuer it to my manne, as sent from his Maister, and will hym to giue hym fourtie pence for his labour.

The matter thus determined, Mistres Doritie sent vp her maide with this emptie Male, wherein she trussed vp the Lawier, and there she left hym lying from fiue of the clocke, vntill it was past eight, and in the Sommer season the weather beyng verie hotte, the Lawier had like to haue been smothered where he laye, at the length accordyng to poinctmente, comes Maister Doctour disguised like a right Porter, with a longe gaberdine doune to the calfe of his legges, and he enquires for a Male that should goe to the Carriers, yea Marie (ꝙ the maide) if you please to come in, it is ready for you, the Doctor beyng a good sturdie lubber, tooke vp the Male verie easily for feare of brusyng the Gentlewomans tender ribbes, whom he had thought he had vpon his backe, and thus forthe of dores he goes, takyng the next waie towardes his lodgyng.

Mistres Doritie with her beloued Souldiour (whom she had made priuie to her deuise) stoode where she might see maister Doctor in his Porters weede, goyng with his carriage, whereat when thei had a while sported them selues, the Souldiour folowed Maister Doctor an easie pase, but onely to kepe the sight of hym, and the Doctour he tooke his waie through the streetes with a maine pase, till he had recouered the feeldes where lookyng aboute hym, to see what companie was stirryng, sawe no bodie neare hym but the Souldiour, whom he did not knowe, and then crossyng the waie from the common pathes, he came to the side of a bancke, and beyng wearie (as he was not to bee blamed, consideryng the knauishe burthen that he had borne vppon his backe) he laiyng doune the Male tenderlie vppon the side of the bancke, seeyng no bodie but the Souldiour, who was but a little distaunce from hym, saied. Ah my sweete wenche, I can see no creature stirryng in al the feeldes, but one manne whiche is commyng this waie, who so soone as he is paste, I will vndoe the Male.

The Lawier in the Male, when he felt the Porter lay hym doune, was in a good hope that he had been in his owne chamber, but hearyng by these speeches that he was in the feeldes, began to coniecture assuredly, that the porter had spoken those wordes to some woman that was in his companie, with whō he was confederate, for the stealyng of suche thynges as thei should finde in the Male, and that when thei should open the Male & finde hym there, thei would not sticke to cute his thote for feare least he should bewraie them, and for the onely spoile of suche thynges as he had about hym, that the Lawier was in suche a perplexitie, that he wiste not for his life what he might doe: one while he had thought to haue cried out for helpe, then he thought it would the soner bryng hym to his ende, and as he continued thus in the middest of his muse, the Souldiour was come to the place, and speakyng to the Doctor, he saied: Porter it seemeth thou haste been knauishly loden, for I perceiue thou

thou art very hot, but what hast thou in thy Male, I praie thee that thou art carriyng this waie so late in the euenyng. Marie (q the doctor) I haue ware there suche as it is, hast thou ware knaue (q the Souldiour) is that a sufficiente aunswere, what ware is it, mennes ware, or womens ware. Sir I knowe not (q the Porter) I haue but the carriyng of it to a Gentlemans house that is here hard by, well (q the Souldiour) vndoe your trusse, for I will se what wares you haue there, before you and I depart, why sir (q the Porter) should I be so bolde to vndoe a Gentlemans Male, that is deliuered me in trust to be caried, no sir you shall pardon me, if you were my Father, and herewithall he tooke the Male vpon his backe, and beganne to goe his waies. But the Souldiour knowyng better what was in the Male, then the Porter hymself that carried it, and beeyng prouided for the purpose with a good Cudgell, let driue halfe a dosen blowes at the Male, as it laie vpon his backe so surely, that the Lawier cries out, alas, alas, alas. Why Porter (q the Souldiour) haue you quicke wares in your Male, no merueile you were so daintie in the shewyng of it.

Here withall the Doctor laied doune his Male, and kneelyng doune to the Souldiour, saied. Ah sir for the loue of God bee content, and I will not let to confesse the whole truthe vnto you: I haue a Gentlewoman in my Male, whiche I haue stolne from her housebande, and seyng you to be a gentleman, but yong in yeres, and impossible but that you should loue the companie of a faire woman, beholde, I will deliuer her vnto you, to vse at your pleasure, and when you shall see tyme, to restore her vnto me againe, desiryng you sir of all courtesie to seeke no other displeasure against vs. You haue saied well (q the Souldiour) but is she suche a one as is to bee liked, faire, freshe, and yong. Trust me sir (q the Doctor) if she bee not as faire, and well likyng as any Dame within the walles of this Citie, make me an example to all other, how thei shall dissemble with a Gentleman suche as you are. Thou saiest well (q the Souldiour) and now I thinke long till I haue a sight of this Paragon, whiche thou haste so praised vnto me. You shall see her straight sir (q the Doctor) and here withall he began

to

to unlase the Male with great expedition, whiche when he had unlosed at the one ende, that he might come to the sight of this Gentlewomans face (as he had thought) he saied to the Souldiour, see here the sight whiche you so muche desire, and pullyng the ende of the Male open with his handes, the Lawier thruste forthe his hedde, and looked with suche a piteous countenaunce, as though he had been readie to bee tourned of the Ladder: But the Doctor seyng a face to appeare with a long beard, was in suche a maze, that he could not tell in the worlde what he might saie. The Souldiour who had neuer more a doe then to forbeare laughter, to see how these twoo, the one beheld the other: saied to the Doctor, and is this the faire gentlewoman whiche thou hast promised me, haste thou no bodie to mocke but me, that with suche commendations thou giuest praise to a woman, whereby to set my teeth an edge, and then in the ende thus to delude me? But I will teache thee how to plaie the knaue againe while thou liueste, and here withall he layed on with his Cudgell, sparyng neither hedde, shoulders, armes, backe, nor breast, and so be bumbasted the Doctor, that for the space of a quarter of a yere after, he was not able to lift an Urinall so hye as his hedde.

The Lawier who had nothyng out of the Male but his hedde, seeyng this fraie, struggeled so muche as he could, to haue gotte forthe, and to haue runne awaie, while the Porter was a beatyng, but it would not bee, his armes were so surely laced doune by his sides, that for his life he could not gette them forthe.

The Souldiour, when he had throughly requited Maister Doctours knauerie, that he had used against his beloued Mistres in his letter, left hym, and beganne to bende hym self towardes the Lawier: The Lawier seyng the Souldiour commyng, had thought verely that he had been some good fellowe that was walkyng there so late, to haue taken some prey, said: O sir for the loue of God spare my life, and take my purse, to whom the Souldiour aunswered: naie villaine, my commyng is neither to take thy life nor thy purse, but to minister reuengemente for thy large speeches, whiche like a discourteous

wretche

wretche thou haste vsed against a woman, and there with all laied vpon hym so long as he was able to fetch any breath, and then callyng the Porter vnto hym, he saied: Let these wordes whiche I minde to speake suffice for a warnyng to you bothe, if euer I maie learne that any of you hereafter this do vse any misdemeanure towardes any woman, either by word or writyng, assure your selues that although I haue but dallied with you at this tyme, I wil deuise some one meane or other to minister reuenge, that all suche as you bee, shall take an example by you. And thus I leaue you, goyng his waie to his sweete harte, tellyng her the whole discourse how he had spedde, by whom he was welcomed with a whole laste of kisses &c.

And now to retourne to those twoo that were lefte in the feeldes, as you haue heard: the Doctor takyng good vewe of the Lawyer, knewe hym verie well, but the Doctor was so disguised in his Porters apparell, that the Lawyer did not knowe hym, but saied vnto hym, a mischeef light of all suche Porters, that when thei bee put in truste with carriages into the Citie, will bryng them into the feeldes to such banquettes as these, Marie qd the Doctor a mischeef take all suche burthens, that when a manne hath almoste broken his backe with bearyng them, and then shall receiue such a recompence for his labour as I haue doen: Villaine (qd the Lawyer) why diddest thou not beare me to my Chamber as thou wert willed when thou diddest receiue me. I would I had carried thee to the gallowes (qd the Doctor) so I had escaped this scouryng, but I perceiue this banquette was prepared for vs bothe, and here withall with muche adoe he got of the Porters coate, and makyng himself knowne to the Lawyer, eache of them conferred with the other, how cunnyngly thei had been dealt withall, and did thinke it not beste for them any farther to deale in the matter, for feare of farther mischeef, but with much adoe got them home, where the Lawier kept his bedde very long after: But the Doctor tooke Sparmaceti, and suche like thynges that bee good for a bruse, and recouered hym self in a shorte space.

Now it fell out afterwardes that this Souldiour, who liued in greate credite with Mistres Doritie (as he had well deserued,

serued, was imployed in the kynges warres against forraine foees, with a greate nomber of othere, where he spent his life in his Princes quarrell, & Mistres Dorinie, sorrowing a long tyme the losse of so faithfull a freende, seeyng the diuersitie of men, that she had made her choise emongst three, and had found but one honest, feared to fall into any further infamie, contented her self to liue orderly, and faithfully with her housband, al the rest of her life, and her housbande who neuer vnderstoode any of these actions, loued her dearely to his dying daie.

And now to saie somethyng of the other brother and his wife, whiche as you haue heard was suche a notable scold, that her housbonde could neuer enioy good daie, nor merie houre: She was suche a deuill of her tongue, and would so crossebite hym with suche tauntes, and spightfull quippes, as if at any tyme he had been merrie in her companie, she would tell hym his mirthe proceaded rather in the remembraunce, of that she had brought hym, then for any loue that he had to her self, if he were sadde, it was for greef she was not dedde, that he might enioye that she had. If he vsed to goe abroade, then he had been spending of that he neuer gotte him self. If he taried at home, she would saie it was happie he had gotten suche a wife, that was able to keepe hym so Ioelly. If he made any prouision for good cheare, or to fare well in his house she would bid hym spende that whiche he hymself had brought. If he shewed hym self to bee sparyng, then she would not pinche of that whiche was her owne. Thus doe what he could, all that euer he did was taken in the worste parte: and seyng that by no maner of faire meanes he was able to reclaime her. In the ende he deuised this waie, hym self with a trustie freend that he made of his counsaill, gotte and pinioned her armes so faste, that she was not able to vndoe them, and then puttyng her into an old Peticoate, whiche he rent and tattered in peeces of purpose, and shakyng her heire loose about her eyes, tare her Smocke sleeues that her armes were all beare, and scratching them all ouer with a Bramble that the bloud followed, with a greate chaine about her legge, where with he tied her in a darke house that was on his backside, and then callyng his neibours about

her,

her, he would seeme with greate sorrowe to lament his wiues distresse, tellyng thē that she was sodainly become Lunatique, whereas by his geasture he tooke so greate greefe, as though he would likewise haue runne madde for companie. But his wife (as he had attired her) seemed (in deede) not to be well in her wittes, but seeyng her housebandes maners, shewed her self in her conditions to bee a right Bedlem, she vsed no other wordes but cursynges and banninges, criyng for the Plague and the Pestilence, and that the Deuill would teare her housbande in peeces, the companie that were about her, thei would exhorte her, good neighbour forget these Idle speeches, whiche doeth so muche distemper you: and call vpon God and he will surely helpe you. Call vpon God for help (qd the other) wherein should he helpe me, vnlesse he would consume this wretche with Fire and Brimstone, other helpe I haue no need of. Her housebande, he desired his neighbours for Gods loue that thei would helpe him to praie for her, and thus altogether kneelyng doune in her presence, he beganne to saie (Miserere) whiche all thei saied after him, but this did so spight and vexe her, that she neuer gaue ouer her railyng, and ragyng against them all. But in the ende, her houseband who by this shame had thought to haue reclaimed her, made her to become from euil to worse, and was glad hym self in the ende, cleane to leaue, and to get hym self from her into a straunge Countrey, where he continued the rest of his life.

Thus to cōclude, besides the matter that I meane to proue menne maie gather example here, when thei goe a wiuyng, not to chose for beautie without vertue: nor for riches without good conditions. There be other examples if thei be well marked, worth the learning: both for men & women, whiche I leaue to the discretion of the reader.

FINIS.

Of Gonſales and his vertuous wiſe Agatha.

The argument of the ſixt Hiſtorie.

¶Gonſales, *pretendyng to poiſon his verteous wife for the loue of a Courtiſane, craued the helpe of* Alonſo *a Scholer ſomethyng practiſed in Phiſicke, who in the ſteade of poyſon gaue hym a poulder, whiche did but bryng her in a ſounde ſleepe duryng certaine howers, but* Gonſales *iudgyng (in deede) that his wife had been dedde: cauſed her immediatly to be buried, The Scholer againe knowyng the operation of his poulder for the greate loue he bare to* Agatha, *went to the vault where ſhe was entombed, about the hower that he knewe ſhe ſhould awake. When after ſome ſpeeches vſed betweene theim, he carried her home to his owne houſe, where ſhe remained for a ſpace, in the meane tyme* Gonſales *beeyng married to his Courtiſane, was by her accuſed to the Gouernour for the poiſoning of his firſt wife, whereof being apprehend he confeſſed the facte, and was therefore iudged to dye, whiche beyng knowne to* Agatha, *ſhe came to the Iudge, & clearyng her houſbande of the crime, thei liued together in perfect peace & amitie.*

here was ſome tyme in the Citie of Siuille in Spaine, a Gentilman named Gonſales, who though he were a man of yeares ſufficient to be ſtaied, and to giue ouer the wanton prankes of youthfull follie. Yet was he by Nature ſo enclined to followe his luſtes, and withall ſo variable and ſo vnconſtant, that he he suffered hym self to be ruled wholy by his passiōs, and measured all his doyng rather by his delightes and pleasures, then by sounde discourse and rule of reason. This Gentleman fallyng in loue with a Gentlewoman of the saied Citie whose name was Agatha, sought all the meanes he could to haue her to wife. And her freendes although thei were well enough enformed of the disposition of Gonsales, wherby thei might haue feared the entreatie of their kinswoman, for that thei knewe him very riche, and her dowrie not to be very greate, thei were well content to bestowe her vppon hym: and thought that thei had in so doyng placed her very well. But before the first yere after their Marriage was fullie expired, Consales followyng his wonted humour, and waxing wearie of loue, grewe to desire chaunge, giuyng thereby a notable example for women to learne how little it is to their commoditie or quiet, to matche them selues to suche, that be rather riche then wise: and how muche it were better for them to bee married to men, then to their goodes.

For beyng come to soiourne in that Streate wherein he dwelt, a notable Courtesane, who to the outward shewe was verie faire, though inwardly she was moste foule, as she that vnder a goodlie personage, did couer a wicked and daungerous minde, corrupted with all vices (as for the moste part all suche women doen.) It was Gonsales chaunce to be one of the first that fell into those snares, whiche she had sette for suche simple mens mindes, as haunte after the exteriour apparance of those thynges, whiche their senses make them to delight in, and not consideryng the daunger whereunto thei commit themselues, by followyng of their disordinate appetites, doe suffer themselues to be entrapped by suche lewde Dames: Emong whiche this (forsoothe) was one that was of singuler skill to captiue mens mindes, whiche by experience and by the naturall disposition of her mynde, bent wholie to deceipte and naughtinesse: had learned a thousande giles and artes, which waie to allure men with the pleasauntnesse of her baites. Wherefore after he was once entangled with her snares, he fell so farre beyond all reason, and past all beleef, to dote vpon this Strumpet that he could finde no reste, nor no contentment, but so long as he was with her. But she beyng as dissolute a Dame as any liued in the worlde, and as greedie likewise of gaine as euer any was of her profession, would not content her self with Gonsales alone, but yelded vnto as many as list to enioye her, if thei came with their handes full, and spared for no coste to reward her liberalitie. Whiche thyng was vnto hym, that was so besotted on her, so greeuous and so intollerable, that nothyng could be more.

There was at that same tyme, a Scholer in the Citie that studied Phisicke: with whom Gonsales had familier acquaintaunce, and the Scholler thereby hauyng accesse and conuersation in his house, beganne so feruently to be in loue with Agatha his wife, that he desired nothing so earnestly in the worlde as to enioye her, and to winne her good will. Wherefore hauyng (as I haue saied) free accesse to her house, and to declare his affection vnto her without suspicion, he ceased not by al the meanes he was able to deuise, to sollicite and to procure her to yeelde vnto his desire. With his endeuour and earneste suite, although it were vnto Agatha noysome and displeasaunt, as she that was disposed to kepe her self honest: and that she could in that respecte haue been very glad, that he would forbeare to frequent her house. Yet knowyng her housbande to be a man of no verie greate substaunce, and but slenderly stuffed in the hedpeece: and that he delighted greatly in the familiaritie of the Scholler, she forced her self to endure with patience, the importunate molestation, whiche he still wearied her withall. Takyng from hym neuerthelesse all hope, to obtaine at any tyme any fauour at her handes, and cuttyng hym shorte from all occasions, as muche as she could, whereby he might haue cause either to molest her, or to looke for any thing to proceade from her, that were lesse then honest.

The Scholer perceiuyng that his owne trauaile, to win her affection was but labour loste, thought best to trie if by the allurement or perswasion of any other, he might happly moue her to shew her self more courteous, and fauourable vnto him. Wherefore hauing founde out an olde mother Elenour, a disciple

ciple of the Spanishe Celestina, suche a one as was most cunnyng and skilfull in mollifying of womens mindes, to worke them afterwarde to receiue the impressions of their louers, he caused her to take acquaintaunce of Agatha, and by degrees (as though she had been moued with pittie and compassion of her case) to declare vnto her the loue which her housband bare vnto the Courtisane: and to shewe her how vnworthie he was that she should be true vnto hym. And in the end passyng from one speeche to an other, she saied plainly vnto her, that it was a greate follie, since her housebande did take his pleasures abroade with other women, to staude to his allowances, and to take the leauyng of his Strumpets, and therewith to bee content: and that, if she were in her case, and had a housebaud that would strike with the sworde, she would vndoubtedly requite hym and strike with the scabberde, so she counselled her to doe likewise.

Agatha beyng a very discrete Gentlewoman, and louyng her housbande as an honest woman ought to doe, saied to her in aunswere of her talke, that she would bee right glad to see her housbande to be suche a man as she wished hym to be, and as he ought to be. But that since she sawe it would not be, and that he could not frame hym self thereto, she would not take from hym or barre hym of that libertie, whiche either the custome of the corrupted worlde, or the priueledge that men had vsurped vnto them selues, had giuen vnto them. And that she would neuer for her parte violate or breake that faithe whiche she had giuen hym, nor slacke or neclect that care and regarde of her honour, whiche all women by kinde and nature ought to haue, as the thing that maketh them to bee moste commended throughout the worlde, let her housbande doe what he list, and like and loue as many other women as pleased hym. And that she thought her self so muche the rather bounde so to doe, because he did not in the rest misuse her any waie, or suffer her to want any thyng that reasonably she could desire or craue at his handes: and for that she had not brought hym in effect any other dowrie worthie to bee accompted of then her honestie. Wherefore she was fully resolued neuer to varie from that

constant

constant resolution. And finally shewyng her self somewhat moued and stirred with choler, she tolde her that she maruailed at her not a little (that beyng a woman of those yeres) that she should rather reprehend and chide yong folke, if she should see them so bent, then encourage them to euill, & mused much she could finde in her harte to giue her suche counsell: whiche she assured her was so displeasant and so vngrateful, as if from hence forthe she durst presume to speake thereof any more, she would make her vnderstande perchaunce to her smarte, how ill she could awaie with suche pandarly practises.

This olde hag hauyng had her head washed thus without sope, departed from Agatha, and came vnto the Scholler and tolde hym in breefe how ill she had sped, and in what sorte the honest Gentlewoman had closed her mouth, whereof the Scholler was very sory: yet for al this, he thought he would not giue ouer his pursute, imaginyng that there is no harte so harde or flintie, but by long loue, by perseuerance, praier, and teares, maie in the ende be mollified and wrought to be tender.

In this meane season, Consales still continuyng his olde familiaritie with the Scholer, and hauyng made hym priuie of the loue he bare vnto the Courtisane, and what a greefe it was vnto him to see her enioyed by any other then by himself: one daie among other talke betwene them of that matter, he saied vnto the Scholer, that it neuer grieued hym so muche to haue a wife as it did then, for that if he had bin vnmaried he would haue taken Alegia (for so was the Courtisane named) to be his wife, without whom he could finde no rest nor quiete in mynde, and so long as euery man hath a share with hym in her, he accompted himself as ill as if he had had no parte in her at all. And thereto saied further, that assuredly if it were not for feare of the Lawe, he would ease hym self of that burden by riddyng of Agatha out of the worlde. Whereunto replied the Scholer, saiyng that in deede it was a grieuous thyng for a Gentleman to be combred with a wife, whō he could not finde in his harte to loue, and that in suche a case, he that did seeke the best waie he could to deliuer hym self of that yoke, was not altogether vnexcusable, though the rigor of Iustice had ap-

poincted

poincted seuere punishementes, for suche as violentlie should attempt, or execute any suche thyng. But that men that were wise, could well enough finde out the meanes, whiche waie to worke their ententes, without incurryng any daunger of the Lawe for the matter. Whiche language in deede he vsed vnto hym, but to feede his humour, and to see whereunto that talke in fine would tende: And accordyng to his desire before it was long. Gonsales hauyng vsed the like speeches, twoo or three tymes, and still findyng hym to soothe his saiyng, tooke one daie a good harte vnto him, and brake his minde vnto the scholer at large and in plaine termes, to this effecte.

Alonso (for that was the Scholers name) I doe assure my self and make full accompt, that thou art my faste freende, as I am thyne, and I doubte not but that the freendship, whiche is betweene vs, doeth make thee no lesse sorie then my self, to see me greeue with this continuall trouble of mynde, wherein I liue, because I can not compasse to take this woman whom I loue so dearely to bee my wife, and by that meanes come to haue the full possession of her vnto my self, whiche is the thing I doe desire aboue all other thinges in the worlde. And for as muche as I dooe perswade my self that by thy meanes, and with the helpe of thy profession, I maie happ to finde some remedie for my greef. I haue thought good to tell thee a conceit, whiche I haue thought on often tymes: wherein I meane to vse thee and thy assistance, for the better accomplishyng of my purpose, in that behalfe. Assuryng my self that thou wilte not refuse, or denie me any fartheraunce that thy skill maie afforde me, or shrinke and drawe backe from the performyng of any freendly offer, whereby I maie come by to finde some ease of minde, and be deliuered of that intollerable torment of spirite, wherwith I am oppressed, for the loue of this Aselgia, in whō I haue fixed and sette all my ioyes and delightes. Thou shalte therefore vnderstande that I am determined, as soone as I can possible, to ridde my handes of Agatha my wife, and by one meane or other to cause her to dye: And I haue been a this good while about the execution of this my entent, but because I could neuer yet deuise the beste waie to performe it, so that her death might not bee laied vnto my charge. I haue delaied it hetherto, and perforce contente to beare the heauie burthen of my greeued mynde till now, whiche hence forwarde I am resolued to beare no longer, if thou wilt accordyng to my truste in thee, and as the freendship whiche is betweene vs doeth require, graunt me thy furtherance and helpyng hande. Wherfore, knowyng that through thy long studie in Phisicke, thou haste attained so greate knowledge, that thou canste deuise a noumber of secretes, whereof any one might bee sufficiente to bryng my purpose to effecte. I doe require thee to fulfill my desire in that behalfe, and to giue me thy helpe to bryng this my desire to passe: whiche if thou doe, I will acknowledge my self so long as I shall liue, to bee so muche bounde vnto thee, that thou shalt commaunde me and all that I haue, in any occasion of thine, as freelie and as boldlie as thou maiest now, any thing that is thine owne.

The scholer when he had heard Gonsales and his demaũde stoode still awhile, as musyng vppon the requeste, and in the meane while discoursed with hym self, how by the occasion of this entente, and resolution of Gonsales, he might perhappes finde out awaie to come by the possession of Agatha, and to haue her in his handes, and at his deuotion. But keepyng secrete his thoughtes and meanyng, he made hym aunswere: That true it was, that he wanted not secrete compositions, to make folke dye with poison, so as it could neuer bee discerned by any Phisition or other, whether the cause were violent, or no, but that for twoo respectes he thought it not good to yeeld vnto his requeste. The one, for that Phisicke and Phisitions were appointed in the worlde, not to bereue menne of their liues, but to preserue them, and to cure them of suche diseases, as were daungerous and perillous vnto theim: The other because he did forsee, in what ieoperdie he should putte his owne life, whensoeuer he should dispose hymself to worke any suche practise, consideryng how seuerely the lawes haue prescribed punishementes for suche offences. And that it might fall out how warely soeuer the thing were wrought, that by some sodaine or vnlooked for accident, the matter might be discouered

(as

(as for the moste parte it seemeth that GOD will haue it) in whiche case he were like to encurre no lesse daunger then Gõsales, and bothe (assured) without remission to lose their liues. And that therefore he would not for the first respect, take vpon hym to doe that, whiche was contrarie to his profession: Nor for the seconde, hazarde his life to so certaine a daunger, for so hatefull a thing as those practises are to all the worlde.

Gonsales verie sorie to heare his deniall, told hym that the Lawes and dueties of freendship, doeth dispence well enough with a manne, though for his freende he straine sometyme his conscience. And therefore, he hoped that he would not forsake hym, in a cause that concerne hym so weightilie as that did. And that neither of those twoo respectes (if thei were well cõsidered) ought to bee able to remoue hym from pleasuryng of his freende. For that now adaies, aswell were thei accompted and estemed Phisitions, that killed their pacientes, as thei that did cure thẽ: and because the thing beyng kept secret betweene them twoo alone, he needed not to doubt, or feare any daunger of his life by the Lawe. For if it should by any mischaunce happen, that he should bee imputed or burthened with poisonyng of his wife, he assured hym that he would neuer whilest he had breathe, confesse of whom he had the poison, but would rather suffer his tongue to be pulled out of his hedde, or endure any torment that might be deuised.

The Scholler at the laste seemyng to bee wonne, by the earnestnesse of his petition: saied, that vpon that condition and promesse, of not reuealyng him at any tyme, he would be content rather to shewe hymself freendlie vnto hym, then a true professor of his Science, or an exact regarder of his cõscience: and that he would doe as he would haue hym.

And hauyng lefte Gonsales verie glad and ioyfull, for that his promesse, he went home, and made a certaine composition of mixture of pouders, the vertue whereof was suche, that it would make them that tooke any quantitie thereof, to slepe so soundlie, that thei should for the space of certaine howers seme vnto all menne, to bee starke deade. And the nexte daie he retourned to Gonsales, and to deliuer it vnto hym, saiyng: Gonsales,

ſales, you haue cauſed me to dooe a thyng, I proteſte I would not dooe it for my life: But ſince you maie ſee thereby, that I haue regarded more your freendſhippe, then my duetie, or the conſideration of that whiche is honeſt and lawfull: I muſte require you eftſones to remember your promeſſe, and that you will not declare to any creature liuyng, that you haue had this poiſon of me.

Whiche thing Gonſales verie conſtauntlie vpon his othe did promiſe hym againe, and hauyng taken the pouder of him, aſked hym in what ſorte he was to vſe it: And he tolde hym, that if at Supper he did caſte it there vpon her meate, or into her brothe, ſhe ſhould dye that night followyng, without either paine or tormente, or any greeuous accidentes, but goe awaie euen as though ſhe were a ſleape. That Euenyng at Supper tyme, Gonſales failed not to put the pouder into his wifes potage, who hauyng taken it, as ſone as Supper was doen feelyng her ſelf verie heauie and drouſie, went to her Chamber and gatte her to bedde (for ſhe laie not with Gonſales, but whē he liſte to call her, whiche had been verie ſeldome, ſince he did fall into loue with the ſtrumpet, and within an hower after, the operation of the pouder tooke ſuche force in her bodie, that ſhe laye as though ſhe had been dedde, and altogether ſenceleſſe, Gonſales in like ſort when he ſawe his tyme went to his bed, and liyng all that night with a troubled minde, thinking what would become of Agatha, and what ſucceſſe his enterpriſe would take, the Mornyng came vpō hym before he could once cloſe his eyes, whiche beeyng come he roſe, not doubtyng but that he ſhould aſſuredlie finde his wife dedde, as Alonſo had promiſed hym. And as ſoone as he was vp, he went out of his houſe, and ſtaied but an hower abroade, and then he retourned home again, and aſked his Maide, whether her Miſtres were vp or no. The Maide made hym aunſwere, that ſhe was yet a ſleape: And he makyng as though he had marueiled at her long liyng in bedde, demaunded her how it happened that ſhe was ſo ſluggiſhe that Mornyng, contrarie to her cuſtome, whiche was to riſe euery Mornyng by breake of the daie, and badd her goe and wake her, for he would haue her to giue hym

ſome

some thing, that laye vnder her keyes. The wenche accordyng to her Maisters commaundement, went to her Mistres bedde side, and hauyng called her once or twise somewhat softely, when she sawe she waked not, she laied her hand vpon her, and giuyng her a shagge, she saied withall, Mistres awake, my Maister calleth for you. But she liyng still, and not awakyng for all that the Maide tooke her by the arme, and beganne to shake her good and hard: and she not withstandyng, neither answeryng, nor stirryng hande or foote. The Maide retourned to her Maister, and tolde hym that for aught she could doe, she could not gette her Mistres to awake. Gonsales hearyng the Maide to saie so, was glad in his mynde: But fainyng hymself to be busied about somwhat els, and that he regarded little her speeche, he bidde her goe againe, and shake her till she did waken. The Maide did so, and rolled and tumbled her in her bed, and all in vaine: Wherefore commyng againe vnto her Maister, she saied vnto hym, that vndoubtedly she did beleeue, that her Mistres his wife was dedde, for she had founde her verie colde, and rolled her vp and doune the bedde, and that yet she stirred not. What? dedde q Gonsales, as if he had been all agaste and amazed, and risyng there withall, he went to her beddes side, and called her, and shaked her, and wrong her by the fingers, and did all that might bee, as he thought, to see whether she were aliue: But she not feelyng any thing that he did, laie still like a dedde bodie, or rather like a stone.

Wherefore, when he sawe his purpose had taken so good effecte, to dissemble the matter, he beganne to crie out, and to lament, and to detest his cruell Destinie, that had so sone bereued hym of so kind, so honest, and so faithfull a wife: and hauing in the ende discouered her bodie, and finding no spot or marke, whereby any token or signe of poisonyng might be gathered, as one that would not seme to omit any office of a louyng husband, he sent for the Phisition to loke vpon her, who hauyng vsed some suche meanes, as he thought mete to make her come to her self: finally, seyng her to remaine vnmoueable, and with out sence, concluded, that some sodaine accident had taken her in the night, whereof she had died, and for dedde he left her.

At whiche his resolutiō, though Gonsales were very glad, yet to the outward shewe declaryng hym self to be verie sorie, and full of woe and heauinesse, he behaued hymself in suche cūnyng sorte, as he made all the worlde beleeue, that he would not long liue after her. And hauyng called her freendes, and lamented with them her sodaine death and his misfortune: In fine, he caused her Funerall to bee verie sumptuouslie and honourably prepared, and buried her in a Vaute, whiche serued for a Toumbe to all his auncestours, in a Churche of a Frierie, that standes without the Citie.

Alonso that was verie well acquainted with the place, and had hym self a house not verie farre from that Frierie, wente his waie that same Night vnto his saied house, and when he sawe the tyme to serue for his purpose, he gatte hym to the Vaute or Toumbe wherein Agatha was laied, with one of these little Lanters, that thei call blinde Lanterns (because thei tourne them, and hide their light when thei liste.) And because he was a yong manne of verie good strengthe, and had brought with hym instrumentes of iron to open the Toumbe, and lifte vp the stone that couered it, he gatte it open, and hauyng vnderpropped it surely: he went into the vaute, and toke the woman straight waie in his armes, minding to bryng her out, and carrie her awaie so a sleape as she was. But the force and vertue of the powder, beeyng finished and spent, assone as he moued her, she awaked out of her sleape, and seyng her self clad in that sorte, emong ragges and dedde bones, she beganne to trēble, and to crie: Alas where am I? Or who hath brought me hether, wretche that I am? Marie that hath your cruell and vnfaithfull housebande, aunswered the Scholer: who hauyng poisoned you, to marrie a common Strumpet, hath buried you here, whether I come to trie if by my skill I could reuiue you, and call backe your soule by those remedies, whiche I had deuised vnto your bodie againe: Whiche if I could not haue doen, as I entended, I was resolued to haue died here by you, and to haue laied my dedde bodie here by yours, to reste vntill the latter daie, hopyng that my Spirite should in the meane while haue come and enioyed yours, where euer it had been.

been. But since the Heauens haue been so fauourable vnto me, as in this extreme daunger wherein you were, to graunt suche vertue vnto the remedies, whiche I haue vsed toward you, as the whiche I haue been able to keepe vndissolued, your gentle Spirite with your faire bodie. I hope (my deare) that you will hence forthe consider, what the affection of your wicked housbande hath been toward you, and how greate good will, and by consideration thereof, discerne and resolue whiche of vs twoo hath beste deserued to be beloued of you.

Agatha findyng her self in that sort buried in deede, did easily beleeue the truthe whiche the Scholer told her, and to her self concluded, that her housebande had shewed hym self in her behalf, a man of all other moste cruell and disloyall. Wherfore tournyng her self toward the Scholer, she saied vnto hym.

Alonso, I can not deny, but that my housebande hath been to me, not onely vnkinde, but cruell alsoe: nor I can not but cōfesse, that you haue declared your self to bee moste louyng and affectioned toward me: And of force I must acknowledge my self beholdyng vnto you, of no lesse then of my life, since (alas) I see my self here emong dedde bodies buried aliue. But for as muche, as though my housebande haue broken his vowe to me, I haue not yet at any tyme failed my faithe to hym. I doe require you, that if you desire that I should esteeme this kind and louyng office of yours, as it deserueth to bee esteemed, or make accompt of this life, whiche you haue giuen me, you will haue due regarde and consideration of myne honestie, and that you will not by offeryng me any villanie (whiche neverthelesse I can not any waie misdoubte, where I haue alwaies found so muche and so greate courtesie) make this your courteous and pitifull acte to bee lesse cōmendable, and praise worthie then it is. Whiche if you doe bridle your vnlawfull and sensuall appetite and desire, will remain the moste vertuous and worthie of honour and fame, that euer courteous Gentleman hath doen for a miserable woman, since the world began.

Alonso failed not with affectuall and manifest argumentes to perswade her, that her housbande had now no more right or title to her at all, and that although he had, yet if she were

wise,

wise, she should not committe her self vnto his courtesie againe, since by this mortall token, he had giuen her a sufficient testimonie of his ranckor, and euill will towardes her, whereby she might well enough bee assured not to escape, when soeuer she should resolue, to putte her self againe into his handes: And that therefore she was not to make any accompt of hym, but to shewe her self thankfull, for so greate a benefite as she had receiued, and to requite hym so with her fauour and courtesie, as he might now in the ende, attaine to gather the fruite of his long and constaunte good will, and of his trauell susteined for the saffegarde of her life. And with those wordes bendyng hymself towarde her, he would haue taken a kisse of her lippes. But Agatha thrustyng hym backe, saied to hym again. If my housebande (Alonso) haue broken those bandes, wherewith I was knit vnto hym by Matrimonie, through his wicked and leude demeanour, yet haue not I for my parte dissolued theim, neither will I at any tyme so long as I shall liue. As for committyng my self vnto his courtesie, or goyng any more into his handes, therein I thinke it good to followe your aduise: not that I would bee vnwillyng to liue and dwell with hym, if I might hope to finde hym better disposed: but because I would be lothe to fall eftsones into the like daunger and greuous perill. And as for requityng you, for this your commendable trauaile in my behalfe, I knowe not what better recompence I am able to giue you, then to rest bounde vnto you for euer, and to acknowledge my self beholdyng vnto your courtesie for my life: Whiche Obligation if it maie satisfie you, I will be as glad and as content, as I maie bee in this miserable state wherein I am. But if your meanyng perchance bee, that the losse of myne honestie, should bee the rewarde and hire for your paines, I dooe beseche you to departe hence out of this Toumbe, and to leaue me here enclosed, for I had rather dye here thus buried quicke, through the crueltie of my housebande, then through any suche compassion or pitie to saue my life, with the losse of myne honour and good name.

The Scholer by those wordes, perceiued well enough the honest disposition of Agatha, whiche he wondered at, conside-

ryng

ryng that the terror of death it self was not able once to moue her from her faithfulnes and constancie of minde. And though it were grieuous vnto him to finde her so stedfast, yet hopyng that by tyme in the ende he might ouercome her chaste and honest purpose, aunswered: that he could not but commende her for her disposition, though he deserued a kinder recompence of his long and feruent loue, and she a more louyng and faithfull housbande. But since she was so resolued, he would frame him self to be content with what she would, and not craue of her any thyng that she would not willingly graunt hym to haue. And therewith helpyng her out of the Sepulcher, he led her home vnto his house, and lefte her there with an olde woman that kept his house, to whom he recommended her, and whose helpe he was assured of, to dispose the good will of Agatha towardes hym, and the next mornyng retourned into the Citie.

Gonsales after a fewe daies, seeming not to be able to liue without a wife to take care of his familie, wedded that honest Dame Aselgia, and made her Mistres of hym self and all that he had. This his newe mariage so sone contriued, caused the freendes of Agatha to maruaile not a little, and to misdoubte that the sodaine death of their kinsewoman, had not happened without some misterie. Neuerthelesse, hauyng no token nor euidence or profe, thei helde their peace. But Gonsales hauyng his desired purpose and liuyng with his newe wife, it befell vnto hym (through Goddes iust iudgement with this his ioly Dame) as it chaunced to Agatha with hym before. For Aselgia that was neuer wont to feede with so spare a diet, as she that had neuer bin contented before without greate chaunge, nor had not bin vsed to that kinde of straightnes (which Gonsales growing ielous of her, began to keepe her in) but had alwaies liued at libertie, and with suche licentiousnesse, as women of her profession are wont to doe, became in shorte space to shewe her self so precise vnto hym, and to hate and abhorre hym in suche extreme sorte, that she could not abide to see, or heare hym spoken of. By occasion of whiche her demeanour towardes hym: Gonsales to his greefe began at last, to knowe and to discerne what difference there is betweene the honest and carefull loue of an honest wife, and the dissemblyng of an arrant Strumpet. Wherefore one daie among the rest, complainyng of the little loue whiche he perceiued she bare hym, and she aunsweryng hym thwartly. Gonsales fallyng into heate of Choler, saied angerly vnto her: haue I thou naughtie packe poysoned Agatha for thy sake, that was the kindest and the louingest wife that euer man had, and is this the rewarde I haue and the requitall thou yeeldest me, to shewe thy self euery daie more despightefull and crabbed then other? Aselgia hauyng heard hym and noted well his wordes, tooke holde of them, and straight waie thought that she had founde the waie to rid her self of Gonsales: wherefore she reueiled his speeches vnto a Ribalde of hers, suche a one as supplied her want of that which Gonsales alone nor ten suche as he were able to satisfie her withall, and induced hym to appeache hym for that facte, assuryng her self that the Lawe would punishe hym with no lesse then death, and thereby she to remaine at libertie to dooe what she list againe, as she had been before. This companion accused Gonsales vpon his owne wordes vnto the frendes of Agatha, who hauyng had halfe a suspition thereof before, went and accused him likewise before the Judge, or hed Magistrate of the Citie. Wherupon Gonsales and his woman were both apprehended and put to their examinations, to searche out the truthe: which Gonsales being halfe conuicted by the confession of the gentle peate his newe wife, but chiefly grieued with the worme of his owne conscience, and to auoyde the torment of those terrors whiche he knewe were prepared for him, confessed flatly, affirmyng that he had poysoned her with a poysone whiche he had kept of long tyme before in his house, perfourmyng yet therein the promise whiche he had made vnto the Scholer: And vpon his owne confession, sentence was giuen against hym that he should loose his hed.

Alonso when he vnderstoode that Gonsales was condemned to dye, was very glad thereof, supposyng that he beyng once dead, Agatha (who all this while for any thyng that the olde woman could saie or alledge vnto her in the behalfe of Alonso, would neuer yeeld or consent to any one poincte where-

in

in her honour mighe haue beene touched or spotted) should remaine at his discretion, and that she would no longer refuse to graunt hym her good will when she should see her self deliuered of Gonsales. But the daie beyng come wherein he was to be put to execution, she hauyng had inteligence of all that had passed, and knowyng that he was appoincted to dye that daie, determined with her self that she would in that extremitie deliuer her disloyall housebande, and giue hym to understande how little she had deserued to bee so entreated by hym as she had been. Wherefore hauyng gotten out of Alonso his house, she hied her unto the Citie as fast as she could, and beeyng before the Justice or Magistrate she saied unto him. Sir, Gonsales whom you haue condenmed and commaunded to be put to death this daie, is wrongfully condemned: for it is not true that he hath poysoned his wife, but she is yet a liue, and I am she. Therefore I beseche you giue order that execution maie be staied, since that your sentence is grounded upon a false enformation and confession is uniust, as you maie plainly discerne by me beyng here.

When the Gouernour heard Agatha speake in this sorte whom he had thought to haue been deade and buried, he was all amazed and halfe afraied to looke upon her, doubtyng that she was rather her spirite or ghoste, or some other in her likenesse then a liuely woman in deede: for she was apparelled in a very plaine and blacke attyre, and was very wanne and pale by reason of the affliction whiche she had indured. First, for her owne ill fortune, and then for the mischaunce of her housband.

In this meane while, the Sergantes and Officers had brought Gonsales before the Justice or Magistrate, to the ende that he (accordyng to the custome of the Citie) should giue them commaundement to leade hym to the place of execution, and there to fulfill his sentence upon hym. But as sone as Agatha perceiued hym, she ranne unto hym, and takyng hym about the necke and kissing him she saied. Alas my deare housebande, whereunto doe I see you brought through your owne folly and disordinate appetite which blinded your iudgement. Beholde here your Agatha aliue and not deade: who euen in this extremitie is come to shewe her self, that louyng and faithfull wife vnto you, that she was euer.

The Iustice or Gouernour seyng this straunge accident, caused execution to be staied, and signified the whole case vnto the Lorde of the Countrey, who at that tyme chaunced to bee at Sciuille: who wonderyng no lesse then the other at the matter, caused bothe Gonsales and his wife to bee brought before him, and demaunded of them how it had chaunced that she hauyng bin buried for deade was now founde aliue. Gonsales, could saie nothyng but that for the loue he bare vnto Aielgia he had poysoned his wife, and that he knewe not how she was reuiued againe. But Agatha, declared how the Scholler with his skill had deliuered her from death, and restored her life vnto her, but how or by what meanes she could not tell.

The Lorde hauyng sent for Alonso, and demaunded hym of the truth, was certified by hym, how that in steede of poison he had giuen to Gonsales a pouder to make her sleape: Affirmyng likewise that notwithstandyng the long and earneste pursuite, whiche he had made to obtaine her loue, and the crueltie and iniurie whiche she sawe her housebande had vsed towarde her, to put her in that daunger and perill of her life, out of whiche he had deliuered her, yet could he neuer by any perswasion or entreatie winne her to fulfill his desire, or bryng her to make breache of her faithe and honestie. By whiche reporte the Lorde knewe verie well, that in an honest woman the regarde and respect of her honour and chastitie, doeth farre exceade any other passion, for any miserie be it neuer so great. And commendyng highly the loue, and constancie of the woman towarde her housebande, and praisyng the pollicie of Alonso, he tourned hym self vnto Gonsales, and saied vnto hym. Full euill hast thou deserued to haue so good, and so verteous a Gentlewoman to thy wife, and in reason she ought now rather to be Alonso his wife then thine: Neither wert thou worthie of lesse then that punishment, whiche the Lawe hath condemned thee vnto, though she be yet aliue, since thou, asmuch as in thee laye, hast doen, to bereue her of her life. But I am content that her vertue and goodnesse, shal so muche be auaile-

able

able vnto thee, that thou shalt haue thy life spared vnto thee for this tyme: Not for thy owne sake, because thou deseruest it not, but for hers, and not to giue her that sorrowe and greefe, whiche I knowe she would feele, if thou shouldest dye in that sorte. But I sware vnto thee, that if euer I maie vnderstande that thou dooest vse her henceforthe, otherwise then louyngly and kindely, I will make thee to thy greeuous paine proue how seuerely I can punishe suche beastly and heinous factes, to the example of all others.

Gonsales imputyng his former offence, to want of witte and Iudgement, made promis vnto the Lorde, that he would alwaies dooe as he had commaunded hym. And accordinglie hauyng forsaken cleane that baggage strumpette, that he had wedded: he liued al the rest of his daies in good loue and peace with Agatha his wife, whose chaste and constant minde, caused Alonso where before he loued her for her exterior beautie, euer after to reuerence her, & in maner to worship her as a diuine creature, for the excellēcie of her vertue. Resoluing with hym self that a more constaunt faithe and honest disposition could not bee founde in any mortall woman.

FINIS.

Of Aramanthus
borne a Leper.

The argument of the vij. Historie.

¶ Aramanthus *soonne to* Rodericke *Kyng of* Tolosia, *beeyng borne a Leper, was sent by his father to the Ile of* Candy *for remedie, and by a tempeste at the Sea, the Shippe was driuen into Turkie, where she was caste awaie, and no manne saued but the childe, whiche was taken vp by a poore Fisherman, and fostered as his owne soonne, and afterwardes seruyng the Turke in his warres, shewed hym self so politique that the Turke by his onely aduise, incroched muche vpon the Christians, and in fine by his meane the Citie of* Tolosia *was taken, his father put in prison, and how in the ende he was knowne to bee the soonne of* Rodericke.

Shall not neede by any long circumstaunce to discribe, how many troubles, tumultes, broyles, Brabbles, Murthers, Treasons, how kingdomes haue been disturbed, how many Countries laied waste: How many Cities haue been sacked, how many Townes haue been rased, and how many mischeefes haue euer happened, sithence the firste creation of the worlde, vntill this present daie, by that monsterous vice Ambition. Consideryng that euery Historie maketh mentiõ, euery Chronicle beareth recorde, and euery age, tyme, and season, haue seen with their eyes, and this our tale that followeth shall some thyng make more euident.

There was sometyme remainyng in the famous Citie of Tolosia a worthie Kyng, whose name was Rodericke: who was

was

was likewise espoused to a moste vertuous Queene called Isabell, and truely a happie Court it might bee called, whiche thei held, aswell for the loue that was betweene the kyng and Queene: As for the vertue and clemencie, wherewith bothe the one and the other were accompanied.

There was remainyng in the Court, the Duke of Caria, who was the onely brother of Rodericke Kyng of Tolosia, this Duke beeyng a greate deale more vicious then his brother was vertuous, practised no other thing, but how he might come by the kyngdome of Tolosia: Knowing that there were no more betweene hym and it but the Kyng, who loued hym more dearely by a greate deale then he deserued. But it fell out the Queene Isabell was knowne to bee with childe, the Duke verie lothe that any other heires should steppe in betwene hym and home, deuised to poyson the Queene, & so had thought to haue dooen, by as many as the Kyng should haue taken to wife (if at any tyme thei proued to be with child) but by the prouidence of God, this poyson tooke no greate effecte in the Queene, sauing that whē she was deliuered of a sonne, the child was founde to be in a notable Leprosie, and the Kyng hauyng intelligence of an excellent Phisition, (but especially for the curyng of that desease) was remainyng in the Ile of Candy, prepared a Ship presently to sende the childe, whiche by the extreamitie of a contrarie winde, was driuen into Turkie, and the Shippe caste awaie vppon the maine, and all the meinie drouned exceptyng the childe, whiche beyng in a Cradle was carried to the shore as it laye. Where a Fisherman founde it, with suche sumptuous furnitures aboute it, with a verie riche Iewell hangyng aboute the necke. He tooke it vp in his armes, and caryyng it home, with Bathes and homely Oyntmentes of his owne deuising, within a very little space, the childe was restored to perfecte health, whom he called Aramanthus, and brought hym vp as his owne sonne, the childe knowyng no other in deede, but that the Fisherman had been his father, and as Aramanthus grewe in yeres, so he proued of a verie comely personage, bnt of a moste excellent and perfecte witte, although he had no other trainyng vp, but

vsed

vsed to goe to the Sea with his father a fishyng.

Now it fell out that the Turke was leauiyng a mightie Armie, to set vpon the Christians, the cause was this, he had twoo children, a sonne and a daughter, the daughter her name was Florella, whose beautie was verie excellent, and mindyng to matche his daughter with some noble Prince, he pretented that suche Countries, Cities, Tounes, Castelles, Fortes, or what so euer he could by conquest get from the Christians, to giue them all for his daughters dowrie.

Aramanthus hearyng of this preparation to the warres, would needes become a Souldier, where at his father the Fisherman was greatly displeased, and beganne to preache vnto his sonne of the incommodities of warre, and with how many miseries Souldiers are besieged. Aramanthus whose basenesse of his bringyng vp, could not conceale the nobilitie of his birthe, would in no wise be perswaded but goe he would, and beyng pressed for an ordinarie Souldier, when he came to the place of seruice shewed hym self so valiant, and in verie shorte space became to be so expert, that, that Captaine vnder whose Ensigne he serued, bare awaie the credite from all the reste: and in the ende was hym self preferred to charge, whiche he gouerned with so greate discretion, and still conducted with suche celeritie and sleight, that who but Aramanthus and his companie had the onely name throughout the Turkes cāpe, and where there was any attempt to be giuen, where valiancie should bee showne, Aramanthus he must giue the charge, and where any policie must bee put in practise, Aramanthus he must laye the platte: that to bee shorte, he grewe into suche credite with the greate Turke hym self, that Aramanthus onely gaue hym cousaill in all his affaires, and there with all had so good successe, that his practises stil preuailed, and came to happie ende, that the Turke by his aduise, had dooen wonderfull spoiles vpon the Christians, and had taken from them many Cities, Tounes, and Prouinces.

And thus leauyng them in the warres for a season, I will conuaye my tale againe to Isabell Queene and wife to Rodericke, who was now the second time knowne to be with child,

whereat

whereat the Duke of Caria beyng wonderfully wrothe, pretendyng to finde a quicke dispatche for all together, he secretly accused the Queene of Adulterie to the Kyng his brother, and with suche allegations, and false witnesses as he had prouided, so enformed the king that his tale was credited: and the rather for that the kyng knowyng his Queene to bee with child, did thinke hym self too farre spent in yeres to dooe suche a deede. And yet the kyng was replenished with so greate pitie, that he could not endure to heare of her death: He therefore by a messenger, commaunded her presently to departe the Court: and in paine of her life, neuer after to come in his presence. These newes did wonderfully amaze the Queene, who with many piteous intercessions, desired to knowe her accusers, and that she might but speake for her self before his Maiestie, and then as he should finde her, to vse her accordyng to her desertes. But all in vaine, for the Duke had so throughlie incensed the Kyng, that he would neither abide to see, nor heare her. The Duke understandyng how matters had passed, came to the Queene, and seemed muche to lamente her case, perswadyng her to holde her self contented for a little season, not doubtyng but in tyme, that he hym self would so perswade with his brother, that she should bee heard to speake in her owne defence, in the meane season, if it pleased her to vse his house in the Countrey, he would prouide for her all maner of necessaries, what soeuer she should want, and for her better comfort, if she had any assured freende, whose companie she desired, that she might secretly sende for theim to holde her fellowshipp, and to passe the tyme, and that he hym self would many tymes visite her, and daiely enforme her how matters did passe in her behalfe, with the kyng his brother.

The poore Queene, thinkyng all had proceaded of good will, whiche this Traitour had proffered, gaue him more then a thousande thankes, reposyng her self and the innocencie of her cause, onely in this Iudas, who practised nothyng els but her death, and the death of that she went withall.

The nexte daie he prouided a couple of Ruffians, suche as he knewe were for his purpose, whiche should haue secretely conueighed her to the Dukes house (as she had thought) but as the Duke had willed them, as thei rode ouer a Forest when thei came to the side of a woode, thei tooke her from her horse, spoiled her of suche thynges as were aboute her, and mynded to haue killed her, and throwne her in some Bushe: But it fell out that there were certaine banished menne in the Woode, whiche liued in that desarte in maner of Outlawes, and hearyng the piteous complainte of the Queene, thei came to her rescue, but the villaines that would haue slain her, perceiuyng them, fledde and left the Queene, where these outlawes came vnto her, vnto whom from poinct to poinct she declared euery thyng, how it was happened vnto her, the Outlawes hauyng greate compassion, when thei knewe her to be the Queene, for that thei had euer heard her to bee noblie reported on, brought her with theim to their Caue, where thei ministered suche releef to her distresse, as menne might doe that were in their estates. The Queene thinkyng that GOD had preserued her life to some better purpose, contented her self for a season to remaine emongest theim: Where she learned to plaie the Cooke, and to dresse their meate, suche as thei brought in, or could prouide for in the Forest. And thus leauyng the Queene with these Outlawes, I will retourne againe to speake of Aramanthus, who was now deuisyng to frame a plotte, how he might betraie the Citie of Tolosa, whereof his Father was kyng, as you haue heard.

For the Turke hauyng intelligence of the pleasauntnesse of this Citie, and of the wonderfull wealthe and riches wherewith it did abounde, and therewithall had learned that is was of suche force and inuinsible strengthe, that there was no maner of hope how it might be subdued, whereat the Turke was verie sorowfull and sadde.

But my yong Fisherman Aramanthus, whose cunnyng neuer failed, where courage could not helpe, caused the Turke with his whole armie by sea, to come before this Citie, whiche is situate faste vpon the sea side, and there to come to an anker, where Aramanthus hymself, as a messenger appoincted from the Turke, came to the kyng of Tolosa, to whom he told this tale.

tale. That the Turke his Maister hauyng been in diuers partes of Christendome, where he had made warres a long space, and vpon diuers consideratio͂s, mindyng to departe with his Armie into his owne Countrey for a season, and beyng vpon the Seas: one night as he was lying vpon his bedde, beholde, a vision appeared vnto hym in a dreame, whiche shewed hym how greeuouslie he had offended the GOD of the Christians in the persecutyng, spoilyng, and the murtheryng of theim, as he had doen in this iourney, and for that he should knowe, that the Christian GOD was the moste high and almightie God in deede, whō with his tyrannie he had so displeased, he should bee creepled of all his limmes from that tyme forthe, till his diyng daie, whiche should verie shortlie followe, with this he awaked, and giuyng a piteous grone, suche as was about him commyng vnto hym, founde hym in a wounderfull maze, and so benummed in all his partes, that he was not able to stirre hande nor foote: The nexte daie callyng his Counsailers and Captaines aboute hym, not able of hymself to come forthe emongest theim, but as he was brought out of his Cabbin on mens backes, he declared vnto theim the whole circumstaunce of the premisses, and beyng striken with a wonderfull remorse in conscience, he determined to saile backe againe, not myndyng to depart from out those partes of Christendome, till he had made satisfaction of all suche spoiles and outrages, as he had committed against the Christians, and hymself with his whole armie to become Christened, and there to be instructed in the true and perfect faith, and as he continued this determination, beholde, a contrary winde hath driuen vs on these partes, where hearyng of the fame of this noble Citie of Tolosia, he hath sent me vnto your grace, desiryng nothyng but your saffe conduct for hymself, and certaine of his cheef Lordes and Counsailers that be aboute hym, that in this noble Citie thei might bee Baptized, and receiue the Christian faithe, promisyng hereafter, not onely to ioyne in league, and perfecte amitie with the Christians, but also to lincke with theim in Religion, hymself, his Countries, Kyngdomes, and Prouinces.

This tale was not so smothly tolde, but there was greate

doubte and suspition had in the matter, in the ende thinkyng thei could receiue no preiudice, by receiuyng of so small a nomber, gaue safe condite for the Turke hymself, and for fiue hundred of his companie, suche as it pleased hymself to appoincte.

The nexte daie, the Turke was brought into the Citie on mennes shulders, with his appoincted companie, where he was worthely receiued by the kyng himself, with the rest of his lordes, and brought into a Pallace of purpose, verie richely furnished, where beyng laied doune vpon a bed, as though he had been able neither to stande nor sit, and giuyng the Kyng with the rest of his companie, greate thankes for his entertainment he desired hym with the Duke his brother (accordyng to the custome) to be his Godfathers when he should be Christened, to whiche request thei bothe willingly agreed: the next daie the Turke hymself was the first that receiued Christendome, and then all the reste of his noble menne that were with hym, the whiche beeyng finished, many godlie exhortations were preached vnto theim by learned men. The Turke seemed in verie gratefull maner to take this courtesie, wherwith the kyng had vsed hym: and thus takyng his leaue hymself withall his companie, departed againe aborde the shippes, the Turke hymself beyng caried vpon mennes backes, making showe as though he had been so feeble and weake, that he had not been able to haue mooued, or stirred any one ioynt without helpe, fainyng that he would haue departed with his companie into Turkie.

The Kyng of Tolosia, with all his people and Citezens, seing with what deuotion the Turke with the rest of his companie had receiue Christendome, beganne to thinke assuredly, that onely by the Deuine prouidence of GOD, the Turke was so conuerted, and doubted nothyng of the tale, whiche Aramanthus before had tolde them, whiche tourned in the ende to their vtter subuersion. For the next daie Aramanthus commyng againe to the Kyng, brought woorde of the death of the Turke, and with a piteous discourse vttered, with a nomber of fained sighes, saied: that aboute twelue a clocke of the night paste, the Turke deceased, and desired at the houre of his death that as in this worthie Citie, he had receiued the true and Catholike

tholike

tholike faithe, so likewise that he might be entoumbed, and receiue Christian buriall in the cathedrall Churche, to the which he had giuen by his Will fourtie thousande Frankes, more to the common Treasure of the Citie a hundred thousande frankes, to the kyng himself as a present of his good will, a riche Jewell, whiche hymself did weare of greate estimation, to the Duke his brother, his owne Armour and furniture. Item, to the releef of the poore within the Citie tenne thousande Frankes, many other thynges (q Aramanthus) he hath bequeathed that I haue not spoken of, the whiche God willing shalbe performed to the vttermoste.

The Kyng seemed greatelie to lamente the death of the Turke, and began to coniecture assuredly, that it was the will of God but to preserue his life till he had receiued christendome but the tyme of his buriall was deferred for certaine daies, till thinges might be prouided, and more readie for the pompe and solempnisyng of his Funerall, and wonderfull cost was bestowed by Aramanthus, who had the onely orderyng of the matter, hopyng in the ende to receiue the whole commoditie: and also to be rewarded with a large and bountifull intrest, the daie of buriall beyng at hande, Aramanthus desired the kyng, that for so muche as the Turke had finished his daies in the middest of his armie emongst his souldiers, that he might likewise be buried like a noble captaine, and accordyng to the maner of the feeld, he might be brought to his graue with certaine bandes, trailing their weapons, as the custome of souldiers is to burie their dedde. This request seemed to bee verie conuenient, and therefore was the readilier graunted: but what should I stand with long circumstaunce to discipher all the Ceremonies that were vsed in this treason. The daie was come that this practise must be put in vre, and an emptie coffin solempnly brought to the Citie, vnder showe of greate sorowe, when thei were al filled with greate ioye and gladnesse, to see what happie successe was like to followe, of that thei had premeditated, and accordyng as Aramanthus had giuen order, fiue thousande of their choise men were appoincted to marche, the one halfe before, and the other halfe after the Coffin, trailyng their Ensignes and weapons, and in this maner thei entered the Citie, where the kyng with his nobles and principalles of the Citie, were readie in mournyng weedes to accompanie the Corse. When Aramanthus sawe his tyme, the Alarum was giuen, and he hymself was the first that laied handes of the kyng his Father, the rest of his nobles were so enclosed, that there could not one of them escape: defence there was none to be made, for the one side were in armes, killyng and murthering of as many as thei could see stirryng in the streates: the other side vnprouided, glad to hide them selues, for the sauegard of their liues: the reste of the fleete were likewise in a readinesse, and rōnyng a lande entered the Citie, where there was no manne to repulse theim. And thus the famous Citie of Tolosia was taken by the Turkes, euen in a moment, without any maner of resistaunce: the Churches and prisons were filled full of Christians, where thei were whipped, racked, and tormented to the death, vnlesse thei would forsake their faithe, the kyng hym self with his brother and all the lordes, were committed to prison, there to be fedd with bread and water (and yet to be scantled with suche short alowance, as it was not able to suffice nature) and so to be dieted, vnlesse thei would forsake their faithe.

Now the Turke, who onely by the meanes of Aramanthus, had conquered from the Christians so many Cities and Townes, for the loue he bare vnto hym, and in respecte of his seruice, determined to make Aramanthus his soonne in lawe, and to giue hym his daughter Florella for his wife, and for her dowrie, all suche partes as he had taken from the Christians by conquest: and vnderstanding that the father of Aramanthus was but a poore Fisherman, he pretended likewise to make hym a Duke, and to giue hym liuyng to maintaine his estate. The Turke therefore withall possible speede, hasted messengers with shippyng, to bryng his daughter, with the olde Fisherman the supposed Father of Aramanthus, to this Citie of Tolosia, where he minded to performe that he had determined

Now it fell out that the miserable Queene Isabel (whom you haue heard was left with child, remainyng with certaine Outlawes) was deliuered of a daughter, whiche she her self

nursed

nursed in the Caue, where she had remained, and hearyng that the Turke had taken the Citie of Tolosia, would needes goe see what was become of the kyng her housebande: Her daughter whiche was not yet fully a yere olde, she committed to the Outlawes, to bee fostered with suche homely Junkettes, as thei could prouide, who seyng her determination, promised to drie Nurse the child so well as thei could, till she should make retourne. Thus preparyng her self in a verie simple attire, with a boundell of Broomes on her hedde, she came to the Citie of Tolosia, where roming vp and doune the streates to sell her Broomes, she learned all that had happened to the Kyng, and how he was readie to perishe, for want of foode and sustenance wherefore, myndyng to giue suche succours, as her habilitie would serue: She deuised in the maner of a poore seruaunt, to gette into the seruice of the Turke, who was the Jailer, and had the custodie of the Kyng, where euery night, as oportunitie would serue, she conueighed to hym through a grate, suche fragmentes as she spared out of her owne beallie, whiche were verie shorte, and there withall muche more homelie, but some thyng the better to amende his cheare. She would leane her self cloase to the grate, and thrustyng in her Teate betwene the Irons, the kyng learned againe to sucke, and thus she dieted him a long season. Neither wiste the kyng what she was, that bestowed on hym so greate grace and goodnesse: yet he blessed her more then a thousande tymes a daie. And although there were many of his companie, that died for wante of sustenaunce, yet he againe with these banquettes, recouered hymself, and began to waxe strong. Where at the Turke beganne to suspecte some parciallitie in the Jailer, and caused a priuie watche to bee kepte: But Isabell suspectyng nothyng, accordyng to her accustomed maner, at Night when it was darke came to her Nurserie, where her order that she so long vsed, was espied, and beeyng apprehended by the watche, the next daie she was presented to the Turke, and in what maner thei had founde her, whereat the Turke wonderfullie agreeued: Sware by Mahounde hymself, that she should presentlie bee tortured, with the greatest tormentes that might be deuised.

ſed. And in the middeſt of his furie, woorde was brought hym that his daughter Florella, with the Fiſherman that was Father to Aramanthus were arriued, and readie to preſent them ſelues before hym, whereat the Turke wonderfullie reioyſed, and callyng Aramanthus, cauſed them to bee brought in, Florella gaue that reuerence to the Turke, whiche bothe appertained to the duetie of a Childe, and alſo as belonged to his eſtate. Aramanthus likewiſe, although he were the greateſte Counſailour, apertinent to the Turke, yet vſed that duetifull reuerence to the Fiſherman his Father, as is to bee requird in a Childe. The Turke imbracyng his daughter Florella, tolde her the cauſe that he had ſent for her, was to eſpouſe her to Aramanthus, who although the Deſtinies had denaied to make Noble by place of birthe, yet through his vertues, valiaunce, and worthie exploites, he had gained the title of true Nobilitie, in deſpite of Fortunes teeth. Florella hauyng heard of the fame and worthineſſe of Aramanthus, was the beſte pleaſed woman in the worlde.

And the Turke tournyng hym towardes the Fiſherman, ſaied, and a thouſande tymes happie art thou old Father, that haſte liued to ſee thy ſelf ſo highly exalted in thy ofſpring: The poore Fiſherman kneelyng doune, ſaied: Moſte mightie, and magnificente Prince, not myndyng longer to conceale the thing, whiche might redounde ſo greatly to the contentation of ſuche worthie perſonages, ſeyng then that Aramanthus, who onely through his owne valiauncie, hath aſpired to ſo greate dignitie and honour. How greatly were I then to be blamed, and how worthely might I be condemned? If I ſhould take vpon me to bee the ſire of hym, who by all likelihoode, is deſcended of Roiall and Princelie race, for better teſtimonie, behold this riche Mantell, and theſe other coſtly furnitures, wherein I founde Aramanthus wrapped, and by ſeemyng ſaued by his Cradell, whiche brought hym a Shoore, from ſome Shippe that was wracked, where I founde hym by the Sea ſide (as I ſaie) wrapped in theſe ſumptuous furnitures, with this riche and precious Iewell about his necke, beyng but an Infaunte, by coniecture not aboue the age of a quarter of a yere,

where

where takyng hym vp in my armes, I brought hym home to my house, called hym by the name of Aramanthus, and thus fostered hym vp as my owne child, vntill the daie that he came to serue your Maiestie in the warres.

The Queene Isabell whiche stoode by, and heard this discourse, and seyng the furnitures and the Jewelles, wherwith she had decked her childe, assuryng her self that Aramanthus was her soonne, could no longer staie her speeche, but saied: And doe I then beholde my sonne with my vnhappie eyes, is he liuyng here in presence, whom I deemed to bee dedde? Oh moste gracious Goddes I yeelde you humble thankes, and would to God my soonne thy commyng had been but halfe so happie, as thy presence is ioyfull to me thy wretched mother. What newes be these (ꝙ the Turke) which I heard, I think the woman be out of her wittes: but what art thou that wouldest challenge Aramanthus for thy sonne, whose parentes now I wel perceiue, are no beggers like thy self. Yes surely (ꝙ the Queene) and much more miserable, then those that goe from doore to doore, and although his father sometyme swaied the sworde of gouernement, and satt in place and seate of Princely Throne. Dispatche then at once (ꝙ the Turke) and tell me who is his father, and what is the miserie wherwith he is perplexed: wherein if thou canst perswade me with a truth, assure thee that onely for Aramanthus sake, I am the man that will minister release.

Beholde then (ꝙ the Queene) Kyng Rodericke is his Father, whom thy self keepest here in pryson, in this miserable maner, and I whom thou seest here am his mother, the wife of the kyng, and sometyme the Queene of this wretched Citie of Tolosia, who beyng deliuered of a soonne, whiche by the pleasure of GOD was visited in my wombe, and borne in an extreame Leprosie: for helpe whereof he was sent by his Father by Shippyng to the Ile of Candy, and till this presente daie there was neuer tidynges heard, either of the Shippe, or of any one man that was in her. And now beholde I see with myne eyes the furnitures wherein I wrapped my childe, and the Jewell whiche I put about his necke, with my owne handes at his departure: the Fisherman verifiyng this tale to bee true, saied in deede that he found him in an extreame maladie, which he cured himself with medicines of his own prouiding.

Aramanthus hauyng heard how matters were sorted out, beganne to teare hym self, saiyng: Ah moste wicked and vnnaturall wretche, what Furies haue saued thee, that thou wart not drouned with the reste, but that thou must be preserued as an instrument to woorke thy parentes wracke: Come come you hellishe Hagges, and shewe your force on hym that hath worthely deserued it. But what hath Tantalus offended, that he should continually bee sterued? Or how hath Sisiphus that rowles the restlesse stone? Or what trespasse hath beene committed by Prometheus, Ixyon, Titias, or Danaus sillie daughters, drawyng water at the welle: That maie bee compared to that whiche I haue dooen, is it possible then that I should escape vnpunished? Or that the sacred Goddes will be vnreuenged of my facte, no no, I haue deserued to bee plagued, and haue merited more worthely to bee tormented then any of these afore rehearsed. Florella ouer hearyng these desperate speeches, fell doune in a sowne for greef to see her Aramanthus so disquieted. The Turke after his daughter was come againe to her self, sorowed to see the heauinesse of Aramanthus, caused the kyng his father, with the Duke of Caria presently to be sent for out of prison: And taking Isabell on the one of his handes, and Aramanthus on the other, he saied to the Kyng, Receiue here noble Prince, a moste louyng and faithfull wife, and a moste valiaunt and worthie soonne: And my self from an enemie, for euer after this, to become thy moste assured and trustie freende.

The Kyng was wonderfully amazed to heare these speeches, did thinke hym self to bee in some dreame: till in the ende he heard the whole discourse how euery thyng had happened, and beyng rauished with gladnesse, he saied.

O happie euill, whiche bryngeth in the ende so greate a good, and welcome bee that sorrowe, whereby is sprong a ioye, muche more surmountyng, then euer was any heauinesse: and with many like speeches, he still embraced his sonne

Aramanthus in his armes, and although he understoode that it was the Queene his wife, which so louyngly had succoured hym, when he was readie to haue famished in the Prison, for want of meate: yet he could not finde in his harte to beare her any countenaunce, considering what he had conceiued against her, by the informatiō of his brother (as before you haue heard) whiche beyng perceiued by the Duke, moste humbly desiring forgiuenesse: he confessed to the kyng al his mischeef, from the beginnyng to the endyng, whereof the Kyng was bothe sorie and glad: Sorie, for that he had so unnaturally dealt with so vertuous and courteous a wife: And glad for that he was so resolued and confirmed in her chastitie, whiche before he had in suspence.

And now the Turke, for the loue that he bare to Aramanthus, and for the likyng that he sawe to bee in his daughter towardes hym, whom he hym self had appoincted to bee her spouse, became in deede to be Christened, with all his retinew that was aboute hym, and then restoryng Rodericke againe to the kyngdome of Tolosia. By al consentes the mariage betweene Aramanthus and Florella, was concluded with great pompe and magnificence: and thus the Turke leauyng this new maried couple in the Citie of Tolosia, and departed with his armie into Turkie.

The Queene Isabell, not forgettyng the greate goodnesse she had receiued by these Outlawes, whiche before had saued her life, and with whom her daughter yet remained, so dealt with the Kyng her housebande, that thei were altogether sent for, and verie ioyfully receiuyng his daughter: restored the Outlawes againe to their libertie: bestowyng of them for recompence, roomes, and offices of credite and estimation.

Thus to conclude, euery one beyng well contented,
thei liued together in quietnesse, with many long and happie daies.

FINIS.

Of Phylotus and Emelia.

The argument of the viij. Historie.

¶Philotus *an olde and auncient Citizen of* Rome, *falleth in loue with* Emelia, *a yong and beautifull virgin the daughter of* Alberto, *who knowyng the wonderfull wealthe of* Phylotus, *would haue forced his daughter to haue maried hym, but in the ende was pretely deceiued by* Phylerno, *the brother of* Emelia, *who maried with* Phylotus *in his sisters steade, and other pretie actions that fell out by the waie.*

T hath many tymes bin had in question, and yet could neuer be decided from whence this passion of extreame loue doeth proceede, whose furie is suche where it once taketh possessiō, that (as thei saie) loue is without lawe, so it maketh the Pacientes to bee as vtterly voide of reason, but in my opinion the self same thyng, whiche is many tymes shadowed vnder the title of loue, maie more properly bee termed and called by the name of luste, but be it loue, or be it luste, the difference is nothyng so muche, as the humour that feedes it, is wonderfull straunge, and hath no maner of certaintie in it exceptyng this, it is without parcialitie, for commonly when it driueth vs to effect, it is doen without any maner of respect, for some tyme it maketh vs to linger after our frendes, somtyme to languish after our foes, yea: betweene whom there hath been had mortall hostilitie: the sonne hath beene seene to fall in loue with the wife of his father, the father again in like maner with the wife of his soonne, the Kyng hath bin attached with the poore and needie Begger, the poore againe in likyng with those of high degree, yea and though there haue been many which haue seen

their

their owne errour, and there with all haue confessed their abuse, yet thei haue not bin able to refraine them selues, from prosecutyng their follie to the ende, and all be it, reason proffereth vs sondrie sufficient causes, why we ought to refraine the appetite of our owne desires, yet fancie then is he that striketh suche a stroke, that reasons rules can naught at all preuaile, and like as those whom loue hath once intangled, the more thei striue the farther thei bee tied, so it is vnpossible that loue should be constrained, where affection breedes not likyng, nor fancie is not fed, but where these two hath once ioyned in election, al other affectes be so dimme and blinded, that euery vice seemeth to vs a vertue, whereof springeth this Prouerbe. In loue there is no lacke, so that in deede to saie the truth, if there be any pitie to be imputed, to this raging loue, it is in that it is not partiall nor hath it any respecte of persones, but bee thei frendes, be thei foes, be thei riche, be the poore, be thei young, be thei olde, bee thei wise, bee thei foolishe, loue is still indifferent, and respecteth all a like, but if any man will thinke that in respecte of beautie, we esteeme not all the reste: I am able to saie it is not true, consideryng how many haue forsaken the better likyng, and haue chosen the worse, so that for my parte the more I consider of it, the more I am amazed, and therefore will beate my braines no more aboute it, but leaue it to the credite of suche as haue bin louers themselues, whose skill in the matter I preferre before mine owne, and will come to my Historie of Phylotus, who beyng an aged man, fell in loue with a yong maiden, farre vnfittyng to his yeares, and followeth in this sorte.

In the gallant Citie of Naples, there was remainyng a yong man, called by the name of Alberto. This Alberto beyng maried not fully out a yeare, his wife was deliuered of a sonne, whom he named Phylerno, and vpon diuers considerations, myndyng to chaunge his habitation, he prepared hym self to goe dwell at Rome, and first takyng order for his sonne Phylerno, who for the tendernesse of his age he left still in Naples at nurse, hym self, his wife, with all the reste of his householde came to Rome, where he had not very long remained, but his wife was likewise deliuered of a daughter, whom he called by the name Emelia, who as she grewe in yeares, she likewise proued to bee very beautifull and faire, and amongst a greate nomber of others, there was dwellyng in Rome an auncient Citizen, whose name was Phylotus, a man very orderly in yeares, and wonderfully aboundyng in goods, this Phylotus hauing many tymes taken the viewe of Emelia, beganne to growe very sore in loue with her, or rather I maye saie in his olde yeares beganne to doate after this yong maiden, for it can not bee properly called loue in these olde men, whose dotage if it were not more then outragious, either their greate discretion would represse it, either their many yeares would mortifie it. But Phylotus in the ende desired Emelia of her father in the waie of mariage, Alberto accordyng to the custome of parentes, that desires to marie their daughters, more for goods, then for good will betweene the parties, more for lucre then for loue, more for liuing then for learning, more for wealth then for wit, more for honour then for honestie, and so thei maie haue great store of money thei neuer consider farther of the man. Alberto in like maner knowyng the wealth wherewith Phylotus was indued, who had neuer a childe but one onely daughter, whose name was Brisilla, gaue his full consent, without any farther consideration of the inequalitie of the yeares that was betweene Phylotus and his daughter, he neuer remembred what strifes, what iarres, what debates, what discontentment, what coūterfaityng, what dissemblyng, what louryng, what loathyng, what neuer likyng, is euer had where there is suche differences betwene the maried, for perfecte loue can neuer bee without equalitie, and better were a married couple to continue without liuyng, thē without loue: and what are the occasions that make so many womē to straie from their housbandes, but when thei bee maried to suche as thei cannot like of: but surely if women did throughly consider how daungerous it is for thē to deale with these olde youthes, I thinke thei would bee better aduised in medling with them, for besides that thei be vnwildie, lothsome, (and sir reuerence of you) very vnlouely for you to lye by, so thei bee commonly

inspired

inspired with the spirite of ielousie, and then thei will looke to you so narrowly, and mewe you vp so closely, that you will wishe a thousande tymes the Prieste had bin hanged that maried you, but then to late.

But to retourne to our Historie: Alberto respecting more the wealth of Phylotus, then the likyng of his daughter, gaue his consent to take him for his sonne in lawe, and tolde Emelia how he had disposed on her, Emelia seeyng what an olde babie her father had chosen to be her housebande, moste humbly desired hym to giue her leaue to chouse for her self, whereat her father beyng very angrie, beganne sharply to rate her saiyng, and arte thou then so muche wedded to thine owne will, that thou skornest to be derected by me thy louyng father, or thinkest thou that thy wisedome doeth so farre surmount my wit, that thou canst better prouide for thy self then I which so carefully haue hetherto brought thee vp, or doth the tendere loue or the chargeable cost which I haue bestowed on thee, deserue no better recompence, then to despise those that I would haue thee to like of.

Emelia fallyng doune of her knees before her father saied, moste deare and louyng father, moste humbly I beseche you, for the affection whiche by nature you beare me, not to thinke me so gracelesse a childe, that I would goe aboute to contrary you, or stubbornly would refuse what soeuer you would think conuenient for my behoofe, and although you shall finde in me suche duetie as is meete for a daughter, and all obedience that is fit for a childe, yet sir consider the harte whiche can not bee compelled, neither by feare, neither by force, nor is not otherwise to be lured, then onely by fancies free consent, and as you haue bestowed on me this fraile and transitori life, so my bodie shall be at your disposition as it shall please you to appoinct it, and will conclude with this humble petition, desiryng you not to bestowe me of any that is not agreable to my fancie and good likyng.

Well (ꝙ her father) then see you frame your likyng to like well of my likyng. I haue promised you to Phylotus in marriage, and Phylotus is he that shall be your housband, and

looke

looke you goe not aboute to contende againste that I haue determined, if you doe, neuer accompt me for father nor frende, and thus he departed.

Emelia hearyng this cruell conclusion of her father, was wonderfully abashed, and beeyng by her self in her Chamber, she beganne to consider of her fathers wordes, and for feare to incurre any farther displeasure, she deuised how she might frame her self to the likyng of her louer, and with a yong womans minde, she first beganne to consider of his wealth, of his callyng, of the reuerence wherewith he was vsed in the Citie, and that likewise in beyng his wife, she should also bee had in estimation, and bee preferred before other women of meaner credite, and to desire superioritie, it is commonly euery womans sicknesse, and therefore this could not chouse but please her very well, then she remembred how commodious it were to marrie one so wealthie as Phylotus, wherby she should not neede to beate her braines aboute the practising of housewiferie, but should haue seruauntes at commaundment to supplie that tourne, this likewise pleased her very well, but because she would well perswade her self, she beganne to coniecture how she should spende the time to her contentment, and therefore she beganne to thinke what a pleasure it was to bee well furnished with sondrie sutes of apparell, that in the mornyng when she should rise, she might call for what she liste to put on, accordyng as the tyme and the fasshion did require, and her fancie serued beste, for thus Phylotus was well able to keepe his wife, and this pleased her likewise very well, & then when she were vp, she might breake her fast with a cuppe of Malmsie, or Muskadine nexte her harte. It was very good for ill ayres in a mornyng, and this she thought was but an easie matter, and likewise pleased her very well: when she had broken her fast, then she might stirre about the house, and looke to this, and see to that, and where she found any thyng amis, not to touche it with her owne fingers, for marryng the beautie of her hande, but to call for Cicelie, Ione, or Cate, and to chide them like sluttes, that thei could not spie a faught but when thei must be tolde: this likewise pleased her very well, then to

haue

haue prouided for Dinner some Iunckettes, that serued beste her appetite, her housebande had good store of coyne, and how could it bee better spent then vpon them selues: to make their fare the better, this likewise pleased her verie well, now when she had dined, then she might go seeke out her examplers, and to peruse whiche works would doe beste in a ruffe, whiche in a Gorget, whiche in a Sleeue, whiche in a Quaife, whiche in a Caule, whiche in a Handcarcheef, what lace would doe beste to edge it, what seame, what stitche, what cutte, what garde, and to sitte her doune and take it forthe by little and little: and thus with her Nedle to passe the after noone, with deuising of thinges for her owne wearyng, this likewise pleased her passyng well, then to prouide for Supper some shift of diete, and sondrie sauces, the better to helpe the stomacke, Oranges, Lemons, Oliues, Caphers, Salades of sondrie sortes, alas a croune will goe a greate waie in suche trifles: This likewise pleased her verie well, when she had supped, to vse some exercise, accordyng to the season: if it were in Sommer, to goe walke with her neighbours to take the aire, or in her garden to take the verdure of swete and pleasaunt flowers, this likewise pleased her verie well, when she was come in, and readie to go to her Chamber, a Cuppe of cold Sacke to bedward, is verie good for digestion, and no coste to speake of where suche abondance doeth remaine, and this likewise pleased her verie well.

But now although she had deuised, to passe the daie tyme with suche contentation, when she remembred at Night, she must goe to bedde to be lubber leapt: and with what cold courtesie she should be entertained by her graie headed bedfelowe, what frosen embracementes he was able to bestowe of her, all was marde, and quite dashte out of remembraunce, and all the commodities before spoken of, that she should receiue in the tyme of the daie, would not serue to counteruaile that one incommoditie, in the season of the Night: Like as wee saie, one vice spilles a greate noumber of vertues. Thus Emelya was now to seeke, and could in nowise frame her self to loue Philotus: But when she had flattered her self with a thousande delightes, that she should receiue in the daie tyme by his wealth, when she remembred bedd tyme, she was as newe to beginne as before. Wherefore she remained in greate perplexitie, thinkyng her happe to bee over hard, and the comforte verie bare, where the beste choice had suche assuraunce of doubtfull ende. For to Marrie after her Fathers mynde, she knewe would breede her lothed life: and to gainsaie what he had determined, would likewise loose her fathers likyng, that she wiste not for her life whereon to resolue, and thus from daie to daie as she continued in this doubte. There happened to hit into her companie a yong Romaine gentleman, whose name was Flanius, who sodainly fell in Loue with Emelia, and takyng the tyme whileste his opportunitie serued: He let Emelia to vnderstande, of the greate Loue he bare her. Emelia, accordyng to the custome of women, made the matter verie coye at the firste, although in her harte she were right gladd, consideryng her case how it stoode. Flanius was so muche the more importunate vpon her, and with suche nice termes as woers be accustomed: he so Courted, and followed Emelia, that she perceiuyng his feruent affection, tolde hym a verie shorte circumstaunce, how her father had disposed her, to one that she could not like of, and therefore, if he would first promise to take her as his wife, and that he could finde suche meanes, to conueigh her from her fathers house in secret sorte (for otherwise she was sure her Father would be a let to hinder their purpose) she was contented to harken to his speeche, and yeelde to his demaunde. Flanius the gladdest man in the worlde, to heare these ioyfull newes, sware vnto her that all should bee accomplished, and that with as muche speede as her self would desire.

There was no more to cōclude of then, but how she might be conueighed from out her fathers house. Flanius deuised that late in an euenyng, or in the night tyme when euery one were quiet in their beddes, if she could finde the meanes to get forth of doores, then he would bee readie to receiue her. But that could not bee, for bothe her Father and Mother neuer failed, to bee at home in the Euenynges, and at nightes she was lodged in her fathers Chamber, that it was impossible for her to get forthe. So that there was no remedie, but that the feate

must

must bee brought in some after noone, when bothe her father and mother vsed to bee abroade about their businesse: and then she knewe not how to come forthe alone, because she had not been accustomed so to doe, and to followe a straunger, it would breede the greater suspition.

But Flauius to auoide all these surmises, deuised the nexte euenyng, to conueigh her in at some backe windowe of her fathers house, a sute of mannes apparell, wherin the next daie in the after noone, her father and mother being abroad, she should shift her self, and so come her waies vnknowne of any to suche a place: where he himself would be readie awaiting for her, and so conueighe her home to his owne house. This deuise Emelia liked passyng well, and accordyng as it was appoincted: The nexte euening Flauius conueighed this sute of apparel in at the windowe, where Emelia was readie to receiue it, and laiyng it vp in safetie, till the nexte daie in the after noone, her father and her mother beyng bothe forth of dores, she quickly shifted her self, into this mannes apparell, and thus forthe of dores she goes to her appointed place, where Flauius was staiyng, who accordyng to promise, cōueighed her home to his owne house.

This matter was not so closely handeled by Emelia, but she was espied by one of her fathers seruauntes, who beyng on the backside through a windowe, sawe her how she was strippyng of her self, and marked how she put on the mannes apparell, whereat the yong fellowe had greate marueile, and stood still beholdyng to see what would fall out in the ende. But whē he sawe her goe forthe adores, he hasted after into the streate: But Emelia was so sodainly gone, that for his life he wist not whiche waies to seeke after her, wherefore in a wonderfull haste, he came to his maister, whom he found in the Citie, in the companie of Philotus, saiyng: Oh sir, I haue verie euill newes to tell you, what is the matter (q his Maister) is any thyng amisse at home? Yea sir (q the seruaunte) your daughter Emelia is euē now departed into the Citie, in the habite of a manne: But whiche waies she went, I could not for my life deuise, for after she gat once forthe of the place where she shifted her, I could neuer more set eye of her.

Is Emelia gone (quod her louer Philotus) Oh GOD what euill newes bee these that I heare, and without any further staye, bothe the Father and the Louer, gatte theim out at the doores together, and aboute the streates thei runne like a couple of madde menne.

Now it fell out, that Phylerno the Sonne of Alberto, and Brother to Emelia, whom you haue heard before, was lefte at Naples, beyng an infant, and had remained there till this time at Schoole, and at this verie instant was come from Naples to Rome, to visite his Father and Mother, of whom he had no maner of knowledge, otherwise then by their names. And it fortuned that Alberto and Phylotus, happened to meete with Philerno in the Streates, who was so like his sister Emelia, that bothe Alberto, and Phylotus assured them selues, that it could bee no other but she. Wherefore Alberto commyng to hym, saied: Staie staie, moste shamelesse and vngracious Girle, dooest thou thinke that by thy disguisyng of thy self, in this maner, thou canste escape vnknowne to me, who am thy Father, ah vile strumpet that thou arte: what punishement is sufficiente for the filthinesse of thy facte? And with this he seemed as though he would haue flune vpon her in the Streate, to haue beate her: But Phylotus thruste in betweene theim, and desired his neighbour to staie hym self, and then imbracyng Philerno in his armes, he saied: Ah Emelia my sweete and louyng wenche, how causte thou so vnkindely forsake thy Philotus, whose tender loue towardes thee is suche, that as I will not let to make thee soueraigne of my self, so thou shalt be dame and Mistres of all that euer I haue, assuryng thee, that thou shalt neuer want for golde, Gemmes, Jewells, suche as be fit and conuenient for thy degree.

Philerno seyng a couple of old doting fooles, thus clusteryng aboute hym, not knowyng what thei were: had thought at the firste thei had been out of their wittes, but in the ende by their woordes, perceiuyng a farther circumstance in the matter, he deuised some thyng for his owne disporte, to feede them a little with their owne follie, saied. Pardon me I beseche you this my greeuous offence, wherein I knowe I haue too farre

straied

ſtraied from the limites and boundes of modeſtie, proteſtyng hereafter ſo to gouerne my ſelf, that there ſhall be no ſufficient cauſe, whereby to accuſe me of ſuche vnmaidenlike partes, and will euer remaine with ſuche duetie and obedience, as I truſt ſhall not deſerue but to be liked duryng life.

Philotus hauyng heard this pitifull reconciliation, made by his Emelia, verie gently entreated her father, in her behalf, well, q her father) ſeeyng you will needes haue me to forgiue this her leudneſſe, at your requeſte I am contented to pardon her, and then ſpeakyng to Philerno, he ſaied.

How ſaie you houſwife, is your ſtomacke yet come doune, are you contented to take Philotus for your houſebande, yea my good father (q Philerno) and that with all my harte, Oh happie newes (q Philotus) and here withall he began to ſette his cappe on the one ſide, and to tourne vp his muſchatoes, and fell to wipyng of his mouthe, as though he would haue falne a kiſſyng of her by and by in the Streates, but remembryng hym ſelf where he was, he brought Alberto with Philerno, into a freendes houſe, that was of his familiare acquaintance, and there the Marriage betweene theim was throughlie concluded, and all parties ſemyng to giue their full conſentes. Philotus deſired his father in Lawe, that he might haue the cuſtodie of Emelia, ſwearyng by his old honeſtie, that he would not otherwiſe vſe her, then his owne daughter Briſilla, vntill the date of his Nuptials, and then to vſe her as his wife: to whiche requeſt Alberto ſeemed verie willyngly to giue conſent: But then becauſe Philotus would not carrie his beloued through the Streates in her mannes apparell, he deſired hir father in Law to go home, & ſende ſome ſuite of her apparell, wherwith to ſhifte her, before he would carrie her to his owne houſe. Alberto ſeyng matters ſo throughlie concluded, tooke his leaue of theim bothe, and goyng his waies home, he cauſed all his daughters apparell to be looked together, and to be ſent to the place where Philotus was remainyng with Philerno, who takyng forthe ſuche as ſhould ſerue the tourne for that preſent Philerno ſo well as he could arraied hym ſelf, in one of his ſiſters ſuites of apparell, and thus departed with Philotus to his owne house, where Philotus callyng his daughter Brisilla, he saied vnto her, beholde here the partie, whom I haue chosen to be your mother, chargyng you of my blessyng, that you honour, reuerence, and obeye her, and with all diligence that you be attendaunt vpon her, and readie at an ynche to prouide her of any thyng, that she shall either want or call for. And you my deare and louyng Emelia, I doe here ordaine and appoint you to bee Mistres of this house, and of all that is in it, desiryng you to accepte of this my daughter, to doe you seruice in the daie tyme, and in the night to vouchsafe her for your bedfellowe, untill our daie of Marriage bee prefixed, and then my self will supplie the roume. Philerno seyng the excellent beautie of Brisilla, was nothyng sorie to haue suche a bedfellowe, but thought euery hower a daie, till night was come, which beyng approched, to bedde thei went, where Philerno did not thinke it his readiest waie, to giue any sodaine attempte, but therefore he brake into this discourse followyng.

My Brisilla, were it not but that we bee founde parciall in the causes of our freendes, but especially where the causes doe touche our parentes, our iudgementes be so blinded by affection, that we can neither see, nor well cõfesse a manifest truthe but if matters might be considered on, without respect of persones with indifference, and accordyng to the truthe and equitie of the cause: I durste then put my self in your arbitremente my Brisilla, and to abide your sentence, whereto I doubt not, but you would confesse the preiudice I sustaine, it is muche intollerable, and almoste impossible, for a yong maide to endure, and the rather, if you would measure my condition, by your owne estate, who beeyng as you see, a yong maiden like your self, and should be thus constrained by my frendes, to the Marriyng of your father, whom I doe confesse to bee worthie of a better wife then my self. But consideryng the inequalitie of our yeres, I can not for my life frame my self to loue hym, and yet I am forced against my will to marie him, and am appointed to be your mother, that am more meete to be your cõpanion and plaie felowe. But that affiance whiche I haue conceiued in your good nature, hath made me thus boldly to speak

vnto

vnto you, desiryng but to heare your opinion with indifferencie, whether you thinke I haue good cause to complaine or naye: and then peraduenture I will saie farther vnto you, in a matter that doeth concerne your owne behoofe.

Brisilla hearyng this pitifull complaint, verie sorowfull in her behalfe, saied: would to God I were as well able to minister releef vnto your distresse, accordyng to your owne contentment, as I am hartely sorie to consider your greef, and do wel perceiue the iuste occasion you haue to complaine.

Ah my Brisilla, said Philerno, I am as hartly sorie in your behalfe, and peraduenture doe vnderstande something, whiche your self doe not yet knowe of, whiche will greeue you verie sore. But first Brisilla, lette me aske you this question, doe you knowe my father, or naie.

No sure (quod Brisilla) I haue no maner of knowledge of him neither did I knowe, whether you had any father aliue, or nay but now by your owne reporte, and as straunge it was to me, to heare the wordes whiche my Father vsed to me this daie, when he brought you home, for that I neuer vnderstoode before, that he went aboute a wife.

Philerno was verie glad to heare these newes, because it serued so muche the better for his purpose, and therefore saied as followeth.

This tale that I minde to tell you (my Brisilla) will seme more straunge then all the reste, and yet assure your self, it is nothyng so strange as true, and therefore giue eare to that I mynde to saie: Doe you not thinke it verie straunge in deede, that the one of vs should bee made bothe mother and daughter to the other, and that our fathers whiche bee now so diescrepit and olde, should bee so ouer haled, with the furie of their fonde and vnbrideled affections, that to serue their owne appetites, thei force not with what clogges of care, thei comber vs that be their louyng daughters, but haue concluded betwene them selues a crosse Marriage, and so in deede it maie well be tearmed, that will fall out so ouerthwarte to our behoofes, who beyng now in our yong and tender yeres, and should bothe of vs be made the dearlinges of twoo old menne, that seekes to preferre

ferre

ferre their owne lust, before their childrens loue, and measure the fierie flames of youth, by the dead coales of age, as though thei were able with their cold and rare imbracementes, to delaie the forces of the fleshe, whose flames doeth excead in these our greene and tender yeres, and as muche possible for vs to continue in likyng, as flowers are seen to agree with Froste, but in plaine tearmes (my Brisilla) & to discipher a very troth, it is contracted betweene our aged parentes, that your father (as you see) should first take me to his wife, whiche weddyng beeyng once performed, then my father in like maner should chalenge you, accordyng as it is concluded betweene them.

Alas (ꝙ Brisilla) these newes bee straunge in deede, and it should seem by your wordes so fullie resolued on, that there is no hope of redresse to be had in the matter.

None in the worlde (ꝙ Philerno) but thus betweene our selues, the one of vs to comfort the other.

A colde comforte (ꝙ Brisilla) wee shall finde in that, but oh pitilesse parentes, that will preferre your owne pleasures with your childrens paine, your owne likyng, with you childrens loathyng, your owne gaine, with your childrens greefe, your owne sporte, with your childrens spoile, your owne delight, with your childrens despight. O how muche more happie had it been, that we had neuer been borne.

Alas my Brisilla (ꝙ Philerno) torment not your self with suche extreame anguishe, for if that would haue serued for redresse, the matter had been remedied, and that long sithence: But I would to GOD my Brisilla, that I were a manne for your onely sake, and hauyng so good leisure, as thus beeyng together by our selues, wee would so handle the matter, that our fathers should seeke newe wiues.

Alas (ꝙ Brisilla) suche wishes are but waste, and vnpossible it is, that any suche thyng should happen.

Impossible (ꝙ Philerno) naie surely Brisilla, there is nothyng impossible, but I haue knowne as greate matters as these haue been wrought: Doe we not read that the Goddesse Venus, transformed an Iuorie Image, to a liuely and perfect woman, at the onelie requeste of Pygmalion, Diana likewise conuerted

conuerted Acteon to a Harte, Narcissus for his pride was turned to a flower, Archane to a Spider, with a greate number of others haue bin trasformed, some into beastes, some into foules, and some into fishes, but amongst the reste of the miracles that haue bin wrought by the Goddesse, this storie falleth out moste meete and fittyng to our purpose.

There was sometime remaining in the Countrey of Phestos a maried couple, the housbande called by the name of Lictus, the wife Telethusa, who beyng with childe, was willed by her housbande so sone as she should be deliuered, if it were not a lad, that the childe should presently be slaine, his wife beyng deliuered at her appoincted tyme, brought forthe a girle, and yet notwithstandyng her housbandes commaundement, brought vp the childe, makyng her housebande beleeue it was a boye, and called it by the name of Iphis, and thus as it grew in yeares, was apparelled like a lad, and beyng after by his father assured to a wife called by the name of Ianthe, a young maiden, and the daughter of one Telest dwellyng in Dictis, Telethusa the mother of Iphis, fearyng her deceipt would bee knowne, deferred of the marriage daie so long as she could, sometymes fainyng tokens of ill successe, sometimes faining sicknesse, sometymes one thyng, sometymes an other, but when all her shiftes were driuen to an ende, and the marriage daie at hand, Telethusa commyng to the Temple of the Goddesse Isis, with her heire scattered aboute her eares, where before the Aulter of Isis, she made her humble supplications, and the gentle Goddesse hauing compassion, transformed Iphis to a man.

Loe here Brisilla, as greate a matter brought to passe as any wee haue spoken of yet, and the Goddesse bee of as greate force and might in these daies, as euer thei were in times past, we want but the same zeale and faith to demaunde it, and sure in my opinion, if either of vs made our request to the Goddes, who co[illegible]ly bee still assistant to helpe distressed wightes, thei would neuer refuse to graunt our reasonable requestes, and I will aduenture on it my self, and that without any farther circumstaunce.

And here with all he seemed with many piteous sighes, throwyng vp his handes to the heauens, to mumble forthe many wordes in secrete, as though he had been in some greate contemplation, and sodainly without any maner of stirryng either of hande or foote, did lye still as it had bin a thing immouable, whereat Brisilla beganne for to muse, and in the ende spake to hym, but Phylerno made no maner of aunswere, but seemed as though he had bin in some traunce, where with Brisilla began to call and with her arme to shake hym, and Phylerno giuyng a piteous sigh, as though he had bin awaked sodainly out of some dreame, saied. O blessed Goddesse Venus, I yeeld thee humble thankes, that hast not despised to graunt my request: and then speakyng to Brisilla, he saied: and now my Brisilla be of good comforte, for the same Goddesse whiche haue not disdained to heare my supplication, will likewise be assistaunt to further our farther pretences, as hereafter at our better leisure we shall consider of, in the meane tyme receiue thy louyng freende, that to daie was appointed to bee thy fathers wife, but now consecrated by the Goddesse to be thy louyng housebande, and here withall imbrasing Brisilla in his armes. She perceiued in deede that Emelia was perfectly metamorphosed, whiche contented her very well, thinkyng her self a thrise happie woman to light of suche a bedfellowe, thus bothe of them the one pleased very well with the other, thei passed the tyme, till Phylotus had prepared and made all thynges readie for his Marriage daie, and then callyng his freendes and neighbours about hym, to the Churche thei goe together, where Alberto gaue Phylerno his soonne, in the steede of his daughter Emelia to Phylotus for his wife: when all the reste of the Marriage rites that are to bee doen in the Churche were performed, thei passed forthe the daie with feastyng and greate mirthe vntill it was night. When the companie beganne to breake vp, and euery one to take his leaue, and Phylotus with his birde were brought into [illegible] Chamber, where Phylerno desiryng the companie to auoide, and makyng fast the doore he saied to Phylotus, there resteth yet a matter to be decided betweene you and me, and seyng we be here

here together by our selues, and that tyme and place doeth fall out so fit, I hold it for the best that it be presently determined.

What is the matter then (q Phylotus) speake boldly my Emelia, and if there be any thyng that hanges in dispence betwene vs, I trust it shall easely bee brought to a good agreement.

I praie God it maie (q Phylerno) and to reueale the matter in breefe and shorte circumstaunce, it is this. You are now my housebande, and I your lawfull wife, and for that I dooe knowe the difference in our yeares, your self being so olde and I very yong, it must needes fall out there will be as greate deuersitie in our conditions, for age is commonly giuen to bee frowarde, testie, and ouerthwart: youth againe to be frolique, pleasaunt, and merrie, and so likewise in all our other conditions wee shall bee founde so contrarie and disagreeyng, that it will be impossible for vs to like the one of the others doynges, for when I shall seeme to followe my owne humour, then it will fall out to your discontentmēt. And you againe to follow that diet whiche your age doeth constraine, will be moste lothsome vnto me, then you beyng my housebande will thinke to commaunde me, and I must be obedient to your will, but I beyng your wife will thinke scorne to be controlde, and will dispose of my self accordyng to my owne likyng, and thē what braules and brabbles will fall out, it were to muche to bee rehearsed, and thus we shall liue neither of vs bothe in quiet, nor neither of vs bothe contented, and therefore for the auoidyng of these inconueniences, I haue deuised this waie, that beyng thus together by our selues, we will trie by the eares whiche of vs shall bee maister and haue authoritie to commaunde, if the victorie happen on your side, I am contented for euer after to frame my self to your ordinaunce and will as it shall please you to appointe: if otherwise the conquest happen on my side, I will triumph like a victor, and will looke to beare suche a swaie, th[illegible]will not be contraried in any thyng, what so euer it shall please me to commaunde.

Phylotus knowyng not what to make of these speeches, and thinkyng the tyme verie long, till he had tasted his firste fruites, ſaied: Come, come my Emelia lette vs goe to bedde. where I doubt not but we ſhall ſo well agree, that theſe mat, ters will eaſely bee taken vp, without any controuerſie, ſuche as you haue ſpoken of.

Neuer while I liue (ꝙ Phylerno) before I knowe where- on to reſolue: and whether you ſhall reſte at my commaunde- ment, or I at yours.

Why (ꝙ Phylotus) dooe you ſpeake in earneſt, or would you looke to commaunde me that am your houſebande, to whom you ought to vſe all duetie and obedience.

Then were I in good caſe (ꝙ Phylerno) that ſhould bee tied to vſe duetie or obedience, to a manne of your yeares, that would not let to preſcribe vs rules of your owne dotage, to be obſerued in ſteede of domeſticall diſcipline.

Then I perceiue (ꝙ Phylotus) wee ſhall haue ſomethyng adooe with you herafter, that will vſe me with theſe tearmes the verie firſte night. But ſee you make no more to dooe, but come on your waies to bedde.

And I perceiue (ꝙ Phylerno) the longer that I beare with you, the more foole I ſhall finde you, and with this vp with his fiſte and gaue Phylotus a ſure wheritte on the eare. Phylotus in a greate rage flies againe to Phylerno: there was betweene them ſouſe for ſouſe, and boxe for boxe, that it was harde to Iudge who ſhould haue the victorie. In the ende Phylerno gettes Phylotus faſte by the graie bearde, and by plaine force pulles hym doune on the flower, and ſo be pomels hym aboute the face, that he was like to haue been ſtrangled with his owne bloud, which guſhed out of his noſe and mouth. Wherefore holdyng vp his handes he cried, Oh Emelia, I yeelde my ſelf vanquiſhed and ouercome, for Gods ſake holde thy handes, and I will neuer more contende with thee du- ryng life.

Phylerno ſtaiyng hym ſelf ſaied, art thou contented then to yeeld me the conqueſt, and hereafter this acco[illegible]s thou haſt ſaied: neuermore to ſtriue with me, neuer to gainſaie any thyng, what ſo euer it ſhall pleaſe me to commaunde.

Neuer while I liue (ꝙ Phylotus) and therefore for Gods ſake

sake let me arise, and chalenge to your self what superioritie you please, whiche for me shall neuer be denaied so long as I shall liue.

Well (q Phylerno) but before I will let you arise, I will haue you promise me to confirme these conditions, whiche folowe in this maner. Firste, that at my pleasure I maie goe abroade with my freendes, to make merie so often as I liste, whither I liste, and with whom I list. And neither at my goyng forthe, to be demaunded whither I will, ne at my returne to bee asked where I haue been. I will farther haue you condescende to this, that for as muche as I haue learned, that it is not onely verie vntothsome, but likewise verie vnwholesome, for youth and age, to lye sokyng together in one bedde. I will therefore make no bedfellowe of you, but at my owne pleasure. And in maner as followeth, that is to saie: this first yere I shall be contented, to bestowe one night in a moneth to doe you pleasure, if I maie see you worthie of it, or that you be able to deserue it: but the first yere beyng once expired, fower tymes a yere maie very well suffice, that is one night a quarter, as it shall please my self to appoinct. There be many other matters whiche I will not now stande to repeate, but these before rehearsed, be the principall thynges wherein I wil not bee controlde, but meane to followe myne owne likyng, how saie you Phylotus, can you bee contented to frame your self herein, to followe my direction.

Alas (q Phylotus) I see no other shifte, I must perforce endeuour my self paciently to abide what soeuer it shall please you to commaunde, and doe yeeld my self as recreant, and ouercome, and wholy doe put my self to your fauour and mercie, readie to receiue whatsoeuer it shall please you to awarde vnto me.

Phylerno, lettyng hym now arise saied, prepare your self then to goe to your bedde, and anon at myne owne leasure, I will come vnto you: and departe againe at myne owne pleasure, when I shall see tyme.

Phylotus, comfortyng hym self with these swete speeches did thinke it yet, to be some parte of amendes, that she had promised

mised to come and visite hym: went quietly to his bedde, there to abide the good hower till Emelia did come.

Phylerno, hauyng prepared one of these marcenarie women (whereof there are greate store in Rome to bee had) conueighed her to the bedd of Phylotus, giuyng her enstructions how to vse her self: and went him self to his beste beloued Brisilla, whom he had made priuie to his whole deuise, and in this maner it was agreed betwene them, thei had thought to haue dieted Phylotus once a moneth with some cast stuffe, suche as thei could hire best cheape in the Towne.

But it fell out that Flauius, whom you haue heard before, had stolne awaie Emelia, beyng at the Churche the same daie that Phylotus was maried, and saw Alberto giue his daughter Emelia to Phylotus for his wife: had thought assuredly that hym self had been deceiued by some Deuill or spirite, that had taken vpon hym the likenesse of Emelia. And therefore hastyng hym self home with all possible speede, came to Emelia, and blessyng hym self he saied: I charge thee in the name of the liuyng GOD, that thou tell me what thou art, and that thou presently departe to the place from whence thou camest. And I coniure thee in the name of the holie Trinitie, by our blessed Ladie the Virgine Marie, by Aungels and Archaungels, Patriarkes and Prophetes, by the Apostles, and fower Euangelistes, Matthewe, Marke, Luke and Ihon, by all the holie Martyres and Confessours, and the reste of the rable and blessed route of Heauen, that thou quietly departe without any maner of preiudice, either to manne, woman, or childe, either to any maner of beaste that is vppon the face of the earth, the foules of the ayre, or the fishes in the Sea, and without any maner of tempest, storme, whirle winde, thunder or lightnyng, and that thou take no maner of shape, that maie seeme either terrible or fearfull vnto me.

Emelia hearyng these woordes, merueilyng muche what thei ment: with a smilyng countenaunce came to[illegible]es Flauius saiyng, why how now Seignior Flauius, what doe you thinke me to bee some Deuill, or any Hagge of hell, that you fall so coniuryng, and blessyng of your self?

I

I charge thee come no nere (q Flanius) stande backe, for these inticementes can no longer abuse me, when I haue seen with myne eyes, my beloued Emelia, maried in the Churche, and giuen by Alberto her Father, to Phylotus for his wife what should I thinke of thee but to be some feende, or sent vnto me by some Inchauntment or Witchcrafte, and therefore I will no longer neither of thy companie, neither of thy conference: And here withall takyng Emelia by the shoulders, he thrust her forthe of doores, and shuttyng the doore after her: He gat hym to his chamber, where he fell to his praiers, thinkyng assuredly that Emelia had been some spirite.

But Emelia, after she had a three or fower daies made what meanes she could to Flanius, and sawe it was in vaine: was driuen to goe to her Father, before whom fallyng vppon her knees, she desired hym moste humbly to forgiue her.

Alberto takyng her vp in his armes saied, that he knewe nothyng wherein she had offended hym, but her suite might easily be graunted.

Deare father (q Emelia) I know I haue offended, and so farre as my facte deserueth, rather to be punished then pitied: the remēbraunce whereof is so lothsome vnto me, that I feare to call you by the name of father, hauing shewed my self so vnworthie a daughter. These wordes she pronounced with such sorrowe, that the teares streamed downe her cheekes, wherewith Alberto moued with natural affection, saied, deare child, I knowe no such offence that ought to be so greeuously taken: but speake boldly what so euer it be, I freely forgiue it.

Emelia verie well comforted with these speeches, began to discourse how she firste disguised her self in Pages apparel, and what greef it was to her conscience, that she should so farre straie from the duetie and obedience of a childe, and to become a fugitiue in a mannes apparell. But her father not sufferyng her further to proceede in her tale, saied: Alas deare daughter if this bee the matter, it is long agoe sithe I haue bothe forgiuen and forgotten these causes: and therefore let these thynges neuer trouble you. But tell me now how doe you like of your bedfellowe, how agree you with him, or he with you, I would

be

be glad to knowe.

Alas deare father (ꝙ Emelia) that is the matter that I come to you, he hath turned me awaie, and wil no longer take me foꝛ his wife, and what is the cauſe that hath moued hym vnto it, I pꝛoteſt befoꝛe God I knowe not foꝛ my life.

Hath he turned thee awaie (ꝙ Alberto) my ſelf wil quickly finde a remedie foꝛ that matter, and without any moꝛe to do (would not tary ſo much as while his goune was a bꝛuſhyng) but out of dooꝛes he goes towards Phylotus, whō by chaunce he met withall in the Streates, and in a greate chafe begins to chalenge hym foꝛ abuſyng of his daughter, ſwearyng that he would make all Rome to ſpeake of his abuſe, if he ment to pꝛoceede in that he had begunne.

Phylotus wonderyng to ſee the man in ſuche an agonie, beganne to wiſhe that he had neuer ſeene hym noꝛ his daughter neither, and that if any bodie haue cauſe to complaine, it is I (ꝙ Phylotus) that haue married ſuche a wife, that is moꝛe like to a Deuill then a woman: and I perceiue now is maintained in her miſchiefe by you that are her father, who ought rather to rebuke her then ſo to take her part, and to incourage her in her leudeneſſe.

What incouragment is this you ſpeake of (ꝙ Alberto) I knowe not what you meane by theſe woꝛdes, but aſſure your ſelf of this, that as I will not maintaine my child in any thing that is euill, ſo I will not ſee her take a manifeſt wꝛong.

Doe you thinke this to bee good then (ꝙ Phylotus) that your daughter ſhould beſtowe ſuche hanſell on her houſbande as ſhe hath all readie beſtowed vpon me, and then pointyng to his face, he ſaied: See here your daughters handie woꝛke, how thinke you, is this requiſite to be boꝛne with all, that you ſtande ſo muche in your daughters defence?

Alberto ſeeyng his face all ſwolne, and the ſkinne ſcratched of, perceiued that Phylotus was at a fraie, and had good cauſe to complaine: And wonderyng that his daughter was ſo ſodainly become a ſhꝛewe, ſaied: If this bee my daughters handie woꝛke, I can neither beare withall, neither will I allowe it in her, ſo to vſe her houſebande. And therefoꝛe I pꝛaie

you,

you, lette me heare the matter debated betweene you: and I doubte not, but to take suche order, as there shall no more any suche rule happen betweene you.

I am contented you shall debate what you will (q Philotus) so it maie be doen with quietnesse, but I will neuer more contende with her for the Maisterie while I liue, she hath alreadie wonne it, I am contented she shall weare it.

I praie you then (q Alberto) that you will goe home to your owne house, and I will goe fetche my daughter, and will come vnto you straight waie, and I doubt not but to take suche order betweene you, as shall fall out to bothe your likynges.

I praie God you maie (q Philotus) and I will goe home and there will staie your commyng.

Alberto likewise went to his owne house, and callyng Emelia, saied neuer a woorde vnto her, but willed her to followe hym: and commyng to the house of Philotus, whom he founde within, taryng his commyng. And by fortune at the same instant, Philerno and Brisilla bothe were gone into the toune to buye certaine thynges that thei had neede of. And Alberto beginning first to rebuke his daughter, that would seme in suche maner to abuse her housebande, & with a long discourse he preached vnto her, with what duetie and obedience, women ought to vse their housebandes withall, and not to take vpon thẽ like maisters, to correct and chastice thẽ. Emelia denaied not onely the fact, but also she denaied Philotus to be her housebande.

What haue wee here to doe (q her father) how canst thou (shamelesse queane) denaye that, whiche within these fower daies was performed, in the face of the whole worlde?

Emelia standyng stiffe to her tackelyng, would in nowise confesse that euer she was Married.

Then her father begã to charge her with her owne wordes, which he had vsed to hym before, how she had disguised her self in mans apparell, and so stole awaie forthe of dores, the whiche Emelia neuer denaied. Why then (q her Father) did not I meete thee in the streates, and at the request of thy housebande here present, did forgiue thee thy fault, to whom I then deliuered thee, and with whom thou hast euer sithence remained.

Emelia made flatte deniall of any of all these saiynges to bee true. Alberto in a greate furie, would haue taken witnesse of Philotus in the matter, but Philotus fearyng an other banquet at night, when he should goe to bedde, durste not in any wise seeme to contrary Emelia: In the ende after greate fendyng and prouyng had in the matter, Emelia from poincte to poincte discoursed to her Father, how she firste fell into the likyng of Flauius, and by his practise, so conueighed her self awaie in his Pages apparell, and had with hym remained all this while, till now he had tourned her awaie.

Her father would in no wise allowe this tale to be true, but Flauius beeyng well knowne to bee a courteous Gentleman, Alberto deuised to sende for hym, who presently at his gentle intreatie, came to the house of Philotus, where he spared not to confesse a truthe, that onely for the loue that he bare to Emelia, he deuised to steale her awaie, and there came one vnto hym in the likenesse of Emelia, and in the same apparell that he had prouided for her, whom he verie chastly kepte, untill suche tyme as he sawe with his owne eyes, that Emelia was Married in the Churche to Philotus, and then assuryng hym self, that he had been deceiued by some Spirite, that had taken vpon hym the similitude and likenesse of Emelia, he presentlie came home, and tourned her awaie, and what was become of her, he could neuer learne.

Alberto muche amazed to heare this tale, saied. Senior Flauius doe you knowe your Emelia againe, if you see her, and then poinctyng to his daughter, he saied: Is not this the same Emelia that you speake of, whiche you haue tourned awaie.

I knowe not (qd Flauius) the one from the other, but sure I sawe with myne eyes twoo Emelias so like, that the one of them of force must needes bee the Deuill.

There is no question (qd Philotus) but that is my wife, if there bee euer a Deuill of theim bothe, I knowe it is she: But alas that euer I was borne, what shall I now doe, I knowe I haue Married a Deuill.

And by fortune as Alberto chaunced to looke forthe of the windowe, he espied Philerno and Brisilla in the Streate commyng

myng homewardes: peace (q Alberto) here commeth the other Emelia, wee shall now trie, whiche of theim is the Deuill (I thinke) before we departe.

By this Philerno was come in, and hearing how matters had been debated, and were falne out, againe knowing Alberto to be his Father, and what preiudice his sister Emelia was like to sustaine, if she should be forsaken by her freende and louer Flauius, confessed the whole matter, humblie desiryng his father to forgiue hym.

When he had a while wondered at the circumstaunce, and the truthe of euery thing laied open, and come to light, all parties were well pleased and contented, sauyng Philotus, for whē he remembred first the losse of his loue Emelia, then how Philerno had beaten hym, what a bedfellowe he had prouided hym, while he hymself went and laie with his daughter: these thynges putte all together, made hym in suche a chafe, that he was like to runne out of his wittes: But when he had raged a good while, and sawe how little helpe it did preuaile hym, he was contented in the ende, that his daughter Brisilla, should Marrie with Philerno, and Flauius verie ioyfully receiued againe his Emelia (when he knewe she was no Deuill) and bothe the marriages consūmat in one daie. And so I praie GOD giue them ioye and euery old dotarde so good successe as had Philotus.

FINIS.

The Conclusion.

Gentle Reader, now thou haſt peruſed theſe Hiſtories to the ende, I doubte not but thou wilte deeme of them, as thei worthely deſerue, and thinke ſuche vanities more fitter to bee preſented on a Stage (as ſome of theim haue been) then to bee publiſhed in Printe (as till now thei haue neuer been) but to excuſe my ſelf of the follie that here might bee imputed vnto me, that my ſelf beyng the firſt that haue put them to the print, ſhould likewiſe be the firſt that ſhould condemne them as vaine: for mine owne excuſe herein I aunſwere, that in the writyng of them, I haue vſed the ſame maner, that many of our yong Gentlemen vſeth now adaies, in the wearing of their apparell, which is rather to followe a faſhion that is newe (bee it neuer ſo fooliſhe) then to bee tied to a more decent cuſtome, that is cleane out of vſe: Sometyme wearyng their haire freeſeled ſo long, that makes theim looke like a water Spaniell: ſometymes ſo ſhorte like a newe ſhorne Sheepe, their Beardes ſometymes cutte rounde like a Philippes Doler, ſometymes ſquare like the Kynges hedde in Fiſhſtreate: Sometymes ſo neare the ſkinne, that a manne might iudge by his face, the Gentleman had had verie pilde lucke, their Cappes and Hattes ſometymes ſo bigge, as will hold more witte, then three of them haue in their heddes: Sometimes ſo little, that it will hold no witte at all. Their Ruffes ſometymes ſo huge, as ſhall hang aboute their neckes like a Carte wheele: ſometymes a little fallyng bande, that makes theim looke like one of the Queenes ſilke women. Their Clokes ſometymes ſo long, as it ſhall trippe on their heeles, ſometymes ſo ſhorte, as will not hang ouer their elbowes; their Jerkinnes ſometymes with hye collors,

buttoned

buttoned close vnder their chinne, sometymes with no collors at all aboute their neckes, like a wenche in a redde wastcoate that were washyng of a bucke: Sometymes with long sausie sleeues, that will be in euery dishe before his maister, sometymes without sleeues, like Scogins manne that vsed to run of sleeuelesse errandes: Their Dublettes sometyme faggotte wasted aboue the Nauill, sometymes Cowebeallied belowe the flanckes, that the Gentleman must vndoe a button when he goes to pisse.

In their Hoose so many fashions as I can not describe, sometymes Garragascoynes, breached like a Beare, sometymes close to the docke, like the Deuill in a Plaie (wantyng but a taile) sometymes rounde like to Saincte Thomas Onions, sometymes petite Ruffes of twoo ynches long, with a close stockyng cleane aboue the nocke of his taile: sometymes disguisyng theim selues after the vse of Spaine, sometymes after the Italian maner, and many tymes thei imitate the Frenche fashion so neare, that all their haire is readie to fall of their heddes.

Now I am sure, if any of theim were asked, why he vsed suche varietie in his apparell, he would aunswere, because he would followe the fashion. Lette this then suffice likewise for myne excuse, that my self seeyng trifles of no accoumpt, to be now best in season, and suche vanities more desired, then matters of better purpose, and the greatest parte of our writers, still busied with the like. So I haue put forthe this booke, because I would followe the fashion.

And nowe freendlie Reader, because I haue entred thus farre to speake of fashions: I will cōclude with a tale that maketh somethyng for my purpose. I haue read it so long agoe, that I can not tell you where, nor the matter is not greate though I doe not tell you whē. But in Englande (as I think) and as it should seme, nere aboute London. There was sometymes dwellyng a Gentleman, though not of verie greate wealth, yet of a verie honest life, and of good reporte emongest his neighbours, whose name was maister Persinus, this gentilman had a daughter, whose name was Mildred, aboute the age of eighteene yeres, of a singulare beautie, verie well trained up by her owne Mother, who was likewise living, and with whom she now remained. It fortuned that a Deuill of Hell called Balthaser, no inferiour Deuill, but a Maister Deuill, a principall officer, and commaunder in Helle, and truste me, if there were euer a Deuill that was an honeste manne, Balthaser was he, sauyng that beyng now an auncient Deuill, and well spente in yeres, he beganne to waxe wanton, and to doate in the Loue of Mistres Mildred: But yet not like our greatest parte of louers now a daies, that still practise their loues unlawfully, more for luste, then for loyaltie: But Balthaser contrariwise, bare his loue honestlie, lawfullie, yea, and in the waie of Marriage, the whiche to bryng to passe, he toke suche continuall care and trauaile in his mynde, that he now confessed the fire of Helle to bee but a trifle, in respecte of the scorchyng flames of Loue. Sometymes coniecturyng in his minde, what bashfulnesse is founde to bee in yong Damselles in these daies, but especially when a manne comes to proffer thē loue, thei are so shamefast, that with a good wil thei would neuer heare of Marriage, till thei were thirtie yeres old at the leaste, and many of theim if it were not for menne, I thinke could bee well contented to leade Apes in Hell: Other whiles he remembred the greedie desire that is generallie in Parentes, who neuer consente to the Marriyng of their faire daughters, without some greate ioynter: Now the Deuill had no landes, and therefore to finde the beste remedie he could, thei saie the Deuill is able to put uppon hym all mãner of shapes, so he tooke upon hym the presence and personage of so gallant a yong Gentleman, as fitted so well the fancie of Mistres Mildred, that without any long circumstãce, she was contented to accept hym for her housebande, the whiche beyng perceiued by her Father and Mother, not mindyng to contrarie their daughters likyng, gaue their free cōsentes, there was no more to dooe, but to appoincte for their Marriyng daie, the whiche beeyng once expired, the Deuill sittyng by his beste beloued, uttered these wordes, or suche like as followeth.

My good Mildred, my deare and louyng wife, I muste

confesse

confesse my self not a little beholdyng vnto you, that neither examinyng my Pedigree from whence I came, neither what I am, neither yet how I am able to kepe you, would notwithstandyng vouchsafe to take me for your housebande, I muste thinke your courtesie proceaded of Loue, and doe accoumpte my self so muche the more beholdyng vnto you, and now to giue you some triall, that you haue not made your choice of a Rascall or a Knaue of no reputation, I am contented to giue you one demaunde what soeuer you thinke beste to require of me, and therefore my deare, aske what you liste, your desire shalbee satisfied, alwaies prouided, that here after you neuer trouble me with any farther requestes.

The yong wife wonderfully well contented with these louyng speeches, of her courteous housebande, desired of hym a little pause and respite: And now commyng to her Mother, to whom she vnfolded the whole contentes of the premises, sittyng theim doune together, to consider of the matter, after a greate nomber of consultations, and as many imaginations had betwene them, in the ende thei concluded, that her request should bee for a sute of apparell of a gallaunt fashion, but euen then newlie come vp, and commyng to her housebande with this demaunde, thei had their wishe presently accomplished, and this sute of apparell laied vp them, so well made and fitted as possibly could bee desired. Thus all partes were well pleased, thei continued in good likyng for the space of one moneth, at whiche tyme an other newe fashion was then come vp, aswell in the attiryng of their heddes, as also in the makyng of their Gounes, Kirtells, and Stomachers. Mistres Mildred, beyng now quite out of conceit, for that she had neuer a goune to putte on her backe but of a stale cutte, and the fashion at the leaste of a monethe olde, who would blame the gentlewoman though she tooke it very greuously: alas her minde was so far out of quiet, that her meate almoste did her no maner of good. Whiche sodaine alteration beyng perceiued by her houseband he beganne to intreate her, to shewe hym the cause of her conceiued greef, the whiche when she had reueiled, the good honest Deuill her houseband saied: well my deare wife, although

when

when I satisfied your last demaũde, my conditions were that you should neuer trouble me with any further requestes, yet once againe to recomforte you, aske of me what you will, I will graunte your desire, but to cutte you of all hope that hereafter this, I wil neuer be troubled again with newe fashions, assure your self that this is the last request, that euer I minde to graunt you.

Mistres Mildred giuyng hym twentie kisses for his kindnesse, went again to her mother with these ioyfull newes, and concludyng as before, thei brought the deuill, an Inuentorie of newe fashions, beginnyng with Cappes, Caules, Quaiues, Ruffes, Partlettes, Sleeues, Gounes, Kirtelles, Peticotes, and there was no Stitche, no Cutte, no Lace, no Garde, nor no fashion that was then in vse, but in this Inuentorie it was to bee founde, and as before, this bill was no sooner presented, but all thinges were in readinesse, so well fitted and fashioned, as if the moste cunnyngest workemen in Englande had been at the makyng. But what should I saie? Before an other moneth was expired, there was a newe inuention, for then came vp newe fashions in their Caps, in their Hattes, in their Caules, newe fashioned Shadowes, then came vp Periwigges, Frizelyng, and Curlyng, then came vp Dublettes, Bombastyng, and Bolsteryng: newe fashions in their Gounes, Kirtelles, and Peticotes, then thei began to weare Crimsin, Carnation, Greene and Yellowe Stockynges: to bee shorte, there was suche alteration in womens apparell, from the top to the toe in a moneth, that Mistres Mildred thought her self now againe to bee cleane out of fashion, the remembraunce whereof brought her likewise to be quite out of countenaunce, but whẽ she remembred how she was prohibited, from makyng any further demaundes, it did so gaule her at the harte, that now she beganne to froune, lumpe, and lowre at her housebande, whiche when he perceiued, he said vnto her: why how now my good Mildred, I feare me thy hedde is troubled againe with newe fashions, from whence commeth these sodaine fittes, what is the matter that breedeth suche alteration in thy manners, tell me I praie thee, what is it that doeth offende thee?

To

The Conclusion.

The poore Gentlewoman not able to speake one woorde for weepyng, at the laste burstyng out into these tearmes, if (ꝙ she) I had made my choise of a housebande worthie of my self, I should neuer haue giuen hym cause thus to wonder at me, nor my self haue had occasion to complaine for suche a trifle, for that I might haue been, as other women doe, and haue followed euery fashion, and euery newe deuise, without either grudgyng, or restraint of my desire, I should not then haue bin inioyned to such a kinde of silence, but I might haue made my housebande priuie to my wantes, I should not then haue bin kepte like Ione of the Countrey, in a tyre of the olde fashion deuised a moneth agoe.

While Mistres Mildred was proceeding in these speeches or suche other like, the Deuill her housebande was stroke in suche a dumpe, that not able any longer to indure her talke, he not onely auoided hym self from her presence, but also deuised with speede to flie the Countrey, and commyng to Douer, thinkyng to crosse the Seas, findyng no shippyng readie, he altered his course and gat hym into Scotlande, neuer staiyng till he came to Edenbrough, where the Kyng kept his Court, and now forgettyng all humanitie whiche he had learned before in Englande, he began againe a freshe to plaie the deuill, and so possessed the King of Scots hym self, with such straūge and vnaquainted passions, that by the cōiecture of Phisitions, and other learned men that were then assembled together, to iudge the Kynges diseases, thei al concluded that it must needes bee some Feende of Hell, that so disturbde their Prince: whereupon Proclimations were presently sent forthe, that who soeuer could giue releef, should haue a thousand crounes by the yere, so long as he did liue. The desire of these crounes, caused many to attempt the matter, but the furie of the Deuil was suche, that no man could preuaile.

Now it fortuned that Persinus, the father of Mistres Mildred, at this present to be at Edenbrough, who by constrainte of some extremitie, was now compelled to practise Phisicke, wherein he had some pretie sight, but there with all so good successe, that who but Persinus the Englishe Phisition, had al the name through the whole Realme of Scotlande. The fame of this Phisition came to the hearyng of the Kyng, who sendyng for Persinus, began to debate with hym of the straungnesse of his fittes, profferyng large sommes of money if he could finde a remedie. To whom Persinus aunswered, that it passed farre his skill: the Kyng notwithstandyng, would not giue ouer, but intreated Persinus to take in hande the cure, whiche when he still denaied, did thinke it rather proceeded of stubbornesse, then for want of experience, wherefore he began to threaten hym, swearyng that if he would not accomplishe his request, it should cost hym his life.

Persinus seyng hym self so hardly besteade, was contented to trie some parte of his cunnyng: and the next daie when the kyng was in his fitte, he was brought in to see the maner how it helde hym. Whom the Deuill perceiuyng to come in at the doore, speakyng to Persinus, he saied in this maner.

My father Persinus, I am glad I see you here, but what winde hath driuen you hether to this place.

Why what arte thou (q Persinus) that callest me thy father.

Marie (q the Deuill) I am Balthaser, that was once maried to your daughter, in deede a Deuill of hell, though you neuer knewe it before, whom your daughter weried so muche with her newe fashions, as I had rather be in Hell, then maried to suche a wife.

And arte thou then Balthaser (q Persinus) why then I praie thee good sonne departe the Kyng of Scots, for he hath threatned me for thy cause, to take awaie my life.

Marie (q Balthaser) euen so I would haue it, it were some parte of aquitaunce, for your daughters kindnesse towardes me.

Persinus seyng the disposition of the Deuill, thought [illegible] good to deale any farther with hym at that present, but [illegible] warde when the Kyng was come to hym self, he requ[illegible] hym but respete for one moneth, and against the [illegible] should then take him in hande againe, he deuised with [illegible] that all the Ordinaunce in the Tower might be shot [illegible]

The Conclusion.

Belles in the Towne might be rong, and that all the Trumpets, Drummes, and all maner of other Instruments might altogether sounde, about the Court and lodging of the king.

These thynges beyng accordingly prepared, and the daie come that was assigned, Persinus being with the Kyng at the beginnyng of his fit, accordyng as it was appointed the Ordinaunce was shot of, the Belles began to ring, Musitions played on euery side, at whiche sodaine noyse, the Deuill beganne to wonder, and callyng to Persinus he saied: why how now father, what meaneth all this noyse. Why (ꝙ Persinus) doest thou not knowe the meanyng, then I perceiue Deuilles doe not knowe all: but because thou must be aquainted with it, I will tell thee afore hande. The laste tyme I talked with thee thou toldest me thou hadst married my daughter, and thy tokens were so true, that I am sure thou didst not lye, for which cause knowing where thy bidyng is, I haue sent for her to the Towne, and this noyse that thou hearest, is her welcome to the Courte.

And is my wife then come hether to seeke me out (ꝙ the Deuill) then I shall be sure to be troubled with new fashions: naie then farewell Scotland, for I had rather get to hell: and thus leauyng the kyng he departed his waie.

Now to conclude, if a sillie woman were able to wearie the Deuill, that troubled hym with newe fashions but once in a moneth, I thinke God hym self will bee wearied with the outrages of men, that are busied with new fangles at the least once in a daie: I can no more, but wishe that Gentlemen leauyng suche superficiall follies, would rather indeuour themselues in other exercises, that might be much more beneficiall to their Countrey, and a greate deale better to their owne reputation, and thus an ende.

FINIS.

VERBAL VARIANTS

THE following list contains the verbal variants from *A* (1581) in *B* (1583), *C* (1594), *D* (1606), and *E* (1846). When the same variant appears in more than one edition, the spelling listed is that of the earliest edition in which the variant occurs. Since the passages in *D* equivalent to those in *A*, pp. 209–11, are reproduced above, pp. lxxvi–lxxvii, the variants in these passages in *D* are not listed here.

3. 9 f. a-little] alittle *B*, *C*: a litle *D*: a little *E*

4. 6 open] *Om. C*, *D*

15 thriste] thirste *B*, *C*, *D*

6. 5 are thei] they are *D*

6 nier] nearer *C*, *D*

7 tourning] turnings *C*, *D*

12 loues] love *E* euill] well *E*

7. 9 Dunce] Daunce *D*

10 at all] a tale *B*, *C*, *D*

18 f. kneles] kneeleth *C*, *D*

9. 12 speede] sped *C*, *D*

13 came] knewe *B*, *C*, *D*

25 towarde] towardes *C*, *D*

26 indeuours] indeuour *C*, *D*, *E*

10. 10 Disciplines] discipline *C*, *D*

12 plattes] plots *C*, *D*

33 in] to *B*: into *C*, *D*

11. 11 vnpossible] impossible *E*

12. 4 my thinke] me thinke *C*: me thinkes *D*

14 long] belong *D*

17 desires] desire *C*, *D*, *E*

26 serues] serue *C*, *D*, *E*

29 waies] way *C*, *D*

33–13. 2 neither made] made neither *C*, *D*

13. 11 falls] falleth *C*, *D*

14 me] he *E*

32 comes] commeth *C*, *D*

14. 8 speake a truth] speake trueth *C*: speake the truth *D*
14 fightes] fight *C*, *D*, *E*
15 settes] set *C*, *D*, *E*
16 disquietes] disquiet *C*, *D*, *E*
25 a] an *B*, *C*
15. 13 comes] come *C*
14 f. should he come] he shold come *D*
16. 5 it] he *B*, *C*
29 The Scottes by custome.] *Om. D*
31 in greate] in some great *D*
32 all owe] allowe *C*, *D*
17. 5 on] in *B*, *C* behalfes] behalfe *C*
11 his displeasure] his heauy displeasure *D*
17 proude] *Om. C* his] *Om. C*
23 corosiued] corosiue *B*, *C*
18. 4 owne] *Om. D*
12 hath] haue *C*
17 the] this *C*
18 tyme] *Om. D*
19. 6 write] wrote *E* write theim] writ to them *D*
20. 22 he by right hath] he right hath *B*: he right due hath *C*
21. 21 Finis. þ B.S.] Finis. B.S. *B*, *C*
22. 14 haue] are *B*, *C*
23. 21 f. looseth] loseth *E*
26. 7 f. dumphes] dumpes *C*
12 any] *Om. C*
17 serueth] serued *C*
30 happes] hearts *C*
27. 15 her] *Om. C*
28. 37 and to] and so *B*
29. 12 conueniente] convenience *E*
30. 33 hoiste] hoised *C*
31. 23 infortunate] vnfortunate *C*
24 auailes] auaileth *C*
25 drounde] droune *B*, *C*
33. 22 should] would *B*, *C*
34. 23 long tyme] long a time *D*

VERBAL VARIANTS

36. 2 The] This *B*, *C*

39. 8 boundes] bonnds *D*

10 was] once *D*

26 fainest] fairest *D*

27 baall] bane *D*

41. 18 to bee] *Om. C*

43. 3 trauaile and] *Om. C*

8 doeth laste] lasteth *C*

45. 9 Thus] This *C*

12 on this] in this *E*

31 f. from the one to the other] from one to other *D*

46. 23 waies] way *C*

47. 5 a] *Om. D*

17 waies] way *C*

34 f. disposest] disposed *D*

48. 15 therefore to haue the greater care] therefore haue greater care *D*

49. 5 and haue] and I have *E*

6 my life] my naturall life *C*

19 had] *Om. C*

29 of Souldiours] of the Souldiers *D*

35 Gentlewomans] gentlewomens *C*

50. 25 same] said *E*

27 Sextẽ] duke *C*

51. 34 Cayoe] Cayre *C*

38 kneele he] kneele downe he *C*

53. 12 therefore] thereof *C*

28 president] present *C*

54. 15 Dutches Messilina] duchesse of Messilina *C*

33 greate] greater *C*

57. 4 presently] priuily *D*

18 this] these *B*, *C*

58. 33 commyng] came *C*

34 especially to] especially vnto *C*: especially by *E*

59. 13 this Valeria] this time Valeria *C*

16 that] *Om. C*

22 see execution] see his execution *D*

59. 33	quite] quit *C*
60. 37 f.	suche crooked] suche a crooked *E*
61. 9	sometyme] sometimes *C*
36	for] of *E*
62. 16	to] vnto *C*
25	infortunate] vnfortunate *C*, *E* knowes] Knoweth *C*
63. 8	frustrate] prostrate *C*, *E*
16	quite] quit *C*
64. 14	and brought] and had brought *C*
32	trickled] trickling *B*, *C*
65. 24	this] thus *E*
67. 9	into] in *E*
35	of the Christians] of Christians *E*
68. 15	deseuered] seuered *D*
69. 3	is] *Om. C*
6	greate familiaritie] greate a familiaritie *C*
29	Feuer] feruer *C*
70. 24	haue passage] haue a passage *C*
71. 12	a] *Om. D*
15	a] *Om. D*
72. 12	her] *Om. E*
23	terrour] tenour *C*
73. 26	Silla thought her self now more] Silla nowe thought herself more *C*
33	neate] neare *E*
37	moste in] in most *C*
75. 10	will] *Om. D*
76. 34	it] *Om. C*
79. 29	hym, feasted] him, and feasted *C*
80. 29	to] vnto *C*
32	proceadeth] proceaded *B*, *C*
36	to] vnto *C*
81. 4	vnto] to *C*
82. 33	not thynges] not but things *C*
83. 29	oughtest thou rather] rather oughtest thou *C*
84. 15	he] it *D*
85. 20	so] most *C*

86. 5 to] vnto *C*
27 the thing] *Om. C*
35 a woman] *Om. C*
87. 27 founde suche] found any such *C*
88. 31 f. that past] that is past *C*: that was past *D*, *E*
89. 15 that] the *D*
90. 16 or blocke] or a block *C*
21 carle] earle *C*: churle *D*
91. 14 high] highest *C*
92. 3 then] them *D*
23 bowe] ow *C*
93. 11 from hym] him from *C*
19 forst] force *D*
30 Nor] No *D*
94. 14 that] the *C*
23 desires] desire *B*, *C*
95. 10 giuyng her self] giuing of herselfe *C*
18 eightene] xviii *B*: 18 *C*
22 those] these *D*
34 hath] haue *C*
96. 18 ruled wholie] wholy ruled *C*
25 leese] loose *C*
97. 32 so content] so [was] content *E*
99. 9 manne to] man for to *C*
11 of] in *D*
21 shall] will *D*
25 nere her] nere here *E*
26 hym] *Om. D*
100. 10 portion] proportion *C*
14 whitte nor more] whit more *C*
23 matche] march *C*
102. 29 2000. pounde] two thousand pounds *C*
103. 23 noble] *Om. C*
30 in maner] in a maner *E*
34 pounde] poundes *C*
104. 11 f. And . . . come] *Om. C*
24 pounde] pounds *C*

104. 34 abstained] abstaining *D*
106. 3 aduenture] aduentures *B*, *C*
27 ofte] often *D*
107. 3 slaked] slacked *D*
108. 2 and especially] and he especially *C*
15 shapes] sharpes *D*
110. 17 was onely] was [not] onely *E*
30 not to feare] not feare *C*
111. 20 desolate] desolute *C*
37 woundyng] wounded *C*
112. 15 their] her *C*
113. 4 brought] bought *E*
114. 21 in] at *B*, *C*
115. 17 vnderstande at] vnderstand more at *C*
33 wrested] wresled *C*
116. 9 cause] haue *D*
10 that if] if that *C*
29 with] and *C*
117. 19 feare, and] feare, now *C*
28 to] into *C*
34 and] or *E*
36 indifferently] indifferent *C*
118. 35 her] a *C*
119. 17 certifiyng of] certifying them of *C*
121. 3 outrage] courage *B*, *C*
5 not] no *C*
10 be bedfellowe] be a bedfellow *C*
27 to] vnto *C*
122. 8 although] though *C*
26 many rowlyng] many a rolling *C*
27 Mistres] M. *C*
35 alone] aboue *C*
123. 7 rightes] rites *C*
9 f. complexitions] complexions *B*, *C*, *E*
124. 27 wife] life *B*
35 $\overset{t}{y}$] yf *E*
125. 16 speake] spake *C*

VERBAL VARIANTS

125. 19 it is] is it *B*, *C*
28 his fill of the banket] the fill of his banquet *C*
126. 37 in maner] in a manner *C*
127. 32 vnto] to *C*
128. 7 faire] some *C*
29 see Fortune] see how Fortune *D*
129. 3 me] *Om.* *C*
8 although] though *C*
14 vnworthinesse] worthiness *D*
130. 5 apposed] opposed *C*
6 hewen] hewed *C*
10 the Loue] his loue *C*
131. 7 liues this] liues at this *C*
10 my] mine *C*
132. 13 wiles] willes *D*
133. 2 f. dishonestly] dishonestie *C*
11 past] pas *C*
36 f. to encountred] to have encountred *E*
134. 20 desolations] desolation *C*
24 the moste beste and purified] the best & most purified *D*
38 out their] out of their *C*
135. 6 f. so at] so that at *C*
8 impossible] vnpossible *C*
21 we saie] say we *C*
26 vnto] to *C*
136. 4 to the] vnto the *C*
5 to] vnto *C*
30 greatly to] greatly for to *C*
137. 11 wright] written *C*: write *D*
13 writte] wrote *C*
24 did neuer] neuer did *C*
25 liues this] liues at this *B*, *C*
37 f. in the settyng of you] in settyng you *B*
138. 10 towarde] towards *C*
38 myne] my *C*
139. 6 to] vnto *C*
10 to] vnto *C*

139. 28	to] vnto *C*
30	to] vnto *C*
140. 25	thus goyng] thus she going *C*
26	shuttes] shutteth *C*
141. 22	goe] got *E*
33	poinctmente] appointment *D*
142. 10	he] *Om. C*
23	Porter lay] porter to lay *C*
24	a] *Om. C*
26	those] these *D*
143. 2	thy] the *B*, *C*
38	sir] waie *B*, *C*
144. 14	whiche] that *B*, *C*
16	an] on *C*
20	be] he *E*
25	gotte] gotten *B*, *C*
31 f.	towardes] toward *C*
145. 4	vnto] to *C*
11	his waie] away *C*
17	his] *Om. C*
25	beare] carrie *B*, *C*
146. 26	not pinche of] not be pincht of *B*, *C*
38	on] in *C*
147. 17	loue] sake *C*
148. 5	Alonso] Alfonso *C*
14	should] would *C*
31	his] their *C*
32	vnconstant] inconstant *C*
149. 5	saied] same *B*, *C*
21	dwelt, a] dwelt [lived] a *E*
23	goodlie] godly *D*
25	doen] doe *C*: done *D*
150. 12	studied Phisicke] studied in Phisicke *B*, *C*
36	happly] happely *C*: happily *D*
151. 11	pleasures] pleasure *C*
22	she] he *C*
31	throughout] through *C*

VERBAL VARIANTS

152. 5 folke] folks *C*
18 long] louing *D*
19 wrought] brought *C*
30 he had had no] he had no *D*
153. 20 vnto] to *C*
29 and] or *C*
30 by] *Om. C*
36 f. been a this good] been a good *B*, *C*: been this a good *D*
154. 8 thy] the *C*
10 sufficiente to] sufficient for to *C*
25 compassions] composissions *B*: compositions *C*
26 folke] folkes *C*
29 requeste] requests *C*
33 in] into *C*
37 warely] warily *C*
155. 2 seemeth] seemes *C*
6 to his] vnto his *C*
13 cause] case *C*
15 of] *Om. C*
20 should] could *C*
22 of] *Om. D*
34 of] or *E*
36 certaine] two *C*
156. 15 were a] were in a *C*
30 And] *Om. E*
33 Maide] Maiden *B*, *C*
35 demaunded her] demanded of her *C*
37 by breake] by the breake *C*
38 wake] awake *D*
157. 9 notwithstandyng] not vnderstandyng *B*, *C*
13 Maide to saie] maid say *C*
23 beddes side] bed side *D*
158. 6 long liue] liue long *B*, *C*
14 that] the *C*
21 gatte] got *C*
26 awaked] awoke *C*
159. 4 toward] towardes *C*

159. 6 I hope] I doe hope *C*
8 toward] towardes *C*
19 affectioned] affectionated *D* toward] towardes *C*
21 f. for as muche, as though] for as muche, although *B*: forasmuch as, although *C*
36 affectuall] effectuall *C*
38 to] vnto *C*
160. 2 vnto] to *C*
14 to] vnto *C*
29 content] wel contented *C*
37 perceiued] perceiuing *D*
161. 4 vnto] to *C*
30 straightnes] straitnesse *C*
163. 17 you giue] you to giue *C*
18 sentence is grounded] sentence grounded *E*
164. 2 this] that *B*, *C*
13 how the] how that the *C*
16 f. demaunded hym of the] demaunded of him the *D*
165. 11 his] her *C*
14 that baggage] the baggage *C*
166. 13 meane] meanes *D*
26 sithence] since *C*
168. 29 platte] plot *C*
169. 13 with] hath *C*
18 neither] neuer *D*
22 f. brother, that] brother, and that *C*
27 freende] freendes *E*
30 in her] in that *C*
32 had proceaded] had to proceede *B*
170. 2 house] houses *B*, *C*
171. 7 vnto] to *C*
172. 18 finished, many] finished with many *D*
23 though] if *C*
33 to] vnto *C*
36 a] of the *C*
36 f. night paste] night last past *C*
173. 5 a] an *B*, *C*

173. 11 shalbe] shall in due time be *C*
23 for so muche] forasmuch *C*
33 to] into *C*
174. 12 f. rõ-nyng] commyng *B*, *C*
20 f. scantled] scanted *C*
175. 35 to] vnto *C*
176. 18 fame and] *Om. C*
31 race, for] race? and for *C*
177. 2 my] mine *C*
36 one] other *D*
38 my] mine *C*, *E*
179. 19 restoryng] restored *C*
23 Tolosia, and departed] Tolosia, departed *C*, *E*
28 f. altogether sent for] all sent for together *C*
180. 26 effect] affect *E*
181. 5 sondrie sufficient] sufficient sundry *C*
182. 3 name Emelia] name of Emelia *B*, *C*
11 bee properly] properly be *C*
13 either] or *E*
16 desires] desire *E*
183. 13 thine] thy *C*
30 lured] allured *C*
184. 9 louer] loue *D*
186. 37 Chamber] Chambers *B*
38 get] go *C*
187. 28 hasted] hastened *B*, *C*
30 waies] waie *D*
189. 22 semyng] seemed *C*
25 otherwise vse her] vse her otherwise *D*
27 willyngly to] willingly for to *C*
190. 12 our daie of] day of our *C*
24 indifference] indifferencie *C*
28 maide] maiden *C*
38 in] to *D*
191. 11 hartly] hartely *B*, *C*, *D*, *E*
30 diescrepit] discrepit *C*: decrepite *D*
38 seekes] seeke *C*

192. 2 f. measure the] measure their *B*, *C*
30 would] should *B*, *C*
193. 22 ill] euill *C*
34 Goddes] goddesses *C*: Goddesse *D*
194. 3 forthe] with *C*
14 and now] *Om. C*
16 haue] hath *C*: has *E*
37 to] vnto *C*
195. 17 for vs] *Om. C*
30 shall bee maister] shalbe the master *C*
38 taked] taken *B*, *C*, *D*
196. 10 f. to whom] vnto whom *C*
23 flies] flieth *C*
26 gettes] getteth *C*
27 pulles] pulleth *C* be] he *E*
197. 26 direction] directions *D*
198. 30 in] of *B*, *C*
38 fall so coniuryng] fall so to Coniuryng *B*, *C*: fall to conjuryng *E*
199. 2 nere] neerer *C*
17 armes] hands *C*
33 in a mannes] in mans *C*
200. 8 and without] and that without *C*
26 a] *Om. D*
201. 16 vnto] to *B*, *C*
18 by fortune] it fortuned *B*, *C*
33 hym] her *B*, *C*
34 stole] stolne *B*, *C*
202. 29 speake] spake *C*
34 euer] neuer *D*
36 a] the *B*, *C*
203. 18 raged] regarded *B*, *C*
28 FINIS] *Om. C*, *D*
205. 8 aboue] about *B*
206. 34 cõsentes, there] consentes, that there *B*
207. 25 partes] parties *E*

EXPLANATORY AND TEXTUAL NOTES

EXPLANATORY AND TEXTUAL NOTES

REFERENCES are to pages and lines of the facsimile text. In addition to the conventional abbreviations for scholarly magazines and reference works the following are also used:

A *Riche His Farewell to Militarie Profession* (1581).

Apperson G. L. Apperson, *English Proverbs and Proverbial Phrases* (London, 1929).

B *Riche His Farewell to Militarie Profession* (1583).

Bond *The Complete Works of John Lyly*, ed. R. W. Bond (Oxford, 1902).

C *Rich His Farewell to Militarie Profession* (1594).

Cinthio Giraldi Cinthio, *Gli Hecatommithi*, reprinted in *Raccolta di novellieri italiani* (Torino, 1853).

Collier *Eight Novels Employed by English Dramatic Poets of the Reign of Queen Elizabeth* [Rich's *Farewell*], ed. J. P. Collier, Shakespeare Society (London, 1846).

Cunliffe *The Complete Works of George Gascoigne*, ed. J. W. Cunliffe (Cambridge, 1907).

Cunningham *Rich's The Honestie of This Age* (1614), ed. Peter Cunningham, Percy Society (London, 1844).

D *Rich His Farewell to Militarie Profession* (1606).

Dyce *The Dramatic Works and Poems of James Shirley*, ed. Alexander Dyce (London, 1833).

Greg *The Weakest Goeth to the Wall* (1600), ed. Sir Walter Greg, Malone Society Reprints (Oxford, 1912).

Grosart *The Life and Complete Works in Prose and Verse of Robert Greene, M.A.*, ed. A. B. Grosart (London, 1881–1886).

HMC Historical Manuscripts Commission.

Linthicum Marie C. Linthicum, *Costume in the Drama of Shakespeare and His Contemporaries* (Oxford, 1936).

Lucas *The Complete Works of John Webster*, ed. F. L. Lucas (London, 1927).

Maidment and Logan *The Dramatic Works of Shakerley Marmion*, ed. James Maidment and W. H. Logan (Edinburgh, 1875).

Mann *The Works of Thomas Deloney*, ed. F. O. Mann (Oxford, 1912).

McKerrow *The Works of Thomas Nashe*, ed. R. B. McKerrow (London, 1910).

Mill *Philotus* (1603), ed. Miss A. J. Mill, Scottish Text Society (Edinburgh, 1933).

Painter William Painter, *The Palace of Pleasure*, ed. Joseph Jacobs (London, 1890).

Pettie George Pettie, *A Petite Pallace of Pettie His Pleasure*, ed. Herbert Hartman (New York, 1938).

PRO Public Record Office.

Rollins *The Paradise of Dainty Devices*, ed. H. E. Rollins (Cambridge, Mass., 1927).

Smith *The Oxford Dictionary of English Proverbs*, ed. W. G. Smith (Oxford, 1948).

Sugden E. H. Sugden, *A Topographical Dictionary to the Works of Shakespeare and His Fellow Dramatists* (Manchester, 1925).

Swaen *How a Man May Chuse a Good Wife from a Bad* (1602), ed. A. E. H. Swaen, *Materialen zur Kunde des älteren englischen Dramas*, Vol. XXXV (Louvain, 1912).

Tilley M. P. Tilley, *Elizabethan Proverb Lore* (New York, 1926).

Wilson *The Plague Pamphlets of Thomas Dekker*, ed. F. P. Wilson (Oxford, 1925).

1. 1. *Riche*] On title pages, in dedications and commendatory poems, in documents, and by Rich's contemporaries his name was spelled in almost every conceivable way: "Barnaby," "Barnabe" (preferred by *DNB*), "Barnabie," "Barnabee," and "Rich," "Riche," "Ritch," "Ritche," "Rych," "Ryche," "Rytch," "Rytche," and "Reche." But "Barnaby Rich" appears a score of times on title pages and elsewhere in Rich's works, often enough, I think, to justify adopting the simplest spelling of the name.

1 f. *Riche . . . profession*] Several scholars, humorlessly supposing that Rich's title was to be taken literally, have soberly observed that Rich did not actually give up soldiering in 1581. See W. M. A. Creizenach, *The English Drama in the Age of Shakespeare* (London, 1916), p. 198; Sir Sidney Lee's article on Rich in *DNB*; and Morton Luce, ed., *Rich's "Apolonius & Silla"* (London, 1912), p. 50. Luce remarks, "The title . . . is misleading, for the author returned eventually to his trade [*sic*] as a soldier."

2. *Militarie profession*] Elizabethans apparently considered the phrase not specific but generic, like certain words designating other occupations—"law," "medicine," "farming," for example. Hence often

no definite article preceded it. Compare Geoffrey Gates, *The Defence of Militarie Profession* (1579) and William Garrard, *The Arte of Warre. Beeing the onely rare booke of Myllitarie profession* (1591). Gates writes (sigs. A3–A3v), "The experience of the troublesome furies of men . . . aduanced Militarie profession." In *The Pathwaie to Martiall Discipline* (1581) Thomas Styward refers (sig. A3) to "all such as haue desire to militare profession." In Vicentio Saviolo's *Practise . . . of the use of rapier a. dagger* (1595) the translator declares (sig. B1v), "Some Authors doo write, that hunting, hauking, wrastling, &c. are things in some sort belonging vnto Militarie profession." Rich himself usually omits the definite article. In *The True Report* (1582) he confesses (sig. A3) that he is "adicted to Militarie profession"; and in *The Second Tome of the Travailes and aduentures of Don Simonides* (1584), he mentions (sig. B1) "the mirrour of Militarie profession" and (sig. E3) "one of the Pillars of the state, I meane Militarie profession." In *The Solace for the Souldier and Saylour* (1592) Simon Harward describes (sigs. B1–B1v) "what comfort and confidence" fighting men "may haue in the lawfull practise of Militarie profession."

2–5. *conteinyng . . . discourses . . . Gathered . . . for*] Either Rich or Walley, the publisher, repeated these formulas on the title page of *The Straunge and wonderfull aduentures of Don Simonides . . . Conteinyng verie pleasaunte discourse: Gathered for the recreation aswell of our noble yong gentilmen, as our honourable courtly Ladieship*, also published in 1581 by Walley.

11 f. *Gentleman*] In the dignification, which usually appears after his name on title pages, Rich took an acute interest. In *Roome for a Gentleman* (1609) he discusses (sigs. B2v, B3) both "the better sort of those that be knowne to be Gentlemen by birth, and others that by their places and professions are gentelized." According to his careful definition (sigs. D1–D1v), "A Gentleman born . . . must be discended from three degrees of Gentry, both by father and mother (for this is the opinion of the Heraldes) otherwise they are called Gentlemen of the first head, nightgrowne, mushrumpes, startvppes and such other." Among those he lists (sig. E1) as eligible to use the title because of their professions are "all Martial men that haue borne office, and haue had commaund in the field. . . . The profession of Armes being honourable, euery ordinary Souldier that hath serued seauen years without reproch,

ought to be accounted a Gentleman." Thus Rich doubtless considered himself doubly "gentelized"—by his captaincy and by his long military service, if not by birth.

13. *Malui . . . vocari*] Most of Rich's title pages from 1578 to 1617 bear this engaging posy: "I have preferred to be rich than to be called so." Such puns on the name were of course hard to resist: in a poem of commendation prefacing Rich's first publication, *A Right Exelent and Pleasaunt Dialogue* (1574), G. Argal advises, "Reade Rich, a booke enricht with goodly store,/ . . . Rich hath enricht his woorke as naught is skant"; in another, commending Rich's *Allarme to England* (1578), S. Stronge writes, "A iewel ritche and gemme of price, the same no doubt doth seeme,/ A ritcher gifte for thy behoofe, he could not geue, I deeme"; in another, prefacing the *Allarme*, Thomas Lupton enjoins, "And thanke thou Riche, that giues this larum bell,/ A richer gifte, he could not giue thee well." Compare also McKerrow, III, 16. Latin quotations and proverbs employing the formula "I prefer [or I should prefer] . . . than" are common, for which see J. A. Mair, *A Handbook of Proverbs, Mottoes, Quotations, and Phrases* (London, n.d.), p. 420, and [Sir Gurney] *Benham's Book of Quotations* (London, 1936), p. 618b. Compare the motto "Malo virum pecunia, quam pecuniam viro indigentem" on the title page of Cyril Tourneur's *The Transformed Metamorphosis* (1600). Since the present tense, *malo*, rather than Rich's present perfect is usual in such mottoes, Philip King may be forgiven for misquoting Rich's posy in *The Surfeit to A.B.C.* (1656), p. 55: "Such [a master of style] in times past was *Barnaby Rich* the *Philologist* with his Motto *Malo me divitem esse*."

14 f. *Imprinted . . . Walley*] Despite the "Imprinted," Walley was the publisher for whom John Kingston printed *A*. See p. lxi, above.

3. 20–22. *profites, though . . . blisse. Yet*] Read *profites. Though . . . blisse, yet*, to clarify the antithesis and balance Rich is here essaying: "Though . . . for a tyme," "yet . . . now"; "bale from blisse," "Cheese from Chalke"; "ouerhaled me . . . that," "warned me, that."

23–24. 4. *I see . . . feeld*] Compare *Much Ado about Nothing*, II. iii. 13–15: "I have known when there was no music with him but the drum and the fife; and now had he rather hear the tabor and the pipe."

4. 15 f. *trauaill, . . . badde lodging, worse fare, vnquiet slepe*] The author of *The Weakest Goeth to the Wall*, based on the first novel in the

Farewell, seems to glance at this passage. He writes, "I am *Barnabie Bunch*, the Botcher. . . . Ile labour for my meate, worke hard, fare hard, lie hard, for a liuing" (Greg, lines 495–98).

19 f. *flappe . . . taile*] The proverb (Tilley, p. 155; Smith, p. 514) seems to have meant "a contemptuous dismissal." It had some connection with "Tom Drum's entertainment" (for which see the notes on 9. 21 f. and 199. 9 f.), according to William Hawkins' *Apollo Shroving* (1626), ed. H. G. Rhoads (Philadelphia, 1936), p. 163, lines 2286 f.: "It shall haue *Tom Drums* entertainement. A flap with a Foxe tayle." A clue to the derivation of the proverb may be lurking in Greene's *A Looking-Glasse for London and England* (1594), Grosart, XIV, 65: "Mis[tresse] these words of yours are like a Fox taile placed in a gentlewomans Fanne."

23 f. *quiet reste*] Read probably *quiet*, *reste*, supplying the comma for which the compositor had no room at the end of the line.

5. 6–9. *contentations, when . . . companies: I*] Read probably *contentations. When . . . companies, I.*

12–6. 12. *As . . . I*] Rich's section on dancing is almost as much cited as Sir John Davies' celebrated comments in *Orchestra*, and may have suggested the interchange on the subject between Sir Toby and Sir Andrew in *Twelfth Night* (I. iii. 127–39), of which Rich's second tale is the principal source. For full details about the dances Rich discusses see A. F. Sieveking, "Dancing," *Shakespeare's England* (Oxford, 1916), II, 437–50.

14. *nor to vse measure in any thyng*] Read *nor vse* or *nor learn to vse*? Compare the proverb "There is a measure in all things" (Tilley, p. 226; Smith, p. 475).

14–25. *measure . . . Ieigge*] Compare *Much Ado about Nothing*, II. i. 72–84: "If the Prince be too important, tell him there is measure in everything, and so dance out the answer. For, hear me, Hero: wooing, wedding, and repenting is as a Scotch jig, a measure, and a cinquepace."

19 f. *trickes and tournes*] No precise description of these terpsichorean embellishments seems to be available, but Rich himself provides a few hints of what they were like in *Faultes* (1606), sig. C4v: "[The professional dancer's wit] will serue him well enough to talke of the *turne* of the toe, of the *caper* aboue ground, of the lofty *tricke*."

Compare Sir John Davies' *Orchestra*, ed. E. M. W. Tillyard (London, 1947), p. 31, "Oft doth she make her body upward flyne/ With lofty turns and caprioles in the air"; *Twelfth Night*, I. iii. 131, "And I think I have the back-trick simply as strong as any man in Illyria"; and Sir John Harington's *An Apologie* (1595), sigs. A1v–A2, "[Tiresome critics] descanted of the newe Faerie Queene and . . . the greatest fault they coulde finde in it, was that the laste verse [the alexandrine] disordered their mouthes, and was like a tricke of xvii. in a sinkapace."

21. *plaine Sinquepace*] The original galliard, which had five basic figures: hence the name *cinquepace*, or *cinque pas*.

23. *make a Capricornus*] *NED* contains no definitions of *capricornus* that provide clues to the meaning of this mystifying expression.

24. *Capre*] Probably from the Italian *capriole*, or "goat's leap," the caper involved jumping into the air and clicking the feet together. For the "*caper* aboue ground" and "lofty turns and caprioles in the air" see the note on 5. 19 f.

6. 6. *nier*] I.e., "nearer."

course] What follows suggests that Rich is playing on the word, to be read (1) course and (2) corse (body).

23 f. *rather . . . liking*] Compare Nashe's *The Anatomie of Absurditie* (1589), McKerrow, I, 24, "It were to be wished, that . . . the praise of the vertuous were . . . prohibited . . . to be so odiouslie extolde, as rather breedes . . . lothing then lyking."

7. 10 f. *whisper . . . eare*] Instead of *at all*, *B*, *C*, and *D* print *a tale*, areading that seems satisfactory in the light of Capulet's speech (*Romeo and Juliet*, I. v. 23–26), "I have seen the day/ That I . . . could tell/ A whispering tale in a fair lady's ear,/ Such as would please." See also "Prepare her ears to hear a wooer's tale" (*Richard III*, IV. iv. 327).

13 f. *newe profession*] I.e., pleasing women, as opposed to his old profession, soldiering, to which he is saying farewell.

26–28. 2. *publishe . . . sauecundites*] A commonplace in dedications. Rich offers the "trifles" in *The True Report* (1582) to Sir Francis Walsingham, "to be safecundited vnder your graue title" (sig. A3). In *The Pathwaie to Martiall Discipline* (1581), dedicated to Lord Howard of Effingham, Thomas Styward expresses the hope (sig. A3) that "[my book] maie vnder the passport and safe conduct of your Honour, be had the more in price." And in *Have with You to Saffron-Walden*

(1596) Nashe assures Richard Lichfield in the dedication (McKerrow, III, 9), "vnder thy redoubted patronage and protection my workes are to haue . . . more than common safe-conduct into the world."

8. 9. *Punie*] A recently admitted pupil in a school, university, or Inn of Court.

13. *Yours . . . honestie*] On this, the most celebrated phrase in the *Farewell*, see pp. liv–lviii, above.

9. 1. *To . . . Souldiours*] Rich similarly honors his military colleagues in the *Allarme to England* (1578) and in *A Path-way to Military Practise* (1587).

17 f. *how . . . regarded*] Compare *2 Henry IV*, I. ii. 190–92: "Virtue is of so little regard in these costermonger's times that true valour is turn'd berod."

21 f. *thrust . . . shoulders*] Rich appears to be thinking of "Jack (or Tom) Drum's entertainment." See his *Don Simonides* (1581), sig. S3, "After she had laughed her fill, [Rome would] giue you Iacke Drommes, entertainment, and thrust the contemner of Beautie . . . out of the doores." *NED* quotes, among others, Withal's *Dictionarie* (1608), p. 104, "Hee thrust him foorth of doores by head and shoulders, as they say, Jacke Drums entertainement." See also 199. 9 f., above.

29–10. 2. *waight. I*] Read *waight, I.*

10. 4. *sir . . . you*] The modern equivalent would be, I think, "if you'll pardon the expression" or "asking your pardon." Rich is fond of using it for humorous effect, as in *Don Simonides* (1581), sig. Q2, "*Andruchio* smilyngly interrupted *Simonides*, and was it . . . all for loue sir reuerence"; in *Faultes* (1606), sig. D1v, "[Panders are] a necessary instrument for the Vsurer, whereby to accomplish a great deale of (sir reuerence of you) K, N, auerie"; again in *Faultes*, sig. F4v, "And call you this loue? I, it is loue sir reuerence"; and in *My Ladies Looking Glasse* (1616), sig. G2v, "See how gastfully hee lookes, his armes crossed, his eyes blubbered, his hatte puld ouer his browes, and all for loue sir reuerence." Compare also Mercutio to Romeo, I. iv. 41 f., "We'll draw thee from the mire/ Of this sir-reverence love," and *The Comedy of Errors*, III. ii. 91–93, "[She is] such a one as a man may not speak of without he say 'sir-reverence.'"

5 f. *my . . . Engıande*] Rich's description of the *Allarme* (1578) as his "last booke" seems to indicate that the *Farewell* was completed

earlier than the first part of *Don Simonides*, also published in 1581 and registered on October 23, 1581.

6. *I . . . thyng*] In the last sentence in the *Allarme* he "promises," sig. L3v, "Thus gentle reader . . . when my time and occasion shall better serue mee, I wil not foreslowe some other thing, the which I trust shall be more to thy liking."

8 f. *decaie . . . discipline*] The final section of the *Allarme* (sigs. H4v–L3v) is entitled "The fourth parte conteining the decay of Martiall discipline."

10–16. *to haue . . . seen them*] Since the places named figured more than once in the wars in the Netherlands from 1572 to 1576, and since the dates Rich fought there cannot be precisely fixed, it is difficult to specify what battles, skirmishes, and fortifications he had in mind or to tell whether his knowledge of them was gained at first or second hand. That he had made preparations for the book which never appeared is suggested by a bit in *A True Discourse Historicall of the Succeeding Gouernours in the Netherlands and the Ciuill Warres There* (1602) by his friend Thomas Churchyard. Here Churchyard says in a marginal gloss (p. 19) that he is indebted for his information to "Captaine Barnabey Rich his notes." This acknowledgment is opposite a paragraph describing military doings in Holland from November, 1572, to August, 1573. In his *Allarme* (1578) Rich speaks (sig. H3) of having seen every street in Flushing full of English ordnance and gives (sigs. K4–L) a detailed, evidently eyewitness account of the tactics of two English "bands" before besieged Zieriksee, which surrendered in June, 1576.

13 f. *Delfte . . . Leiden*] After the Spanish captured The Hague in October, 1573, Colonel Morgan's English regiment occupied a position between Delft and Rotterdam, "alwayes readie to thrust into Delft, Rotterdam, Delfts hauen, or Maeslandt Sluce," while the "garrisons wrought continually to fortifye" Delftshaven and Maaslandsluice, "especially Delfts hauen, which was not easily to be woon, hauing necessaries fit for a fort . . . for the better assurance of Leyden," according to Edward Grimeston, *A Generall Historie of the Netherlands* (1627), pp. 407 f. But Maaslandsluice gave up in May, 1574, and five hundred Englishmen (Rich among them?) under Colonel Edward Chester, refused admittance by the citizens of Leyden, surrendered and were returned to England. The siege of Leyden was in full swing by May 26,

1574. See J. L. Motley, *The Rise of the Dutch Republic* (Everyman ed., London, 1930), II, 440–44, and (for accounts of this phase of the war by Rich's contemporaries) Churchyard, *A True Discourse Historicall*, sig. E3; Geoffrey Gates, *The Defence of Militarie Profession* (1579), sigs. D4–E; Sir Roger Williams, *The Actions of the Lowe Countries* (1618), pp. 110–14; and I. D. L.'s French translation of van Meteren, *L'Histoire des Pays-Bas* (1608), vol. I, fols. 74v–75, 105.

14. *the Breylle . . . Gorcoum*] Before *Gorcoum* a comma should be inserted. By the "hedde" of "den Briel" (as the island is called in Dutch—hence Rich's "*the* Breylle"?) Rich may have meant that part closest to the mouth of the River Maas, though "head" can also mean a projecting point of the coast. Count de la Marck and his Sea Beggars captured Brielle for the Protestants on April 1, 1572. Rich evinces a lively interest in this sector in his *Allarme*, where he observes (sig. L3) that after the Spanish had taken Zieriksee in June, 1576, they should have attacked "*Bryel Island* . . . the which coulde not haue beene defended, if the Spaniards had once beene commaunders of the Plaate. The firste thing the Spaniards would there haue sought for, should haue been the *Bryel* head, which is now verie strongly fortified, but at that instant nothing begun: which if they had once taken, *Holland* had beene no longer able to haue holden out, for their trade by sea would haue beene soudeinly cutte off, without the which they may not endure, considering it is the onely wealth of all their townes, that are to bee accompted of, as *Skeydame*, *Delftes* hauen, *Roterdame*, *Delfte*, . . . *Gorcom.*" In *A Path-way to Military Practise* (1587) Rich tells (sig. B4) a humorous, probably apocryphal tale about a mercenary stationed at Gorcum "about" 1576.

15. *Gouldfluce, Maaselandefluce, the Crympe*] The first two words should be read *Gouldsluce*, *Maaselandesluce*, "two verie strong Forts, either of them manned with fiue Companies of English" under Colonel Edward Chester, according to Edward Grimeston's *A Generall Historie of the Netherlands* (1627), pp. 434 f. Valdez' Spanish troops first attacked Goudasluice, but were repeatedly beaten back by the English under Captain Gainsford. Since the two forts blocked the only means of entry into Holland for the Spanish cavalry, however, Valdez persisted, finally drove the English out, and on May 17, 1574, cut them "in peeces." For further details about the fall of Maaslandsluice see the

note on 10. 13 f. Grimeston also records (p. 466) that on February 11, 1576, the Protestants captured the "great fort called Crimpen [Rich's *the Crympe*, the modern Dutch *Krimpen*], in the gulph of the riuer of Lecke." For another account of its fall see Thomas Stocker, *A Tragicall Historie of the . . . Ciuile Warres of the Lowe Countries* (1583?), fol. 139.

19. *louyng Histories*] I.e., "love stories." Compare "Histories, all treatyng . . . of loue" (10. 4).

20 f. *before . . . Morice*] I.e., before July 16, 1579, when James Fitzmaurice Fitzgerald, the "arch traitor," landed at Dingle, Kerry, with three ships and two emissaries from the Pope and tried fruitlessly to wrest Ireland from the English heretics. For further details of his invasion, see the account of him in *DNB*; R. Bagwell, *Ireland under the Tudors* (London, 1890), III, 12–24; and E. M. Hinton, *Ireland through Tudor Eyes* (Philadelphia, 1935), pp. 35 f. Like Rich, John Derricke may also have been forced by military emergencies to lay aside his literary interests in 1579 and 1580, since on the title page of *The Image of Irelande* he describes his book as having been "Made and deuised . . . *Anno 1578*, and now published and set forthe . . . this present yere of our Lorde *1581*."

22 f. *thei saie*] Rich's usual formula, sometimes slightly varied, to introduce proverbs and sententious remarks, as at 13. 9, 13. 16, 16. 5, and 185. 34. The author of the comedy *The Return from Parnassus* (1597), ed. W. D. Macray (Oxford, 1886), p. 43, makes extravagant fun of the phrase: "Luxurio, as they say, a man of God's makinge, as they saye, came to my house, as they saye, and was trusted by my wife, a kinde woman, as they saye, for a dozen of ale, as they saye, and he a naughtie felowe, as they saye, is run away, as they saye; for even as an emptie barrell soundeth moste, as they saye, even so Luxurio came to my house and was welcom, as they saye, and even as a pot of ale and a puddinge are good in a frostie morninge, even soe Luxurio . . . hath overrune the reckoninge. My wife and I, twoo honest folkes, as they saye, ment no harme, but even as the ape wanteth a tale, as they saye, even so wee wanted all malice, as they saye." Shakespeare also evidently considered the phrase inelegant and laughable, for he often puts it into the mouths of such comic characters as Bardolph: "And being fap, sir [the gentleman] was, as they say, cashier'd" (*The Merry Wives of Windsor*, I. i. 183 f.); Mistress Quickly: "I defy all angels (in any such sort, as they

say) but in the way of honesty" (*The Merry Wives of Windsor*, II. ii. 74–76); Mistress Quickly again: "Old folks, you know, have discretion, as they say, and know the world" (*The Merry Wives of Windsor*, II. ii. 134–36); Elbow: "a bad woman, whose house, sir, was, as they say, pluck'd down in the suburbs" (*Measure for Measure*, II. i. 64 f.); Dogberry: "As they say, 'When the age is in, the wit is out'" (*Much Ado about Nothing*, III. v. 37 f.); Costard: "Go to; thou hast it . . . at the fingers' ends, as they say" (*Love's Labour's Lost*, V. i. 81 f.); Salerio: "Many a tall ship lie buried, as they say" (*The Merchant of Venice*, III. i. 6 f.); Clown: "But, as they say, to hear music the General does not greatly care" (*Othello*, III. i. 17 f.); Nurse: "if ye should lead her into a fool's paradise, as they say, it were a very gross kind of behaviour, as they say" (*Romeo and Juliet*, II. iv. 175–77).

11. 4. *at my . . . London*] Probably early in February, 1580. See the note on 11. 32 f.

4–12. 11. *It . . . witte*] In *The Seventeenth Earl of Oxford* (London, 1928) B. M. Ward quotes this extended passage and argues (pp. 192–94) that it was a "lampoon directed against Lord Oxford" which, "there can be no doubt," was instigated "by the Vice-Chamberlain [Sir Christopher Hatton]. Moreover, Hatton belonged to Leicester's faction in opposing the French match [between Elizabeth and the Duc D'Alençon], and Riche's description of a man in a French muff, a French cloak, and a French hose makes it practically certain that he is caricaturing Lord Oxford. . . . There can surely be little doubt that the Elizabethan reader would see in Riche's lampoon a picture of the chief supporter of the Anjou match." See also Eva T. Clark, *Hidden Allusions in Shakespeare's Plays, a Study of the Oxford Theory* (New York, 1931), pp. 384 f.

6. *footeclothe*] The cloth that hung over the saddle far enough down on the sides to guard the feet from the mud was a mark of affluence, sometimes of pretentiousness. See Sir Francis Bryan's translation of Guevara's *A Looking Glass for the Court* (1575), sig. D8v, "[Fortunate village-dwellers] neede no Mule nor Horse with a foote clothe"; Nashe's mention of "surfit-swolne Churles, who now ride on their footcloathes" in his section on Gluttony in *Pierce Penilesse* (1592), McKerrow, I, 201; Dekker's *The Wonderfull Yeare* (1603), Wilson, p. 34, "Sextons gaue out, if they might (as they hoped) continue these doings

but a tweluemoneth longer, they and their posteritie would all ryde vpon foote-cloathes to the ende of the worlde"; and Webster's *The White Devil* (1612), I. ii. 47 f., Lucas, p. 114, "But call his wit in question, you shall find it/ Merely an Asse in's footcloath." See also Nashe's *Have with You to Saffron-Walden* (1596), McKerrow, III, 79, and M. M. Knappen, *Tudor Puritanism* (Chicago, 1939), p. 195.

32 f. *in . . . Februarie*] February, 1580, if the phrase and "at my last beyng at London" (11. 4) refer to the trip mentioned in a declaration of the account of Sir Thomas Heneage (Declared Accounts, A.O. 1/383/18, PRO). According to this entry (to which F. B. Williams, Jr., kindly directed me), on February 20, 1580, Walsingham signed a warrant to pay Rich "for bringing of letteres in poste for her Majesties affaires, from Sir William Pellham knighte lorde Justice of Irelande, being then at Dublin to the Courte at Whitehall xxx^{mo} Januarii," 1580.

12. 4–7. *Frenche . . . warmer*] The hood was fashionable for men in the fourteenth and fifteenth centuries, for women in the sixteenth. The French hood covered the head and the neck. Its mode declined before 1603, and it definitely passed "out of fashion for all classes by 1630" (Linthicum, pp. 216, 217).

16–22. *to please women . . . armours*] There is a curious parallel to this passage in *The Return from Parnassus* (1597), ed. W. D. Macray (Oxford, 1886), p. 53: "Since souldierye is not regarded, I'le make the ladies happie with enjoyinge my youth, and hange up my sworde and buckler to the behoulders." Compare also *1 Henry VI*, V. iv. 173 f.:

> So, now dismiss your army when ye please,
> Hang up your ensigns, let your drums be still;

and *Richard III*. I. i. 5–13:

> Now are our brows bound with victorious wreaths,
> Our bruised arms hung up for monuments,
> Our stern alarums chang'd to merry meetings,
> Our dreadful marches to delightful measures.
> Grim-visag'd War hath smooth'd his wrinkled front,
> And now, instead of mounting barbed steeds
> To fright the souls of fearful adversaries,
> He capers nimbly in a lady's chamber
> To the lascivious pleasing of a lute

22 f. *hang . . . walles*] Rich uses this curious expression again in *Roome for a Gentleman* (1609), sig. B2v: "We call it a happy peace . . . when our Drummes and warlike instruments . . . are hanged by the wals." Compare the idiom "to lie by the walls," i.e., "to remain idle, unused."

24 f. *lye to*] Read *lye, to*, supplying the comma for which the compositor had no room at the end of the line.

31. *the Militarie profession*] See 1. 2n.

13. 6. *vnrewarded. Is*] Read *vnrewarded, is.*

6 f. *Iacke . . . office*] Read *Iacke out of office*, the usual form of the proverb (Smith, p. 246)? Compare *1 Henry VI*, I. i. 175, "But long I will not be Jack out of office!"

16 f. *one Lawyer . . . Shire*] Though not listed by Smith or Tilley, the expression sounds proverbial and is preceded by the formula with which Rich usually introduces proverbs (see the note on 10. 22 f.). Rich's opinion of lawyers was consistently low. Compare his "Anothomy of Ireland" (1615), ed. E. M. Hinton, *PMLA*, LV (1940), 87: "They say souldyers & lawyers could neuer thryve both togyther in one shyre."

23. *steale . . . wares*] About the contraband in which dishonest merchants dealt Rich is more specific in his *Allarme* (1578), sig. C3v: "In *Englande* once a yeere wee fynde the extremitie, eyther for wante of corne, lether, hydes, tallowe, butter, cheese, bacon, beefe, biere, & many other such lyke, which by her Maiestie are prohibited: but no restrainte may serue against those theeues . . . of their owne countrey." Even after the bans on certain exportations were lifted, Rich continues to complain in *Opinion Diefied* (1613), sig. E1, "in this time of peace the Marchant findeth libertie, to carry away Corne, Beere, Butter, Cheese, Leather, Tinne, Ordinance, Cloath, Wooll, and all other such commodities, so that our store and plenty, by these meanes are turned to penury," and in *The Honestie of This Age* (1614), Cunningham, p. 13, "And he that robbes the realme of corne, and of all other commodities, transporting it beyond the seas, is hee not an honest trading marchant, and what is he that dares call him theefe?"

14. 11–15. *pinchyng . . . Lawyers*] Rich voices the same complaint in *A Path-way to Military Practise* (1587), sig. B4v: "[For absurd lawsuits citizens] will not sticke to spende more poundes, then for the

releefe of a souldiour, or defence of their countrye they are willinge to giue pence."

24 f. *Maister*] Literally or figuratively? If the former, Rich's duties may have included serving Hatton as a courier and sending him advices from Ireland.

25. *vpholder*] If this means that Rich received financial support from Hatton, such support may have been given for services rendered in Hatton's employ or for Rich's literary efforts. Rich dedicated to Hatton the *Allarme to England* (1578) and both parts of *Don Simonides* (1581, 1584). The fulsome praise in the *Farewell* (14. 23–15. 23) doubtless also gratified Sir Christopher, who, let us hope, regarded these compliments as tantamount to a dedication, and hence worthy of reward. For a clue to the amount Rich could have hoped to receive from his dedicatee, see G. M. Vogt, "Richard Robinson's *Eupolemia* (1603)," *SP*, XXI (1924), 636. For "his Booke Dedicatory," Robinson reports, Hatton gave him "6 Angels iij li" (i.e., "six angels plus three pounds" or "six angels—that is, three pounds"?). Hatton's liberality, Robinson continues, "kept me from trubling my frendes abrode for one whole yeares space afterwardes." My friend V. B. Heltzel has kindly allowed me to consult his unpublished files on literary patronage, which contain a list of forty-four books dedicated to Hatton by twenty-eight authors, including Rich's friends Thomas Churchyard and Thomas Lupton. On Hatton as "upholder" of soldier-authors see E. S. Brooks, *Sir Christopher Hatton* (London, 1947), Chapter XIII, "A Lover of Learned Men."

26. *Holdenby*] On this magnificent estate, the "Holmby" which James I bought in 1605, and in which Charles I was imprisoned in 1647, see Brooks's biography (cited immediately above), Chapter XVI.

30. *Pallas of pleasure*] Also probably much indebted to Painter's *Palace* and certainly to Pettie's *Petite Pallace*, Greene similarly alludes to one or both in *Mamillia* (1583), Grosart, II, 18: "He had made a Metamorphosis of himselfe from . . . the castle of Care, to the pallace of pleasure."

31 f. *no . . . handes*] In this extravagant judgment even Lord Burghley, master of the rival estate Theobalds, seemed to concur (see Brooks, pp. 157 f.).

33. *not . . . finished*] Apropos of this passage Brooks says (pp.

159 f.), "It may be conjectured that 1583 was the date when the last touches were given to the building, and Hatton's heraldic achievement, bearing that date, was put up over the entrance gates." For a picture in which this date on the gate is visible, see Francis Grose, *The Antiquities of England and Wales*, VIII (1787), 117. The great archways, practically all of Holdenby that still survives, also bear the date 1583 (Brooks, p. 164).

15. 4–7. *greate . . . smokes*] Stingy masters of great houses kept fires only in their own quarters and neglected to provide heat for the rest of the household and for guests. Some of the chimneys on such houses were evidently only dummies, put up for display. Thus Charles Gibbon, *Not So New, As True* (1590), p. 14, "We haue now sumptuous houses, but slender hospitallitie: for all the smoke comes out of one chimney." See also Greene's *A Quip for an Upstart Courtier* (1592), Grosart, XI, 272.

6. *sundrie Chimneis*] Even the Parliamentary commission which surveyed Holdenby after Charles I's execution were sufficiently impressed to comment on the "many costly and rare chimney-pieces" (quoted by Brooks, p. 161).

17. *giueth . . . wante*] Hatton's charity was legendary. John Phillips celebrated his "kindliness and helpfulness to the poor" (quoted by Brooks, p. 353); by this "purse-bearer vnto the poore" the indigent "were neuer at their need denaid," according to Greene, *A Maidens Dreame* (1591), *The Plays & Poems*, ed. J. C. Collins (Oxford, 1905), II, 230; and Camden called him "a great reliever of the poor" (quoted by Brooks, p. 19), "for almesdeeds of all others most bountifull" (*Brittania*, trans. Philemon Holland, p. 508). A hundred poor people marched before his body at his funeral in St. Paul's (Brooks, p. 353).

30–32. *it . . . repentaunce*] Among the "signes and miracles" Rich could have had in mind were the floods of January, 1580, the earthquake of April 6, 1580, the apparitions in Cornwall about May 18, 1580, and the comet of October 10, 1580, all celebrated in a spate of broadsides and pamphlets. See H. E. Rollins, *An Analytical Index to the Ballad-Entries* (Chapel Hill, 1924), No. 1079 (on "the harmes of the great floodes"), Nos. 327, 663, 1838, 2224, 2714 (on the earthquake), No. 2444 (on the apparitions in Cornwall), Nos. 22, 807, 2630 (on the comet); and William Ringler, *Stephen Gosson* (Princeton, 1942), pp. 70 f.

16. 3. *see*] Read probably *say* to conform with the usual formula, "like as wee saie," as at 16. 5. See the note on 10. 22 f.

5 f. *as . . . other*] The observation sounds proverbial and is introduced by the formula which usually precedes Rich's aphorisms and proverbs (see the note on 10. 22 f.), but it is not listed in the standard collections of proverbs. Compare, however, Thomas North, *The Dial of Princes* (1568), sig. **2, "For seldom times one poison hurteth another: but it driueth out the other," and Nashe, *Strange Newes, of the Intercepting Certaine Letters* (1592), McKerrow, I, 256, "Sloth is a sinne, and one sinne (as one poison) must be expelled with another."

18–25. *For . . . vs*] Compare *Richard II*, II. i. 40–50:

> This royal throne of kings, this scept'red isle . . .
> This happy breed of men, this little world,
> This precious stone set in the silver sea,
> Which serves it in the office of a wall,
> Or as a moat defensive to a house,
> Against the envy of less happier lands;
> This blessed plot, this earth, this realm, this England.

29. *The Scottes by custome*] On the disappearance of this phrase in *D* see p. lxxiv, above.

32. *all owe*] Read probably *allowe* with *C* and *D*.

17. 20. *blondie*] Read *bloudie*.

24. *the . . . published*] "The Bishops' Bible," or "Matthew Parker's Bible," published in 1568, was highly esteemed by Elizabeth.

28 f. *treasons . . . Papistes*] Rich is elsewhere more explicit: thus in *The True Report* (1582), sig. E4, "Did not *Campion* sell Pardons to imploye his money against her Maiestie? did not thei of that confederacie, sell the death of her highnesse," and in *A True and a Kinde Excuse* (1612), sig. B1, "It is . . . defended by *Iesuites* to murther Princes, and this is holden by their greatest doctors, as *Sanders, Parsons, Alline*." Nicholas Sanders (1530?–1581) and William Allen (1532–1594) were members of James Fitzmaurice Fitzgerald's expedition against Ireland in 1579, to which Rich refers above (10. 20 f.).

18. 10 f. *as . . . also*] Source: Gascoigne's "Councell given to master Bartholmew Withipoll," Cunliffe, I, 344:

What was I saying? sirra, will you see
How soone my wittes were wandering astraye?
I saye, praye thou for thee and for thy mate,
So shipmen sing.

Rich adapts the first two lines of the verse at 24. 21 f.

19. 6. *write*] I.e., "writ." Compare "quite" for "quit" (59. 33, 63. 16) and "spitfull" for "spitefull" (122. 13).

8 f. *to . . . vse*] If this testimony is to be believed, the stories in the *Farewell* presumably were circulated in manuscript among Rich's friends.

10 f. *forsed . . . Printer*] I.e., "to send them from Ireland"? If so, Rich himself could not see the book through the press, and Robert Walley, the publisher, is only doing Rich justice in blaming (22. 14–17) the typographical errors not on the author but on the printer's haste.

17. *L. B.*] See pp. xxii–xxvi, above.

18–26. *I . . . merie*] A conventional precaution? Compare Philemon Holland's recommendation to the readers of his translation of Suetonius, ed. Charles Whibley, Tudor Translations (London, 1899), I, 3, "if happlie in prosecuting of this point, he [Suetonius] hath recorded ought that may be offensive to chaste and modest mindes, yee shal do well to glaunce over with your eye such places lightly, as I with my pen touch unwillingly."

24–26. *Trustyng . . . merie*] The participial phrase makes sense when read with either the preceding or succeeding sentence.

20. 1. *W. I. Gentleman*] Though this poet's identity can probably never be conclusively established, the following seem the likeliest candidates: (1) Captain William Jenkins, like Rich a soldier in Ireland, is mentioned in the *Calendar of the State Papers Relating to Ireland . . . 1574–1585* (pp. 247, 343, 363, 366, 544), where his name is twice linked with that of Rich's friend Captain Thomas Maria Wingfield (on whom see my note, "Thomas North at Chester," *HLQ*, XIII [1949], 93 f.). (2) William Jones (Johnes), whose name also appears in the *Calendar of the State Papers Relating to Ireland* for the same years (pp. 519, 537, 540, 559, 583, 584). From Dublin, Jones wrote more than once to Walsingham, complaining, like Rich, of the abuses of the Anglican clergy in Ireland. (3) William Jones, Gentleman, the translator of Lipsius' *Sixe Bookes of Politickes* (1594) and *Nennio, or A Treatise of*

Nobility (1595). Since the *Nennio* contains a commendatory verse by Spenser, perhaps Jones was a member of the Spenser-Sidney-Bryskett circle in Ireland with which Rich was also connected. (4) W. I., author of *The Whipping of the Satyre* (1601). He refers (sig. A2) to satirists and others who "would shortly haue proued as mischieuous to the Inhabitants of England, as Tyrone hath bene to the Frontiers of Ireland."

6 f. *place. As*] Read *place, as.*

22. *he by right hath*] The readings of this phrase in *B* and *C* reveal an entertaining probability: omitting the *by*, the compositor of *B* spoiled the meter of the line; noticing the defective meter in *B*, the compositor or proofreader of *C* did not refer to *A* for the correct reading, but rendered the phrase "he right due hath" and thus restored the meter by an addition of his own devising. For a similar treatment of one of Dekker's texts see Wilson, p. xxxiii.

21. 1. *Baptiste Starre*] A student by this name matriculated as a pensioner from St. John's College, Cambridge, at Michaelmas Term, 1565 (John Venn and J. A. Venn, *Alumni Cantabrigienses* [Cambridge, 1927], Part I, vol. IV, p. 151). According to an entry in the Middlesex Sessions Rolls for Michaelmas Term, 1585, a number of victualers were indicted "for allowing unlawful games, contrary to the statute for the maintenance of archery; among them were . . . Baptist Starr, the constable of Ratcliffe, who was also outlawed" (Mark Eccles, *Christopher Marlowe in London* [Cambridge, Mass., 1934], p. 96). In 1589 William Grene, the collector for the Hundred of Farnham, Surrey, swore that "Baptist Starr late of Tilforde within the Hundred aforesaid . . . was removed & departed from Tilforde aforesaid unto what place he knoweth not," leaving behind "not any goodes cattelles landes or tenementes within this County of Surrey" on which to levy eight shillings in taxes which Starre owed (Certificates of Residence, E 115/337/89, PRO). From the records of a case tried in January, 1607, Israel Lea, son and heir of Richard Lea, deceased, *v.* Thomas Westarrey and James Culliner (formerly Req 2/301, PRO; the bundle is being renumbered) we learn that one Baptist Starre, citizen and cooper of London, and his wife, Mary, had entered into bonds with the late Richard Lea. With this Lea, Rich was also closely connected: he was a kinsman of Lea's wife, served Lea as a real-estate broker, and deposed in Lea's favor in two litigations. Lea returned the compliment and deposed in Rich's

favor at another trial. (For the cases in which both were involved see Req 2/55/12, Req 2/64/83, and C 24/282/47 in the PRO, references which Leslie Hotson generously gave me.) If all these are the same Baptist Starre—and it seems improbable that many could have borne precisely this charming name—then we have an engaging though sketchy picture of him from 1565 to 1607: Cantabrigian, poetaster and friend of Captain Rich, constable of Ratcliffe, outlaw, fugitive from a tax collector in Surrey, cooper in London, and debtor to Rich's cousin Lea.

7. *Whose . . . praise*] For a sample of the praise see Captain Christopher Levens' letter to Sir Robert Cecil, March 9, 1601, recommending "rewards for services done on the occasion of the late rebellion," and citing Rich among the "most deserving" (HMC, *Salisbury MSS.*, XI, 117).

22. 1. *Printer*] I.e., "publisher," Robert Walley. See above, p. lxi.

4. *Spider . . . gaule*] A commonplace, as in Deloney's *Jack of Newbury* (1597?), Mann, p. 19, "(like the Spider) ye turne the sweete flowers of good counsell into venemous poyson."

10–13, 18–21. *Misconster . . . wright*] Walley evidently wrote his commendatory poem specifically for Rich's collection instead of pulling out some stock verse. Note the reference to "These pleasaunt Stories." Observe also that Walley shares Rich's fear of offending the overly sensitive reader and hence, in "Misconster not," etc., echoes Rich's nervous reference (19. 18–26) to improprieties which he trusts will be forgiven because they were after all written to induce merriment, not shock.

14–21. *And . . . wright*] Walley expresses the same sentiments in his "Printer to the courteous Reader" commending Rich's *Don Simonides*, which he also published in 1581. In fact, he often repeats the same phrases (which I italicize below), though in iambic pentameter rather than in ballad stanzas:

> If decent *mirthe* bemixt with pleasaunt stile,
> Maie *moue thy minde* good reader *to delight:*
> Accept his will, *reward his paine with praise,*
> *Whiche did this* fine and *pleasaunt storie wright.*
>   Wherein thou shalt, of witte and learnyng finde,
>   Sufficient store to please, thy courteous minde.

The *faultes* are myne, *that passed haue the Presse*,
The praise is his, that tooke the paine to penne:
Yet paines to bothe, of truthe I must confesse,
A thanklesse woorke, to please all kinde of menne.
Yet as it is receiue, and there an ende,
A woorke well likte of all, is wisely pende.

23. 1 f. *Sappho . . . Mantona*] In his *Poetical Decameron* (London, 1820), II, 163, Collier observes, "Shakespeare is charged by the commentators with the heinous offence of confounding the sex which ought to belong to the name of Baptista. Rich seems to have been guilty of the same error in the name of Sappho." Rich's hero could be named, not for the poetess, but for Psapho (or Psaphon), of whom Nashe writes (McKerrow, I, 230), "The Libian Sapho . . . taught little birds that were capable of speech, to pronounce distinctlie, *Magnus Deus Sapho*; that is to saie, *A great God is Sapho*." More likely, however, Rich saw the name in Painter (see 23. 5–9 n.) and considered it appropriate for a man since it ends in *-o*. Compare the names of other male characters in the *Farewell*—Phylerno, Alberto, Alonso, Fineo, and Silvio.

The *Mantona*, which is not geographically identifiable, may be derived from a passage in Painter's "Rhomeo and Juletta" (p. 233 of the first edition, 1567), a principal source of Rich's story: "[Rhomeo] vsed such expedition, as without hurt hee arriued at Mantona." This obvious misprint for *Mantoua*, as Mantua is spelled elsewhere in the story, probably furnished Sappho with his mellifluous title.

5–9 *Claudius . . . Phylene*] All these characters' names Rich seems to have drawn from his favorite source, Painter's *Palace*—Messilina, the Emperor Claudius, and Sappho from "Faustina the Empress," II, 260 f.; Aurelianus from "Zenobia Queen of Palmyres," II, 311; and Phylene from "Two Maidens of Carthage," II, 264. Since the latter immediately succeeds "Faustina" in the *Palace*, and since "Zenobia" is only two short selections removed from "Two Maidens," one suspects that when the time came to christen his characters Rich opened a volume of Painter at this particular place and thumbed through a few pages, selecting handsome names.

6. *prowest*] Perhaps a misprint for *prowess*, perhaps the result of Rich's effort to spell the word as it sounded to him.

11. *ende, restored*] Read perhaps *ende, were restored.*

25–30. *vncertain . . . aduersitie*] Source: Painter's "Sophonisba," II, 239.

24. 18–21. *please . . . all*] Compare *3 Henry VI*, I. iv. 128–31:

> 'Tis beauty that doth oft make women proud;
> But God he knows thy share thereof is small.
> 'Tis virtue that doth make them most admir'd;
> The contrary doth make thee wond'red at.

21 f. *see . . . square*] Source: Gascoigne's "Councell given to master Bartholmew Withipoll," Cunliffe, I, 344:

> What was I saying? sirra, will you see
> How soone my wittes were wandering astraye?
> I saye, praye thou for thee and for thy mate,
> So shipmen sing.

See 18. 10 f. and 38. 15 f.

32–25. 2. *his . . . golde*] I suspect that Rich borrowed this passage, which is curiously poetic in mood and diction, from some verse I have not been able to discover. Note that most of the lines scan, and that the rhymes "beare-weare," "awaie-araie," and "brought-thought" seem also to be poetic vestiges. Observe how (with a little tampering) the lines fall into far from contemptible iambic verse, predominantly hexameter and complete with cesura:

> His head which had been vsed, the loftie Helme to beare,
> Had now forgotten quite, the waueryng Plumes to weare,
> Betossed with euery winde, and readie to blowe awaie.
> His bodie moste ineured, to weare a coate of steele,
> Could not be brought to yield, vnto this queint araie.
> His necke he thought more fit, to paise the trustie targe,
> Then to bee hanged with Gemmes, or Chaines of golde. . . .

34 f. *waueryng . . . winde*] Perhaps Rich intended "waueryng" in the sense of "inconstant, faltering in allegiance," had in mind the court plume attached to the hat to symbolize dignity or rank, and was thinking of the proverbial weathercock in the wind. The gist of this highly figurative passage might then be, in literal language, "Sappho had forgotten how to be a courtier, who must be inconstant, undependable, and quick to shift his loyalties."

37. *paise*] I.e., "peise," "to hold suspended."

25. 6–8. *His . . . foe*] Compare *King Lear*, II. ii. 104 f.:

He cannot flatter, he!
An honest mind and plain—he must speak truth!

9. *Pauion*] I.e., *pavan* (also spelled *pavin* or *paven*), a dignified, stately, processional dance. Compare *Twelfth Night*, V. i. 206 f.: "*To.* Then he's a rogue and a passy measures pavin."

11. *Carpet trade*] Rich's use of the expression is the only one quoted in *NED* (under *carpet*, *sb.* 6), which glosses, "the occupations and amusements of the chamber or boudoir." Compare the very common phrase "carpet knights," so called "because (for the most part) they receiue their honour from the Kings hand, in the Court, and vpon Carpets," according to Francis Markham, *Booke of Honour* (1625), p. 71.

20–22. *likyng . . . hate*] Compare *Richard II*, III. ii. 135 f.:

Sweet love, I see, changing his property,
Turns to the sourest and most deadly hate.

26. 27. *Duchesse of Messilina*] Read probably *Duchesse Messilina.*

37. *chalke . . . doore*] Where innkeepers usually kept, perhaps on a slate, a record (or "score," as in the next line) of what the guest owed. In *The Weakest Goeth to the Wall* (1600), which is based on Rich's "Sappho," the innkeeper is a Dutchman, and Rich's words become a curious mixture of English and Dutch: "keck [behind] dore . . . see de creete de chalke" and "keck see dore de skore" (Greg, lines 760 f., 825).

27. 15 f. *that her honourable*] Probably in an effort to clarify a paragraph the elements of which defy construction, the editor of *C* omitted *her* and thus changed *that* from a conjunctive adverb to a demonstrative pronoun. As it stands, *that* may be taken as either. If it is construed as the latter, then *estate* is in apposition with it.

35 f. *praie . . . paie*] Compare the proverb "He that cannot pay, let him pray" (Smith, p. 156).

28. 5. *chorle*] I.e., "churl," "one who is sordid, 'hard,' or stingy in money-matters" (*NED*).

6 f. *had . . . for*] The general sense of this difficult passage seems to be "had with malice aforethought contrived the plot which was now taking effect as he had expected it would."

20. *that you*] I.e., "that which you."

21. *wife in paune*] This detail may be borrowed from the Eustace-Placidas legend, some version of which Rich undoubtedly used. The wife held in pawn by an evil creditor appears, for example, in John Partridge's *The Worthie Hystorie of the Moste Noble and Valiaunt Knight Plasidas* (1566), ed. H. H. Gibbs, Roxburghe Club (London, 1873), pp. 23 f.:

> Why Plasidas the Master sayd,
> thy wife Ile haue away:
> If that thou wilt not out of hand,
> my duetie to me pay.

24. *that is*] I.e., "that which is." See 28. 20 n.

38–29. 18. *This . . . farewell*] Source: Painter's "The Duchess of Malfy," III, 23.

29. 21. *Cayre*] A frequently used Elizabethan form of "Cairo." For examples from Marlowe and Peele see Sugden, pp. 88 f.

22–25. *passed . . . desert*] Probable source: Pettie's "Admetus and Alcest," p. 137.

24. *Hippes, Hawes, and Slowes*] Hips were proverbially linked with either haws or sloes. Smith (p. 288) quotes "Many haws, many sloes: many cold toes" and "Many hips and haws, many frosts and snaws."

31. *oppressed . . . with trauaile*] Compare *The Tempest*, III. iii. 15–17:

> For, now they are oppress'd with travel, they
> Will not nor cannot use such vigilance
> As when they are fresh.

35 f. *hauyng . . . Stagge*] Probable source: Painter's "Dom Diego and Ginevra," III, 226.

30. 11 f. *the pretie aunswere*] Compare Shakespeare's *Troilus and Cressida*, I. ii. 168 f.: "They laugh'd not so much at the hair as at his pretty answer."

23. *vp sat choole*] Read *vp at schoole.*

33. *hoiste*] Read *hoisteth* to conform with the reading in the source (Painter, III, 100), here followed almost verbatim, and to make the form parallel with *throweth* (line 35), as in Painter: "Fortune, who

in a moment hoisteth a man vp to the hyghest degree . . . and by and by, in lesse space than in the twynckeling of an eye, she throweth hym downe agayne."

33–31. 13. *who . . . abode*] Source: Painter's "Rhomeo and Juletta," III, 100. On such passages Shakespeare made the appropriate comment in *As You Like It*, II. vii. 13–17,

> As I do live by food, I met a fool,
> Who laid him down and bask'd him in the sun
> And rail'd on Lady Fortune in good terms,
> In good set terms.

Though Painter translated his tale almost literally from Boaistuau, who in turn was freely rendering Bandello, the passage is somehow connected with the final speech of the chorus in Gascoigne's *Jocasta*, translated from Dolce's Italian paraphrase of Euripides' *Phoenissae*. These versions may be compared in Gascoigne's *Works*, Cunliffe, I, 324; Lodovico Dolce, *Giocasta*, *Teatro italiano antico* (Milan, 1809), VI, 118; and Pierre Boaistuau, *Les Histoires tragiques* (Lyon, 1616), vol. I, fol. 56.

31. 9 f. *from . . . vacabonde*] Compare Bolingbroke's speech to York, *Richard II*, II. iii. 118–22:

> O, then, my father,
> Will you permit that I shall stand condemn'd
> A wandering vagabond, my rights and royalties
> Pluck'd from my arms perforce, and given away
> To upstart unthrifts?

13–32. *Oh . . . sustenaunce*] For proof that some of Rich's words in addition to his plot fared well as drama, compare this passage with the play based on "Sappho," *The Weakest Goeth to the Wall* (1600), Greg, lines 960–68 (the italics are mine):

> Imperious *fortune* . . .
> To *losse of honour*, daunger of my life:
> To the endaungering of my life, thou addest
> *A seperation twixt my wife and me*. . . .
> And now thou tak'st from me my strength of limmes,
> *Infeebling me for lack of sustenance*.

19 f. *bereue . . . age*] Compare Shirley's *Love Tricks* (of which Rich's eighth tale is the main source), Dyce, I, 84:

> [My son] slain! hapless Cornelio;
> My hopes were treasur'd up in him, the staff
> And comfort of my age; and he is gone?

20–22. *O Death . . . life*] This apostrophe to death (source: Painter's "Rhomeo and Juletta," III, 119) is echoed by Sir Aminadab, the pedant in *How a Man May Chuse a Good Wife from a Bad* (1602), though this learned character, true to his type, furbished Sappho's speech with a little Latin: "O death come with thy dart, come death when I bid thee,/ *Mors vem veni mors*, and from this misery rid mee" (Swaen, lines 1278 f.).

26 f. *preseruest . . . aduersities*] Source: Painter's "Rhomeo and Juletta," III, 100.

28. *brinishe . . . streamed*] Probable source: Gascoigne's "Dan Bartholmewes Dolorous discourses," Cunliffe, I, 115, "the flowing streames,/ Of brinishe teares their wonted floods do make."

31 f. *sustenaunce. He*] Read *sustenaunce, he.*

32. 2. *subbes*] Read probably *sobbes.* The spelling *subbes* is not listed in *NED.*

3–6. *when . . . hym*] Source: Underdowne's translation of Heliodorus' *Aethiopica* (1569), ed. Charles Whibley, Tudor Translations (London, 1895), p. 13.

32. *to . . . doe*] Probably a verbal reminiscence of Cinthio's story of Cesare Gravina, the source of this portion of Rich's plot. Cinthio writes (II, 255; the italics are mine), "[Cesare] acconciosi con uno de' primi gentiluomini di quel luogo, *e servendo il meglio che poteva* . . . passava pazientemente la sua miseria."

35. *in Hucsters handelyng*] This use of the phrase is the earliest cited in *NED*, which glosses, "in a position in which it is likely to be roughly used." But see Churchyard, *A General Rehearsal of Wars* (1579), sig. Bb1, "In hockstars hands, where lawe was made of will,/ (And hauocks mouthe), I daiely hapned still."

36. *assaies*] Possibly "trials imposed to test her virtue," but more probably "military attacks." Compare the elaborate trope based on military terms which follows immediately, 32. 37–33. 8.

37–33. 15. *like . . . Batterie*] D. T. Starnes observes (*SP*, XXX [1933], 469) that, though "the figure of the lover likened to a captain leading his soldiers to the storming of a fort . . . is recurrent in the stories of Painter and Pettie, Rich's elaboration of it echoes passages from [Painter's] 'The Lorde of Virle,'" III, 161, 163.

33. 23–27. *enforced . . . debt*] Her gallant reaction to the threat of poverty seems to have suggested the similar economic measures to which the heroine of *How a Man May Chuse a Good Wife from a Bad* (1602) is driven (Swaen, lines 523–28):

> My husband in this humor, well I know
> Plaies but the vnthrift, therefore it behoues me
> To be the better huswife here at home,
> To saue and get, whilst he doth laugh and spend:
> Though for himselfe he riots it at large,
> My needle shall defray my housholds charge.

Rich's "Agatha," the sixth story in the *Farewell* and the principal source of *How a Man May Chuse*, lacks these details.

34. 5. *to . . . romer*] I.e., "to let the ship roam where it would"? The expression, used again at 72. 29, is not to be found in *NED*. Perhaps it is a technical nautical term that Rich, who was listed in 1586 as qualified to be a sea captain, learned from practical experience. See T. M. Cranfill and Dorothy H. Bruce, *Barnaby Rich: A Short Biography* (Austin, Texas, 1953), pp. 36 f. Compare *The Tempest*, I. i. 8 f.: "Blow till thou burst thy wind, if room enough!"

32–34. *began . . . birthe*] Probable source: Painter's "Two Maidens of Carthage," II, 269.

35. 2–10. *cõmyng . . . happie*] This phase of Sappho's career, the nadir, was closely followed by the author of *The Weakest Goeth to the Wall* (1600), Greg, lines 998 f., 1056–65 (my italics indicate verbal borrowings):

[Sir Nicholas]

> This is no Vniuersitie, nor Schoole,
> But *a poore Village*. . . .
> And for my *Parishioners*, they are husbandmen,
> Nor do I know of any lacks a *seruant*.
> But this, the *Sexton* of our Church *is dead*,

And we do lacke an honest painfull man,
Can make a graue, and *keepe our Clock* in frame,
And now and then *to toule a* passing *bell:*
If thou art willing so to be emploid,
I can befriend thee. . . .

[Lodowick]

Oh withall my heart,
And *thinke me treble happie* by the office.

7 f. *keepyng . . . Clocke*] In running order and properly set? This chore should evidently be added to caring for the fabric of a church and its contents, ringing bells, and digging graves, the traditional duties of a sexton. Compare *The Puritaine or the Widdow of Watling-streete* (1607), ed. C. F. Tucker Brooke, *The Shakespeare Apocrypha* (Oxford, 1908), p. 232, "all worldly Clockes, we know, goe false, and are set by drunken Sextons."

9 f. *thinkyng . . . happie*] Rich was fond of this expression: see 71. 23 and 194. 23 f. Compare Pettie, p. 6, "I thinke him *Terq*[*ue*] *quaterq*[*ue*] *beatum*, *qui a consortio mulierum se conhibere potest*" (*Aeneid*, i. 94), and Greene's *Mamillia* (1583), Grosart, II, 37 f.

18. *remember you*] Rich here "reminds" the reader of a detail he has neglected to mention earlier.

22–29. *Siluanus . . . other*] His virtues seem to be patterned after those of Painter's hero in "Alerane and Adelasia," I, 250 f. Compare *Cymbeline*, I. i. 40–50:

The King he takes the babe
To his protection, calls him Posthumus Leonatus,
Breeds him and makes him of his bedchamber,
Puts to him all the learnings that his time
Could make him the receiver of; which he took,
As we do air, fast as 'twas minist'red
And in's spring became a harvest, liv'd in court
(Which rare it is to do) most prais'd, most lov'd,
A sample to the youngest, to th' more mature
A glass that feated them, and to the graver
A child that guided dotards.

24. *good letters*] I.e., "literature in general," *belles lettres. NED*

quotes among others (under *letter*, *sb.* II 6b) John Northbrooke, *A Treatise against Dicing, Dancing, Plays, and Interludes* (1577), ed. J. P. Collier, Shakespeare Society (London, 1843), p. 54, "Learning and good letters to yong men bringeth sobrietie."

36. 2. *The*] Read probably *This* to conform with the catchword at 35. 39.

hauyng . . . reporte] According to the Elizabethans the power of good "report"—a good reputation—was hard to overestimate. See Lodowick Lloyd, *The Pilgrimage of Princes* (*ca.* 1590), sig. Ss3v: "For as *Cicero* doeth write, we are more moued by reporte oftentymes to loue, then by sighte," and Hoby's translation of Castiglione's *The Courtier*, ed. Sir Walter Raleigh, Tudor Translations, XXIII (London, 1900), 142–45.

15–22. *beyng . . . hewe?*] Sources: Painter's "Alerane and Adelasia," I, 253, and "The Duchess of Malfy," III, 8.

17. *force perforce*] I.e., "despite forceful efforts to resist"? Though not listed by Tilley or Smith, the phrase may be proverbial. See *A Mirror for Magistrates*, ed. Lily B. Campbell (Cambridge, 1938), p. 313, lines 42–44,

destinie was so sterne
As force perforce, there might no force auayle,
But she must fall;

and *2 Henry VI*, I. i. 258: "And force perforce I'll make him yield the crown." Rich uses "perforce" again in this sense at 69. 4 and in his "Epitaph vpon the death of syr William Drury," *The Paradise of Dainty Devices*, Rollins, p. 123,

In *Edenbrough* he wan there Mayden tower
By fyrst assault, perforce the scotishe power.

On this use Rollins comments (p. 267), "This word evidently means 'in spite of,' a meaning not given in the *N.E.D.*"

18 f. *straiyng . . . Chastitie*] See 41. 8–10 n.

20. *luste, frõ*] Read probably *luste? Frõ.*

whence] Read as an interrogative to conform with the reading in the source (Painter, I, 253): "Ah, what passion is it that . . . ingendreth an obliuion of that which was wont to . . . contente me? From whence commeth this new alteration, and desire vnaccustomed . . .?"

22–37. 21. *ah . . . mā*] Source: Painter's "The Duchess of Malfy," III, 9, 12–14.

36 f. *of what . . . yearth*] Compare *Much Ado about Nothing*, II. i. 60–63:

Leon.

Well, niece, I hope to see you one day fitted with a husband.

Beat.

Not till God make men of some other metal than earth.

37. 17 f. *for . . . contentation*] By changing a declarative to an interrogatory sentence, Rich improves his source (Painter, III, 13 f.): "But these honors be nothyng worth, where the Mynd is voyd of contentation."

38. 5–20. *How . . . me*] Source: Painter's "The Duchess of Malfy," III, 11.

12 f. *Goddes . . . Narcissus*] For Rich's knowledge of Ovid in Golding's translation see pp. 320, 349, below.

14 f. *what . . . life*] Source: Painter's "The Duchess of Malfy," III, 10.

15 f. *see . . . straie*] An echo of a poem by Gascoigne. See the note on 24. 21 f.

18. *on me*] Read perhaps *in me*.

39. 5–28. *No . . . this*] In thus "beautifying" with verse his fiction here and in *Don Simonides* (1581) Rich seems to be happily following the example of a favorite model, Belleforest. Rich uses the same six-line iambic pentameter stanza, rhyming *ababcc*, in *Don Simonides* and in "An Epitaph vpon the Death of Sir William Drury," *The Paradise of Dainty Devices*, Rollins, pp. 121–24. Of this stanzaic form Rollins observes (p. 192), "Spenser had used [it] in the first and last eclogues of *The Shepherds' Calendar* (1579), Thomas Howell in many pieces in his *H. His Deuises* (1581), and Shakespeare in *Venus and Adonis* (1593). It is the favorite stanza in the *Paradise*, no fewer than seventeen poems being written in that form."

Note that the cesura in each line of the poem is marked with a comma, even though the comma may come between a subject and its verb (as in lines 11, 12, 15, 20) or a verb and its object (as in lines 6, 9, 19, 26). Rich probably had so marked the medial pause in his manuscript. His friend Thomas Churchyard similarly insisted on marking the cesura. See M. St. Clare Byrne, "Thomas Churchyard's Spelling," *The Library*, Fourth Series, V (1925), 248.

On the quality of the poetry, Collier has made the only discoverable critical comments. In his manuscript "Extracts from and Criticisms upon Rare Books" (in the Folger Shakespeare Library), III, 832, he quotes these verses and pronounces them "the best" of the poetry in the *Farewell*, "though not of first rate excellence." In his *Poetical Decameron* (London, 1820), II, 163 f., he quotes the poem again and has two of his critics remark, "Rich probably is to be placed in the class of smooth versifiers, but, according to this specimen, he has no claim to any rank among original poets. . . . You have correctly ascertained and stated his merits in a sentence."

8, 10, 26, 27. *boundes . . . was . . . fainest . . . baall*] *D* prints, respectively, *bonndes . . . once . . . fairest . . . bane*. A turned letter could have resulted in *bonndes* for *boundes*, and the compositor's misreading could have produced *fairest* instead of *fainest*. But *once* for *was* and *bane* for *baall* can scarcely be thus explained. It is furthermore remarkable that all four of *D*'s substitutions make sense within their contexts. Only two very likely explanations for the changes occur to me. (1) Rich himself made them. This theory is supported by the fact that he evidently made extensive revisions elsewhere in *D* (see above, pp. lxxiv f.). (2) An officious "corrector" was responsible for them. If so, he took surprising liberties with Rich's text. If there were more evidence indicating that texts were sometimes dictated to compositors, one might be tempted to argue that the compositor of *D* misheard the dictation of these four words and consequently set up *once* instead of *was*, etc. All of *D*'s readings except *fairest* Collier evidently accepted without suspicion in his reprint of the poem from the Malone copy in the *Poetical Decameron* (see 39. 5–28 n.), where he comments (p. 164), "*fairest* . . . is probably a misprint for *fainest*."

17–22. *O . . . gall*] Though this stanza is obviously a tissue of poetic commonplaces, certain expressions in it seem to have been drawn specifically from two lyrics by Gascoigne and from a selection by Francis Kinwelmarsh in *The Paradise of Dainty Devices*. Compare Gascoigne's "The Recantacion of a Lover," Cunliffe, I, 52 (the italics are mine):

> [Women's] beauties blaze are *baites* which seeme of pleasant *taste*,
> But who devoures the *hidden hooke*, eates poyson for repast;

Gascoigne's "Dan Bartholmew his second Triumphe," I, 103:

> To *taste* (sometimes) a *baite* of bytter gall . . .
> Doth much encrease mens appetites by reason:
> And make the *sweete* more *sugred* that ensewes,
> Since mindes of men do styll seeke after newes;

and Kinwelmarsh's "Most happy is that state alone," *The Paradise*, Rollins, p. 21:

> By painted woordes, the silly simple man,
> To trustlesse *trappe*, is *trayned* now and than.
> And by conseyte, of sweete alluring tale,
> He bites the *baites*, that *breedes* his *bitter bale*.

32. *a . . . well*] Probable source: Painter's "Dom Diego and Ginevra," III, 239.

40. 10. *intentiue eare*] Compare *Othello*, I. iii. 149 f., 154 f.:

> She'ld come again, and with a greedy ear
> Devour up my discourse . . .
> Whereof by parcels she had something heard,
> But not intentively.

This is Shakespeare's only use of the word *intentively*.

20–23. *beyng . . . seruice*] Source: Painter's "The Duchess of Malfy," III, 12. Compare what John Webster made of the same lines from the *Palace* in his version of the story, I. i. 507 f., Lucas, II, 50: "The misery of us, that are borne great!—/ We are forc'd to wo[o], because none dare wo[o] us."

24 f. *an other . . . bushe*] Compare Shirley's use of the proverb (Smith, p. 340) in *Love Tricks* (of which Rich's eighth tale is the principal source), Dyce, I, 90, "Jenkin has peat the pushes, and Rufaldos has get the pirds."

30–33. *my . . . right*] Source: Painter's "The Duchess of Malfy," III, 15.

32. *discerne of*] I.e., "tell the difference between."

33–41. 4. *I . . . freendship*] Source: Painter's "The Duchess of Malfy," III, 13.

41. 5–8. *And . . . suters, I*] Read *And . . . suters? I*, to conform with the source of the passage, Painter, III, 12: "Shall a Lady of sutch bloud

as I am, be constrayned to sue, where all other be required by importunate instance of their Suters?"

8–10. *I . . . bee thought . . . modestie*] Probable source: Pettie's "Admetus and Alcest," p. 131, "I might bee thought perchaunce to transgresse the law and limyttes of modesty." Rich was infatuated with the formula "stray from (exceed, pass) the limits and bounds of modesty (chastity)": see 36. 18 f., 43. 35 f., 80. 31, 188. 38–189. 2. The phrase evidently made an impression on the author of *How a Man May Chuse a Good Wife from a Bad* (1602), the play based on the sixth story in the *Farewell*, since the dramatist writes (my italics), Swaen, lines 1975–81:

So your demand may be no preiudise
To my chast name . . .
I yeeld vnto it, but *to passe the bands of modestie & chastitie*,
First will I bequeath my selfe againe
Vnto this graue, and neuer part from hence,
Then taint my soule with blacke impuritie.

Compare *Romeo and Juliet*, IV. ii. 25–27:

I met the youthful lord at Laurence' cell
And gave him what becomed love I might,
Not stepping o'er the bounds of modesty.

11–30. *but . . . well*] Compare Emilia's complaint of the double standard, *Othello*, IV. iii. 96–106:

Let husbands know
Their wives have sense like them. They see, and smell,
And have their palates both for sweet and sour,
As husbands have. What is it that they do
When they change us for other? Is it sport?
I think it is. And doth affection breed it?
I think it doth. Is't frailty that thus errs?
It is so too. And have not we affections,
Desires for sport, and frailty, as men have?
Then let them use us well; else let them know,
The ills we do, their ills instruct us so.

18. *wee . . . vesselles*] In 1 Peter 3: 77. Compare *Love's Labour's Lost*, I. i. 274, "For Jaquenetta (so is the weaker vessel called)."

19 f. *more . . . Hercules*] Compare *Love's Labour's Lost*, I. ii. 68–73:

[*Arm.*] What great men have been in love?
Moth. Hercules, master.
Arm. Most sweet Hercules! More authority, dear boy, name more. . . .
Moth. Samson, master.

27. *firme*] I.e., "secure."

36 f. *the . . . deme*] Source: Painter's "The Duchess of Malfy," III, 13.

38–42. 3. *mynde . . . wrathe*] Source: Painter's "Euphemia of Corinth," II, 320.

42. 5 f. *gentleman . . . riches*] Source: Painter's "The Duchess of Malfy," III, 17.

10–18. *I . . . Fortune*] Source: Painter's "Anne Queen of Hungary," II, 396 f.

18–23. *I . . . vices*] Source: Painter's "The Duchess of Malfy," III, 17.

27–43. 21. *seekyng . . . shamefastnesse*] Sources: Painter's "The Duchess of Malfy," III, 14, "Anne Queen of Hungary," II, 403, and "Rhomeo and Juletta," III, 85 f.

31. *desolued*] Thus in all four early editions and in Collier. But read *resolued* to conform with the source, Painter, III, 14: "A certaine naturall shamefastnesse, which of custome accompanieth Ladies, did close hir mouth, and made hir to deferre . . . the effect of hir resolued minde."

43. 9. *ioye and contentation*] The phrase was a favorite of both Painter and Rich. Compare "Rhomeo and Juletta," III, 85 (the source of this passage), 94, and 58. 17, 78. 4 f., 88. 33, 104. 30, and 119. 4 f.

19. *still*] Either "motionless" or, if it modifies "beholdyng," "without interruption."

23–32. *Beyng . . . pretence*] Source: Painter's "The Duchess of Malfy," III, 14 f. Morton Luce, *Rich's "Apolonius & Silla"* (London, 1912), p. 47, compares *A Midsummer Night's Dream*, II. ii. 104 f.,

Transparent Helena! Nature shows art,
That through thy bosom makes me see thy heart,

but in my opinion goes too far in regarding Shakespeare's lines as "Possibly . . . a condensation" of Rich's. See also *The Winter's Tale*, IV. iv. 90–97:

> So, over that art
> Which you say adds to nature, is an art
> That nature makes. . . . This is an art
> Which does mend nature—change it rather; but
> The art itself is nature.

34. *me in*] Read perhaps *in me.*

35 f. *exceadyng . . . modestie*] See 41. 8–10 n.

44. 7–14. *Thinke . . . life*] Source: Painter's "Salimbene and Angelica," III, 316, 321.

8. *freend of Fortune*] I.e., "adventuress" or "opportunist"? See *Willobie His Avisa* (1594), ed. G. B. Harrison (London, 1926), p. 34:

> *Shores* wife, a Princes secret frend,
> Faire *Rosomond*, a Kings delight:
> Yet both haue found a gastly end,
> And fortunes friends, felt fortunes spight.

Compare the commonplace "Fortune's foe."

14–26. *And . . . maner*] Sources: Painter's "Alerane and Adelasia," I, 257, "The Duchess of Malfy," III, 18 f., and "Dom Diego and Ginevra," III, 235.

29–33. *I . . . Princes*] Source: Painter's "Anne Queen of Hungary," II, 388 f.

45. 2–9. *if . . . euer*] Source: Painter's "The Duchess of Malfy," III, 19.

9. *Thus*] Read perhaps *This.*

9 f. *takyng . . . deuotion*] Source: Rich's *A Right Exelent and Pleasaunt Dialogue* (1574), sig. 16.

14–20. *I . . . accomplished*] Source: Painter's "The Duchess of Malfy," III, 17.

21–25. *your . . . Parentes*] Source: Painter's "Rhomeo and Juletta," III, 89.

24 f. *obedience . . . duetie . . . Parentes*] A favorite theme with Rich. See 55. 36–38, 176. 8, 10–12, 183. 27 f., 189. 5, 199. 32.

25. *Parentes*] In the story there is no further hint that Valeria's

mother is alive, and this allusion to her would not have appeared had not Rich exercised his usual fidelity in following his source (Painter, III, 89): "Without any regard to the obedience and reuerence that I owe to my Parentes . . . I wyll make you . . . Mayster [ouer me]."

25–27. *I am . . . me*] Source: Painter's "Rhomeo and Juletta," III, 86.

26. *dispose*] Read *disposed.*

37–46. 2. *the . . . eare*] Probable source: Painter's "The Duchess of Malfy," III, 20 f.

46. 6. *woodes. And*] Read probably *woodes, and.*

7–9. *willed . . . Vasconia*] Probable source: Pettie's "Scilla and Minos," p. 152. Compare *As You Like It*, I. iii. 42–47:

> *Duke.* Mistress, dispatch you with your safest haste
> And get you from our court!
> *Ros.* Me, uncle?
> *Duke.* You, cousin.
> Within these ten days if that thou beest found
> So near our public court as twenty miles,
> Thou diest for it.

23–25. *Wherefore . . . theim*] Compare *Othello*, I. i. 176–83:

> Call up my brother. . . .
> Some one way, some another.—Do you know
> Where we may apprehend her and the Moor? . . .
> At every house I'll call;
> I may command at most.—Get weapons, ho!
> And raise some special officers of night.

31 f. *by greate . . . GOD)*] Rich's parenthetical addendum to *Fortune* reflects the conventional Elizabethan attitude toward that goddess. See George More, *A Demonstration of God in his Workes* (1597), sig. R1v, "blinded by the darke mist of ignorance, we make Fortune the Author of that, whereof God is the dooer, and ascribe to Chaunce, whatsoeuer is performed by the prouidence of the Almightie."

47. 5–10. *fell . . . Nature*] The passage is, I suspect, based on an item in Rich's commonplace book which again yielded a bit in *The Adventures of Brusanus* (1592), where (sig. E3) Prince Dorestus fails to

recognize his father but is nevertheless attracted to him: "Whether it were by som secret instincte of nature, or what other motion it was that moued him, he fell into a most affectionat liking of *Corynus*."

8. *doemed*] I.e., "deemed."

27–29. *gladdyng . . . delightes*] Source: Painter's "Rhomeo and Juletta," III, 94: "After they had gladded and cherished themselues with al kinde of delicate embracements which loue was able to deuise, Rhomeo . . . tooke possession of the place, which was not yet besieged with sutch *ioy and contentation* as they can iudge which haue assayed like delites." I have italicized a phrase Rich especially fancied and consequently used again and again, at 43. 9, 58. 17, 78. 4 f., 88. 33, 104. 30, and 119. 4 f.

33. *into . . . heauinesse*] Source: Painter's "A Lady of Bohemia," III, 197.

38–48. 4. *his wife . . . discontentment*] Probable source: Painter's "A Lady of Bohemia," III, 200.

48. 7–28. *my . . . comforte*] Sources: Painter's "A Lady of Bohemia," III, 198, and (for lines 16–19) Pettie's "Germanicus and Agrippina," p. 72.

14. *or*] Read probably *of.*

16–18. *maintaine . . . contentmente*] Source: Pettie's "Germanicus and Agrippina," p. 72.

26 f. *in . . . teethe*] I.e., "in defiance of Fortune." Compare *The Merry Wives of Windsor*, V. v. 131 f., "a receiv'd belief, in despite of the teeth of all rhyme and reason," and the quotations in *NED* under *tooth*, *sb.* 5.

34–49. 16. *The . . . sad*] Sources: Painter's "A Lady of Bohemia," III, 199, 201, and "Rhomeo and Juletta," III, 93, 101.

49. 12. *lenefie*] I.e., "soothe," "appease." See 54. 7 n.

35. *in Gentlewomans*] Read *in a Gentlewomans* or *in Gentlewomens.*

50. 13–17. *Without . . . Region*] Source: Painter's "The Earl of Angiers," I, 169.

20. *heard*(] Read *heard*).

20 f. *Churche*, *as*] Read *Churche* (*as.*

51. 16 f. *many his freendes*] *NED* cites several uses of "many" followed by a possessive, but none so early as this example.

27–52. 6. *gaue . . . opinion*] Compare the Duke's speech to Bertram, *All's Well That Ends Well*, III. iii. 1–3:

> *Duke.* The General of our Horse thou art; and we,
> Great in our hope, lay our best love and credence
> Upon thy promising fortune.

34. *Cayoe*] Read perhaps *Cayre*, with *C*. Earlier in the story, however, Cayre appears to be free of Turks, since Sappho sets out for it (29. 20 f.) and Messalina intends to follow him there (33. 29 f.).

36–52. 6. *God . . . opinion*] Source: Painter's "Dom Diego and Ginevra," III, 224 f.

38–52. 2. *made . . . ensignes*] Compare Painter's "A Lady of Bohemia," III, 204, where the hero, as a reward for valor, "was made Colonell of a certain number of footmen."

52. 6–12. *whereof . . . theim*] Source: Painter's "The Lord of Virle," III, 184 f.

21. *Turke. The*] Read probably *Turke, the.*

22. *manne well*] Read perhaps *manne was well.*

23. *deserued. Siluanus*] Read probably *deserued, Siluanus.*

53. 6 f. *Chirona*] Consistently spelled *Cherona* elsewhere in the story.

10 f. *hautie enterprises*] An echo of Painter's "Alerane and Adelasia," I, 264.

17–31. *Sir . . . behalf*] Sources: Rich's *A Right Exelent and Pleasaunt Dialogue*, sigs. L5–L5v, and (11. 22 f.) Painter's "A Lady Falsely Accused," I, 209.

26–28. *wofull . . . Theefe*] Compare *Othello*, I. ii. 62, "O thou foul thief, where hast thou stow'd my daughter?" and also I. i. 79, 81, I. ii. 57. With the "mischiuous inticementes" compare "thou hast enchanted her . . . practised on her with foul charms" (I. ii. 63, 73).

28. *president*] I.e., "precedent." *C*'s reading, *present* (i.e., "present occasion," "affair in hand") is also possible here. For a similar choice between *president* and *present* in *1 Henry IV*, II. iv. 32, see the edition of J. Dover Wilson (Cambridge, 1946), pp. 35, 106, 146, and the review of this edition by J. G. McManaway, *Shakespeare Survey* (Cambridge, 1948), p. 128.

54. 7. *lenifie . . . harte*] Source: Painter's "The Lord of Virle," III, 161. Not in Painter is the phrase "and soften," probably added by

Rich to clarify the meaning of "lenifie" for uninformed readers. For similar clarifications see 118. 29, 152. 19, and the notes on 94. 31, 149. 16, 152. 5, and 155. 33 f.

8. *father. He*] Read *father, he.*

55. 34–38. *Madam . . . them*] Source: Rich's *A Right Exelent and Pleasaunt Dialogue*, sig. K4.

36–38. *duetie . . . them*] See the note on 45. 24 f.

56. 20. *tht*] Read *the* or *that.*

23. *in . . . of*] A favorite idiom with Rich. Compare his celebrated "in the waie of honestie" (8. 13) and 56. 38–57. 2, 71. 17, 133. 5, 182. 15, 206. 14.

38–57. 2. *in the . . . Marriage*] See 56. 23 n.

57. 14. *single*] In a legal sense, "without further qualification or addition."

18. *this presentes*] Properly, either "this present" or "these presentes."

35–38. *taking . . . wife*] Compare *The Comedy of Errors*, V. i. 295, 300: "*Æge*. Why look you strange on me? You know me well. . . . But tell me yet, dost thou not know my voice?"

39. *Obliga-*] Though the catchword and the word it indicates (58. 2) differ, the capital is consistent with the usage at 57. 14, 17, 19, 20, and 22.

58. 7. *vnder couert barne*] A legal term, used of a married woman who is under the cover or protection of her husband. Though *barne* is a frequent spelling, *baron* is commoner.

59. 9. *nise . . . daintie*] Echoed by the author of *Philotus* (1603), who borrowed wholesale from other tales in the *Farewell* (see p. xlii above): "Yon daintie Dame scho is sa nyce/ Sche'ill nocht be win be na deuyce" (Mill, p. 114).

13. *By this*] I.e., "By this time"; "in narrative, the time just mentioned" (*NED*).

28–30. *your . . . awaie*] Compare *Othello*, I. iii. 113 f., where a senator inquires whether Othello seduced Desdemona, "Or came it by request, and such fair question/ As soul to soul affordeth?"

33. *quite*] I.e., "quit." See 19. 6 n.

36–60. 4. *it . . . Tyraunt*] Source: Painter's "Ariobarzanes," II, 199.

60. 6. *calleth. Then*] Read probably *calleth, then*, though not even wholesale changes in punctuation could clarify the untidy syntax of this paragraph.

7. *extended vppon*] I.e., "inflicted on."

33 f. *O . . . quiete*] Source: Painter's "Sophonisba," II, 245.

38–61. 5. *countenaunce . . . contrary*] Observe that "countenaunce of greatest credite" is balanced against "losse of life," as "hoped tyme" is balanced against "his contrary."

61. 3. *cooked*] Read *crooked.*

3–7. *What . . . follies*] An extremely difficult passage, its difficulty being aggravated by the generous sprinkling of astrological terms. It may perhaps be paraphrased: "What evilly disposed star has so guided my doings that the time I hopefully spent in military service should thus end with misfortune, the very opposite of what I hoped for, and that I should be forced as if by fate to endure the result of the misfortune, a result for which, I admit, I was predestined to be partly responsible because of my follies."

5. *his contrary*] The "his" refers to "hoped tyme."

12–14. *in . . . Death*] Source: Painter's "Rhomeo and Juletta," III, 102.

14–17. *O . . . Sunne*] Source: Painter's "Sophonisba," II, 245.

20–24. *not . . . displeased*] Source: Painter's "Euphemia of Corinth," II, 331.

27–30. *Is . . . Adultrie*] Source: Painter's "The Duchess of Malfy," III, 36.

30–32. *seeyng . . . rage*] Source: Painter's "Dom Diego and Ginevra," III, 250, 283.

32. *mitigate your rage*] Borrowed verbatim by the author of the comedy *Philotus* (1603): "Sweit father, mitigate your rage" (Mill, p. 118).

62. 3–16. *coole . . . desertes*] Source: Painter's "The Duchess of Malfy," III, 32 f.

4 f. *I . . . detestable*] Borrowed by the author of *Philotus* and versified thus (Mill, p. 127):

> I sall hir ane exampill mak,
> To trumpers all durst vndertak
> For to commit sa foull ane fack.

9. *vnder a Bushe*] "In secret," "sub rosa."

13–15. *I vowe . . . blood*] Compare *3 Henry VI*, IV. iii. 4–6:

> [The King] hath made a solemn vow
> Never to lie an take his natural rest
> Till Warwick or himself be quite suppress'd.

21–27. *let . . . prouocation*] Source: Painter's "Dom Diego and Ginevra," III, 282.

29. *pretie peate*] Compare Katherina's ejaculation, *The Taming of the Shrew*, I. i. 78:

> A pretty peat! it is best
> Put finger in the eye, an she knew why.

30. *an . . . Parrat*] The proverbial reply to any comment that was ill-advised, too glib, vapid, prolix, or nonsensical—parrot-like, in a word. For copious examples see McKerrow, IV, 461, and Smith, p. 40. Compare Shakespeare's *Troilus and Cressida*, V. ii. 194–96: "The parrot will not do more for an almond than he for a commodious drab."

How . . . strompette] Borrowed verbatim by the author of *Philotus* (1603): "How durst thow trumper" (Mill, p. 117, where the Variant Readings show that in the 1612 edition of the play "trumper" is replaced by "strumpet," a reading to be preferred in the light of the source).

31. *chalenge . . . Father*] I.e., "lay claim to me as your father."

31–34. *That . . . straunger*] Source: Painter's "Dom Diego and Ginevra," III, 278.

35–63. 6. *thinke . . . aliue*] Source: Painter's "Dom Diego and Ginevra," III, 282.

63. 7. *giltlesse*] Thus in all editions, though the context seems to call for "guilty."

8. *frustrate*] Though this reading in *A*, *B*, and *D* makes sense, the substitution of "prostrate" for "frustrate" by *C* and Collier has much to recommend it, since the "once againe fallyng" which immediately precedes appears to refer to Valeria's previous descent at 62. 18 f.

9–14. *I . . . satisfie*] Source: Painter's "Dom Diego and Ginevra," III, 277 f.

16. *quite*] I.e., "quit." See 19. 6 n.

19. *whose . . . sorrowe*] Probable source: Gascoigne's "Dulce bellum inexpertis," Cunliffe, I, 165, "My heavie harte within my bellie weepes."

26–34. *O . . . frendes*] Source: Rich's *A Right Exelent and Pleasaunt Dialogue*, sig. K1v.

64. 5–13. *The . . . request*] Compare Richard Edwards' "Iustice. Zaleuch and his Sonne," *The Paradise of Dainty Devices*, Rollins, p. 58.

24. *shewed . . . was*] See 83. 20 n.

35 f. *gladde . . . father*] Compare the final scene of recognition and reconciliation in Francis Sabie's *Flora's Fortune* (1595), sig. G1v: "And woondrous glad that *Flora* had found out,/ So braue a Knight."

66. 1. *Apolonius and Silla*] Rich could have named his hero either after the hero of the ancient tale "Apollonius of Tyre," which he of course knew, or after the philosopher Apollonius, whom he quotes in *Opinion Diefied* (1613), sig. D1v. Scilla is the heroine of a story in Pettie's *Petite Pallace*, from which Rich never hesitated to borrow. Decade I, Novel 10, in another of Rich's happy hunting grounds, Cinthio's *Gli Hecatommithi*, is introduced (I, 223), "Silla ama Silvia" (compare Silvio, the name of Silla's brother).

7. *Pontus*] Well known to Elizabethans as a place name (it was a section of Asia Minor on the Pontus, or Black Sea: see Sugden, pp. 417 f.). Because it ends in *-us*, Rich doubtless considered it appropriate for a man's name.

15–19. *There . . . errour*] Compare A. Arnauld, *The Arrainment of the Whole Society of Iesuits in France* (1594), sig. D2, "The tender age of Children drinketh vp error with the first milke."

67. 8. *loue. Those*] Read *loue, those.*

8–10. *Those . . . daie*] Compare *Macbeth*, IV. ii. 39 f.:

> *Son.* Nay, how will you do for a husband?
> *Wife.* Why, I can buy me twenty at any market.

11–15. *to loue . . . reason*] Compare *The Two Gentlemen of Verona*, IV. ii. 14 f.:

> Yet, spaniel-like, the more she spurns my love,
> The more it grows, and fawneth on her still.

16. *Wherefore . . . gentilwomen*] Such direct addresses to the

lady readers are due to Pettie's influence, which is pervasive in this, the fifth, and the eighth tale. Compare 69. 24–29, 74. 28, 84. 5–13.

18 f. *a Leishe . . . femalles*] In sporting parlance a leash was a set of three. Rich carries out the figure of speech consistently, writing not "a man and two women," but "a male and two females," as if they were a dog and two bitches.

22 f. (*who onely . . . will*] Either omit the perplexing parenthesis or read *who* (*onely . . . will*).

28–30. *I . . . long*] An apt self-criticism with which few modern critics would disagree. But that Rich himself felt called upon to apologize for the prolixity of his first tale is remarkable, because in his day brevity does not seem to have been considered a virtue in fiction.

30. *long. From*] Read *long, from.*

34 f. *During . . . Christians*] Mohammed II took it from the Christians in 1453.

68. 2–4. *leuied . . . Turke*] From personal experience Rich no doubt knew of similar instances of generosity (on a much smaller scale) in fighting for religious causes. See the testimony of his friend Thomas Churchyard, *A General Rehearsal of Wars* (1579), sig. K2v, "Now is to be noted, that M. Henry Champernowne of Deuonshire . . . serued in the cause of the Protestantes of Fraunce, of his own proper charges in the second Ciuile warres, with xij. gentlemen or more." See also Painter's "Camiola and Roland," III, 355, where various lords raised an army "vpon their own proper costes, and charges."

13–17. *beeyng . . . Ile*] On the similarity between this episode and *Othello*, II. i, see p. li, above.

29 f. *who . . . allurement*] Source: Painter's "Rhomeo and Juletta," III, 97.

31. *attached*] I.e., "seized," "attacked."

32–37. *nothyng . . . Countrey*] Compare the Princess Olivia in Margaret Tyler's translation of Ortuñez' *The Mirrour of Princely Deedes and Knighthood*, Part I (1578), sig. O2 (my italics): "*Nothing might ease hir* highnesse *but* Rosicleers *presence*, . . . galling hir most to thinck that *seing he was a straunger* in ye land, he would ere long *retourne to his own countrey.*"

69. 4. *self. So*] Read probably *self, so.*

perforce] "Despite." See 36. 17 n.

13–17. *But . . . youth*] Compare Pettie's "Icilius and Virginia," p. 105, and *1 Henry VI*, IV. i. 167 f.:

> Go cheerfully together and digest
> Your angry choler on your enemies.

24 f. *promise*] See 67. 30–33.

24–29. *Gentlewomen . . . Feuer*] On such Pettie-like teasing and flattering of the gentlewomen readers see 84. 5–13 n.

26. *long . . . discourse*] A reference to a deplorable four-page poem, the "Compleinte" of Nicole, the heroine deserted by the hero in the principal source of "Apolonius," Belleforest's *Histoires tragiques*, IV (Lyons, 1616), 214–18. Presumably of Belleforest's own composition, the "Compleinte" appears in no other version of the much-treated "Apolonius" story, as H. H. Furness was the first to observe in *New Variorum Twelfth Night* (Philadelphia, 1901), p. xviii. Rich was wise to leave the details of Nicole's lament to the reader's imagination and get on with his story.

Probable source of "dolorous discourse": Pettie's *Petite Pallace*, p. 42. Compare Greene's *Mamillia* (1593), Grosart, II, 177, "Can these thy dolorous discourses cure thy care?"

29. *Feuer*] I.e., "intense nervous excitement, agitation."

35–37. *Pedro . . . trust*] Source: Painter's "Rhomeo and Juletta," III, 92.

70. 37–71. 3. *Captaine . . . Starre*] Probable source: some version of the Eustace-Placidas legend. According to John Partridge's *The Worthie Hystorie of the Moste Noble and Valiaunt Knight Plasidas* (1566), ed. H. H. Gibbs, Roxburghe Club (London, 1873), pp. 20 f.

> The Master of the ship doth like,
> the beautie of the wife,
> Of Plasidas, and doth delight,
> his wauering wanton minde.

71. 17. *break with*] I.e., "broach the subject to."

in . . . mariage] See 56. 23 n.

23. *thinke . . . happie*] See the note on 35. 9 f.

26–29. *for . . . self*] Source: Pettie's "Germanicus and Agrippina," p. 70.

72. 7 f. *determined . . . abused*] Source: Painter's "Salimbene and Angelica," III, 317 f.

12. *suffer her*] Either "bear with her" or "leave her."

17–22. *drue . . . GOD*] Sources: Painter's "The Rape of Lucrece," I, 24, "A Chaste Death," II, 30, and "The Lords of Nocera," III, 392.

21 f. *reconciliation to GOD*] Compare *Othello*, V. ii. 25–29:

> *Oth.* Have you pray'd to-night, Desdemona?
> *Des.* Ay, my lord.
> *Oth.* If you bethink yourself of any crime
> Unreconcil'd as yet to heaven and grace,
> Solicit for it straight.

29. *to put romer*] See 34. 5 n.

30–33. *were . . . Casks*] Compare Belleforest's version of the ancient tale of Apollonius of Tyre (for whom Rich named his hero?), *Histoires tragiques*, VII (Lyons, 1595), 74 (my italics), "En fin *le nef* ayant rencontre vn escueil *fut mise en pieces. Cest icy que chacun tasche a sauuer sa vie, l'vn prenant vn ais*, l'autre s'efforçant de gagner l'esquif qui embrassoit vn auiron, ou vne piece de la nef rompue."

73. 30–32. *beganne . . . hym*] Source: Painter's "Francis the French King," II, 81.

33. *neate aboute hym*] Though *neate* meaning "skilful and precise in action" (*NED*) fits well enough here, Collier's emendation to *neare* seems respectable in the light of a passage from Rich's "Fineo"—whom the Turk took "to his seruice in good place nere his own persone" (113. 5)—and of a passage from Painter's "Francis the French King" (II, 81), Rich's probable source here: "[Count Guillaume] was in sutche good fauour with the king, as he tooke him not onely into seruice, but vsed him so nere his persone, as he made him of his priuy chamber."

33–35. *in . . . Chamber*] May be read as modifiers of either the preceding or the succeeding sentence.

74. 2. *a widowe*] Giving in his diary an account of a performance of *Twelfth Night* which he witnessed in 1602, John Manningham speaks of Olivia as a widow, "a possible indication that Shakespeare, who presents her as a spinster in the extant comedy, gave her in a first draft the status with which Riche credited her" (Sir Sidney Lee, *A Life of William Shakespeare* [London, 1925], p. 331 n.).

4–6. *Lady . . . reuenues*] Of this passage one of the conclave in Collier's *Poetical Decameron* (London, 1820) complains (II, 151), "Rich does not scruple to be guilty of tautologies."

5. *Iulina*] The name of one of the heroines in Francis Sabie's *Flora's Fortune. The Second Part and Finishing of the Fishermans Tale* (1595).

9–19. *the . . . carefully*] Compare *The Two Gentlemen of Verona*, II. i. 17–27:

Val. Why, how know you that I am in love?
Speed. Marry, by these special marks: first, you have learn'd . . . to walk alone . . . to sigh like a schoolboy . . . to weep like a young wench . . . to speak puling like a beggar.

11–13. *sendyng . . . what*] The author of the comedy *Philotus* (1603), after borrowing his plot from the eighth tale and a major character from the sixth, seems also to echo this bit of the second: "Giue hir this Tablet and this Ring,/ This Pursse of gold and spair nathing" (Mill, p. 105).

11–21. *must . . . write*] Sources: Pettie's "Pygmalion's Friend," p. 241, and "Alexius," p. 259.

24–26. *And . . . manne*] Compare *All's Well That Ends Well*, III. vi. 121–23:

[*Ber.*] . . . but I sent to her,
By this same coxcomb that we have i' th' wind,
Tokens and letters, which she did resend.

28. *Now gentilwomen*] On such digressions see 84. 5–13 n.

30–32. *her self . . . self*] Compare *The Two Gentlemen of Verona*, where Julia complains, IV. iv. 104 f.:

And now am I (unhappy messenger!)
To plead for that which I would not obtain.

75. 3–8. *Siluio . . . all*] Compare *Twelfth Night*, III. i. 117–21:

Oli. O, by your leave, I pray you!
I bade you never speak again of him;
But, would you undertake another suit,
I had rather hear you to solicit that
Than music from the spheres.

17 f. *heard coniectured*] Read *heard, coniectured,* thus supplying the comma for which the compositor had no room at the end of the line.

76. 16. *cceipt*] Read *conceipt.*

22–27. *Siluio . . . proffered*] Source: Rich's *A Right Exelent and Pleasaunt Dialogue,* sig. I1v.

26. *a poincte of*] I.e. "an instance of." See 130. 16 n.

77. 19 f. *thought . . . Sunne*] Compare *The Tempest,* IV. i. 30, where the ardent, impatient Ferdinand complains, "I shall think . . . Phoebus' steeds are founder'd."

20 f. *some . . . stande*] Compare Painter's "Rhomeo and Juletta," III, 92, where the lovers wish for the power "to commaund the Heauens (as Iosua did the Sunne)."

22. *Phaeton . . . whippe*] Compare in Golding's translation of Ovid, ed. W. H. D. Rouse (London, 1904), p. 44, lines 168–70, Phoebus' counsel to Phaeton:

> (And if thou canst) at least yet this thy fathers lore obay:
> Sonne, spare the whip, and reyne them hard, they run so swift away
> As that thou shalt have muche a doe them their fleeing course to stay.

78. 3–10. *where . . . diet*] Omitted (as indelicate) by Furness in his reprint of the tale in the *New Variorum Twelfth Night* (Philadelphia, 1901), pp. 328–39. Collier, less strait-laced, not only prints the passage in his edition (p. 79) but comments on it with evident relish in his *Poetical Decameron* (London, 1820), II, 154 f., "If Shakespeare were wrong in making Olivia not a widow, he was right in not carrying her love to Cesario or to the man she fancied was he, to such an extreme as Rich represents it. . . . Rich, as you will find, has no scruple of that sort, for Julina afterwards proves to be in the family way. . . . Julina . . . finding the consequences of her intercourse with the brother but too apparent, is in a state of great alarm"; and again (II, 160), Silvio "left Julina in what family men call 'a hopefull condition.'"

8. *fourtie wekes after*] Compare Rich's *My Ladies Looking Glasse* (1616), sig. G3v, "The next day she begins to breed child, and then for forty weeks after, what queasinesse, what squeamishnes, what curiosity."

a . . . women] Source: Painter's "The Countess of Celant," III, 56.

12. *Siluano*] An understandable slip for *Siluio* from the hand

of a compositor who had set up *Siluanus* dozens of times in the preceding story.

16–18. *tooke . . . Silla*] Compare *The Comedy of Errors*, I. i. 132–36:

> Five summers have I spent in farthest Greece,
> Roaming clean through the bounds of Asia . . .
> Hopeless to find, yet loath to leave unsought
> Or that, or any place that harbours men.

24. *he*] Read *she*.

79. 7. *like . . . liste*] Compare Pettie's "Minos and Pasiphae," p. 216.

24–28. *debatyng . . . manne*] In the opinion of R. G. White, "A reminiscence [of this passage] plainly appears in *Sir Andrew Aguecheek's* complaint to *Sir Toby* [II. ii. 6–8], 'Marry, I saw your niece do more favours to the Count's serving man, than ever she bestow'd upon me'" (*The Works of William Shakespeare*, V [Boston, 1857], 150 f.).

80. 6. *meditation*] Presumably an error for "mediation."

19–21. *perceiuyng . . . beallie*] Source: Painter's "The Duchess of Malfy," III, 24.

22 f. *become . . . honour*] Source: Painter's "The Duchess of Malfy," III, 27.

30–36. *Sir . . . that*] Source: Painter's "The Countess of Celant," III, 74.

31 f. *passe . . . modestie*] See 41. 8–10 n.

81. 6–8. *I . . . myndes*] Her assertion may have suggested a similar one in Shakerley Marmion's *A Fine Companion* (1633), of which Rich's eighth tale is the principal source (Maidment and Logan, p. 110):

> My mind was never yet ambitious,
> And there is nothing but your company
> Can satisfy, or limit my desires.

16 f. *thou . . . tongue*] Source: Painter's "Rhomeo and Juletta," III, 96.

82. 5. *certifie a trothe*] See 83. 20 n.

22–25. *is . . . persone*] Source: Painter's "The Duchess of Malfy," III, 29.

26–34. *Siluio . . . complaine*] Compare *Twelfth Night*, V. i. 146–51:

> [*Oli.*] Cesario, husband, stay.
> *Duke*. Husband?
> *Oli.* Ay, husband. Can he that deny?
> *Duke*. Her husband, sirrah?
> *Vio.* No, my lord, not I.
> *Oli.* Alas, it is the baseness of thy fear
> That makes thee strangle thy propriety.
> Fear not, Cesario; take thy fortunes up.

28–31. *will . . . likyng*] Source: Painter's "The Countess of Celant," III, 52.

83. 8–15. *I . . . infamie*] Sources: Rich's *A Right Exelent and Pleasaunt Dialogue*, sigs. K6v–K7, and Painter's "The Duchess of Malfy," III, 4.

13. *degraduation*] The only example cited in *NED*, which glosses, "Degradation, abasement from rank of dignity." Rich's "degraduation of her honour" is the result of Painter's "denigration of hir honour," III, 4.

20. *confesse a trothe*] A great favorite with Rich, the phrase sounds proverbial but is not listed by Tilley, Apperson, or Smith. Rich employs it, or variations of it, at 64. 24, 82. 5, 177. 24, 190. 22, and 202. 16. See also his *True Report* (1582), sig. B1, "She was become penitent, confessed a truth, and . . . detested her errour," and *Faultes* (1606), sig. D1, "And what can I do but confesse a troth?" Compare *Othello*, V. ii. 68: "Let him confess a truth."

26 f. *beeyng . . . me*] Again compare *Twelfth Night*, V. i. 146 f.:

> [*Oli.*] Cesario, husband, stay.
> *Duke* Husband?
> *Oli.* Ay, husband. Can he that deny?

26–31. *beeyng . . . GOD*] Source: Painter's "Camiola and Roland," III, 360.

38–84. 4. *swearyng . . . conscience*] Source: Painter's "The Countess of Celant," III, 75.

84. 5–13. *I . . . deceiued*] In thus interrupting his narrative with a teasing remark, Rich is happily following the example of Pettie, who is

much given to regaling his lady readers with short, spicy commentaries on the action, commentaries now confidential and insinuating, now coy, now saucy in tone; "like a Master of Ceremonies in the Pump Room," as one scholar wittily observes (in a criticism that applies equally well to Rich), Pettie "bows and smirks and rallies." For other arch digressions see 67. 16, 69. 24–29, 74. 28, 126. 8–11, 130. 19–21, 133. 27–38, and 136. 14–17.

19–26. *What . . . housbande*] Source: Painter's "The Duchess of Malfy," III, 32 f.

28–35. *but . . . scourges*] This rousing bit, piecing out a paragraph taken largely from Painter, sounds homiletic and was, I suspect, borrowed from a sermon. In *The Excellency of Good Women* (1613) Rich confesses, sig. B2v, that to "adorne" his subject he has borrowed from a sermon by "a learned diuine."

32. *righteous true*] Read probably *righteous, true.*

85. 7–10. *thus . . . come*] Source: Painter's "The Lord of Virle," III, 192.

11–18. *ah . . . treason*] Source: Painter's "Dom Diego and Ginevra," III, 243.

19–22. *ah . . . name*] Source: Painter's "Salimbene and Angelica," III, 315.

33–38. *How . . . honour*] Source: Painter's "Dom Diego and Ginevra," III, 278.

86. 30–32. *And . . . teates*] Studying the relationship of *Twelfth Night* to its source, Collier comments on this passage in his *Poetical Decameron* (London, 1820), II, 158, "Such an *eclaircissement* could scarcely take place on the stage, and this might be one reason why Shakespeare omitted the incident."

32 f. *and . . . self*] Omitted by Furness in his reprint of the tale, *New Variorum Twelfth Night* (Philadelphia, 1901), p. 338.

87. 27–36. *Where . . . vnfained*] Sources: Painter's "Two Gentlewomen of Venice," III, 154, and "Sophonisba," II, 249.

88. 31 f. *that past*] Read *that was past* to conform with Rich's scenes of reconciliation elsewhere: "desiryng bothe . . . to forgiue what was past" (64. 38–65. 2), "please it you to pardon what is paste" (76. 34), "contented to beare with you for that whiche is alreadie paste" (28. 14 f.), and "desired his mother to beare with all that was paste" (55. 23).

89. 1. *Nicander*] *Nicandro* in the original. Why the change I do not know. Sappho, Silvio, Alonso, Phylerno, and Alberto indicate that Rich considered names ending in -*o* suitable for his male characters.

8 f. *2000. crounes*] "2000. pounde," according to 102. 29, on which see the note.

13–16. *In . . . Ferrara*] Source: Cinthio, II, 309. On Alfonso I (1476–1534), whose chief distinction seems to be that he married Lucrezia Borgia in 1502, see E. G. Gardner, *Dukes & Poets in Ferrara* (London, 1904), Chapter XIV. An account of his reign was available to Elizabethans in William Thomas' *The Historye of Italye* (1561), fol. 212.

19–22. *but . . . deserue*] In Cinthio only two words, "ma povera" (II, 317).

22 f. *prime and flower*] In Cinthio a single word, "fiorire" (II, 317).

90. 6. *and the woman*] Read *and then the woman* to conform with the source, "e poi la donna" (II, 317).

10. *languished . . . loue*] A somewhat effusive version of "miseramente si amassero" (II, 317).

14 f. *without . . . honor*] Not in Cinthio.

16. *as . . . blocke*] The alliterative phrase has no counterpart in Cinthio.

17–19. *liued . . . other*] Less moving than Cinthio's simpler "si struggeano di desiderio l'uno dell' altro" (II, 317).

19 f. *sorte eche daie, with . . . other*] Read *sorte, eche daie with . . . other* to conform with the source, "meno felice il facea di giorno in giorno l'avarizia" (II, 317).

20 f. *th' old carle*] An amusing version of "vecchio" (II, 318). "Carle," which means, specifically, "one who is churlish or mean in money matters, a grabber," is apt here. Compare "chorle," 28. 5.

21 f. *Don . . . heire*] Ercole II (1508–59), son of Alfonso and Lucrezia Borgia, became Duke of Ferrara in 1534. Since he was a patron of Cinthio, it is not surprising that Ercole appears in a flattering light throughout the tale. For the relationship between the Duke and the novelist see Angelo Solerti, *Ferrara e la corte estense* (*Città di Castello*, 1900), p. lxxxiii.

22 f. *passing . . . dwelt*] Not in Cinthio.

26 f. *the . . . beautie*] The phraseology of this expansion of "la

bellezza della giovane" (II, 318) is highly characteristic of Rich. Compare "the comeliness of his personage" (32. 4 f.), "comely in his personage" (35. 24), "comeliness of personage" (67. 7), and "a verie comely personage" (167. 37).

37. *Princes*] I.e., "Princess"—"reina" in Cinthio (II, 318).

91. 6 f. *although . . . matche*] A badly confused version of "quantunque vedesse il giovane, che non era convenevole al grado suo, ch'egli la si piagliasse per moglie" (II, 318). Nothing in the Italian justifies the infinitives "to wishe, or to procure." The English makes sense, however, if "to bee farre" is read "to bee too farre."

10 f. *But . . . For*] Not in Cinthio. The addition is characteristic of Rich. Compare "but all in vaine, for" (80. 13) and "But all in vaine, for" (169. 17).

15. *as . . . considered*] In this perplexing clause, the counterpart of a present participle, "parendole" (II, 318), "that" may be considered a demonstrative pronoun with "mishappe" as its antecedent. Had the compositor been guilty of simple verbal metathesis, the clause would begin "as that [i.e., 'because'] she." The passage is rendered neither more clear nor more agreeable stylistically by the fact that it contains the first two of a spate of "that's"—six within five lines.

18. *Nicander should . . . perceiue*] Read *should Nicander . . . perceiue* to conform with the conditional clause in the source: "se forse Nicandro si avvedesse" (II, 318).

18 f. *hunted . . . haunte*] A colorful rendering of "le desse l'occhio" (II, 318).

22–25. *she . . . house*] Rich here omits a reference to attending mass but compensates for the omission by specifying when any reasonably devout maiden may be expected to go to church. The Italian reads, "[Lucilla] si ristrinse in casa, di maniera che non appariva mai, se non quanto ella andava ad una chiesetta, vicina alla sua casa, a messa" (II, 318).

26 f. *that . . . hym*] To Cinthio's "che Lucilla non l'avesse lasciato" (II, 318) Rich has added a version of the proverb (Tilley, p. 335) probably inspired by Pettie's "o waveryng of women" (p. 92). Parentheses serve as quotation marks distinguishing the proverb also at 45. 32 f. and 121. 36 f.

36–92. 5. *The . . . I*] On the six-line iambic pentameter stanza and on Rich's interpolation of poetry in his fiction see 39. 5–28 n. Except in the first stanza, however, the rhyme scheme in Nicander's complaint is *abcbdd* rather than the more popular *ababcc*.

92. 9. *beste, beloued*] On the marking of the cesura, even between two such closely related words, see 39. 5–28 n.

20. *to . . . close*] Source: Pettie's "Icilius and Virginia," p. 125, "good god how cloasely then will hee [your elderly husband] mew you up." Compare 183. 3.

22–24. *If . . . holde*] Three hexameter lines in the midst of an otherwise regular pentameter poem.

34. *loue, to thee . . . can tell*] Since the comma marks the cesura as in the lines above, "to thee" probably modifies "love," not "can tell."

93. 13–16. *The . . . fight*] This modified ballad stanza, rhyming *abcb*, Rich uses consistently throughout Lucilla's reply.

18. *By . . . will*] This poetic passing of the buck is based on "La giovane . . . dava la colpa alla madre" (II, 318 f.).

33–94. 2. *frame . . . take*] Highly characteristic of Rich, who works this formula overtime. See 5. 6, 85. 38, 94. 11 f., 109. 4, 183. 36, 185. 36, 190. 34, 195. 32, and 197. 25 f.

94. 19. *mouther*] Read *mother*.

27. *in . . . pleasure*] The phrase, which has no counterpart in Cinthio, echoes Painter's "Giletta of Narbonne," I, 176, "Wherefore I purpose, *for recompense of the pleasure*, which you shall doe for mee, to giue so muche readie money to marie her honourablie, as you shall thincke sufficient" (my italics).

31. *Artificer . . . man*] In Cinthio a single word, "artefice" (II, 319).

95. 5. *punished with pouertie*] An alliterative rendering of "astretta . . . dall' estrema povertà" (II, 320) that doubtless gratified so forthright a euphuist as Rich.

20 f. *I . . . graue*] The trope is more effective than the original "aspetto . . . la morte" (II, 320). Compare Greene's *Mamillia* (1593), Grosart, II, 165, "nothing is so certaine in old age as euerie day to looke to die."

26. *bring . . . spoile*] Franker than the original "la farebbe divenir femina del mondo" (II, 320).

36 f. *forced . . . ouercome*] The phraseology of this greatly expanded version of Cinthio's "son stata . . . vinta" (II, 320) is unquestionably Rich's. Compare "I yeelde my self vanquished and ouercome" (196. 30 f.) and "[I] yeeld my self as recreant, and ouercome" (197. 29 f.).

96. 9 f. *will minister . . . releefe*] The phraseology of this rendering of "darò . . . tal sostentamento" (II, 320) is, again, undoubtedly Rich's. Compare "minister releef" (31. 38), "ministered suche releef" (170. 16 f.), and "minister releef" (191. 7 f.). He is so infatuated with the phrase, in fact, that he once again produces the sound, if not the meaning, of it: "minister release" (177. 26).

14. *froward Fortune*] Cinthio's "malvagia fortuna" (II, 320). Though Cinthio manages to vary the adjective, Rich usually reacts to "fortuna" with the same cliché. Compare "frowarde Fortune" (102. 5) from "nimica fortuna" (II, 324); "Fortune . . . froward" (114. 30) from "fortuna . . . contraria" (I, 302); and "froward Fortune" (119. 27) from "ria fortuna" (I, 305).

25. *whereby . . . name*] Not in Cinthio.

29. *open my lippes*] An interesting figure of speech and more effective than the original "movesse parola" (II, 321).

36 f. *since my . . . me*] Not in Cinthio.

97. 2. *a lowe Chamber*] In Cinthio "una camera terrena" (II, 321)—literally, "a room on the ground floor."

11 f. *You . . . alone*] The latter word modifies the former. For the agreement referred to see 96. 21 f., 26 f.

23–25. *that not . . . meane*] The *and* which seems to be missing between *commyng* and *did* is present in the Italian, here rendered very freely: "che non solo non ne fusse contentà, ma nè anche consapevole; e molto disse, per non accettar tal condizione" (II, 321).

32. *and so content*] Read *and so was content*, with Collier, to conform with the source, "e fu contento" (II, 321).

37. *As . . . peepe*] An engaging figure of speech and an improvement over the stilted "Tosto che il sole menò il nuovo giorno" (II, 321).

98. 6. *is extreame hotte*] In Cinthio "si sentiva il caldo ardentissimo" (II, 321). The earliest adverbial use of "extreme" cited in *NED* is dated 1593.

10–12. *with . . . bodie*] In the light of Rich's pretensions to delicacy (see 19. 17–24), this ardent expansion of "che meravigliosa vaghezza le aggiungeano" (II, 322) is amusing.

21–23. *beganne . . . peece*] An animated rendering of "sè stesso lodò, che di sì rara bellezza si fusse acceso" (II, 322).

28. *this ouer*] Read *thus* ouer.

29 f. *a greate skritche*] Cinthio's "un gran grido" (II, 322).

99. 2 f. *like . . . mornyng*] A more effective trope than "quasi stille di rugiada su mattutine rose" (II, 322).

5 f. *Trouble . . . not*] A felicitous expansion of "Non vi turbate" (II, 322).

11 f. *a . . . glad of*] This boast probably suggested the following in *Philotus* (Mill, p. 107), whose author borrowed heavily from other tales in the *Farewell* (see above, p. xlii):

> Now thair is twentie into this toun . . .
> That wald be glaid for to sit doun,
> Vpon thair kneis to grip him [a desirable suitor].

The doublet "dooe wishe and would bee glad of" is the result of Cinthio's "è desiderata" (II, 322).

17–22. *For . . . satisfaction*] A more eloquent plea than Cinthio's "Però che dandovi a me, non vi date ad un plebeo, ma ad un signore, che vi ha fatto servo la vostra bellezza" (II, 322).

20–22. *and . . . satisfaction*] Not in Cinthio.

24 f. *two . . . Iuorie*] Very little if any improvement over the original "due acerbetti pomi" (II, 322).

29 f. *or . . . will*] This addition, designed to increase the weight and poignancy of the original, "Signore, vi prego . . . che vi piaccia di non mi far forza" (II, 322), seems bathetic.

100. 10. *portion*] Read *proportion*, with *C*, to conform with the original "convenienza" (II, 323).

14. *is . . . am*] Here there may be some corruption in the text. The curious "no . . . nor" has no basis in the original "non è però più nobilmente nato, che io mi sia" (II, 323).

32 f. *by Gods help*] Not in Cinthio. The addition is very characteristic of Rich, who continually thus alludes to the power of Providence, as at 16. 24, 46. 31 f., 72. 37 f., 100. 36, 109. 2 f., and 161. 26.

36. *by the grace of God*] Again Rich's addition.

37–101. 2 *to giue . . . Praier*] Rich here omits Cinthio's reference to espousing God but compensates for the omission by adding the bit about fasting and prayer. The Italian reads, "darmi vergine a Iddio, e lui prendermi per isposo, ed a' servigii suoi finire vergine la vita mia" (II, 323).

101. 23–102. 12 *This . . . daughter*] A greatly reduced version of the original, omitting Cinthio's references to a previous story and to Pope Adrian (II, 324).

26 f. *of . . . quiuer*] A "poetic" rendering of the already sufficiently poetic "ch' avesse Amore" (II, 324).

102. 5. *frowarde Fortune*] See 96. 14 n.

29. *2000. pounde*] More munificent and closer to Cinthio's "tre mila fiorini d'oro" (II, 324) than the "2000. crounes" specified at 89. 8 f.

32. *And . . . you*] Not in Cinthio. The addition provides a rhetorically effective transition to the direct discourse.

103. 23. *noble desires*] The careful qualifying adjective seems unintentionally ironical.

30. *in maner*] The phrase, a favorite of Rich's (see 108. 19, 126. 37, and 165. 18), means "so to speak," "as it were."

104. 21. *Yes Marie*] An eminently Elizabethan rendering of the decorous "anzi si" (II, 326).

33–36. *continence . . . daughter*] Of these particular anecdotes the Elizabethans seemed never to tire. For other versions see Hoby's translation of Castiglione's *Courtier* (1561), ed. Sir Walter Raleigh, Tudor Translations, XXIII (London, 1900), 250, 253, 255 f.; Painter, II, 166–71, 355; Lodowick Lloyd, *The Pilgrimage of Princes* (1573?), sig. O1v; and North's *Plutarch*, ed. George Wyndham, Tudor Translations, XI (London, 1895), 321 f., 334, and XII (London, 1896), 401, 419. Rich himself relates the story about Scipio in his first publication, *A Right Exelent and Pleasaunt Dialogue* (1574), sigs. D6v–D7, and again in *Roome for a Gentleman* (1609), sig. O1v. In the former he mentions the locale of the story, "in Spaine," as in line 35, where the phrase is an addition to Cinthio's version, otherwise here translated with reasonable fidelity.

105. 5. *bathyng . . . blisse*] The alliterative phrase has no counterpart in Cinthio.

24–34. *And . . . liberties*] Not in Cinthio. By thus supplying a conventional, lived-happily-ever-after ending, Rich transfers the final emphasis from virtuous, continent Don Hercules to Nicander and Lucilla, where it belongs in a narrative that bears their names.

106. 8. *whereby*] Read *where by*.

10 f. *one . . . Italie*] Not in Cinthio.

15 f. *Gauona*] Read *Sauona*.

16–18. *a Citie . . . miles*] On this explanation, which does not appear in Cinthio but was added by either L. B. or Rich, see p. xxiv, above.

23 f. *refused . . . to*] The doublet is the result of "fosse . . . contrario" (I, 298).

24–31. *For . . . them*] On this passage, which has no counterpart in Cinthio, see p. xxxii, above. The father's attitude seems to have been characteristic of the Genoese. Compare Fynes Moryson's comment of 1594 in his *Itinerary* (Glasgow, 1907), I, 360, "It is proverbially said of this City . . . Genoa superba: That is . . . Genoa the proud . . . and as Florence is called the faire for the building, so I thinke Genoa is called the proud."

27. *childe*] Read *chide*. Compare "reprehend and chide" (152. 5).

32–107. 2. *or . . . frendes*] Not in Cinthio.

107. 6. *stout and valiant*] In Cinthio a single word, "valoroso" (I, 298).

7–9. *and . . . vnto*] Not in Cinthio.

14–16. *very . . . weapon*] Compare *1 Henry VI*, I. iii. 75–79: "We charge and command you, in his Highness' name . . . not to wear, handle, or use any sword, weapon, or dagger henceforward, upon pain of death."

15 f. *and . . . weapon*] This rigorous detail has no counterpart in Cinthio.

17 f. *for . . . Citie*] Cinthio's "per essere l'uno e l'altro di loro capo di fanterie" (I, 298 f.), a passage that could scarcely fail to quicken the interest of Captain Rich and set him to augmenting the original.

19–36. *And . . . prisoner*] There are curious (and amusing) parallels between this adventure and one which Rich himself maintains he suffered in Dublin. Compare "The orygynall whye the Lord Chancellor and his brother the Bishoppe of Meathe conceyved ferst displeasure agaynste me," Rich's report to the Privy Council, July 15, 1592, printed by E. M. Hinton, *Ireland through Tudor Eyes* (Philadelphia, 1935), pp. 87 f. (my italics): "Nicholas Walshe (*accompanied with sundrye persons . . .*), *he came unto me as I passed through the street and gevinge me most shamefull wordes*, too tedyous & moste undecente to be heere rehearsed, who seeing that his rayling speeches would not prevail to draw me to that he looked for which was to quarrel, he sodaynly struck me with hys fist, and drawing his dagger stabbed at me three or foure times and *withall he drew his sword*, and being driven to defend my selfe *I gave him a small hurt*, the which hys master hearing of sent his warrant to the Sergeant-at-Arms that he should *forthwith carry me to prison.*"

21. *to . . . language*] I.e., "to abuse him." Compare Thomas Lodge's testimony that his brother William "gave [him] . . . dyvers and sundrye evill and malicious words" (C. J. Sisson, *Thomas Lodge and Other Elizabethans* [Cambridge, Mass., 1933], p. 89). An antonymous expression was "to give good words, or language," i.e. "to flatter." See Dekker's *The Wonderful Year* (1603), Wilson, p. 4, "theres . . . sound law to make you giue good words to the *Reader.*" Rich's expression is the result of Cinthio's "a svillaneggiarlo" (I, 299).

23 f. *saied . . . againe*] A vigorous expansion of "gli rispose" (I, 299).

28. *not to*] Read *not) to.*

29. *beare no Coales*] This fine old proverb (Smith, p. 502), meaning "put up with no affront," is the result of "non ero uomo da patire ingiuria" (I, 299). Compare Nashe's *Have with You to Saffron-Walden* (1596), McKerrow, III, 53, "Wee will beare no coales, neuer feare you"; *Romeo and Juliet*, I. i. 1, "Gregory, on my word, we'll not carry coals"; and *Henry V*, III. ii. 50, "I knew by that piece of service the men would carry coals."

34. *though but lightly*] The specific detail, lacking in Cinthio's "ferì . . . su la mano" (I, 299), adds reality to the duel.

36. *enuironed hym*] This sensible prelude to his capture has no counterpart in Cinthio.

108. 3. *was . . . heade*] Cinthio's "fu condannato . . . ad essere morte" (I, 299). By specifying the means of execution Rich renders the sentence more immediate and terrible.

8. *no worse*] Read *not worse?* The Italian is here so freely

rendered that it is no help in establishing the reading. Cinthio writes, "e fu condannato a pena poco men dura della morte" (I, 299).

8–22. *hauyng . . . cease*] Compare *The Tempest*, I. ii. 144–51:

> [Our enemies] hurried us aboard a bark,
> Bore us some leagues to sea; where they prepar'd
> A rotten carcass of a butt, not rigg'd,
> Nor tackle, sail, nor mast. . . .
> There they hoist us,
> To cry to th' sea, that roar'd to us; to sigh
> To th' winds, whose pity, sighing back again,
> Did us but loving wrong.

14 f. *diuerse and sondrie*] The cliché, from Cinthio's "varie" (I, 299), would be hard to resist even today.

15. *stormes and shapes*] In Cinthio a single word, "imagini" (I, 299), in the light of which Collier's suggestion (p. xv) that *formes and shapes* is the correct reading seems apt.

19. *in maner*] I.e., "so to speak." See 103. 30 n.

21. *Whiles . . . tormented*] Not in Cinthio, the clause provides a neat transition from the preceding paragraph.

24. *Moores . . . roauyng*] A lusty rendering of "Mori, i quali erano usati di andare in corso" (I, 299). According to Sugden, p. 528, "During the Turkish rule [of Tunis, annexed to the Ottoman Empire in 1575] it became notorious for the daring and cruelty of its pirates."

26. *happely*] I.e., "haply," "by chance," not "happily," so Cinthio's "forse" (I, 299) indicates.

27. *gaine and bootie*] From Cinthio's "guadagno" (I, 299).

29. *prey . . . profite*] Again, from Cinthio's "guadagno" (I, 299).

37. *though . . . Infidels*] Not in Cinthio.

109. 2 f. *through . . . GOD*] This pious version of Cinthio's "in sorte" (I, 299) is very characteristic of Rich. Compare 16. 24, 46. 31 f., 72. 37 f., 100. 32 f., 100. 36, and 161. 26.

4 f. *He . . . captiuitie*] A felicitous expansion of "tollerava quella cruda servitù pazientemente" (I, 299 f.).

7. *beleeuyng . . . dead*] Though Rich often lets a participial phrase stand for a sentence, the reading in the source indicates that

"beleeuyng" may have been a slip for "beleeued": "tenne certo, ch'egli si fosse morto" (I, 300).

10 f. *and . . . daies*] Not in Cinthio.

30–32. *and . . . together*] Not in Cinthio.

36–110. 2. *wherein . . . beautie*] On this information, which is not in Cinthio but was added by either L. B. or Rich, see pp. xxiv f., above. In *A Tour through Italy* (1791), pp. 56, 13, 62, Thomas Martyn corroborates the testimony in Rich, remarking that "The Genoese have sumptuous country houses or villas," that en route from Savona to Genoa one passes "many villages, villas, and magnificent palaces belonging to the Genoese nobility," and that "From Genoa to Sestrì there is a continued chain of country houses for six miles together."

110. 12 f. *to . . . commaunde hym*] The phraseology of this version of "fare poscia di lei quel ch'ella gli imporrebbe" (I, 300) is very characteristic of Rich. Compare "to obeye whatsoeuer she would . . . commaunde him" (70. 19 f.), "what so euer it shall please me to commaunde" (195. 35 f.), and "to abide what soeuer it shall please you to commaunde" (197. 28 f.).

17. *was onely thankefull*] Read *was not onely not thankefull* to conform with the original "non pure non n'ebbe grazia alcuna" (I, 300).

20. *Kyng . . . sellyng*] According to Sugden, p. 528, Tunis' "chief source of revenue was the sale of Christian slaves."

22. *mischeeuous knave*] Cinthio's "manigoldo" (I, 300), a very strong epithet in Italian.

23 f. *when . . . sleape*] Not in Cinthio. The clause endows Fiamma with considerable practical sense and lends an air of premeditation and *savoir faire* to the flight which follows.

26 f. *the knaue . . . coast*] A nautical detail lacking in Cinthio.

27. *Ligorno*] Cinthio's "Livorno" (I, 300), as the town is spelled in modern Italian. "Its original name was Ligorno, whence the Hobson-Jobson Leghorn" (Sugden, p. 302).

35 f. *who . . . Gentlewomans*] Not in Cinthio.

111. 4. *protracted*] Read perhaps *protracting* to conform with "hauyng" (line 3) and "shifting" (lines 4 f.). The Italian is here so freely rendered that it is no help in establishing the reading. Cinthio writes, "Ma avendo più volte sollecitato la donzella il Moro, ed egli tuttavia addottole sue favole . . . " (I, 300).

8. *or... Sea*] Not in Cinthio. Before the addition of the rational, practical element to her plan, Fiamma's behavior seems fatuous indeed.

16–19. *and . . . meanes*] An analysis of his motives lacking in Cinthio.

24. *repented*] Read *repenting* to conform with Cinthio's "pentita" (I, 301) and with "blamyng" (line 23).

33. *and boorded it*] Not in Cinthio.

37. *woundyng*] Read *wounded*, with *C*, to conform with Cinthio's "gli dieron di molte ferite" (I, 301).

112. 31. *aduentures. Neuerthelesse*] Read *aduentures, neuerthelesse* to conform with the original "sciagure, nondimeno" (I, 301).

33 f. *and . . . hym*] An expansion of "e così fece ella" (I, 301).

113. 8. *Cube*] A coinage from Cinthio's "cuba" (I, 301). It is not listed in *NED*.

8 f. *whiche . . . Serraqlio*] Not in Cinthio, the explanation was doubtless as welcome to readers in 1581 as it is to us. For *Serraqlio* read *Serraglio* to avoid the improbable *q* not followed by a *u*.

11–13. (*who . . . ouercame*) . . . *condition*] Read (*who . . . ouercame . . . condition*).

18–20. *whiche . . . theim*] Not in Cinthio.

26–31. Read "The maner [or] custome of the Kyng was, to cause his [concu]bines to come vnto him, and to lye with them by order, [as] thei had been bought or come to his handes: By reason of [w]hiche custome, for that there were very many bought before [t]he commyng thether of Fiamma, there was alreadie a whole [ye]are. . . ." In square brackets are letters taken from *B* to replace those which are scarcely legible or torn away in *A*. The missing letters appear correctly in Collier's edition of 1846, when the unique copy of *A*, which he reprinted, may have been legible in these places.

32–34. *But . . . her. Fineo . . . greefe*] Read *But . . . her, Fineo . . . greefe* to conform with the source, "Ma avanzandovene sol tre, si stava in grandissimo dispiacere Fineo" (I, 302).

37. *tenne thousand folde*] This impressive degree is not specified in the original—"e gli accresceva la pena il timore" (I, 302).

114. 16–18. *and think . . . might*] Not in Cinthio.

27–29. Read "Thei beyng returned safe vnto Sauona, deliuered [the let]ters vnto the father and brother of *Fineo*, who with the r[est] of his freendes, and in effecte all the whole Citie, were ve[rie] glad that his Fortune had not been altogether so froward t[o]ward. . . ." The bracketed letters are taken from *B*. See 113. 26–31 n.

30. *Fortune . . . froward*] See 96. 14 n.

33. *a . . . Fregat*] An affectionate rendering of what Cinthio calls, with the detachment of a landlubber, "una barca" (I, 302).

34 f. *Marchaundize . . . Gentlewomen*] An attractive expansion of "merci da uomini e da donne" (I, 302).

37 f. *some . . . price*] A complete reversal of Cinthio's "alcuni doni pregiosi" (I, 302).

115. 13 *as . . . firste*] The meaning of the phrase, which has no counterpart in Cinthio, is not clear. Since "gentle" when used to modify "things" meant "noble," "excellent," perhaps the "gentle present" is to be contrasted to "some one trifle." The sentence might then be paraphrased, "To all the women Fineo and his brother gave some trifle, and to the most distinguished ['the firste'] a handsome present."

15. *very . . . Pearle*] Cinthio's "una borsetta bellissima" (I, 303); the embroidery is Rich's addition.

29 f. *when . . . slept*] Not in Cinthio. The addition lends Fiamma a practicality and *sang-froid* she lacks in the original. Compare the note on 110. 23 f.

32. *which . . . purpose*] Not in Cinthio.

33. *brake and wrested*] The doublet, the result of "ruppero" (I, 303), suggests that Rich understood, perhaps from personal observation, the practical problems involved in getting through a jail window.

37. *and . . . daie*] Not in Cinthio.

38–116. 4. *Fiamma . . . awaie*] In Cinthio there is no hint of the king's deductions; he is merely informed of the flight—"il re intese la costor fuga" (I, 303). Why the parentheses, or whether they are Rich's or the compositor's, I do not know.

116. 5 f. *certaine . . . vesselles*] More specific than Cinthio's "alcune navi sottili" (I, 303).

9 f. *would . . . buried*] Cinthio's "volea fare ardere" (I, 303). I know no way to discover whether the change from "burned" to "buried" was intentional, whether it resulted from a misreading of manuscript, or whether it was a typographical error. But being burned alive or being buried alive—either fate is sufficiently gruesome.

15–17. *Fortune . . . arise*] This considerably expanded version of "la fortuna . . . fe' levare un vento contrario" (I, 303), seems to reflect a knowledge of Painter's "Poris and Theoxena," where certain details are much the same as in "Fineo." Attempting to rescue his family, Poris "priuely embarked himselfe and them. . . . But his intent was cleane altered and chaunged, for . . . at that instant *a contrary winde and tempest rose*, that brought him backe again" (II, 253 f.). The italics indicating words Rich appears to echo are mine. See also Rich's "the extremetie of a contrary winde" (34. 4 f.), "the extreamitie of a tempest" (68. 14), "the extreamitie of a contrarie winde" (167. 25), and "a contrary winde" (171. 29).

19–22. *with . . . people*] In *Cent excellentes nouvelles* (1584), Gabriel Chappuys' version of *Gli Hecatommithi*, the translator seldom betters the original, but here his irony is more effective than either the Italian or the English: "auec tel plaisir que peut imaginer celuy qui cognoist la cruauté des gens de ce pays" (Vol. II, fol. 237v).

21. *crueltie and barbarousnesse*] In Cinthio a single word "crudeltà" (I, 303). Rich again magnifies this facet of the Mohammedan character at 116. 24 f.

24 f. *or els . . . Infidels*] Not in Cinthio. See the preceding note.

26. *Cockboate*] A technical nautical term, from Cinthio's "palischermo" (I, 303), suggesting a knowledge of the sea that is something more than rhetorical, while Chappuys' translation (see 116. 19–22 n.) of the same word, "le petit batteau" (vol. II, fol. 237v), suggests that he was at home on no body of water more extensive than the Seine.

117. 5–7. *drewe . . . death*] This phraseology, despite Cinthio's "messa mano al coltello . . . se volle uccidere" (I, 303), is most characteristic of Rich. Compare "Silla . . . drue out her knife readie to strike her self to the harrt" (72. 17 f.), doubtless in emulation of Painter's noble Lucrece, who "drewe a knife . . . and stabbed her selfe to the harte" (I, 24).

9 f. *the . . . me*] See the note on 162. 27 f.

17 f. *But . . . saied*] A felicitous expansion of "Ma Fineo le disse" (I, 304).

21–23. *therefore . . . dedde*] A greatly expanded version of "Però lasciate me morire, e voi vivete" (I, 304).

33 f. *at . . . freendlie*] Not in Cinthio, the addition aptly illustrates the "muche milder maner" just referred to.

34 f. *in . . . ha*[l]*fe*] The length of time of her incarceration is not specified in Cinthio.

35. *indifferently well*] Ever-practical Rich, who had been exposed for years to Dutch and Celtic, probably felt obliged to add this qualification to Cinthio's flat statement, "già appresa avea la lingua" (I, 304).

36–118. 3. *That . . . doen*] Direct discourse in Cinthio.

118. 3 f. *she . . . loue*] Not in Cinthio, these details increase the poignancy of her recital.

6. *their . . . ende*] Not in Cinthio.

26. *since your Fortune*] Recognizing the inconsistency in the original, "Poscia che Iddio" (I, 304), Rich snatches the word "Iddio" from the infidel's mouth and replaces it with "Fortune."

32. *I doe . . . bothe*] Not in Cinthio.

34. *with this ryng*] An agreeable though sentimental touch that is not in Cinthio.

37. *the kynges courtesies*] The irony the phrase supplies is lacking in Cinthio's "ch'altro non attendevano dal re che la morte" (I, 304).

119. 18. *God and Nature*] A more respectful word order than Cinthio's "la natura e Iddio" (I, 305).

27. *froward Fortune*] See 96. 14 n.

120. 2. *and their wiues*] An interesting variation of the title was suggested by a reader, probably Rich's contemporary, who wrote in *B* (copy 1) opposite this line "brethren and theire Madam." The first part of the suggestion is trimmed away.

24–26. *question . . . woman*] Rich was still exploring much the same question in 1617 in *The Irish Hubbub*, sig. C3v, "It were much better for a mans owne credit to marry a wise harlot, then a foolish honest woman."

31–121. 5. *auncient . . . mynde*] The opinion of the Romans in this matter was preserved, I suspect, in Rich's notebook. He invokes the same passage (the source of which has escaped me) for authority in *The Honestie of This Age* (1614), Cunningham, pp. 15 f. (the italics are mine), "And the *ancient Romans* banished out of their cittie, all women that were found to be dishonest of their tongues, yet tollerating with those others, that were well knowne to be dishonest of their bodies, thinking the first to bee more pernicious then the last, because *the infirmity of the one proceeded* but *from the frailtie of the flesh, but the wickedness of the other from an vngracious and a wicked minde.*"

121. 5. *it is*] Read probably *is it.*

19. *the harte . . . not*] The usual form of the proverb was "What the eye seeth not, the heart rueth not" (Smith, p. 569; Tilley, p. 141).

20 f. *from . . . douneward*] Rich is less anatomical in *The Honestie of This Age* (1614), Cunningham, p. 16, "Will you see now a womans honestie is pent vp in a litle roome, it is still confined but from her girdle downewards."

26. *a famous Citie*] London, so 128. 9–12, 131. 7, and 137. 25 indicate.

122. 4. *after . . . sorte*] I.e., "just average."

5–8. *so . . . wife*] Source: Painter's "A Lady of Turin," I, 241.

13. *spitfull*] I.e., "spitefull." See 19. 6 n.

24 f. *to beholde . . . gentlewoman*] Source: Rich's *A Right Exelent and Pleasaunt Dialogue*, sig. I4v.

25–34. *lent . . . tende*] Compare Falstaff's boasts, *The Merry Wives of Windsor*, I. iii. 47–53, 65–69, 72–78:

Briefly, I do mean to make love to Ford's wife. I spy entertainment in her: she discourses, she carves, she gives the leer of invitation. I can construe the action of her familiar style, and the hardest voice of her behaviour (to be English'd rightly) is "I am Sir John Falstaff's." . . . I have writ me a letter to her; and here another to Page's wife, who even now gave me good eyes too, examin'd my parts with most judicious illiads. Sometimes the beam of her view gilded my foot, sometimes my portly belly. . . . O, she did so course o'er my exteriors with such a greedy intention that the appetite of her eye did seem to scorch me up like a burning glass! Here's another letter to her. She bears the purse too. She is a region in Guiana, all gold and bounty. I will be cheaters to them both, and they shall be exchequers to me.

26. *looke*] Read *lookes* to conform with "rowlyng lookes" at 45. 36 and "amarous lokes" at 77. 30.

27–34. *practised . . . perceiue*] Source: Rich's *A Right Exelent and Pleasaunt Dialogue*, sig. I4v.

32. *fourtie . . . hundred*] An exorbitant rate of interest even in

the usurious Elizabethan age. See Thomas Wilson, *A Discourse upon Usury* (1572), ed. R. H. Tawney (London, 1924), p. 227, "[Most vices] have not more harmed . . . the moste of men, then thys filthye usurye hath doone. . . . A man taketh upp a thousande poundes at one tyme, and payeth for the same twentye, thyrtye, naye shal I saye fourtie in the hundred sometymes."

123. 7. *rightes*] "Rights" or "rites"? Either is possible in the context, though "rites" seems the more probable here.

9 f. *complexitions*] Read *complexions* ("physical constitutions") with *B*, *C*, and Collier. Specifically, "complexion" meant "the combination of the humours of the body in a certain proportion" (*NED*).

12–14. *the . . . children*] Source: Rich's *A Right Exelent and Pleasaunt Dialogue*, sig. K5v.

22. *rather . . . giue*] A curious perversion of "It is more blessed to give than to receive."

34. *set . . . edge*] Read probably *set his teeth an edge*, i.e., "excite his appetite," as at 144. 16. The usual meaning of "set the teeth on edge" ("cause an unpleasant tingling in the teeth") seems impossible in this context.

124. 9. *restored) am*] Read *restored) I am.*

10 f. *Galen, Hypocrates, Auicen*] Probable source: Painter's "The Lord of Virle," III, 186, where the hero's physicians, unable to cure his dumbness, cursed "their Patrones, Galen, Hypocrates, and Auicen."

11. *Plinij*] Read probably *Plinie* or *Pliny*. Or did Rich write the genitive form as it stands in scores of titles beginning *C. Plinii Secundi*?

12. *a . . . malladie*] Compare Lyly's *Euphues* (1578), Bond, I, 208, "O ye gods haue ye ordayned for euerye maladye a medicine."

20. *sorted out*] I.e., "turned out."

20–24. *Mistres . . . comfort*] Compare the strategy which Mistress Page proposes to Mistress Ford, *The Merry Wives of Windsor*, II. i. 97–100: "Let's appoint him [Falstaff] a meeting, give him a show of comfort in his suit, and lead him on with a fine-baited delay."

29. *linckt . . . freendship*] See the note on 171. 35 f.

33–35. *knowyng . . . paradize*] Source: Pettie's "Amphiaraus and Eriphile," p. 88.

125. 6 f. *quieted . . . hope*] Compare *The Merry Wives of Windsor*,

III. iii. 205–208, "Shall we . . . give him another hope, to betray him to another punishment?"

9–12. *moste . . . you*] Source: Pettie's "Curiatius and Horatia," p. 168.

126. 7. *one . . . mercy*] Compare *Othello*, IV. ii. 52 f., "I should have found in some place of my soul/ A drop of patience."

8–11. *How . . . selues*] On such interruptions of the story to banter the lady readers *à la* Pettie see 84. 5–13 n.

23 f. *counterfecte*] I.e., "counterfeit," "portrait."

26. *distaine*] "Tint, stain, coloring."

37. *in maner*] I.e., "as it were." See 103. 30 n.

127. 3. *life . . . libertie*] Compare Greene's *Mamillia* (1593), Grosart, II, 210, "I think my lands, life, nor libertie halfe sufficient to requite thy curtesie."

11–19. *And . . . cause*] Sources: Gascoigne's celebrated lyric, "The Arraignment of a Lover," and a bit from Pettie's "Sinorix and Camma," which is evidently also based on Gascoigne's poem. A comparison of all three passages will reveal almost where Rich left off borrowing from Pettie's prose and consulted Gascoigne's verse. The italics indicating the places Rich echoes are mine. Gascoigne writes (Cunliffe, I, 38):

At Beautyes barre as I dyd stande,
When false suspect accused mee,
George (*quod the Judge*) holde up thy hande,
Thou art arraignde of Flatterye:
Tell therefore howe thou wylt bee tryde?
Whose *judgement* here wylt thou abyde?

My Lorde (*quod I*) this Lady here,
Whome I esteeme above the rest,
Doth knowe my guilte if any were:
Wherefore hir *doome* shall please me best,
Let hir bee *Judge* and Jurour boathe,
To trye mee guiltlesse by myne oathe.

Quod Beautie, no, it fitteth not,
A Prince hir selfe to judge the *cause*:
Wyll is our Justice well you wot,
Appointed to discuss our Lawes:

If you wyll guiltlesse seeme to goe,
God and your countrey quitte you so.

Pettie writes (p. 17): "at the *bar* of your *beauty I humbly holde up my handes*, meaning *to be tried by your courtesy and mine owne loyalty*, and minding *to abide* your sentence." Like Rich, John Grange also used both Gascoigne's and Pettie's version as sources for a bit in *Grange's Garden*, appended to *The Golden Aphroditis* (1577), sig. O3: "I haue bene arraigned at Dame Venus hir barre, in which arraignment (Lady) as guiltlesse I haue helde vp my hande, standing to your curtesie as one accused I know not whereof but for loyalty. Thus as a poore prysoner haue I helde vp my hande, answeryng at the iudges call, and appealyng to your curtesie onely for some sparke of grace." He again alludes to the lyric in *The Golden Aphroditis*, sig. F3, "I see thy tongue is made of . . . *Calcedon*, which greatly befriendeth your secte in pleadyng your cause at Dame *Venus* hir barre." In *Mamillia* (1583), Grosart, II, 127, Greene made use of the same passage in Pettie, but his borrowing was more literal than Rich's: "I appeale to your good grace and fauour, minding to be tried by your curtesie, abiding either the sentence of consent vnto life, or denial vnto death." See also his *Mamillia* (1593), II, 197 f., "I am forced by loue to pleade for pardon at the barre of thy bounty . . . till either the sentence of life or death be pronounced vpon me"; Deloney's *Jack of Newbury* (1597?), Mann, p. 66, "Yes faire Widow (quoth hee) as you are a clyent to the law, so am I sutor for your loue: and may I finde you so fauorable to let mee pleade my owne case at the barre of your beauty"; and Lodge's *Rosalynde* (1590), ed. Sir Walter Greg (London, 1931), p. 70, "[If I could find Rosalynde] and plead before the bar of her pity . . . hope tells me she would grace me with some favour."

13 f. *holde . . . handes*] Compare Nashe, *Strange Newes* (1592), McKerrow, I, 261, "Hold vp thy hand, *G. H.*, thou art heere indited," and McKerrow's explanation, IV, 159, "At a trial the accused person was called upon by the clerk to hold up his hand before the indictment was read to him. This was presumably intended either to distinguish the accused to whom the particular indictment had reference, or possibly to make sure that he was aware of what was going on."

18 f. *it . . . Iusticer*] Source: a passage borrowed from Painter and quoted more exactly at 59. 36 f. (on which see the note).

21–25. *if . . . likyng*] Source: Pettie's "Amphiaraus and Eriphile," pp. 88 f.

27. *he . . . place*] Source: Pettie's "Pygmalion's Friend," p. 240. The same inelegant *double entendre* is in Barry's *Ram-Alley* (1611), IV. i, *A Select Collection of Old Plays*, ed. I. Reed and O. Gilchrist (London, 1825), V, 428:

> Your action entered first below shall shrink,
> And you shall find, sir Serjeant, she has friends
> Will stick to her in the common place.

28 f. *Maister . . . her*] Again an indelicate *double entendre* (compare line 27). Compare Massinger's *The Bondman* (1624), I. ii, ed. H. Coleridge (London, 1848), p. 75:

> You are no sooner out of sight, but she
> Does feel strange qualms; then sends for her young doctor,
> Who ministers physic to her on her back,
> Her ladyship lying as she were entranced.

128. 11 f. *Kyng . . . feelde*] Henry defeated the French at Agincourt on October 25, 1415, returned to Dover on November 16, and entered London on November 23.

16. *greate*] Read *greater*.

24–28. *he . . . tearmes*] Compare Falstaff's letter to Mistress Page, "Let it suffice thee, Mistress Page—at the least, if the love of a soldier can suffice—that I love thee. I will not say, pity me,—'tis not a soldier-like phrase; but I say, love me" (II. i. 10–14), and his speeches to Mistress Ford, "I cannot cog, I cannot prate, Mistress Ford. . . . Come, I cannot cog, and say thou art this and that, like a many of these lisping hawthorn buds that come like women in men's apparel and smell like Bucklersbury in simple-time. I cannot. But I love thee" (III. iii. 50 f., 76–80). See the notes on 129. 33 f. and 130. 6.

30 f. *she . . . aire*] Source: Pettie's "Curiatius and Horatia," p. 167.

129. 17 f. *I . . . tende*] Her feigned naïveté may have inspired the real ingenuousness of the heroine of the comedy *Philotus* (1603), based on Rich's eighth tale. To certain burning proposals in the comedy Emily replies, "I wait not weill sir quhat ye meine" (Mill, p. 104).

28 f. *marche . . . Venus*] Compare Pettie's "Curiatius and Horatia," p. 174, "make mee marche under *Venus* banner."

33–35. *I . . . vp*] The conventional plea of the soldier again. See the notes on 128. 24–28 and 130. 6; *Othello*, I. iii. 81 f., "Rude am I in my speech,/ And little bless'd with the soft phrase of peace;" and Gervase Markham and Lewis Machin, *The Dumb Knight* (1608), sig. C4, "Mistresse *Prat*, I am a souldier, and can better act my loue then speake it."

35 f. *likyng. Please*] Read *likyng, please.*

35–38. *if you . . . feined*] His proposal may have suggested the following in Shirley's *Love Tricks* (of which Rich's eighth story is the principal source), Dyce, I, 11:

> If my affection be suspected, make
> Experience of my loyalty, by some service,
> Though full of danger; you shall know me better,
> And so discern the truth of what you see not.

130. 5. *apposed*] I.e., "opposed," "confronted."

6. *blunt and plaine*] For his own bluntness and plainness, the traditional "failings" of the soldier, Rich apologizes to Queen Elizabeth in the dedication of *A Path-way to Military Practise* (1587), "Pardō me (most gracious Princesse) in discharging my dutie, though simplie yet truely, Souldiours are but blunte, but sure they looue plainnes." Compare *King Lear*, II. ii. 98, "Sir, 'tis my occupation to be plain," and II. ii. 101–106,

> This is some fellow
> Who, having been prais'd for bluntness, doth affect
> A saucy roughness. . . . He cannot flatter, he!
> An honest mind and plain—he must speak truth!
> An they will take it, so; if not, he's plain."

See also the notes on 128. 24–28 and 129. 33–35.

9 f. *perceiued . . . Loue*] Source: a passage borrowed from Painter and quoted more exactly at 43. 10 f. See 42. 27–43. 21 n.

16. *a poinct of*] I.e., "an instance of." Compare Greene's *Mamillia* (1583), Grosart, II, 30, "it were a poynt of meere folly to trust a friend in loue," and 76. 26, above.

19 f. *what . . . you*] Compare Gascoigne's poem in "The Adventures of Master F. J.," Cunliffe, I, 413, where the hero's mistress grants him, first, kisses, second, embraces, and—"What followed next, gesse you that know the trade." On such Pettie-like chaffing of the gentlewomen readers see 84. 5–13 n.

22. *pleased*] "Satisfied sexually"? Compare Gervase Markham and Lewis Machin, *The Dumb Knight* (1608), sig. B3, "He is euen . . . as waspish as an ill pleased bride the second morning."

38–131. 21. *And . . . you*] Rich derived the idea for the letter which may be punctuated, hence interpreted, two ways and some of his words from Nicholas Udall's *Ralph Roister Doister* (1567), *Chief Pre-Shakespearean Dramas*, ed. J. Q. Adams (Cambridge, Mass., 1924), p. 448 (my italics indicate words Rich echoes):

> Sorie to heare report of your good welfare.
> For (*as I heare say*) suche your *conditions* are
> That ye be worthie fauour of no liuing man.
> To be *abhorred* of euery honest man;
> *To be taken for* a woman enclined *to vice*;
> Nothing at all *to vertue* gyuing hir due price.
> Wherfore concerning mariage, ye are thought
> Suche a fine paragon, as nere honest man bought.
> And nowe by these presentes I do you *aduertise*
> That I am minded to marrie you in no wise.

How the letters become billet-doux when repunctuated may be seen in Udall, pp. 451 f., and at 137. 19–138. 2. Rich could also have found the letter in both its forms in Thomas Wilson's popular textbook *The Rule of Reason*, where it was first included in the third edition, 1553, fols. 66–67v.

131. 6 f. *as . . . Bridewell*] The deadliness of this insult was no doubt apparent to most Elizabethan readers, to whom the word *bridewell* had come to mean not merely the notorious prison for loose women but any prison for such culprits.

18 f. *enemie . . . vice*] A perversion of a stock euphuistic antithesis. Compare Greene's *Mamillia* (1593), Grosart II, 192, "He is . . . a protested foe to vice and a professed friend to vertue," and II, 200, "shee became such a foe to vice, and such a friend to vertue."

20. *in . . . forth*] "In giving a detailed account of you."

20 f. *will . . . you*] A commoner form of the proverb (Tilley, pp. 161 f.) was "Here I found you and here I leave you."

22–31. *This . . . reuengemente*] See 136. 18–20 n.

23. *sware . . . Beggers*] I.e., "made up her mind so firmly that no amount of begging from any source whatsoever could induce her to change it"? Compare Rich's *Don Simonides* (1584), sig. M1v, "*Sertorius* . . . Bedlem mad with anger . . . sweares by no Beggers he would be reuenged"; Nashe's *Have with You to Saffron-Walden* (1596), McKerrow, III, 89, "*Gabriell* . . . protests by no bugges he owes him not a dandiprat"; *George a Greene* (1599), *The Plays & Poems of Robert Greene*, ed. J. Churton Collins (Oxford, 1905), II, 189, "[George] by no beggers swore that we were traytours"; and Dekker's *The Wonderfull Yeare* (1603), Wilson, p. 12, "Onely the Souldier . . . swore by no beggers that now was the houre come for him to bestirre his stumps." See also the editorial comments of McKerrow, IV, 346; of Wilson, who paraphrases, p. 256, "to swear fiercely"; and of Collins, who explains, II, 369, "that is, swore by no mean people; the phrase is from the Romance, 'Hee swore by no beggars but by the lyfe of good King Richard.'"

32. *tenure*] I.e., "tenor."

34 f. *Maie . . . thee*] Source: a passage borrowed from Painter and quoted more precisely at 85. 11 f. See 85. 11–19 n.

132. 3. *fained, faunyng*] Read *fained faunyng*.

3 f. *O fained . . . dissimulation*] Source: Pettie's "Pygmalion's Friend," p. 232.

4–6. *what . . . woman*] Source: Pettie's "Pygmalion's Friend," p. 231. If Rich did not here echo Pettie so clearly, it would be hard to decide whether his source was Pettie's version or that of Gascoigne, who writes in "Don Bartholmew of Bathe," Cunliffe, I, 98:

> But that at last (alas) she was untrue,
> Which flinging fault, bicause it is not new,
> Nor seldome seene in kits of Cressides kind,
> I marvaile not, nor beare it much in mind.

Evidently borrowing from Pettie or Rich, Greene repeats the formula in *Mamillia* (1583), Grosart, II, 16, "[Florion] knew very well, that there was litle constancy in such kites of Cressids kind," and in the *Carde of Fancie* (1587), Grosart, IV, 132, "what curtesie is there to bee found in such Kites of Croesus [*read* Cressid's] kinde? Or what constancie is there to be hoped for in . . . Dames?" Compare also *A Gorgeous Gallery of Gallant Inventions*, ed. H. E. Rollins (Cambridge, Mass., 1926), p. 18,

> Thy fawning flattering wordes, which now full falce I finde,
> Perswades mee to content my selfe, and turne from *Cressids* kinde.

The most famous use of the phrase is of course Shakespeare's, in *Henry V*, II. i. 80 f.,

> Fetch forth the lazar kite of Cressid's kind,
> Doll Tearsheet, she by name.

28 f. *more coie . . . then*] Source: Pettie's "Scilla and Minos," p. 156.

35–37. *with . . . hope*] Source: Pettie's "Amphiaraus and Eriphile," pp. 91 f.

133. 5. *in . . . Mariage*] See 56. 23 n.

11–13. *once . . . man*] Compare *The Two Noble Kinsmen*, II. iv. 6 f.:

> What pushes are we wenches driven to [to get a man]
> When fifteen once has found us!

27–38. *Gentlewomen . . . perceiue*] On such imitations of Pettie's raillery see 84. 5–13 n.

36 f. *encountred*] Read *encountre.*

134. 10. *subtill Lawyer*] The adjective takes on more force when read in the light of a passage from Rich's *My Ladies Looking Glasse* (1616), sig. I1, "[Lawyers] haue such a number of subtill subtillties, that they do yet make more subtill by their subtill handling, that they be able to set the Lawes themselues togither by the eares."

23–25. *For . . . drosse*] Source: Pettie's "Alexius," pp. 261 f., a passage Rich may have had in his commonplace book since signs of it appear also in *Don Simonides* (1581), sig. R4, "Sith their [women's] firste creation, thei still shewed them selues to bee altogether brittell," and in *The Excellency of Good Women* (1613), sig. A4, "let vs examine their [women's] first creation, wherein is to be noted the substance whereof they were formed which was of the purified mettall of man." Such theorizing was of course traditional. See David Clapham's translation of Cornelius Agrippa, *A Treatise of the Nobility and Excellency of Womankind* (1542), sigs. B1v–B2, "A woman doth passe a man in the materiall substance of her creation. For she was not made of . . . the vyle clay or dyrte, as the man was, but of a matter purified and lyuely. . . . Furthermore . . . the woman . . . was onely made of god, full stedfast and perfite in all thinges," and Edward Gosynhill, *The Prayse of All Women* (*ca.* 1540), sig. B3, "[Women were created] Not of vyle erthe out of the lake/ But of a rybbe."

135. 4. *netified*] I.e., "made neat." *NED* quotes another example of this charming word—and the charming thought it develops—from Chapman's *Iliad*: "That which he addeth is onelie the worke of a woman, to netifie and polish."

12. *beguile . . . thoughtes*] Source: a passage borrowed from Painter and quoted more extensively at 49. 14. See 48. 34–49. 16 n.

17–28. *but . . . companions*] Rich borrowed this entertaining formula and many of the words (which I italicize in the source quoted below) from two passages in *Euphues: The Anatomy of Wit* (1578), Bond, I, 195, "if one bee harde in conceiuing, they pronounce him a dowlte, . . . if *merrye* a iester, if *sadde* a Sainct, if *full of wordes*, a sotte, if *without speach*, a Cypher"; "If he be *cleanly*, then terme they him *proude*, if meane *in apparel*, a slouen." Notice that Rich's "merrie," "sad," "talkatiue," and "silent" follow the same order as Lyly's "merry," "sad," "full of words," and "without speech." Lyly's model may have been "Egloga Septima" in Barnaby Googe's *Eglogs, Epytaphes, and Sonnettes* (1563) ed. E. Arber (London, 1871), pp. 60 f.; and Rich's "sheepe" (line 24) and "naught" (line 22) seem also to echo this poem by his friend Googe (see the italics which I supply below):

For yf they [women] show but gentle words
    you [men] thynke for loue they dye.
And yf they speake not whan you list,
    than strayght you say, they are hye.
And that they ar, disdainfull Dames.
    and yf they chaunce to talke.
Than cownt you them for chatring Pies
    whose tongs must alwayes walke.

And yf perhaps they do forbeare,
and Sylence chaunce to keepe,
Than tush, she is not for company,
she is but a symple *sheepe.*
And yf they beare good wyll to one,
then strayght are iudged *nought.*

Rich makes delightful use of the formula again at 146. 15–27. See also North's translation of *The Dial of Princes* (1568), fol. 111v, "If he speake, they saye he is a bragger. If he holde his peace, they saye he is a dissarde. If he laughe, they saye he is a foole. If he laughe not, thei say he is solempne"; Greene's *Mamillia* (1593), Grosart, II, 292, "If his young wife be merie she is immodest, if sober sullen, . . . if pleasant inconstant"; Deloney's *Thomas of Reading*, Mann, p. 217, "who doe sooner empeach their credite, then their husbands, charging them, if they doe but smile, that they are subtile; and if they doe but winke, they account them wiley, if sad of countenance, then sullen; if they bee froward, then they are counted shrewes: and sheepish if they bee gentle"; and *Much Ado about Nothing*, III. i. 59–67:

I never yet saw man,
How wise, how noble, young, how rarely featur'd,
But she would spell him backward. If fair-fac'd,
She would swear the gentleman should be her sister;
If black, why, Nature, drawing of an antic,
Made a foul blot; if tall, a lance ill-headed;
If low, an agate very vilely cut;
If speaking, why, a vane blown with all winds;
If silent, why, a block moved with none.

27. *cruell . . . Bugges*] Compare Greene's *Mamillia* (1593), Grosart, II, 261, "[Some men affirm] that they [women] bee . . . as cruell as Tygres, and what not?"

136. 14–17. *But . . . sake*] On such persiflage in the manner of Pettie see 84. 5–13 n.

18–20. *those . . . reuenged*] With her powerful lust for revenge (which Rich also dwells on above, 131. 22–31) compare the same passion which Falstaff's letters inspire in Mistress Page and Mistress Ford. In the course of a single scene Mistress Page says, "How shall I be reveng'd on him? for reveng'd I will be, as sure as his guts are made of puddings" (II. i. 30–32); then Mistress Ford, "How shall I be revenged on him? I think the best way were to entertain him with hope till the wicked fire of lust have melted him in his own grease" (II. i. 67–70); and again Mistress Page, "Let's be reveng'd on him" (II. i. 96 f.).

23–27. *he . . . will*] Compare Mistress Ford's speech, *The Merry Wives of Windsor*, IV. iv. 26 f.:

> Devise but how you'll use him [Falstaff] when he comes,
> And let us two devise to bring him thither.

38. (*Maister Doctor qþ*] Read *Maister Doctor* (*qþ*.

137. 9 f. *moste . . . countrey*] Compare Nashe's *Strange Newes*, McKerrow, I, 324, "the onely reasty iade in a country." McKerrow comments (IV, 192), "It may be remarked that in similar contexts the phrase 'in *a* country' was usual, where we now say 'in *the* country,'" and refers to other examples by Nashe, Greene, and Lodge.

11. *wright*] I.e., "writ," "written."

14. *No have?*] "No" was often thus used "in a rejoinder or retort having the form of a negative question" (*NED*).

36 f. *enemie . . . vice*] See the note on 131. 18 f.

138. 8 f. *misconsteryng of*] *NED* quotes one other example, from Greene's *Pandosto* (1588): "He then began to . . . misconsture of their too priuate familiarity."

12–140. 12. *my . . . hower*] Between this portion of the story and *The Merry Wives of Windsor* there are striking parallels. Like Mistress Dorothy, Mistress Ford pretends to be in mortal terror of her jealous husband and makes an appointment—by the clock—with her victim, at an hour when her husband is to be away from home. See II. ii. 83–96:

> *Quick.* Marry . . . [Mistress Ford] gives you to notify that her husband will be absence from his house between ten and eleven.
>
> *Fal.* Ten and eleven.
>
> *Quick.* Ay, forsooth . . . Master Ford her husband will be from home. Alas, the sweet woman leads an ill life with him! He's a very jealousy man. She leads a very frampold life with him, good heart!
>
> *Fal.* Ten and eleven. Woman, commend me to her. I will not fail her.

See also III. iii. 209 f., "Let him be sent for to-morrow eight o'clock" (the very hour Mistress Dorothy's doctor is bidden to arrive), and III. v. 46–48, Mistress Quickly to Falstaff, "[Mistress Ford] desires you once more to come to her, between eight and nine."

18. *requite. I*] Read *requite, I.*

37 f. *hym . . . eyes*] Source: Painter's "Two Gentlewomen of Venice," III, 154.

139. 24. *make . . . deliuer*] "Deliver without causing any trouble."

140. 18–141. 25. *sodainly . . . Male*] To this amusing scene there are, again, striking similarities in *The Merry Wives*, and in Shakespeare's text there appear to be even verbal echoes (to which my italics call attention). In the comedy Mistress Ford has received Falstaff at his appointed hour and is engaging him coyly in conversation when a servant interrupts to announce Mistress Page, who then bursts in, "sweating and blowing and looking wildly" (III. iii. 101–50):

Mrs. Page. O Mistress Ford, what have you done? You're sham'd, y'are overthrown, y'*are undone* for ever! . . .

Mrs. Ford. Why, *alas*! what's the matter?

Mrs. Page. Your husband's coming hither, woman, *with* all the officers in Windsor. . . . *You are undone!*

Mrs. Ford. 'Tis not so, I hope.

Mrs. Page. Pray heaven it be not . . . but if you have a *friend* here, *convey*, *convey* him out! . . .

Mrs. Ford. What shall I do? . . . I had rather than a thousand pound he were *out of the house.*

Mrs. Page. For shame! . . . Look, *here is a basket.* If he be of any reasonable stature, he may *creep in here.* . . .

Mrs. Ford. He's too big to go in there. What shall I do?

Fal. Let me see't, let me see't, O, let me see't!—I'll in, I'll in! . . . Help me away! Let me *creep in here.*

The echoes continue in Falstaff's report of the incident to Ford (III. v. 84–88) and in the second scene of surprisal (IV. ii. 42–75):

[*Fal.*] As good luck would have it, comes in one Mistress Page . . . and, in her *invention* and Ford's wive's distraction, they *convey'd* me into a buck-basket.

Mrs. Ford ['surprised' a second time with Falstaff]. *I am undone!* The knight is here. . . .

Fal. What shall I do? I'll *creep up* into the chimney. . . .

Mrs. Page. Creep into the kiln-hole. . . .

Mrs. Ford. He will seek there, on my word. Neither press, *coffer*, *chest*, *trunk*, well, vault, but he hath an abstract for the remembrance of. . . .
Fal. Good hearts, *devise* something.

21–23. *who . . . feare*] Compare *The Merry Wives of Windsor*, III. iii. 38–41:

[*Mrs. Ford.*] Mistress Page, remember your cue.
Mrs. Page. I warrant thee. If I do not act it, hiss me.

22. *was . . . plaie*] "Needed no instruction in how to act."

27. *readie . . . self*] Though "bewray" could mean "betray," I suspect Rich had in mind the less delicate meaning "befoul," to quote McKerrow's gloss on Nashe's use of the word (I, 319; V, 225): "I note that thou [Gabriel Harvey] beeing afraide of beraying thy selfe with writing, *wouldest faine bee a mute?*" In *Have with You to Saffron-Walden* (1596), III, 38, Nashe prints an illustration with the legend "The picture of Gabriell Haruey, as hee is readie to let fly vpon Aiax," and explains, "Those that bee so disposed to take a view of him . . . here let them behold his liuely counterfet . . . with his gowne cast off, vntrussing, and readie to beray himselfe, vpon the newes of the going in hand of my booke." See also *The Rare Triumphs of Love and Fortune* (1589), *A Select Collection of Old English Plays . . . Published by Robert Dodsley*, ed. W. C. Hazlitt, VI (London, 1874), 176, "Will you not give one leave to pull down his points? what, an a should his breeches beray?"

28. *crepte . . . bedde*] Probable source: Painter's "Philenio Sisterno," II, 21, where the hero, "seeing the daunger, wherein both he and the wife were . . . crept vnder the bed."

141. 29 f. *Male . . . Lawier*] Probable source: Painter's "Alexander di Medici," II, 414, where there are plans that a character "be trussed vp in a Maile and brought hither."

30–33. *liyng . . . laye*] Compare his plight with that of Falstaff crammed into the "buck-basket," III. v. 116–24.

34 f. *disguised . . . legges*] The gaberdine was "a long coat, worn loose or girdled, with long sleeves—a useful garment for soldiers, horsemen, or travellers. . . . Lesser folk—yeomen, mercers, fishmongers—and women of several classes of society wore gaberdines of tawny, medley, and other cloths" (Linthicum, p. 201). To the list of "lesser

folk" we may add porters, whose habitual garb, so this and a later passage (142. 7) indicate, was the gaberdine.

142. 7. *in . . . weede*] See the preceding note.

15–17. *beyng . . . backe*] Compare *The Merry Wives of Windsor*, IV. ii. 114–18:

> *1. Serv.* Come, come take it up.
> *2. Serv.* Pray heaven it be not full of knight again.
> *1. Serv.* I hope not; I had as lief bear so much lead.

32–34. *in . . . doe*] Compare Falstaff's terror, III. v. 103–11.

143. 2–10. *what . . . depart*] With the soldier's interrogation and irascible repetition of *ware* compare Ford's behavior under similar circumstances, III. iii. 161–69. Of the servants carrying the basket (and Falstaff) the "jealious rascally knave" inquires:

> How now? Whither bear you this?
> *Servant.* To the laundress forsooth.
> *Mrs. Ford.* Why, what have you to do whither they bear it? You were best meddle with buck-washing!
> *Ford.* Buck? I would I could wash myself of the buck! Buck, buck, buck! Ay, buck! I warrant you, buck!

17 f. *backe so surely, that*] Read probably *backe, so surely that.*

38. *straight*] I.e. "straightway."

144. 8. *tourned . . . Ladder*] Those condemned to hanging were made to climb the ladder, i.e., the steps to the gallows, and then "turned off."

9 f. *long . . . maze*] Compare Evans on Mother Prat of Brainford, *The Merry Wives of Windsor*, IV. ii. 203–205: "I like not when a oman has a great peard. I spy a great peard under his muffler."

14 f. *haste . . . me*] Probably proverbial. Compare *Mankind* (*ca.* 1450), quoted in *NED* (under *mock*, *v.* 1), "Haue ye non other man to moke, but euer me?" and *Jack Juggler* (1562), ed. E. L. Smart and Sir Walter Greg, Malone Society Reprints (London, 1933), line 923, "Why canst thou fynde no man to moke but mee?"

16. *set . . . edge*] The idiom evidently means "whet my appetite." See 123. 34.

20. *be bumbasted*] Adding the intensifying prefix "be" to "bum-

basted," or "thrashed thoroughly," strikingly underlines the severity of the doctor's punishment.

21 f. *he . . . Eurinall*] Doubtless a great misfortune for a doctor, who would no longer be able to "cast the waters" of his patients and thus would be professionally incapacitated. This spelling of "urinal" is not listed in *NED.* With the doctor's fate compare Evans' threatened treatment of Doctor Caius, *The Merry Wives of Windsor*, III. i. 14, 90 f.: "I will knog his urinals about his knave's costard"; "I will knog your urinals about your knave's cogscomb."

33. *good fellowe*] Obviously ironical. In a note on the expression McKerrow quotes (IV, 440) Heywood's *1 Edward IV*, sig. E4, "*King Ed.*: Why, dost thou not love a good fellow? *Hobs*: No, good fellows be thieves."

145. 13. *with . . . &c.*] Rich is less subtle in *Don Simonides* (1581), sig. Q2v. "[My mistress] rewarded me with kisses, sometymes with bed pleasures."

34. *kept . . . after*] There is an amusing parallel between his fate and that of two ministers in Ireland, one of whom, Rich reports in his "Remembrances of the State of Ireland" (1612), ed. C. L. Falkiner, *Proceedings of the Royal Irish Academy*, XXVI (1906), 140, interfered with a Roman Catholic burial service in Wexford and "was beaten that he kept hys bed many monethes after. And now very lately a mynyster at Waterford comynge to churche to haue preched was ther assaulted & so beaten that he kept hys bed a long tyme after." Again using the same expressions he originally devised as fiction, Rich repeats as fact the stories of the unfortunate Anglican priests in Ireland in his "Anothomy of Ireland" (1615), ed. E. M. Hinton, *PMLA*, LV (1940), 85.

35. *Sparmaceti*] "A fatty substance . . . found in the head of the sperm-whale . . . used largely in various medicinal preparations" (*NED*). See Hotspur's celebrated speech in *1 Henry IV*, I. iii. 57 f., "And telling me the sovereignest thing on earth/ Was parmacity for an inward bruise."

35 f. *suche . . . bruse*] Including perhaps "A wonderfull drinke agaynst brusings" that Thomas Lupton describes in *A Thousand Notable Things* (1595), sig. Z1: "Take Egremonye, Bettony, Sage, Planten, Iuy leaues, Roseparslie, stamp them together, and mixe Wine thereto: giue the patient it often to drinke, till he be whole. A true and tryed

medicine." Lupton recommends another prescription, sig. B1v: "The iuce of Mullen leaues (of some called Hedgetaper, and of some Longworte,) put to any parte that is brused . . . and the stamped leaues therof, then put vpon the same, a tyed fast on with a cloth: if you let it lye so a whole day and a night vnremoued, it will heale finely."

38–146. 2. *de-serued,*] Read *de-serued*).

146. 15–27. *if . . . owne*] A variation of a formula borrowed from Lyly's *Euphues: The Anatomy of Wit.* See 135. 17–28 n.

29. *her. In*] Read *her, in.*

31. *pinioned*] Compare *The Merry Wives of Windsor,* IV. ii. 127–29: "*Page.* Why, this passes, Master Ford! You are not to go loose any longer; you must be pinion'd."

34. *Smocke*] For a description and photograph of the sixteenth-century smock, which served as underwear and sleeping gown, see Linthicum, p. 189 and opposite p. 190.

37. *tied . . . house*] Standard Elizabethan treatment of lunatics. Compare Malvolio's fate, *Twelfth Night,* III. iv. 131–49, and Marston's *What You Will* (1607), sig. G3v, "Shut the windowes, darken the roome . . . the fellow is madde, hee . . . talkes idly, lunatique."

147. 9–16. *criyng . . . Brimstone*] Compare *The Comedy of Errors,* V. i. 182 f., where Antipholus, declared insane by his wife, "cries for you and vows, if he can take you,/ To scorch your face and to disfigure you."

12. *Idle speeches*] Compare *The Comedy of Errors,* IV. iv. 132: "*Luc.* God help poor [mad] souls! How idly do they talk!"

13. *call vpon God*] So those possessed by the devil and rendered insane were generally urged to do. See King James's *Dæmonologie* (1597), ed. G. B. Harrison (London, 1924), p. 72, "the casting out of Deuilles, is by the vertue of fasting and prayer, and in-calling of the name of God," and *The Merry Wives of Windsor,* IV. ii. 130 f., 162 f., "*Evans.* Why, this is lunatics! This is mad as a mad dog! . . . Master Ford, you must pray, and not follow the imaginations of your own heart."

148. 25. *a Gentilman*] In Cinthio a "nobil uomo" (II, 46). The scholar in the story is similarly reduced in rank (see 150. 11 n.). Why these demotions I do not know, unless Rich feared that his characters might otherwise suggest some powerful English noblemen.

26. *Gonsales*] Rich probably considered this eminently Spanish

name more appropriate for a citizen of Seville than Consalvo, as it is in the original. He was no doubt ignorant that in Spanish Gonsales is a patronymic, not a Christian name.

26–149. 4. *who . . . reason*] A more adequate preparation for the shocking career which follows than the brief, euphemistic passage upon which it is based, "il quale più lascivo e più mutabile era, che a nobil uomo non era convenevole" (II, 46).

29 f. *follie. Yet*] Read *follie, yet.*

149. 7–9. *although . . . kinswoman*] Not in Cinthio.

13. *Consales*] Read *Gonsales.* The *C* for *G*, which occurs again at 152. 20, may be Rich's slip, not the compositor's. Since the name in Cinthio is Consalvo, it would have been easy for Rich absent-mindedly to write "Consales" for "Gonsales."

13 f. *followyng . . . humour*] Not in Cinthio. The addition further underlines Gonsales' lustful disposition, described at 148. 26–149. 4 and mentioned again at 163. 37 f.

16. *commoditie or quiet*] In Cinthio a single word, "giovevole" (II, 46).

18 f. *better . . . goodes*] Compare Greene's *Mamillia* (1593), Grosart, II, 108, "rather wishing . . . to marrye my daughter to a man, then to money," and II, 269, "determined . . . to marrie her rather to a man than to monie."

21–25. *who . . . doen*] These sermonic comments are not in Cinthio.

26–34. *whiche . . . naughtinesse*] Another brief homily without counterpart in Cinthio.

150. 3–5. *as dissolute . . . profession*] A voracious expansion of "femina dissoluta ed avida del guadagno" (II, 46).

7. *with . . . full*] A racier phrase than "con copia di danari" (II, 46).

11. *a Scholer*] In Cinthio his rank is specified—"uno scolare . . . di nobil casa" (II, 46). See 148. 25 n.

25 f. *but . . . hedpeece*] An engaging addition to the original, though inconsistent with the craft Gonsales later displays, particularly at 156. 34 f. and 157. 13–15.

35. *labour loste*] The proverb has no counterpart in Cinthio.

38. *mother Elenour*] Probably named after the principal character

in Skelton's "The Tunning of Elynour Rumming," whose proclivities she shares, so it presently transpires. In *The Elizabethan Stage* (Oxford, 1923), IV, 402, Sir E. K. Chambers mentions a lost comedy entitled *Mother Rumming*, and remarks "Elinor Rumming . . . might well have made a play-theme." In Cinthio the character is introduced simply as "una vecchia" (II, 46).

151. 2. *the Spanishe Celestina*] Not in Cinthio, the reference is to Fernando de Rojas' *Celestina*, part of which John Rastell adapted in the interlude *Calisto and Melibœa* (1525), and which James Mabbe translated as *The Spanish Bawd, Represented in Celestina* (1631). Rich mentions Rastell by name in *The True Report of a Late Practise Enterprised by a Papist* (1582), sig. E3.

2–17. *suche . . . likewise*] The author of the Scottish comedy *Philotus* (1603), who took his plot from Rich's eighth tale, borrows from the sixth this panderess and her technique. See *Philotus*, Mill, pp. 105–14.

15 f. *strike . . . scabberde*] The proverb (Smith, p. 171) has no counterpart in Cinthio.

19. *as . . . doe*] This moral pronouncement has no counterpart in Cinthio.

34–36. *because . . . handes*] These hard, practical reasons for being faithful have no counterpart in the Italian. Only the English Agatha is a good woman and a good economist as well.

152. 2–11. *shewyng . . . practises*] This noble reaction the author of the comedy *Philotus* (1603) seized upon and set in the middle of a plot borrowed from Rich's eighth tale. The heroine of the play, also beset by panderly blandishments, loftily asserts (Mill, p. 114):

all is bot vaine ye seik,
To mee of sik maters to speik,
Your purpois is not worth ane leik,
I will heir you na mair:
Mark Dame, and this is all and sum,
If euer ye this earand cum,
Or of your head I heir ane mum,
Ye sall repent it sair.

5. *reprehend and chide*] In Cinthio a single word, "riprendere" (II, 47). The wisdom of attaching to "reprehend" a simple synonym is

made apparent by a bit of dialogue from *Love's Labour's Lost*, I. i. 182–85:

> *Dull.* Which is the Duke's own person?
> *Ber.* This, fellow. What wouldst?
> *Dull.* I myself reprehend his own person, for I am
> his Grace's farborough.

"Reprehend" is commonly misused "by ignorant speakers for 'represent' and 'apprehend'" (*NED*).

10 f. *how . . . practises*] The racy, colloquial flavor of this passage is lacking in the original "quanto simili ragionamenti le fossero spiacevoli" (II, 47).

12. *This olde hag*] A very spirited rendering of "la vecchia" (II, 47).

12 f. *hauyng . . . sope*] The phrase, which has no counterpart in Cinthio, is proverbial, according to Apperson, who paraphrases (p. 668), "having been well scolded." Compare the proverb "To give one's head for the washing" (Smith, p. 515) and McKerrow's note, IV, 397, "The phrase was not uncommon in the sense of 'submit to insult.'"

14 f. *and . . . mouth*] Not in Cinthio.

17–19. *there . . . mollified*] Compare Thomas Heywood, *A Woman Killed with Kindness* (1607), III. i. 66 f., ed. Katherine L. Bates (New York, 1917), p. 44 (my italics): "Thy *teares* are of no force to *mollifie*/ This *flinty* man."

20. *Consales*] Read *Gonsales.* See 149. 13 n.

22 f. *and . . . himself*] Not in Cinthio.

29–31. *and . . . all*] Not in Cinthio.

32 f. *he . . . worlde*] An effective expansion of "le darebbe morte" (II, 47).

153. 6–8. *Whiche . . . tende*] The sinister, ulterior motives here described have no counterpart in Cinthio. The phraseology of "wherevnto that talke . . . would tende" is highly characteristic of Rich. Compare "whereto tendeth those vowes" (83. 21), "whereto those lookes did tende" (122. 34), "whereto these speeches pretended" (126. 27 f.), and "wherevnto your speeches doeth tende" (129. 18).

11. *brake his minde*] An amusing rendering of the simple "disse" (II, 47) into a common Elizabethan idiom.

13. *Alonso*] Risti in the original. The scholar, like Gonsales, is rechristened with an eminently Spanish name. Rich was doubtless unaware that Risti, or Rystis, means "Liberator" in Greek, and that Cinthio with great appropriateness thus called the man who later rescues Agatha from the tomb. Though Rich retains the names Agatha and Aselgia, the fact that in Greek they signify "Virtuous" and "Unchaste" also probably escaped him. On Cinthio's preciosity and pedantry in naming his characters (the most famous is Disdemona, from the Greek *dys daimôn*, "Unhappy") see Henri Hauvette, *La Morte vivante* (Paris, 1933), p. 32.

19–21. *and . . . worlde*] Not in Cinthio.

27–154. 17. *Assuryng . . . owne*] This eloquent if perverted appeal to friendship, Elizabethan style, is largely an addition to the original, though a few sentences and phrases from Cinthio (II, 48) are woven into it.

30. *come by to*] Read perhaps *come to* with *C*.

36 f. *a this good while*] Perhaps omit *this* with *B* and *C*. Cinthio provides no clue to the correct reading.

154. 19. *stoode . . . requeste*] Not in Cinthio, the addition smacks of a stage direction.

25. *compassions*] Read probably *compositions* to conform with "composition" at 155. 33. *NED* lists "compassioun" used erroneously for "composition." Collier lets "compassions" stand in his edition, but suggests in *A Bibliographical and Critical Account of the Rarest Books in the English Language* (London, 1866), III, 304, "Here 'compassions' ought to be *confections*."

27. *any Phisition*] An addition to Cinthio's "non . . . alcuno" (II, 48) that magnifies the potency of the feat.

31 f. *and . . . theim*] Not in Cinthio.

35 f. *consideryng . . . offences*] A legal detail with no counterpart in Cinthio.

155. 4. (*assured*)] Why the parentheses, unless perhaps for emphasis, I cannot say.

10. *and . . . freendship*] Not in Cinthio.

11 f. *straine . . . conscience*] More effective than Cinthio's "si partisse dall'onesto" (II, 48).

22–25. *he assured . . . deuised*] This delightfully expanded version of "gli prometteva egli di non dir mai che da lui avesse avuto il veleno" (II, 48) is rhetorically effective. The figure of speech "whilest he had breathe" adds force to the "non . . . mai."

26 f. *seemyng . . . petition*] Another addition to the original which recalls a stage direction.

30. *or . . . cõscience*] Not in Cinthio.

33 f. *composition of mixture*] Collier's reading, *composition or mixture*, is preferable in the light of Cinthio's "mescolanza" (II, 48) and Rich's habit of thus doubling single words in the source and linking a fairly complicated word with a simple synonym, as at 94. 31, 118. 29, 149. 16, 152. 5, and 152. 19. Rich's doublet rather than Cinthio's single word seems to have suggested the "compound mixture" in *How a Man May Chuse a Good Wife from a Bad* (Swaen, line 1354).

34–37. *pouders . . . dedde*] An expansion of "polvere da far talmente dormire, ch'altri sarebbe giudicato morto" (II, 48), which is reminiscent of certain details in Painter's "Rhomeo and Juletta," one of Rich's favorite sources.

37. *starke dedde*] In Cinthio the single word "morto" (II, 48). Compare Hoby's "fell starke dead" for Castiglione's "cadde morta," quoted by F. O. Matthiessen, *Translation: An Elizabethan Art* (Cambridge, Mass., 1931), p. 43.

156. 9 f. *verie . . . againe*] These additions greatly intensify the original, "Così gli promise Consalvo di fare" (II, 49).

12. *caste*] An athletic version of "ponesse gentilmente" (II, 49).

13 f. *without . . . tormente*] Livelier than Cinthio's "così acconciamente" (II, 49).

19 f. *she . . . seldome*] Echoed in *How a Man May Chuse a Good Wife from a Bad:* "Come not too neare me, till I call thee wife./ And that will be but sildome" (Swaen, lines 280 f.).

20 f. *since . . . str[u]mpet*] The clause and the explanation of Gonsales' neglect delicately implied in it are not in Cinthio.

21–23. *within . . . sencelesse*] Not a literal rendering of "non passò l'ora, che la prese così profondo sonno, che pareva veramente morta" (II, 49). Rich's "operation" and "sencelesse," which have no counterpart in Cinthio, seem to be repeated in the "cold and senceles sleepe,/ Of . . . approued operation" of which Master Arthur speaks in *How a Man May Chuse a Good Wife from a Bad* (Swaen, lines 1285 f.).

25–29. *liying . . . dedde*] An admirably expanded version of "stando tuttavia colla mente travagliata, aspettò con grandissimo desiderio il giorno, tenendo certo di ritrovare la moglie morta" (II, 49). Though perhaps not a masterpiece of insight and perspicacity, the English nevertheless indicates more adequately than the Italian the state of mind of a man who has poisoned his wife at dinner.

34 f. *makyng . . . bedde*] Not in Cinthio. The histrionic ability and craft Gonsales displays here, at 157. 13–15, and at 157. 28 f. are inconsistent with the simple-mindedness with which Rich, not Cinthio, endows him at 150. 25 f.

157. 5 f. *laied . . . awake*] A pleasingly rowdy version of "le pose le mani addosso, e toccandola gentilmente, le disse: Levatevi, madonna" (II, 49).

8. *that*] I.e., the "shagge" and the maid's spoken injunction.

9–11. *she . . . foote. The . . . hym*] Read *she . . . foote, the . . . hym* to conform with the reading in the source: "non rispondendo la donna, nè movendosi punto, se n'andò [la Giovane] a Consalvo, & dissegli . . ." (II, 49).

13–15. *But . . . speeche*] Not in Cinthio. See the note on 156. 34 f.

28 f. *to dissemble . . . lament*] Not in Cinthio. See the note on 156. 34 f.

34. *the Phisition*] The restraint of this version of "quanti medici erano in Siviglia" (II, 50) is unwonted; Rich's usual method is to add to, not subtract from, the original.

158. 4 f. *he . . . sorte*] Not in Cinthio. See the note on 156. 34 f.

10 f. *Frierie*] Cinthio specifies the Roman Catholic order—"frati dell' Osservanza" (II, 50).

17. *blinde Lanterns*] After Cinthio's "lanterna cieca" (II, 50), though the usual Elizabethan phrase was "dark lantern." Rich's is the only example listed in *NED*, which explains, "A lantern with a slide or arrangement by which the light can be concealed." These contrivances were "of sinister association" for Elizabethans, and there was "a vulgar error that their use was unlawful," according to Lucas, II, 153.

17 f. *because . . . liste*] Not in Cinthio.

20. *instrumentes of iron*] A prudent version of the vague "alcune cose" (II, 50). Alonso's "instruments" may have included a crow-

bar, a mattock, and a spade—if Friar Laurence's "iron crow" (V. ii. 21) and "mattock and . . . spade" (V. iii. 185) and Romeo's "mattock and . . . wrenching iron" (V. iii. 22) provide a reliable indication of the tools usually employed by tomb-breakers.

21 f. *and hauyng . . . surely*] A characteristically practical addition to the original, "ed entrato in esso [il sepolcro] . . ." (II, 50).

23 f. *minding . . . was*] Not in Cinthio.

32. *whether I come*] Read *whether I came* to conform with the source, "son io qui venuto" (II, 50).

37–159. 2. *hopyng . . . been*] Something much like this hope for a spiritual honeymoon, which is Rich's addition to Cinthio, reappears in *How a Man May Chuse a Good Wife from a Bad* (1602), and is one indication that the comedy is based on the English rather than the Italian version. In the play Alonso's counterpart, entering the sepulcher, explains (Swaen, lines 1908–12):

> My comming is with no intent of sinne,
> Or to defile the bodie of the dead,
> But rather to take my last farewell of her,
> Or languishing and dying by her side,
> My ayrie soule post after hers to heauen.

159. 22. *muche, as though*] Read *muche as, though.*

23. *hym. I*] Read *hym, I.*

36. *affectuall*] Quoted in *NED* and defined as "earnest"; but its counterpart in the source is "efficaci" (II, 51), i.e., "effective."

160. 27 f. *and . . . life*] Not in Cinthio.

33 f. *for . . . quicke*] Far more dramatic than the original "chè io voglio più tosto ricever morte" (II, 51).

161. 7–9. *though . . . housbande*] Not in Cinthio.

18. *to . . . familie*] Not in Cinthio, this hint that Gonsales had children is not elsewhere pursued.

18 f. *that honest Dame*] A touch of irony without counterpart in Cinthio.

19 f. *and made . . . had*] Not in Cinthio.

23 f. *Neuerthelesse . . . peace*] Not in Cinthio.

26. *through . . . iudgement*] Not in Cinthio. The addition is very characteristic of Rich, who continually thus acknowledges the

power of Providence, as at 16. 24, 46. 31 f., 72. 37 f., 109. 2 f., 100. 32 f., and 100. 36. The author of *How a Man May Chuse a Good Wife from a Bad*, of which "Agatha" is the source, seems to echo Rich's addition when Gonsales' counterpart in the comedy, being abused by his new wife, exclaims, "I had a wife would not haue vsde me so,/ But God is iust" (Swaen, lines 2219 f.).

26. *ioly*] Probably "jolly" in the sense of "wanton," though it may be simply ironical—"fine," "pretty."

28. *was . . . diet*] An imaginative version of "essendo costei usa non ad un uomo" (II, 52).

30. *straightnes*] I.e., "straitness"—Cinthio's "diligenza" (II, 52).

37–162. 3. *Gonsales . . . Strumpet*] The passage may have suggested the title of *How a Man May Chuse a Good Wife from a Bad*, the comedy based on this story.

162. 5. *aunsweryng hym thawartly*] An eminently Elizabethan version of "rispondendogli . . . orgogliosamente" (II, 52). "Thawartly" is a variant of "thwartly," i.e. "perversely."

6–10. *haue . . . other?*] These most effective rhetorical questions are based on declarative sentences in Cinthio, II, 52. Philemon Holland, "the translator general in his age," was similarly given to turning statements into questions. See F. O. Matthiessen, *Translation: An Elizabethan Art* (Cambridge, Mass., 1931), p. 186.

6 f. *thou naughtie packe*] A very spirited rendering of "Scellerata" (II, 52). The two words "naughty" and "pack" were almost inseparable in Elizabethan English, according to *NED* which gives many examples (under *pack*) and quotes a charming passage from Hyrde's translation of Vives' *Instruction of a Christen Woman* (1557): "Calle hir a naughtie packe: withe that one woorde thou haste taken all from hir, and haste lefte hir bare and foule."

11 f. *and . . . them*] Not in Cinthio, this addition reminds one of Rich's activities as an informer.

14–16. *such . . . withall*] I agree with Baskervill (*PMLA*, XXIV [1909], 712) that this definition of the functions of a "Ribalde," which has no counterpart in Cinthio, suggested the character of the contemptible Brabo in *How a Man May Chuse a Good Wife from a Bad*, the comedy based on "Agatha."

23–33. *Whervpon . . . hed*] Here Rich has rearranged the order of the original. After Gonsales is apprehended, his trial is interrupted in Cinthio (II, 52 f.), who returns to the scholar and Agatha before Gonsales can be convicted and sentenced. By relegating the former to the succeeding paragraph, Rich allows the trial and sentencing, in which the reader is most interested at the moment anyhow, to proceed uninterrupted.

24–29. *examinations . . . flatly*] Compare *How a Man May Chuse a Good Wife from a Bad*, where the judge says, "Here comes your sonne accused, & your wife the accuser: stand forth both. *Hugh* be readie with your pen and Inke to take their examinations and confessions" (Swaen, lines 2533–36).

25–29. *being . . . flatly*] Not in Cinthio.

27 f. *the . . . him*] This addition to the original is an interesting echo of another of the "Italian Histories." Compare "the cruell tormentes, that I knowe this Infidell hath prepared for me" (117. 9 f.), from Cinthio's "fieri supplicii, che so che mi apparecchierà questo crudele" (I, 304).

163. 13–18. *Sir . . . staied*] This dramatic utterance becomes very creditable blank verse in *How a Man May Chuse a Good Wife from a Bad*, where Agatha's counterpart informs the justice (Swaen, lines 2654–56):

> This man is cõdemd for poysoning of his wife,
> His poysoned wife yet liues, and I am she:
> And therefore iustly I release his bands.

19. *confession is*] Read perhaps *confession and is.* The Italian is here so freely rendered that it is no help in establishing the reading. Cinthio writes, "però non lasciate che proceda più oltre la sentenza data da voi, essendo ella, come chiaramente potete vedere, ingiustissima" (II, 53).

24 f. *or some . . . likenesse*] Not in Cinthio. Compare "[Flanius] thought assuredly that hym self had been deceiued by some Deuill or spirite, that had taken vpon hym the likenesse of Emelia" (198. 15–17).

26. *and was . . . pale*] Not in Cinthio.

37 f. *disordinate . . . iudgement*] Not in Cinthio. The addition is

consistent with those underlining this element in Gonsales' character at 148. 26–149. 4 and 149. 13 f.

164. 5. *caused . . . staied*] Not in Cinthio.

6 f. *who . . . Sciuille*] Not in Cinthio.

28. *any other passion, for any miserie*] Read *or* instead of *for* to clarify an otherwise badly confused passage, which is a very free rendering of "tutte le ingiurie" (II, 53).

165. 6–10. *But . . . others*] This version of "Ma ti giuro bene, che se mai mi venirà alle orecchie, che tu meno che amorevolmente tratti ti farò provare quanto io sappia punire così fatti delitti" (II, 54) reflects a knowledge of Painter's "Alexander di Medici" (my italics): "swearing once agayne before thee, that if *I vnderstand*, thou *vse* her *otherwise*, than a Wyfe ought to bee of hir husband, I will deale sutch punishment . . . ouer thee, as *all men* in time to come *shal take* example" (II, 427).

14. *baggage strumpette*] A spirited rendering of "meretrice" (II, 54).

16 22. *chaste . . . woman*] This pious finale seems to be echoed in *How a Man May Chuse a Good Wife from a Bad* (Swaen, lines 2268–70):

> Wonder of women: why hark you M. *Arthur*,
> What is your wife a woman or a Saint?
> A wife, or some bright Angell come from heauen?

18. *in maner*] I.e., "so to speak." See 103. 30 n.

166. 19 f. *broyles, Brabbles*] Compare *Henry V*, IV. viii. 68 f.: "I pray you to serve God, and keep you out of prawls, and prabbles."

21. *how kingdomes*] Read *how many kingdomes* to conform with "how many troubles," "how many Countries," "How many Cities," "how many Tounes," and "how many mischeefes" (lines 18 f., 22, 23, 24, 25 f.).

167. 23 f. *Ile of Candy*] By "Candy" "for the most part the Elizabethans mean . . . the whole island," though Shakespeare uses it correctly (*Twelfth Night*, V. i. 64) to designate the town, not the island, of Crete (Sugden, p. 96).

31 f. *Bathes . . . Oyntmentes*] Compare Thomas Lupton, *A Thousand Notable Things* (1595), sig. H2: "Many haue beene helped that haue had fowle and leprous faces, onely with the washing of the same

with distilled water of Strawberries: the Strawberries first put into a close glasse, and so putrified in Horse dung."

168. 6. *Florella*] Compare Florilla, the name of the Puritan wife in Chapman's *A Humorous Day's Mirth* (1597) and Florello in *Die Tugend- und Liebesstreit* (acted 1608), of which the second tale in the *Farewell* is the source (see pp. xliii f., above).

15–17. *Aramanthus . . . birthe*] Compare *Cymbeline*, III. iii. 82–84:

> [Cymbeline's sons] think they are mine, and though train'd up thus meanly
> I' th' cave wherein they bow, their thoughts do hit
> The roofs of palaces.

19–22. *shewed . . . charge*] Here Rich appears to echo a principal source for this tale, Cinthio's Decade I, Novel 1, *Gli Hecatommithi*, I, 156 (my italics), "[Avventuroso] *in poco spazio di tempo nelle* cose della guerra *divenne così esperto e così valoroso*, *ch'*essendo morto il *capitano* di que' soldati, fu . . . eletto in luogo del capitano."

20. *so expert, that, that Captaine*] Read the first *that* with *so*, the second with *Captaine*.

30. *the greate Turke*] The Sultan of Turkey was commonly so called. Compare "the Great Khan" and "the Great Mogul."

170. 5. *spoiled . . . aboute her*] Compare *The Two Gentlemen of Verona*, IV. i. 3: "*p. Out*[*law to Valentine*]. Stand, sir, and throw us that you have about ye!"

16–21. *to . . . Cooke*] Compare *Cymbeline*, IV. ii. 164, "You and Fidele play the cooks," and IV. ii. 298 f.,

> [*Imo.*] For so I thought I was a cave-keeper
> And cook to honest creatures.

171. 22. *premisses*] "Previous events."

35 f. *ioyne . . . lincke*]. Compare Pettie, p. 127, "enter into league and amitie with." Closer to Rich's version than to Pettie's are two passages by Greene: "linked . . . in the perfect league of amitie" (*Mamillia* [1593], Grosart, II, 153), and "lincked togither in the league of amitie" (*The Myrrour of Modestie* [1584], III, 13). Rich gives a variation of the phrase at 124. 29.

172. 9 f. *Pallace of purpose, verie richely furnished*] Read probably

Pallace, of purpose verie richely furnished—i.e., "purposely furnished very elegantly (for the occasion)."

35. *discourse vttered, with*] Read probably *discourse, vttered with.*

173. 4. *more*] Often used in Elizabethan account books and legal documents to mean "in addition to what has already been specified."

6. *president*] I.e., "precedent," "sign," "earnest," "indication."

8–10. *to . . . Frankes*] If a more modest sum in pounds were substituted for "tenne thousande Frankes," this item might have been drawn from any well-to-do Elizabethan's will, where a clause remembering the poor was often included as a matter of course. See for examples C. J. Sisson, *Thomas Lodge and Other Elizabethans* (Cambridge, Mass., 1933), pp. 118 f., 123.

26. *might . . . bandes*] Source: Belleforest's Story 79, *Histoires tragiques*, IV (Lyons, 1616), 829, where the ambassador observes that a king "conduisant vne grande armee soit conduit au tombeau par les bandes qui luy obeyssent."

31–174. 4. *The . . . Corse*] These obsequies bear an amusing relationship to "An Epitaph vpon the death of sir William Drury," a poem by Rich published in the 1580 edition of *The Paradise of Dainty Devices.* According to Rich's main source for "Aramanthus," Belleforest's *Histoires tragiques*, IV (Lyons, 1616), 831, the Lunigians, agreeing to give Hadding a Christian burial, deck themselves in mourning clothes to receive the funeral cortege; then (my italics) "*quand ce vint le lendemain*, on voit les troupes *armee descendre* en terre . . . & *les enseignes ployees, les picquiers trainans leur bois.*" Compare both Rich's passage and its source with "An Epitaph," Rollins, p. 122, where "Report" is seen arrayed (like Belleforest's Lunigians and Rich's Tolosians) "in mourning weed" and where (my italics)

> Then might I see, a warlik crew appeare,
> Came *marching* on *with weapons traylde on ground*,
> Their outward *show* bewrayde their inward cheare,
> Their droms and tromps did yeeld a dolefull sound,
> They *marched* thus in sad and *solemne* sort,
> As men amasde to heare this late Report.

Notice that "Then might I see, a warlik crew" recalls Belleforest's "on voit les troupes," and "weapons traylde on ground" his "armee descendre en terre." In the course of a long career in the army Rich had doubtless become familiar with military etiquette at funerals, and he may have been himself a mourner when Drury was buried in St. Patrick's, Dublin. But, regardless of what he had seen, it is obvious that the rites for Hadding in Luny and for the Turk in Tolosia were important precedents for those of Sir William. Compare *Coriolanus*, V. vi. 148–51:

> Take him up.
> Help three o' th' chiefest soldiers; I'll be one.
> Beat thou the drum that it speak mournfully.
> Trail your steel pikes.

32. *put in vre*] I.e., "put into practice or performance," a very common phrase.

174. 20 f. *scantled*] I.e., "stinted."

175. 21. *cheare. She*] Read probably *cheare, she.*

22 f. *thrustyng . . . sucke*] For a discussion of this ancient theme, "Roman Charity," see pp. 347 f., below.

37. *Sware by Mahounde*] I.e., "by Mohammed," often vaguely imagined to be a god and so worshiped. Compare Sir John Harington, *Orlando Furioso* (1591), XVI. liv. 125, "By Macon [Mahound] . . . he doth sweare," and *The Faerie Queene* (1596), VI. vii. 47, "the Carle . . . oftentimes by Turmagant and Mahound swore."

176. 8–12. *duetie . . . Childe*] See the note on 45. 24 f.

17. *in . . . teeth*] I.e., "in defiance of Fortune." Source: Painter's "A Lady of Bohemia," III, 198, quoted more extensively at 48. 7–28. See the note on 48. 26 f.

177. 24. *perswade . . . truth*] See 83. 20 n.

26. *minister release*] Read probably *minister releafe* to conform with "minister releef" (31. 38), "minister suche releefe" (96. 9 f.), "ministered suche releef" (170. 16 f.), and "minister releef" (191. 7 f.).

178. 11–14. *Tantalus . . . Titias*] This array inspired a passage in the comedy *Philotus* (1603), of which Rich's eighth tale is the principal source. Observe the echo of "restlesse stone" in the Scottish verse (Mill, p. 122):

> Releiue your Sysiphus of his restles stane:
> Your Titius breist that dois full ryfely bleid,
> Grant grace thairto, befoir the grip be gane:
> Cum stanche the thrist of Tantalus anone.

11–15. *But . . . welle*] Source: Golding's translation of Ovid (1567), which was also useful to Rich in his eighth story. See *Shakespeare's Ovid Being Arthur Golding's Translation of the Metamorphoses*, ed. W. H. D. Rouse (London, 1904), pp. 92 f., lines 553 f., 565–74, and p. 349, below. Many of the references to the illustrious tormented I have seen appear to echo the passage in Golding which attracted Rich, and which in popularity must have been on a par with Gascoigne's "The Arraignment of a Lover" (see 127. 11–19 n.) if one may judge from the following examples: Lodowick Lloyd, *The Pilgrimage of Princes* (1573), sig. Q1v, "*Ixion* for his telling of tales vppon *Iuno*, is no lesse tormented in turnyng of his wheele in Hell, than is *Sisiphus* in rowlyng of his stone, or *Danaus* daughters in fillyng of their emptie Tubbes. The paine of *Prometheus* in *Caucasus*, the punishment of *Titius* is duely appoynted"; H. C., *The Forrest of Fancy* (1579), sig. M4,

> How *Sisiphus* dowth rowle the restlesse stone,
> which to the top attaind, turnes back againe,
> How silly *Titius* making mestful mone,
> Unto a Rock fast tyde, doth stil sustaine, . . .
> How *Tantalus* amidst the streame that standes,
> Up to the chin, is like for drouth to dye, . . .
> How *Danaus* daughters doe themselues apply,
> with pailes that bottomes want, a tubbe to fill;

Brian Melbancke, *Philotimus* (1583), sigs. Dd4–Dd4v, "and *Sisyphus* with thy rowling restles stone, waile ye no more"; Richard Turner, *The Garland of a Green Wit* (1595), sig. B4, "were it . . . to roule the restlesse stone with *Siciphus*, I would rest at your commaund"; John Hind, *The Most Excellent Historie of Lysimachus and Varrona* (1604), sig. G2, "let the torments of *Tantalus*, *Tytius*, *Sysiphus*, and all the ruthfull rout of hell be heaped vpon me"; and John Kennedy, *The History of Calanthrop and Lucilla* (Edinburgh, 1626), sig. C2v,

> Not *Sysiphus*, who roules the restless stone,
> Nor Ixion, who turnes the toylsome wheele,
> Such griefe possesse as he.

21. *fell . . . sowne*] "Sound" for "swoon" was very common, especially in the phrase "to fall in a sound."

179. 20. *Tolosia. By*] Read probably *Tolosia*, *by*.

23. *Tolosia, and departed*] Read probably *Tolosia, departed* with *D* and Collier.

25–31. *The . . . estimation*] Compare *The Two Gentlemen of Verona*, V. iv. 152–59:

> *Val.* These banish'd men that I have kept withal
> Are men endu'd with worthy qualities.
> Forgive them what they have committed here
> And let them be recall'd from their exile.
> They are reformed, civil, full of good,
> And fit for great employment, worthy lord.
> *Duke.* Thou hast prevail'd. I pardon them and thee.
> Dispose of them as thou know'st their deserts.

180. 11–19. *It . . . reason*] Source: Rich's *Allarme*, sig. H2v.

26. *effect*] I.e., "affect," "fall in love."

181. 13. *Prouerbe. In*] Read *Prouerbe, in.*

15. *pietie*] I.e., "virtue"?

16–19. *is . . . indifferent*] Rich is here freely paraphrasing a bit from his own *Allarme*, sig. H2v. Compare also Pettie's "Admetus and Alcest," p. 140.

17. *the*] Read *thei.*

24. *beate . . . aboute it*] Compare Pettie's "Scilla and Minos," p. 155, "[Scilla] was busely beating her braines here about," and *Hamlet*, V. i. 63–65, "*Clown.* Cudgel thy brains no more about it, for your dull ass will not mend his pace with beating." Rich uses the phrase again at 184. 18.

182. 12 f. *either . . . either*] I.e., "either . . . or."

12–14. *if . . . it*] Source: Pettie's "Admetus and Alcest," p. 124.

15. *in . . . mariage*] See 56. 23 n.

17–34. *more . . . of*] Sources: Pettie's "Germanicus and Agrippina," p. 74 and "Amphiaraus and Eriphile," p. 101.

35. *olde youthes*] For a similar ironical phrase, see Nashe, *The Terrors of the Night* (1594), McKerrow, I, 379, where, after describing some hideous devils who haunted a sick man, the author refers to them as "These louely youths and full of fauour." Compare "olde babie," 183. 9.

183. 3. *mewe you vp*] Apparently the figure of speech had legal overtones. See Sir Thomas Smith, *De Republica Anglorum* (1583), sig. O4v: "Although the [English] wife be . . . *in manu & potestate mariti*, by our lawe yet they be not kept so streit as in mew and with a garde as they be in Italy and Spaine." For Rich's source for the phrase see 92. 20 n. Compare Bianca's fate in *The Taming of the Shrew*, I. i. 188 f.:

> And therefore has he closely mew'd her up
> Because he will not be annoy'd with suitors.

9. *disposed on*] Either a misprint for *disposed of* or a use of the idiom (meaning "disposed of") fifty years earlier than any listed in *NED.*

olde babie] See the note on "olde youthes," 182. 35.

10 f. *humbly . . . self*] Source: Pettie's "Admetus and Alcest," p. 125.

13. *wedded . . . will*] Compare Greene, *Mamillia* (1593), Grosart, II, 166, "you haue abused this law of libertie, wedding your self to your own wil & despising my fatherly care."

13–30. *arte . . . consent*] This interchange inspired two passages in one of the comedies based on "Phylotus," Shakerley Marmion's *A Fine Companion* (1633), where, first, Littlegood, Alberto's counterpart, thus upbraids his recalcitrant daughter Valeria (Maidment and Logan, p. 112):

> *Lit.* Are you so well resolv'd? but I may cross you.
> *Val.* Oh me, my father, I am quite undone!
> I am no body.
> *Lit.* Yes, you are the wickedst,
> The most ungracious child that ever lived
> Under so good a government. . . .
> Have I—what should I say?—cherisht you up,
> With tenderness and costly education,
> To have you made a sacrifice to beggary;

and, second, the Æmilia of the play remonstrates with her father (p. 131), "Good sir, think your power may command my duty, but not my affection."

16–19. *carefully . . . recompence*] Source: Pettie's "Germanicus and Agrippina," p. 73, a passage which apparently also impressed John

Hind, *The Most Excellent Historie of Lysimachus and Varrona* (1604), sig. G4, "when we haue brought them [children] vp with great care and cost . . . they wish an end of our liues." Rich's friend Thomas Lodge, on the other hand, in *A Margarite of America* (1596), ed. G. B. Harrison (Oxford, 1927), p. 147, seems to echo Rich's rather than Pettie's version (my italics): "Ah, my deere Philenia . . . who hast *cost* me many broken sleepes *to bring thee vp*, many *carefull* thoughts to *bestow thee*."

22–35. *moste . . . likyng*] Source: Pettie's "Germanicus and Agrippina," pp. 73 f.

27 f. *duetie . . . childe*] See the note on 45. 24 f.

31–35. *my . . . likyng*] Compare *A Midsummer Night's Dream*, I. i. 41 f., 56 f., 117 f.:

> [*Ege.*] I beg the ancient privilege of Athens—
> As she is mine, I may dispose of her. . . .
> *Her.* I would my father look'd but with my eyes.
> *The.* Rather your eyes must with his judgment look. . . .
> For you, fair Hermia, look you arm yourself
> To fit your fancies to your father's will.

184. 7–13. *she . . . estimacion*] Her reflections suggested the following in Marmion's *A Fine Companion*: "I'll tell you what you shall do, be advis'd; refuse not a good offer, think of old Dotario, think how to love him, think of his wealth, think of his honour, think of me, think of yourself" (Maidment and Logan, p. 132).

14 f. *to . . . sicknesse*] Compare Thomas North's translation of *The Dial of Princes* (1568), fol. 109v, "There is no woman that willingly can suffer to haue any superiour, nor yet scarcely can endure to haue any equal."

18. *beate her braines*] See 181. 24 n.

29 f. *Malmsie, or Muskadine*] Emelia's taste in wine is elegant and expensive. See John Florio, *First Fruites* (1578), sig. D3, "What sortes of wine haue they [the English]?/ They haue claret wine, red wine, Sacke, Muscadel [Rich's 'Muskadine'] and Malmesey./ Is it deare, or cheape?/ Claret wine, Red and White, is sold for fiue pence the quart, and Sacke for sixe pence, Muscadel, and Malmesey for eight."

29–185. 9. *she . . . Caule*] The author of the comedy *Philotus* (1603) allots this part of the debate between the ambitious and the sensible Emelia to the "Macrell" whom he borrowed from "Agatha" (see 151. 2–17 n.). His panderess thus tempts the Emily of the play with the joys of the wealthy (Mill, pp. 108 f.):

Than tak to stanche the morning drouth,
Ane cup of Mauesie for your mouth,
For fume cast sucker in at fouth,
  Togidder with a Toist. . . .
To sie your seruantes may ye gang,
And luke your Madynis all amang,
And gif thair onie wark be wrang,
  Than bitterlie them blame,
Than may ye haue baith Quaiffis and Kellis,
Hich Candie Ruffes and Barlet Bellis,
All for your weiring and not ellis,
  Maid in your hous at hame.

30. *nexte her harte*] I.e., "on an empty stomach." Compare Rich's *Greenes Newes* (1593), sig. E2v, "*Margery* and this Taylors wife . . . agreed . . . they would euery morning next their harts, take a phisical dyet."

36. *Cicelie, Ione, or Cate*] Stock names for servant girls or country wenches. See Skelton's "The Tunnyng of Elynour Rummyng," *Workes of Maister Skelton* (1568), sig. K2v:

Earelye and late
Thither commeth Kate
Cislye and Sare;

Gervase Markham and Lewis Machin, *The Dumb Knight* (1608), sig. F3v, "What . . . Sislie, neere a maid within"; *Love's Labour's Lost*, III. i. 207, "Some men must love my lady, and some Joan," and V. ii. 930, "greasy Joan doth keel the pot"; and Rich's "Ione of the Countrey," 209. 12.

185. 8. *Quaife*] I.e., "coif," or small linen cap to be worn indoors. For Elizabethan fashions in the coif see Linthicum, pp. 223 f.

9. *Caule*] For Elizabethan fashions in cauls, tightly fitting hair nets of gold thread or hair, see Linthicum, p. 223.

10. *stitche . . . garde*] For multifarious stitches, or kinds of embroidery, and for Elizabethan fashions in the guard, an ornamental band or border, see Linthicum, pp. 147 f., 150–52.

17 f. *This . . . well, when*] Since the refrain is to be read with

the preceding menu of delicate cates, read probably *this . . . well. When.*

26–31. *But . . . marde*] This observation of the sensible, as opposed to the ambitious, Emelia becomes part of the dialogue in *Philotus*, where Emily replies to the panderess (Mill, p. 113):

I grant all day to be weill tret, . . .
But quhat intreatment sall I get,
I pray yow in my bed?
Bot with ane lairbair for to ly.

28–30. *goe to . . . embracementes*] Compare Shirley's *Love Tricks* (of which "Phylotus" is the principal source): "Can you submit your body/ To bed with ice and snow, your blood to mingle" (Dyce, I, 27).

186. 10. *doubte. There*] Read probably *doubte, there.*

11. *Flanius*] A proper name I have not seen elsewhere. Collier apparently regarded it as a misprint for *Flavius*, which he prints consistently. *Flavius* it is also in the Scottish play *Philotus*, of which this tale is the source. But if *Flanius* is a misprint, all four early editions persisted in the original error, for like *A* they print *Flanius* throughout.

187. 14. *appoincted. The*] Read probably *appoincted, the.*

28. *adores*] A common phonetic reduction of "o'doors," "of doors," and "at doors," properly written separately "a doors."

188. 25–30. *Ah . . . Iewells*] This passage caught the eyes of two dramatists. The author of *Philotus* (1603) paraphrases thus: "For Gold nor geir ye sall not want,/ Sweit hart with me thairs be na scant" (Mill, p. 104); and in *Love Tricks* (licensed 1625, published 1631) Shirley writes, "Nay, she shall want nothing my wealth can purchase.—O my sweet Selina!" (Dyce, I, 26).

38–189. 2. *I haue . . . modestie*] See the note on 41. 8–10.

189. 5. *duetie and obedience*] See the note on 45. 24 f.

12. *is . . . doune*] I.e., "have you got over being froward?"

29. *hir*] Read *his.*

190. 3–7. *beholde . . . for*] The following will give some notion of how this passage (and many others from "Phylotus") fared in the Scottish dialect and verse of *Philotus* (Mill, p. 132):

Brisilla Dochter myne giue eir,
A Mother I haue brocht the heir,

To mee a wyfe and darling deir,
I the command thairfoir
Hir honour, serue, obey and luif,
Wirk ay the best for hir behuif,
To pleis hir sie thy pairt thow pruif,
With wit and all devoir.

22. *cõfesse . . . truthe*] See 83. 20 n.

191. 11. *hartly*] Perhaps a misprint for "hartely," though *NED* lists "heartly" as a separate word meaning "earnestly, sincerely."

30. *diescrepit*] Read perhaps *diecrepit*. Or did Rich confuse "decrepit" and "discrepant"?

38. *dearlinges . . . seekes*] Compare the proverb "Better be an old man's darling than a young man's warling" (Smith, p. 63).

38–192. 3. *seekes . . . age*] Source: Pettie's "Admetus and Alcest," p. 138, a passage also copied by John Hind, *The Most Excellent Historie of Lysimachus and Varrona* (1604), sig. G2v, "O pittiles parent! to prefer his own hate before his childs loue . . . to measure the firie flames of youth by the dead coals of age."

192. 2 f. *measure . . . age*] Compare *2 Henry IV*, I. ii. 196–99: "You that are old consider not the capacities of us that are young. You do measure the heat of our livers with the bitterness of your galls."

4–6. *with . . . yeres*] Source: Rich's *A Right Exelent and Pleasaunt Dialogue*, sig. I4v.

12. *chalenge*] I.e., "lay claim to."

18–20. *oh . . . paine*] Source: Pettie's "Admetus and Alcest," pp. 137 f.

20. *you*] Read *your*.

36–38. *Doe . . . Pygmalion*] The author of *Philotus* combined this and another bit from "Phylotus," 193. 28 f., to make a compact stanza (Mill, pp. 134 f.):

That Iphis was a Mayd we reid,
And swa did for hir prayers speid,
For verie reuth the Goddes indeid,
Transformde hir in ane man:
Pigmaleons prayer purchast lyfe,
Unto his new eburneall wyfe.

Compare Shirley's *Love Tricks* (of which "Phylotus" is the principal source): "I have read of a painter named Pygmalion, that made the picture of a woman so to the life, that he fell in love with it" (Dyce, I, 16).

193. 3. *Archane*] Read *Arachne.*

8–29. *There . . . man*] Source: Arthur Golding's translation of Ovid's *Metamorphoses*, ed. W. H. D. Rouse (London, 1904), p. 198, lines 833 f., p. 199, lines 901–907.

28 f. *the gentle . . . man*] Echoed in *Philotus*. See 192. 36–38 n.

31. *Goddesse*] Read probably *Goddes* (as at line 34). Since "Goddes" seems to have been Rich's normal spelling for both "Goddess" and "Gods," the compositor may be excused for selecting whichever word helped him justify the line. See the note on 194. 15 f.

194. 6–9. *immouable . . . traunce*] Source: Painter's "The Duchess of Savoy," I, 321.

15. *Goddesse*] Read probably *Goddes.* See 193. 31 n.

22. *armes. She*] Read probably *armes, she.*

23 f. *thinkyng . . . woman*] See 35. 9 f., 71. 23, and the note on the former.

35. *birde*] Read probably *bride*, though "bird" can mean "girl," "maiden."

195. 35. Read "swaie, t[hat I] will." The bracketed letters are taken from *B*.

38. *taked*] Cited in *NED* as one of two examples of a rare form of the past participle; but possibly a misprint for *taken.*

38–196. 2. *thinkyng . . . bedde*] His impatience seems to be echoed in Shirley's *Love Tricks* (Dyce, I, 29):

> Rufaldo, thou art mine, all time, methinks,
> Is slow, till we be actually possest
> Of mutual enjoying.

196. 20 f. *the . . . finde you*] Compare W. Wager's *A very mery a. pythie commedie called The longer thou liuest, the more foole thou art* (1569).

22. *wheritte*] A "sharp blow," especially "a box on the ear or slap on the face" (*NED*).

35. Read "accor[ding a]s." The bracketed letters are taken from *B*.

197. 7–11. *Firste . . . been*] The author of *How a Man May Chuse a Good Wife from a Bad* (1602), who took his plot from Rich's "Agatha," also borrowed these ill-natured conditions, which read in dramatic form (Swaen, lines 2179, 2183, 2188–91):

> Not haue my will, yes I will haue my will,
> Shall I not goe abroad but when you please?
> Can I not now and then meete with my friends,
> But at my comming home you will controwle me?
> Marrie come vp. . . .
> What am not I of age sufficient
> To go and come still when my pleasure serues,
> But must I haue you sir to question me?
> Not haue my will? Yes I will haue my will.

"Going abroad" was a privilege accorded wives only by exceptionally lenient husbands. See *The Puritaine or the Widdow of Watling-streete* (1607), I. i. 106, ed. C. F. Tucker Brooke, *The Shakespeare Apocrypha* (Oxford, 1908), p. 222, "[My husband] was vnmatchable,—vnmatchable! . . . [I] spent what I would, went abroad when I would, came home when I would, and did all what I would."

16–21. *this . . . quarter*] This ultimatum Marmion borrowed for *A Fine Companion*: "I will lye with you the first year once a-month, as a parson uses to instruct his Cure, and yet not be question'd for neglect, or non-residence: marry the next year, if you live so long, once a quarter shall suffice you" (Maidment and Logan, p. 137).

198. 10. *cast*] I.e., "cast off."

17. *had . . . Emelia*] Compare Nashe, *Pierce Penilesse* (1592), McKerrow, I, 234, "[Evil spirits can] take on them the induments of anie liuing bodie what soeuer, & transform themselues into all kind of shapes."

19. *blessyng hymself*] A standard precaution. According to R. H.'s translation of Ludwig Lavater, *Of Ghostes and Spirites* (1572), p. 204, among the primitive Christians "It was a common custome . . . to blesse themselues with the signe of the Crosse, when they met with these things [spirits], which many also vse at this day."

19 f. *I . . . art*] Compare Nashe, *Pierce Penilesse* (1592), McKerrow, I, 240, "diuels haue no power to lie to a iust manne, and if they adiure them by the maiestie of the high God, they will not onlie con-

fesse themselues to be Diuels, but also tell their names as they are," and R. H.'s translation of Lavater, *Of Ghostes and Spirites* (1572), p. 211, "[a certain monk,] blissing himself with the sign of the holy crosse, adiured them in the name of the holy and vnseparable Trinitie . . . to declare vnto him who they were."

19–27. *I . . . departe*] Compare *The Comedy of Errors*, IV. iii. 66–68:

> *S. Ant.* Avoid, thou fiend! . . .
> Thou art, as you are all, a sorceress.
> I conjure thee to leave me and be gone;

and IV. iv. 57–60:

> *Pinch.* I charge thee, Satan, hous'd within this man,
> To yield possession to my holy prayers,
> And to thy state of darkness hie thee straight.
> I conjure thee by all the saints in heaven.

20 f. *that thou presently . . . camest*] Compare William Lithgow, *Rare Adventures and Painefull Peregrinations* (1632; reprinted at Glasgow, 1906), p. 29, "Another time . . . I saw an old Capuschin Frier conjuring the Divell out of a possessed woman. . . . The Frier stood up before her . . . and sayd, laying his formost finger on her brow; In nomine Patris, &c. . . . I charge thee to shew me for what cause thou hast possessed the soule of this poore wretch, and I adjure thee to goe backe unto these places from whence thou camest."

22–27. *I . . . departe*] Here Rich evidently follows the traditional rite of exorcism. According to a fifteenth-century manuscript *Forma exorisandi dæmonia* (in the Houghton Library, Harvard), an evil spirit may be effectively conjured by "the Holy Trinity, angels, archangels, patriarchs, prophets, apostles, martyrs, [and] confessors" —who appear in the order in which Flanius invokes them. For the ritual now in use, in which most of the celestial luminaries mentioned by Rich are called on, see *Rituale Romanum* (Malines, 1873), pp. 305–309. See also the ceremony for expelling Satan, who it was assumed possessed all children unregenerated by baptism, in *The First Prayer Book of King Edward VI*, ed. V. Staley (London, 1903), p. 304.

Once, and once only, the author of *Philotus* succeeds in surpassing his original. In the tale Flanius' exorcism is amusing; in the comedy it is hilarious. In addition to invoking the very powers to whom Flanius appeals, his counterpart in the comedy adds functionaries and symbols drawn from the unreformed church, classical mythology, fairy lore, medieval magic, and even Mohammedism, and achieves a climax by rhyming Matthew, Mark, Luke, and John with Lethe, Styx, and Acheron. See *Philotus*, Mill, pp. 139–41.

31 f. *tempest . . . lightnyng*] In *Pierce Penilesse* (1592), McKerrow, I, 231, Nashe warns that evil spirits "by the helpe of *Alrynach*, a Spirite of the West, . . . will raise stormes, cause earthquaks, whirlwinds, raine, haile or snow. . . . The spirits of the aire will mix themselues with thunder & lightening, and so infect the Clime where they raise any tempest, that suddenlie great mortalitie shall ensue," a caveat which King James also in part delivers in his *Dæmonologie* (1597), ed. G. B. Harrison (London, 1924), p. 46, "[Devils] can rayse stormes and tempestes in the aire, either vpon Sea or land." For further information on the subject see L'Estrange Ewen, *Witchcraft and Demonianism* (London, 1933), pp. 89 f.

32 f. *take . . . me*] Miles, Friar Bacon's man, utters a parody of this sort of injunction in *The Famous History of Fryer Bacon*, *Early English Prose Romances*, ed. W. J. Thoms (London, 1858), I, 44:

> But I will have you take no shape
> Of a bear a horse, or ape:
> Nor will I have you terrible,
> And therefore come invisible.

Compare, however, King James's sober warning in the *Dæmonologie* (1597), ed. G. B. Harrison (London, 1924), p. 52, "[The Devil] appeares to diuers . . . in diuers formes. . . . For he deluding them with vaine impressiones in the aire, make himselfe to seeme more terrible to the grosser sorte, that they maie thereby be moued to feare and reuerence him the more." See also 198. 17 n.

38. *fall so coniuryng*] Read perhaps *fall to coniuryng* or *fall so to coniuryng* (as in *B* and *C*). The usual idiom is "to fall *to* doing something."

199. 2. *nere*] I.e., "nearer." Compare "nier" at 6. 6.

9 f. *takyng . . . doores*] I.e., he gives her "Jack (or Tom) Drum's entertainment." See the note on 9. 21 f.

13 f. *made what meanes*] I.e., "registered what complaints." *NED* defines "mean" as "lament, complaint" and quotes the ballad "Mary Hamilton": "'Make never meen for me,' she says."

15–24. *was . . . daughter*] This tender exchange inspired the following speech in *Philotus* (Mill, p. 144):

> I will vnto my father ga,
> Befoir his feit to fald:
> Father sa far I did offend,
> That I may not my mis amend,
> And am ouir pert for to pretend
> Your dochter to be cald.

28. *boldly what*] Read probably *boldly: what.*

30. *Pages apparel*] Elsewhere described simply as "mannes apparell" (187. 9, 187. 19, 187. 25 f., 189. 29, 199. 33), but here Rich apparently recalls a detail from his principal source, Belleforest's story of Nicole, prefaced by a summary beginning "[Nicole] se vestant en page."

32. *duetie . . . childe*] See the note on 45. 24 f.

200. 9. (*would . . . brushyng*)] Apparently proverbial, since proverbs are similarly indicated by parentheses, the Elizabethan equivalent of quotation marks, at 45. 32 f., 91. 26 f., and 121. 36 f.

28. *hansell*] Literally, "gift expressive of good wishes on entering upon any new condition."

201. 30. *standyng . . . tackelyng*] I.e., "stoutly maintaining her position."

33. *he*] Read *she.*

202. 16. *confesse a truthe*] See 83. 20 n.

30. *sure*] Apparently an Irishism.

34–36. *Out . . . Deuill*] Echoed by Phylotus' counterpart in Shirley's *Love Tricks:* "Oh, I have married a devil!" (Dyce, I, 63).

204. 7 f. *on . . . been*] A tantalizing confession. If he had specified which tales had appeared as plays, mentioned titles and names of authors, and told a bit about performances and dramatic companies, he might have added considerably to our knowledge of Tudor drama. A dramatic version of the Eustace-Placidas story, a principal source of Rich's first tale, was recorded in 1534 in the churchwarden's accounts at Braintree, Essex (Rich's native county). See Miss G. M. Sibley, *The*

Lost Plays and Masques (*1500–1642*) (Ithaca, 1933), p. 123, and Sir E. K. Chambers, *The Mediæval Stage* (Oxford, 1903), II, 451. For the plays more or less closely analogous to the "Apolonius and Silla"—*Twelfth Night* story see *Rich's "Apolonius & Silla,"* ed. Morton Luce (London, 1912), p. 7. But that Rich had any of these or the Essex play in mind when he made his assertion must be considered only a possibility, not even a likelihood.

22. *Philippes Doler*] The English name for the peso, or piece of eight, current in the Spain of Philip II.

22 f. *like . . . Fishstreate*] I.e., like the beard of the King on the sign at the King's Head. For abundant references to this tavern in New Fish Street, "where roysters do range," and whither, according to Thomas Heywood, the gentry repaired, see Sugden, p. 294. Kenneth Rogers, *Signs and Taverns round and about Old London Bridge* (London, 1937), p. 72, remarks, "From Henry VIII.'s time, the sign-board doubtless displayed the well-known features of 'Bluff King Hal.' The tokens of the tavern . . . have the head of Henry VIII. on the obverse."

25. *pilde luck*] "Pilled" and "peeled" often meant "miserable," but why a close-cropped beard should indicate wretched luck is not clear.

25–27. *Cappes . . . little*] For the big ones whose crowns came "peaking vp like the spere, or shaft of a steeple standyng a quarter of a yarde aboue the crowne of their heades," according to Stubbes, and for the little ones, the "pinked porringers," "silken pies," and "velvet dishes" of which Shakespeare and Jonson made fun, see Linthicum, pp. 218 f.

28 f. *Ruffes . . . wheele*] For the "cartwheel ruff" see Linthicum, p. 159.

29–31. *fallyng . . . silke women*] A brand-new fashion when Rich wrote the passage, for it was introduced about 1580, according to Linthicum, who describes and gives a photograph of a gentleman's falling band (p. 155 and opposite p. 160). Made of linen, the *rabat*, or French fall, "consisted of a 'stock' or strip fastened to the shirt by pins, a straight collar made to fit the neck by darts or 'clocks,' and strings to tie it in front." About the Queen's silk-women no details seem to be discoverable. Elizabeth's household accounts contain no mention of them, and there is no record that the Queen was interested in sericulture. One can only guess that the silk-women were somehow connected with the royal wardrobe. *NED* quotes (under *silk-woman*) information from the *Encyclopædia Metropolitana* to the effect that Henry VI had silk-women "who were . . . probably only employed in needlework of silk."

31–33. *Clokes . . . elbowes*] For fashions in Elizabethan cloaks great and small see Linthicum, pp. 193–95.

205. 2. *with no collors*] In her discussion of jerkins (pp. 202 f.) Linthicum does not mention the collarless type.

3 f. *wenche . . . bucke*] Such wenches apparently washed in dishabille; according to Linthicum (p. 214) the waistcoat was an undergarment in which a "woman did not appear . . . unless she were a strumpet."

4 f. *long sausie sleeues*] According to Linthicum (p. 172), the "long, open sleeves hanging to the knee or foot . . . an Italian fashion, were called hanging or pendant sleeves [and] were in favour from the eighties until about 1620."

6 f. *Scogins . . . errandes*] To Rich, "sleeveless" must have meant "difficult" or "impossible to perform" if he had in mind the following from *The Jests of Scogin*, *Shakespeare Jest-Books*, ed. W. C. Hazlitt (London, 1864), p. 61: "On a time, Scogin did send Jacke to Oxford to market, to buy a penny-worth of fresh herring. Scogin said: bring foure herrings for a penny, or else bring none. Jack could not get four herrings but three for his penny: and when he came home, Scogin said: how many herrings hast thou brought? and Jacke said: three herrings, for I could not get foure for a penny." The phrase "sleeveless errand" was proverbial (Smith, p. 27; McKerrow, IV, 410). Official messengers bent on purposeful errands wore in the cap a sleeve which assured them safe-conduct. "Without the sleeve they might never be able to perform the errand," Bond explains (III, 503), basing his explanation on a passage from Lady Charlotte Guest's translation of the *Mabinogion*. Compare Shakespeare's *Troilus and Cressida*, V. iv. 5–9: "I would fain see them meet, that that same young Troyan ass that loves the whore here, might send that Greekish whore-masterly villain with the sleeve back to the dissembling luxurious drab of a sleeveless errand."

7–10. *Dublettes . . . pisse*] For a discussion of narrow-waisted ("faggotte wasted" ?) doublets, "Peascod" or Dutch "dublets with great belly," and doublets with fourteen to thirty-four buttons up the front that could be "three hours a buttoning," see Linthicum, pp. 198 f. Compare L. Wright, *A Summons for Sleepers* (1589), sig. D4: "doublets with great burssen bellies, as though theyr guts were ready to fall out."

12. *Garragascoynes . . . Beare*] The usual spelling was *galligaskins* or *galligascons*. For this style of hose, which were often fitted at the hips but full at the knee (hence "breached like a Beare") see Linthicum, pp. 204 f., 208 f.

13 f. *close . . . taile*] For the form-fitting "devil's breeches" see Linthicum, p. 204.

14 f. *rounde . . . Onions*] For "the trunk, or round or French breeches, 'not unlike Saint Omer's onions' . . . 'big as good barrels'" see Linthicum, p. 205. Rich's "Saincte Thomas Onions" is evidently a corruption of "Saint Omer's Onions." Though *NED* quotes this passage from the *Farewell* (under *onion*), the confusion between the two saints is not explained. See, however, the explanation under *saint*: "St. Omer's (corruptly *St. Thomas*) worsted." "St. Thomas Onions" is used as a code word for Middleburgh, Holland, in a letter of intelligence from an unknown informer to Peter Hallins (HMC, *Salisbury MSS*, V, 26 f.).

14–19. *sometymes . . . fashion*] Compare Don Pedro's description of Benedick, *Much Ado about Nothing*, III. ii. 31–37: "There is no appearance of fancy in him, unless it be a fancy that he hath to strange disguises; as to be a Dutchman to-day, a Frenchman to-morrow; or in the shape of two countries at once, as a German from the waist downward, all slops, and a Spaniard from the hip upward, no doublet."

15 f. *petite . . . taile*] Since Rich is quite specific about the length of the "Ruffes" (i.e., "ruffles" ?) and other details, he doubtless had seen the fashion, but I have been unable to find a fuller description or photograph of it. See, however, Nashe, *The Unfortunate Traveller* (1594), McKerrow, II, 227: "I was no common squire . . . I had . . . my longe stock that sate close to my docke."

30. *a tale*] Many scholars have implied or asserted that Rich adapted the delightful tale which follows from Machiavelli's "Belphegor." See Collier, p. xvi; E. Koeppel, "Studien zur Geschichte der italienischen Novelle in der englischen Litteratur," *Quellen und Forschungen*,

LXX (1892), 49, 99; E. Meyer, *Machiavelli and the Elizabethan Drama* (Weimar, 1897), pp. 30 f.; Miss M. A. Scott, *Elizabethan Translations from the Italian* (Baltimore, 1895), pp. 26 f.; and W. E. A. Axon, "The Story of Belfagor in Literature and Folk-Lore," *Transactions of the Royal Society of Literature of the United Kingdom*, XXIII (1902), 108. But a more recent critic, with whose judgment I agree, observes that Rich's source was the version of the story in Straparola's *Le piacevoli notti* (Night II, Novel 4). See D. W. Thompson, "Belphegor in *Grim the Collier* and Riche's *Farewell*," *MLN*, L (1935), 99–102. Whether Rich used the original Italian or Jean Louveau's French translation of Straparola is difficult to determine, since the French is a faithful translation of the Italian. The two versions may be compared in *Les facétieuses nuits de Straparole: traduction Jean Louveau*, ed. J. de Marthold (Paris, 1907), I, 106–15, and *Le piacevoli notti*, ed. G. Rua, *Scrittori d'Italia* (Bari, 1927), I, 87–95.

32 f. *I . . . whẽ*] Without noting the source or the date of the entry, in other words, he probably summarized the tale in his commonplace book, on which see p. xix, above. Compare his *Path-way to Military Practise* (1587), sig. B4v, "I remember longe sithens, (when I was a little bookishe) I reade a History in our English Chronicles, and although I canne not set you downe the place, yet as I can I will tell you the matter."

206. 14. *in . . . Marriage*] See 56. 23 n.

23. *to . . . Hell*] The proverbial fate of old maids (Tilley, pp. 239 f.; Smith, p. 336). See Beatrice's assertion, *Much Ado about Nothing*, II. i. 43 f.: "I will even take sixpence in earnest of the berrord and lead his apes into hell."

26. *ioynter*] I.e., "jointure," "dowry."

207. 25. *partes*] I.e., "parties," "persons interested in the matter."

208. 12. *Caules, Quaiues*] See the notes on 185. 8 and 185. 9.

13. *Partlettes . . . Kirtelles*] For Elizabethan fashions in the partlet, a garment which covered the upper part of the chest and neck only, and which went out of style about 1580, and in the kirtle, used as an outside dress over the petticoat and farthingale, see Linthicum, pp. 162 f., 185 f.

14. *Stitche . . . Garde*] See 185. 10 n.

22. *Shadowes*] For Elizabethan fashions in the "shadow," or

"bongrace," "a projecting front brim or shade worn with bonnets, caps, or coifs to protect the wearer from the sun and so preserve her good grace or beauty," see Linthicum, pp. 235 f.

25 f. *Carnation*] For a discussion of this shade of red, which "resembled incarnate," see Linthicum, pp. 37 f.

26. *Yellowe Stockynges*] Compare *Twelfth Night*, II. v. 165–66: "Remember who commended thy yellow stockings and wish'd to see thee ever cross-garter'd."

33. *lumpe, and lowre*] The two words, almost synonymous and meaning "to look sulky or angry," are "always in collocation" in early quotations (*NED*).

209. 12. *Ione . . . Countrey*] See 184. 36 n.

APPENDIX

SOURCES AND ANALOGUES

APPENDIX

SOURCES AND ANALOGUES

A "Sappho Duke of Mantona"

Into the making of "Sappho" went about two dozen sources.[1] Rich drew the main outline of his plot and many of his words from *Aethiopica, or Theagenes and Chariclea*, Thomas Underdowne's translation of Heliodorus' Greek novel, from William Painter's "The Duchess of Malfy," and from three variations of the St. Eustace–Placidas legend: Giraldi Cinthio's "Cesare Gravina" (Decade V, Novel 8, in *Gli Hecatommithi*), Painter's "The Earl of Angiers," and "Ariobarzanes," also in *The Palace of Pleasure*. Since some of the experiences of Sappho's wife occur in none of these tales yet appear in older versions of the Eustace legend, Rich may also have consulted one or more of the latter.

For further details of plot and character, for names and titles, and for hundreds of words, Rich repaired to thirteen additional stories in Painter's *Palace*; "Alerane and Andelasia," "A Lady of Bohemia," "Dom Diego and Ginevra," "Salimbene and Angelica," "Sophonisba," "A Lady Falsely Accused," "Two Maidens of Carthage," "Anne Queen of Hungary," "Rhomeo and Juletta," "Zenobia Queen of Palmyres," "Euphemia of Corinth," "The Lord of Virle," and "Faustina the Empress." Indeed, through borrowings great and small, Painter is represented on two-thirds of the pages of "Sappho."

Still other words in the tale came from widely scattered sources: from two stories in George Pettie's *Petite Pallace of Pettie His Pleasure*, "Germanicus and Agrippina" and "Admetus and Alcest," and perhaps from a third, "Scilla and Minos"; from Rich's own translation of Belleforest's "The Lady of Chabry," which he included in his first publication, *A Right Exelent and Pleasaunt Dialogue, betwene Mercury and an English Souldier* (1574); from two lyrics by George Gascoigne, "Councell given to master Bartholmew Withipoll" and "Dan Bartholmewes

[1] According to two investigators of the subject, whose findings this section briefly summarizes. For full particulars of Rich's borrowings in "Sappho," see D. T. Starnes, "Barnabe Riche's 'Sappho Duke of Mantona': A Study in Elizabethan Story-Making," *SP*, XXX (1933), 455–72, and T. M. Cranfill, "Barnaby Rich's 'Sappho' and *The Weakest Goeth to the Wall*," *University of Texas Studies in English, 1945–1946*, pp. 142–71.

Dolorous discourses," and perhaps from a third, "Dan Bartholmew his second Triumphe." Finally, Rich seems also to echo two selections from *The Paradise of Dainty Devices*: Francis Kinwelmarsh's "Most happy is that state alone" and Richard Edwards'. "Iustice. Zaleuch and his Sonne."

B "Apolonius and Silla"

There is such a galaxy of analogues to the plot of "Apolonius" that it would be perplexing to decide which is Rich's immediate source if the evidence indicating his use of Belleforest's version of the story were not substantial.[1] As several scholars have already observed,[2] the most striking clue to his dependence on Belleforest is to be found in the following passage: "Gentlewomen accordyng to my promise, I will heare for breuities sake, omit to make repetition of the long and dolorous discourse recorded by *Silla*, for this sodaine departure of her *Apolonius*" (69. 24–27). Now, the only author who does bother to repeat the lament of the heroine deserted by the hero is Belleforest. Departing from Bandello's *novella*, he adds four pages filled with deplorable verse of his own composition.[3]

On the basis of this evidence it has long been argued that Belleforest's tale is the immediate source of "Apolonius." But no one has yet noted how greatly the argument is reinforced by the fact that Rich twice showed his devotion to Belleforest elsewhere. He inserted a translation of another tale from the *Histoires tragiques*, "The Lady of Chabry," in his very first publication, *A Right Exelent and Pleasaunt Dialogue*,

[1] The analogues which antedate the *Farewell* include the anonymous *Gl'Ingannati* (acted 1531, published 1537); Charles Estienne's *Les Abusez* (1534), a translation of the Italian play; Niccolò Secchi's *Gl'Inganni* (acted 1547, published 1562); Matteo Bandello's prose version of the original play, Part II, Story 36, in the *Novelle* (1554); Lope de Rueda's *Los Engaños* (acted 1556, published 1567); the anonymous play *La Española de Florencia* (n.d.); Giraldi Cinthio's Decade V, Novel 8, in *Gli Hecatommithi* (1565), which is probably based on the original play; and François de Belleforest's *Histoires tragiques*, Volume IV (1570), Story 59, a translation of Bandello's tale. Though I can think of no reason why Rich could not have known all of these, an examination of every version mentioned except the anonymous Spanish play has failed to unearth proof that he was familiar with any except Cinthio's and Belleforest's. For the best accounts of the story in its various forms, see *Lælia*, ed. G. C. Moore Smith (Cambridge, 1910), pp. xxiii–xxvi, and *Rich's "Apolonius & Silla,"* ed. Morton Luce (New York, 1912), pp. 7–50.

[2] The first was H. H. Furness, *New Variorum Twelfth Night* (Philadelphia, 1910), p. xviii.

[3] *Histoires tragiques*, IV (Lyons, 1616), 214–18.

betwene Mercury and an English Souldier (1574). In this translation, as in his adaptation of the story of Nicole, he wisely skipped a good deal of Belleforest's verbiage, which interrupts the narrative without ornamenting it. Furthermore, still another of Belleforest's stories, in the same volume which contains the original of "Apolonius," served as a principal source for the seventh tale in the *Farewell.*[1]

In writing "Apolonius" Rich also returned to a number of the sources he had used in "Sappho," including his own *A Right Exelent and Pleasaunt Dialogue*, which yielded two brief passages in "Apolonius" after having done yeoman's service in the first tale. For various tribulations suffered by Silla he seems to have found hints in two other old friends, Cinthio's "Cesare Gravina" and the Eustace-Placidas legend. In the *novella* Cesare's son leaves a young lady pregnant, and his daughter, mistaken for her brother, is apprehended, accused of his misdeed, and imprisoned. The similarity of Silla's predicament to that of Signorina Gravina is striking.[2] And in several versions of the Eustace-Placidas story (in John Partridge's, for example) the heroine, like poor Silla, finds herself aboard a ship whose captain forces on her his wicked, lustful attentions.

For minor details of plot and characterization in "Apolonius"—and, above all, for words—Rich resorted again to the unfailing Painter. The influence of thirteen tales from the *Palace* is clearly to be seen in Rich's second tale: "The Duchess of Malfy," "Rhomeo and Juletta," "The Lord of Virle," "Dom Diego and Ginevra," "Sophonisba," "Salimbene and Angelica," "The Rape of Lucrece," "A Chaste Death," "The Lords of Nocera," "Francis the French King," "Camiola and Roland," "The Countess of Celant," and "Two Gentlewomen of Venice." The first six of these Rich had already employed in "Sappho."

Finally, the influence of Pettie's *Petite Pallace* on "Apolonius" is also marked. Apart from the Pettie-like digressions, attitudinizings, and euphuistic flights in "Apolonius" already commented on,[3] Rich borrowed details of characterization and words from Pettie's "Icilius and Virginia," "Alexius," "Pygmalion's Friend," and "Germanicus and Agrippina."

[1] See below, p. 348.

[2] The parallel is noted by B. E. Boothe, "The Contribution of the Italian Novella to the Formation and Development of Elizabethan Prose Fiction, 1566–1582" (University of Michigan dissertation, 1936), p. 400.

[3] See above, pp. xviii, 274 f.

C "Two Brethren and Their Wives"

Rich took the outline of "Two Brethren" from Giovanni Straparola's *Le piacevoli notti*, Night VIII, Novel 2, an account of the married lives of Silverio and Pisardo. The barest abstract of the *novella*, which Rich used again in his eighth tale, will allow a sufficiently nice appraisal of how much Rich's brothers owe to Silverio and Pisardo:

Two soldiers, sworn brothers, are in the service of the pope. Silverio, the younger, marries Spinella, the daughter of a tailor. She is beautiful, but he spoils her so badly that she becomes incorrigible. Within a year Pisardo, the elder, marries Fiorella, the tailor's other daughter. Immediately after the marriage feast Pisardo gives his bride a cudgel, takes one himself, and proposes that whichever wins in combat shall wear the breeches (which he brings with the cudgels). Fiorella declines to fight, meekly replying, "Are you not the husband, and I the wife, and ought not the wife always to bear herself obediently towards her husband?" Pisardo warns her never to question his authority; and shortly thereafter he takes her to his stables, and, in her presence, slays a horse that will not obey him. Fiorella, terrified, remains a dutiful and obedient wife. Seeing his brother's success in marriage, Silverio tries a similar experiment on Spinella, who laughs him to scorn and becomes more shrewish than ever. He bitterly accepts the failure and gives up the task of improving her disposition as hopeless.

For other important developments in his plot—Dorothy's reception of sundry lovers, her subsequent longing for revenge, the feigned surprisal by a jealous husband, the concealment of a lover in a trunk, and the beating of two lovers by a third—Rich seems to have searched further in Straparola and in Cinthio's *Gli Hecatommithi*, Belleforest's *Histoires tragiques*, and Painter's *Palace of Pleasure*, all collections to which he obviously repaired time and again. A short synopsis of each analogue will show how it anticipated "Two Brethren."

Three of Straparola's stories in addition to that of Silverio and Pisardo are suggestive of "Two Brethren." The first (Night I, Novel 5) concerns Dimitrio, a merchant, whose wife, Polinessa, apparently agrees with Mistress Dorothy that "store is no sore," for she is carrying on an extramarital affair with a priest. Instead of wearing horns as gullibly as

Dorothy's husband, however, Dimitrio disguises himself and manages to surprise his wife with her lover. Polinessa conceals the priest in a clothes coffer (in which, one hopes, Straparola's man of God was more comfortable than Rich's lawyer in his "male with stuffe"). But her presence of mind and ingenuity are of no avail. Dimitrio invites her brothers to dinner, exposes the priest, and then sends Polinessa home with her brothers, who kill her.

As Rich read Straparola's Night II he must have been in a mood for note-taking, for the next analogue, the story of Simplicio di Rossi (Night II, Novel 5), immediately succeeds a tale of which he made considerable use in his "Conclusion."[1] When Simplicio makes mild advances to Giliola, she tells her husband, Ghirotto, who coaches her in her replies to Simplicio and directs her to make an assignation with him. Overjoyed, Simplicio visits her one evening and is told that her husband has been called away for the night. The husband appears in the courtyard, and Giliola, pretending to be terrified, orders Simplicio to crawl into an empty sack (which she and her husband have handy for this purpose). Ghirotto drags the sack out of the house, takes a cudgel which he has duly prepared, and administers such a frightful beating that not a square inch of Simplicio's body is left unscathed. Aching from head to foot, Simplicio painfully makes his way home, the victim of a fate so suggestive of the painful retribution which overtakes Rich's lawyer and doctor that one hesitates to dwell on it.

The third parallel to "Two Brethren" in *Le piacevoli notti* is the story of Nerino, the King of Portugal's son, and his innamorata Genobbia (Night IV, Novel 4). More fortunate than either Simplicio or Rich's lawyer, Nerino does not become the object of a beating after he is surprised with Genobbia by her husband: his quick-witted mistress hides him, first in a chest, then in a wardrobe, summons four strong porters, and orders the wardrobe carried to his own lodgings. Thus he effects the escape for which Mistress Dorothy's lawyer was hoping.

The woman of easy virtue is a type common in Straparola, and one is not surprised to find in *Le piacevoli notti* three heroines so closely akin to Dorothy. But it is a little startling to meet two abandoned women, clearly members in good standing of the sisterhood of Mistress Dorothy, Genobbia, and Polinessa, in the *Hecatommithi* of Cinthio, who usually

[1] See 205. 30 n.

concerns himself with noble, long-suffering ladies and gentlemen like Desdemona and Cesare Gravina. Vana, the first of these (Decade I, Novel 2), is, like Dorothy, far from content with only one man; in fact, "when she had had ten, she was not satisfied." She is hence in a receptive mood when one of her husband's blunt farmhands (in an interview quite suggestive of that between Dorothy and her soldier) proposes himself as a lover in straightforward, homely language. Eventually the husband returns home unexpectedly, surprising Vana and the bumpkin abed together, and Vana saves herself by hiding her lover in a chest.

Cinthio's second unprincipled heroine, Bice (Decade III, Novel 3), becomes embroiled with two lovers at a time. One of these, Panfilo, calls on her while she is entertaining the second, a judge. But like the other quick-witted women of her kind, Bice manages to save herself embarrassment by concealing the judge in a chest. This is subsequently borne off on the shoulders of day laborers, who find it very heavy.

In "Sappho" and "Apolonius" there appear some of the words of the translation of Belleforest's "The Lady of Chabry" that Rich published in his first book, *A Right Exelent and Pleasaunt Dialogue, betwene Mercury and an English Souldier*. But in "Two Brethren" there are notable reminiscences of the Bandello-Belleforest-Rich plot as well as verbal echoes. Both the Lady of Chabry and Dorothy are wanton and lustful; and both relieve the tedium of life with an ailing husband by taking as a lover a gentleman whose business it is to render the husband professional services. Thus in important respects Mistress Dorothy is a comic counterpart of the lewd mistress of Chabry.

After examining the wholesale borrowings from Painter in "Sappho" and "Apolonius," one need scarcely observe that Rich's knowledge of the stories in *The Palace of Pleasure* was almost as intimate as if he had written them as well as "The Lady of Chabry." Hence analogues to "Two Brethren" in *The Palace*, though general, are worthy of note. For example, the notorious Countess of Celant, though she is the heroine of a tale as sanguinary and tragic as "The Lady of Chabry," nevertheless suffers from the same nymphomaniac virus that infects Dorothy: in the course of the story she accepts three lovers. Two of them enjoy her and then "slander" her; whereupon she and the third, a soldier, plan revenge on her "maligners." The parallel to this plot in Rich's fabliau is exact.

Painter's "The Lords of Nocera," another tale of lust, infidelity, and horrendous vengeance, also contains motifs which receive a comic treatment in "Two Brethren." When Lord Nicholas Nocera approaches the wife of his lieutenant, she is pleased with his proposal; yet, using the coy technique of Mistress Dorothy, she temporizes a bit before she assents. Without doing violence to Rich's context one could substitute the playful debate that ensues for Dorothy's conversations with her doctor and lawyer. The behavior of the lieutenant, who is naturally hungry for revenge when he discovers his wife's unfaithfulness, is also suggestive of Dorothy's lust for vengeance and gratitude for aid in securing it.

More nearly akin in spirit to Rich's story are "A Lady of Bohemia" and "Philenio Sisterno," two more tales in *The Palace* that anticipate certain details in "Two Brethren." Like Dorothy, the merry Lady of Bohemia thoroughly dupes two unwanted suitors, shutting them up in locked rooms, where one is compelled to spin, the other to reel yarn. An even closer parallel may be seen in Painter's account of how Emerentiana gulls poor Philenio Sisterno: first she invites him to her house in her husband's absence; next she takes him to a bedroom; and then her husband comes home "suddenly" and "unexpectedly." Feigning extreme fear, she begs him to hide under the bed. Like Dorothy's lawyer, he complies with little urging.

The lawyer's extrication thence was suggested, I suspect, by still another of Painter's tales, "Alexander di Medici," where the friends of a dissolute young man advise him that the best way to gain possession of a miller's daughter by whom he is attracted is to truss her up in a "mail" and kidnap her. The same means of transporting the lawyer out of her bedroom occurs to Dorothy.

Rich tapped three other stories in Painter's *Palace*, not for plot but for words. "Two Brethren" contains short but clear verbal echoes of Painter's "Two Gentlewomen of Venice," "The Lord of Virle," and "A Lady of Turin." For even more rhetoric Rich turned again to Pettie's *Petite Pallace* and appropriated words from seven of the twelve tales in that collection: "Amphiaraus and Eriphile," "Scilla and Minos," "Minos and Pasiphae," "Pygmalion's Friend," "Alexius," and "Sinorix and Camma."

Finally, for several passages in "Two Brethren" Rich was indebted to George Gascoigne's celebrated lyric "The Arraignment of a Lover," to two passages from John Lyly's *Euphues: The Anatomy of Wit*, and to Nicholas Udall's *Ralph Roister Doister.*

D "Aramanthus, Borne a Leper"

From the welter of intrigue and action in "Aramanthus" it is possible to extricate a number of migratory motifs that appear and reappear in literally scores of folk tales and medieval romances. Virtuous queens accused of adultery, children born in forests dangerously removed from civilization, kindly outlaws, scheming and ambitious brothers-in-law, waifs who float to safety and are succored by lowly foster parents, mothers who recognize long-lost children by means of costly garments and jewels, heroes who render great services to pagan rulers, heathens converted to Christianity—all are rife in popular medieval literature. A few specific examples, of the dozens that might be cited, will show that Isabel, Aramanthus, and the rest are types that were far from unprecedented in 1581.

In *The Sultan of Babylon* the daughter of a heathen ruler receives baptism, marries the hero (Sir Firumbras), and gets all Spain for a wedding present; in *The Lay of Havelock* a fisherman adopts the hero, who works earnestly at menial tasks with his foster father; in *William of Palerne* a wicked uncle plots to dispose (by poison) of the hero, who is heir to the throne; in *Sir Bevis of Hampton* the hero renders great services to a heathen potentate, whose daughter he marries after she embraces Christianity; in *The Tale of Gamelyn* the king forgives a group of kindly outlaws and gives them good offices; and in *Sir Eglamour of Artois* the hero's mother recognizes him by means of the rich mantle in which he had been set adrift as a baby. There are really striking parallels to "Aramanthus" in the early folk tale *Hirlanda of Brittany*: the heroine's persecutor is a malevolent brother-in-law prompted by ambition to get his brother's throne; the first royal child is separated from his parents by the villain's machinations and grows up away from them; the prospect of the birth of another child prompts the brother-in-law to accuse the queen years later of infidelity; and, finally, the return of the first child is the occasion of the queen's vindication.[1]

[1] For summaries of the romances mentioned, see J. E. Wells, *A Manual of the Writings in Middle English, 1050–1400* (New Haven, 1926), and Margaret Schlauch, *Chaucer's*

Neither *Hirlanda* nor any other analogue cited is to be considered an immediate source of "Aramanthus." Yet the parallels show how characteristic of the romance and folk tale many of Rich's themes appear to be, and one can only suspect that both the motifs and the archaic flavor of "Aramanthus" are due somehow to Rich's reading in medieval literature.

For that part of his tale in which Isabel saves her imprisoned husband from starvation by suckling him through the bars Rich was indebted to some version or versions of the ancient and widespread story of "Roman Charity." This appears, with minor variations, in the folklore of a dozen lands, in Latin literature, in the romance, in medieval collections of *exempla*, in the drama, in poetry, in painting, in the ballad, and in fiction, Elizabethan and modern.[1]

Of the versions I have been able to examine, Jaques de Vitry's has most details in common with "Aramanthus," but it seems hardly probable that Rich consulted this author.[2] More readily accessible to him were such accounts in English as those in William Caxton's *The Game*

Constance and Accused Queens (New York, 1927). Also parallel to "Aramanthus" are portions of the following: *Emaré*, the Flemish play *Esmoreit*, *Theseus de Cologne*, *Le Bone Florence de Rome*, *Doon de la Roche*, and *Doon de Maience*. My attention was called to several of these analogues by D. T. Starnes, who was kind enough to let me read an unpublished paper on "Aramanthus" by Frances E. Oliver.

[1] According to some variants, the young matron suckles her father instead of her husband. In others her mother is the beneficiary of this solicitude. To cite only a few versions of the tale, for "Roman Charity" in folklore see "La fille qui allaite son père," *Recueil de contes populaires grecs*, ed. Émile Legrand (Paris, 1881), pp. 47–51, and "The King of Portugal," *Roman Legends*, ed. R. H. Bush (Boston, 1887), pp. 322 f. In Latin literature, see Festus, *Concerning the Meaning of Words*, L, 14 (under *Pietati*); Valerius Maximus, V, 4, 7; Solinus, VI, in *The Excellent and Pleasant Worke of Iulius Solinus Polyhistor* (1587), trans. Arthur Golding, sig. E4; and Pliny, *Natural History*, VII, 36. In metrical romance, see the Old French *Girart de Rossillon*, lines 3053–80. In medieval collections of sermons and *exempla*, see *Scala Celi* and *Dialogus creaturarum*, 94. For dramatic treatments of the theme, see Metastasio's *Issipile*, Belloy's *Zelmire*, and Arthur Murphy's *The Grecian Daughter*. Byron tells the story in *Childe Harold's Pilgrimage*, IV, 148–50. The subject has been painted by Rubens, Honthorst, and Luca Giordano. See also the ballad "A worthy example of a vertuous wife, who fed her father with her own milk, [he] being condemned to be famished to death," *The Roxburghe Ballads*, ed. J. W. Ebsworth (London, 1897), VIII, 4–6. Two of Rich's contemporaries also made use of the tale: William Averell cites Valerius Maximus' account in *A Dyall for Dainty Darlings* (1584), sigs. D3v–D4; and in *The Unfortunate Traveller* Nashe alludes (McKerrow, II, 280) to the prison "wher the man that was condemned to death, and coulde haue no bodie come to him and succour him but was searcht, was kepte aliue a long space by sucking his daughters breasts." Some index of the vitality and usefulness of "Roman Charity" is provided by the fact that a version of it appeared as late as 1939, in John Steinbeck's *The Grapes of Wrath*.

[2] See *The Exempla of Jaques de Vitry*, ed. T. F. Crane (London, 1890), pp. 99 f., 232 f.

and Playe of the Chesse (*ca.* 1475)[1] and in I. A.'s translation, *A Summarie of the Antiquities, and Wonders of the Worlde, Abstracted out of the Sixtene First Bookes of the Excellente Historiographer Plinie* (1566).[2] A final possibility is that he knew the tale in ballad form.[3]

Another source of "Aramanthus" was Cinthio's *Gli Hecatommithi*, Decade I, Novel 1. Rich echoes a few of Cinthio's words and adopts much of his plot. In the *novella* the heroine, Lippa, fearing the wrath of her father and brothers because she has become pregnant by one of her lovers, repairs to the bank of a river to bear her child secretly. Then she deserts the baby, a son. From this point the *novella* parallels "Aramanthus" very closely indeed. The child is rescued by a shepherd (the counterpart of Rich's fisherman), christened Avventuroso (as resonant a name as Aramanthus), and reared by his foster father. Despite his bucolic upbringing, the lure of the military life is so great that the youth goes off to war, where he distinguishes himself for his expertness and valor. After a short period of service he is promoted to a captaincy. In a successful campaign he takes his parents (of whose identity he is unaware) prisoners of war. Eventually his mother and father become known to him, he frees them, the parents (who have been long separated) become reconciled, and all "live a happy life together."

For the particulars of Aramanthus' military coup against Tolosia Rich relied on Story 79, "Rvse avec laquelle le Roy des Normands Haddingue prist la cité de Luny en Italie," in the fourth volume of Belleforest's *Histoires tragiques*, the volume containing the tale upon which Rich based "Apolonius." He follows Belleforest's account of the wily Hadding's exploits with such fidelity and at such length that Story 79 may be declared the most important single source of "Aramanthus." Over a third of Rich's tale is merely a retelling of Belleforest's, and Rich occasionally availed himself of Belleforest's phraseology as well as plot.

[1] Edited by W. E. A. Axon (London, 1883), p. 62. Caxton's account is based ultimately on that of Valerius Maximus.

[2] Sig. C3v. Another version of "Roman Charity" is to be found in the *Gesta Romanorum* (No. 215), which Rich may have known in Richard Robinson's English translation (1577), now lost. In *A True and a Kinde Excuse Written in Defence of That Booke, Intituled A Newe Description of Irelande* (1612), Rich writes, sig. 4, "[Some] are better practised, in *Gesta Romanorum* . . . then they be in the *Bible*."

[3] For ballads on "Roman Charity," see H. E. Rollins, *An Analytical Index to the Ballad-Entries (1557–1709) in the Register of the Company of Stationers of London* (Chapel Hill, N.C., 1924), Nos. 779, 3042.

Finally, Aramanthus' outburst of self-recrimination shows the influence of Golding's translation of Ovid, a source that Rich also employed in his eighth tale.

E "Phylotus and Emilia"

For much of the plot of "Phylotus" Rich turned, as often, to *novelle* that had served him before. In Belleforest's story of Nicole, whose influence several scholars have already remarked,[1] he found the brother and sister indistinguishable in appearance and the confusion which ensues when one dresses in the clothes of the other. In Cinthio's "Cesare Gravina," another parallel to "Phylotus" that has been previously noted,[2] he found the youth who dresses himself like a woman and has his way with a girl by gaining admittance, under false pretences, to her father's house and to her bed. And in Straparola's tale of Silverio and Pisardo, as no one has yet observed, he found the suggestion for a combat between husband and wife to decide which is to be master of the household.

Having maneuvered Phylerno into Phylotus' house and Brisilla's bed (in emulation of Cinthio), he then borrowed copiously from Golding's translation of Ovid, charmingly and ingeniously fitting the story of Iphis, and many of Golding's words, into his own plot.

The influence of still another old friend, George Gascoigne, may be detected in "Phylotus." Reminiscences of his poetry are unmistakable in Rich's prefatory matter, in "Sappho," and in "Two Brethren." In "Phylotus," however, Rich is apparently indebted to Gascoigne's *Supposes* (1566), the earliest extant comedy in English prose. The obligation, though slight, is clear.

Rich apparently also found no reason to desert two other sources which had served him before—his own *A Right Exelent and Pleasaunt Dialogue, betwene Mercury and an English Souldier* (1574) and the *Allarme to England* (1578). Several passages from these he transferred very handily to "Phylotus."

[1] See J. S. Weld, "Studies in the Euphuistic Novel (1576–1640)" (Harvard University dissertation, 1940), p. 17; Boothe, p. 404; G. C. Moore Smith, "Riche's Story 'Of Phylotus and Emilia,'" *MLR*, V (1910), 342–44; and the preface to *Gl'Ingannati degli accademici intronati di Siena*, ed. J. Purves (Edinburgh, 1943), pp. 7 f.

[2] By Weld, p. 40, and Boothe, p. 404.

Finally, from Pettie's *Petite Pallace* again, Rich borrowed hundreds of words. Five of Pettie's tales, "Admetus and Alcest," "Scilla and Minos," "Pygmalion's Friend," "Amphiaraus and Eriphile," and "Germanicus and Agrippina," are represented in "Phylotus," and from some of them Rich culled phrases in wholesale lots.

INDEX

INDEX

INDEX

INDEX

INDEX

INDEX

INDEX

AT THE UNIVERSITY PRESS, OXFORD
BY VIVIAN RIDLER
PRINTER TO THE UNIVERSITY

www.ingramcontent.com/pod-product-compliance
Lightning Source LLC
Chambersburg PA
CBHW031630130726
47900CB00018B/63